Biting the Error

Biting the Error
Writers Explore Narrative

Edited by
Mary Burger
Robert Glück
Camille Roy
Gail Scott

Coach House Books

first edition, fifth printing

The editors of *Biting the Error* owe a debt of gratitude to the Poetry Center at San Francisco State University for housing our web journal, *Narrativity*, from which much of this anthology is derived; to Alana Wilcox at Coach House Books for her vision, hard work and patience; to Michelle Rollman for lending us the drawing on page 303; and to Chris Johanson for lending us a lovely image for our cover.

LIBRARY AND ARCHIVES CANADA CATALOGUING IN PUBLICATION

Biting the error : writers explore narrative / edited by Mary Burger ... [et al.].

ISBN 1-55245-142-9

I. Narrative (Rhetoric) I. Burger, Mary, 1963-

PE1425.B58 2004   809'.923   c2004-905555-0

Contents

Introduction

What is a story?

What is the best way to tell a story?

How do our cultures describe themselves? Which of us and what parts of each of us are left out of that description?

How is the self organized?

What are the uses of and reasons for the fragment?

What is the present? The present has never been described – how should we describe it? What are the politics of narration; that is, what is power, including the power of seduction?

How does time operate in fiction? Or, better, the temporal measures each story contains, including its relation to history and to the reader?

What is the relationship between reader and writer: performer and audience? Tyrant and slave? Co-conspirators?

This book speaks to these questions. We want to create a public forum to discuss story, fiction and narration. We have a certain kind of ambition for literature: that it should know itself and its complex function in society. For the writers collected here, form and subject matter are not givens. If innovative prose writers speak to you and to each other, what kind of language will we use? What will we talk about? Dodie Bellamy will discuss the body as uproar and overflow; Kathy Lou Schultz and Betsy Andrews will discuss the sentence; Magdalena Zurawski and Chris Kraus will discuss shame and syntax; Laura Moriarty and Kathy Acker will talk about time and wonder; Bruce Boone and Derek McCormack will explore popular genres where the culture stores so much feeling; Carla Harryman will show us the pleasurable modulations between the opacity and transparency of language, sense and nonsense that coexist with the recognition of intolerable contradiction; Douglas Rice and Robin Tremblay-McGaw will show us the body, which is hidden and revealed in story; Dennis Cooper, Lawrence Braithwaite and kari edwards will discuss the 'performance' of outlaw subject matter.

Here is an offering of the ways we writers describe our engagement with language and with the world.

– Robert Glück

In some sense, the writer is always already dead, as far as the reader is concerned. And yet the minds of reader and writer are bound through the eroticism of the story. In the moment of reading, during that act of holding attention, a ghost is present – it sparkles in the night air, even though it's nowhere clearly visible.

This mystery is attractive! I couldn't shrug it off despite the fact that the poetry community had notably more interesting conversations. I arrived in the Bay Area during the Language Poetry Wars of the eighties, and what I observed during those years was the birth of a discourse. As a prose writer, I envied poetry's sumptuous discourse, from online bulletin boards to theory journals.

Unsurprisingly, many of our contributors are poets. Narration joined the discussion as a fellow traveller because innovative fiction had developed only the rudiments of self-description. While understanding how to read poetry often calls for critical knowledge outside the poem, most fiction comes with a frame already understood by readers. This means readers often feel entitled to find in fiction an immediately recognizable world. Of course there was New Narrative, but that existed mainly inside the terrain of innovative poetry. There it was greeted warmly, but the seminal moment of New Narrative was not recognized elsewhere.

Thus, this cannot be a New Narrative anthology. That moment has passed. It is also not an anthology of a nationality or generation or other identity category: those boundaries are trespassed in our collection. Instead, we've gathered a cadre for radical narrative. The possibilities of narrative are not exhausted by mainstream fiction – indeed, they are not even suggested. Our intent with this anthology is not to normalize a body of work but to broaden and deepen the questions we can ask of the field of fiction. We hope to jump-start a community of discourse. With such a community, transformation is possible: of the premises, social relationships and formal structures of fiction.

– Camille Roy

When I got there (eventually, to San Francisco), I found there were other writers who, like me, were at that time calling ourselves poets but doing a kind of writing that often looked like prose, and talking a lot about *narrative*.

Narrative meant that you could be a person having experiences and you could admit and affirm in writing that you, the writer, had experiences and thought about them and the meaning of them; that personhood itself, if a fiction, was no less useful for not being 'true'; that in fact its very artifice made it a fruitful literary conceit; and that all this – the being, the experiencing, the thinking, the meaning, the artifice – could be the stuff of your work.

And, though personhood might be avowedly fictional, narrative was not the same thing as fiction, which insisted on wholesale invention (with resemblance to persons living or dead etc. etc. ritually denied); it was not the same thing as autobiography or memoir, with their adherence to what was (again, troublesomely) 'true.'

We had started from the point of poetry (or migrated to it) because, I'd say, we were interested in the distillation of semantics, of texture and tone and image and rhythm and sound, the scrupulous attention – to the point of stall-out – to the operations of meaning and representation and power all afforded by the form called *poem*. A poem allowed for a semantic self-examination that could become an end in itself, in a way that narrative forms – conventionally, at least – didn't allow.

But the potentially closed circuit of semantic or material attentiveness in poetry also turned out to be a convention, a limitation that couldn't support some kinds of meaning. In particular, what I wanted from narrative were the tools for exploring being in time. I needed writing about being a person among other people being in time – the knotty, sustained working-through, the confusion and thrill, the impossibility and necessity, of existing in a world with others.

Writers I knew then (in the 1990s) who were exploring the fulcrum between narrative and poetry had behind us the strenuous self-situating discourse of Language Poetry, the self-mining storytelling of New Narrativists and the inter-genre investigations of a variety of their contemporaries. We knew these groups had battled one another, but for us the lines of difference they left behind were more like paths than walls. The New Narrative practice of interrogating the subject by exposing its simultaneous self-effacement and self-aggrandizement, by representing event or identity or experience while taking apart the materials of representation, looked like a counterpoint to Language Poetry, which interrogated the semiotics of meaning and the materiality of language at the level of the sentence, the word, the phoneme.

9

The projects of my peers that have emerged since that time gamely recombine practices that were once (and are still, in many other venues) relegated to either poetry or prose. Works by Betsy Andrews, Taylor Brady, Aja Couchois Duncan, Michael du Plessis, Renee Gladman, Rob Halpern, Laird Hunt, Pamela Lu and Maggie Zurawsky, to name just a few, push us to understand that narrative can merge artifact and artifice and a deep awareness of the two.

Social identity, political argument, philosophical questioning can mingle with travesty, delusion, fantasy, audacious claims to reality, among the media of image and description and figure and sound. To break with the unexamined assumptions of the story, and to bring the poem out of its timeless solitude, call for open-ended conversation on what narrative writing can be. This anthology is a conversation about such possibilities.

– Mary Burger

Like the daily news, much contemporary fiction fails to say what must be said. The field has been left open to experimental prose writers, tracking – using the sentence as sensor – the shadows on the horizon of everyday life and contemporary thinking. Less a school than a continental cat's cradle crossing borders, mother tongues, generations, genres, what most of this work shares is that story-making is art, a *language* art that deals, ultimately, with the positioning of the storyteller and her work in the aesthetic (re)production of social relationships.

My line on this grid first ran between San Francisco and Montréal, twin cities in a way, with their traditions of radical politics and aesthetics, their relative tolerance for eccentricity, even their outside staircases. One fall in the mid-nineties, Camille Roy came to read in Montréal, and the conversation ensued about how our prose was read as failed straight prose by both progressive poets and the mainstream. For the latter, feeling was not supposed to really think; for some of the former, thinking that risked emoting was suspect. Our prose invited new approaches to reading: it was cut up, partical, informed by contemporary art's investigation of the failure of representation and by its pillaging of poetic avant-gardes as well as of theory and popular culture. Camille, who writes software, said: We need a web magazine.

Soon *Narrativity* went up, hosted by the Poetry Center at San Francisco State. Most of these essays first appeared on the website.

It made sense that the Canadian end of the project should be located in Montréal. Not long after Bob's seminal New Narrative workshops started in the late seventies (in part as a queer response to the absent author of late-century avant-garde poetics), Montreal's 'fiction/theory' group took on issues of writing-in-the-feminine (l'écriture au féminin) in response to French formalism's death of the author. In both cases, identity was *about* experimentation. Like the U.S. writers, our group in Québec would not repress the instability – we called it fluidity – of the word *identity*. North and south, an emphasis on texture, techné and freedom with respect to genre seemed a shared strategy. Parataxis was located somewhere else than in the relationship of sentence to sentence or word to word as foregrounded by Language Poetry. Yet it was with avant-garde writing, not fiction, that we conversed.

Canada, the USA, Mexico: these borders, cultural origins, languages do inform our writing. If my early experience of experimental prose was Québec based and feminist inflected, my experience of amassing this initial sampling has underscored for me the eccentricity of Canadian experimental prose. One could hypothesize that north of the 49th, the repressed French referent in English-language writing, which is political as well as linguistic, frequently encourages a particular slipperiness of address – morphing towards poetry (Nathalie Stephens) or laconic self-mocking speaking subjects (Corey Frost). One might say that Canadian writers downplay popular-culture tropes (Daphne Marlatt, Nicole Brossard) – a staple for the older U.S. New Narrative writers. But, oppositely, some younger Canadian writers seem preoccupied with these tropes (Derek McCormack, Anne Stone). And anyone familiar with how post–Quiet Revolution Québécois political culture translates into aesthetic concerns will be struck with the parallels in Mexican writer heriberto yépez's piece. Multi-faceted, complex, our dialogues with various continental communities and body politics, and with the larger culture, seem to create narratives reminiscent of storytelling's relationship to audience: infinitely subject to new outcomes, new beginnings and endings. Our audience is splayed throughout culture, anywhere there is resistance and the love of surprise.

– Gail Scott

The Killers
Kathy Acker

Let me start, since we're talking about narration, by telling you a story. Very simple. My story begins with my friend Bob Glück, who, one day, once upon a time, as story structure goes, told me that he has a certain habit – a habit of circumventing his own habits by asking his friends to give him a reading lesson. What should he, Bob Glück, read? Perhaps in order to improve himself, or perhaps in order to do the opposite. So Bob Glück goes to Kevin Killian, another friend, 'Kevin, what do you want me to read?'

Kevin replies, '"The Killers," by Ernest Hemingway.'

Upon hearing this story, for this is a story, I replied, 'Oh, Bob, how weird – Hemingway?'

'Not weird,' replied Bob. 'All the English students at San Francisco State love Hemingway.'

Two nights after this happened, I had the following dream. First, I have to tell you a few details about my childhood and about before my childhood in order to elucidate this dream for you. I never met my father. Though he was married to my mother, he left her when she was three months pregnant with me.

When I was twenty-six years old, through an accident, I traced my father's family. I wrote to them and they wrote back that they would accept me into their family and we arranged to meet. I thought that I was going to meet my real father, but I only met the first cousin. He told me (and I think he was a little crazy – well, not crazy but eccentric, because rich people are never crazy) that perhaps I should not meet my father. Why? Because my father had murdered someone who was trespassing on his yacht. After he had remained six months in a lunatic asylum, the state had excused him of any murder charge. My father then disappeared. No one now knew where he was, said the first cousin. And so I abandoned my search for my father, for my life at that time was hard enough and this new trouble was simply not worth it.

When I was thirty years old, my mother suicided.

Enough of my childhood.

I had the following dream: I dreamt that I was looking for my real father. In my dream, I knew that it was dumb for me to do this because my father was dead. Since I'm not dumb, I, or the dreamer, thought, I must be trying to find my father so that I can escape from this house which is being run by a woman. I go to a private detective. He calls me a dame.

I say, 'I'm looking for my father.'

The private detective, who might be a friend, replies that my case is an easy one. I like that I'm easy. We begin our search. According to his instructions, I tell this private eye everything that I know about my mystery. It takes me several days to recount all the details. It was summertime in Dallas. Everything was yellow. I didn't remember anything about this first period of my life, about my childhood. After this not remembering, I remembered jewels. As soon as my mother passed away, a jewel case was opened. The case, consisting of one tray, had insides of red velvet. Perhaps I'm dreaming my mother's cunt. I'm given a jewel which is green. I don't know where that jewel is now. I have no idea what happened to it. This is the mystery of which I'm speaking.

The private eye pursues my matter. A couple of days later he comes up with my father's name: Olen. This name means nothing to me.

'Olen. Your father's name is Olen. Furthermore, your father killed your mother.'

I think, in order to dismiss thought, that's possible. The detective continues to give me details about my father. He's from Iowa, and of Danish blood. All this could be true, because how can I know anything?

Now, when I woke up out of this dream, I remembered details about my mother's suicide. She had killed herself eight days before Christmas. A note in her handwriting, lying beside her dead body, said that her white poodle was staying with such-and-such veterinarian. Nothing else. But despite this note the cops were convinced that my mother was murdered by a man whose name wasn't known. Nevertheless, it was Christmas and there wasn't going to be any police investigation because the cops wanted to return to their homes, Christmas warmth and holiday.

For the first time ever in my life I had the following thought: My father could have murdered my mother. After all, what if my real father is crazy? At that moment I became very scared. If my father did murder my mother, he could now be planning to murder me.

Now, last week I was touring around and I found myself on a gig in Roanoke, Virginia, where I met this absolutely wonderful writer, Richard Dillard, and Richard told me that when he had been a boy he had encountered his first proposition by a man during a showing of *The Killers* at a local Roanoke theatre.

That's the end of the story.

Also I should mention that in 'The Killers,' the name of the Swede who's about to be slaughtered by those killers is Olen.

Now, is this a story, what I've just told you? Certainly it's narrative, right? And each incident actually did happen. That is, it was real. But a story? Stories are about something. And what I've just told you – it's not about anything. It's not even about me. A story, you see, a story has something to do with realism, and what I've just told you, though each little bit was real or had happened, has nothing to do with realism.

Listen to another voice as we proceed on this treasure hunt, or narration. The voice of Julio Cortázar.

'Almost all the stories I have written belong to the genre called fantastic, for lack of a better word, and are opposed to that false realism that consists of believing that everything can be described and explained, as was assumed by the optimism of nineteenth-century philosophy and science. That is, as part of a world governed more or less harmoniously by a system of laws, principles, cause and effect relations, well-defined psychologies, etc.' That lovely world order – that governing harmoniously by all these principles – we all know is now over.

Okay, a little more on realism. Richard Dillard rightly calls that narrative structuring named realism 'reductive.'

'But isn't that the central story of nineteenth-century realistic fiction?' he exclaims in his review of Alasdair Gray's marvellous novel *Poor Things*. 'The central story of realistic fiction: we are born, we are misshaped by biological inheritance, economic forces beyond our control and cultural biases beyond our recognition, and finally we die with our failed dreams on our dry lips.'

Realism: reductive and dehumanizing.

'There's another order,' says Cortázar, 'more secret and less communicable. That the true study of reality lay not in laws but in the exceptions to those laws has been the guiding principle in my personal search for literature beyond all naive realism.'

Now return to the narration that I told you. I can't even say what it's about: Bob Glück's conversation, my dream about my real father, Richard Dillard's memory. Where in this narration lies the real? It lies in the connections between the three sections, in the connections between the 'real' events and the holes, the silences. In the slippages. Slippages into what?

In *Moby-Dick*, Melville speaks of reality as the interstices through which all of us fall. There's another, a further, way of putting this, of proceeding on our treasure hunt. These interstices can be named chaos, or places where language cannot be, or death. When story-telling, humans attempt to cling to meaning. I think of narration, or the narrative that tries to encounter the real, as that which is negotiating between two orders of time: clock time and chaos. I must say the more I think about it, the more I think writing is about time. The writer is playing – when structuring narrative or when narrative is structuring itself – with life and death. He or she is manoeuvring between order and disorder, between meaning and meaninglessness, and so is making literature.

However, these movements between clock time and chaos in written narrative are more complex. To begin, consider one aspect of time in the novel: the time it takes to write a novel. A novel's a big thing. It usually takes at least a year, often many years. During that time the writer's life changes. So there's the time of all the actual changes the writer is going through – the time it takes to write the novel.

It takes time to read a novel. A novel is very rarely something you read in one sitting. So, that time incorporates all the reader's memories, all the interstices, the time lapses between readings, all the returns to earlier parts of the novel, etc. Finally: the fictive time. The time within the story or the narration. Even in *Hopscotch* there's fictive time. So in this sense a novel, structurally, is a time triad.

I want to quickly consider realism again. Within the realm of realism lies the assumption that language mirrors all that isn't language, right? That's what a narrative is about: telling what is or should be true. A narrative mirrors reality.

Now, do I need to say – how simplistic. I want to ask, why bother being so simplistic? Why bother with the lie of realism? Why bother being so miserable, so reductive, when one could play? If I'm going to tell you what the real is by mirroring it, by telling you a story that expresses reality, I'm attempting to tell you how things are. By letting you see through my own eyes, I give you my viewpoints, moral and political. In other words, realism is simply a control method. Realism doesn't want to negotiate, open into, even know, chaos or the body or death, because those who practice realism want to limit their readers' perceptions, want to limit perceptions to a centric – which in this society is always a phallocentric – reality. 'I am the one,' says the realistic writer. 'I'm telling you reality.' I have the same quarrel about narrowing anything to single identity.

In other words, behind every literary or cultural issue lies the political, the realm of political power. And whenever we talk about narration, narrative structure, we're talking about political power. There are no ivory towers. The desire to play, to make literary structures that play into and in unknown or unknowable realms, those of chance and death and the lack of language, is the desire to live in a world that is open and dangerous, that is limitless. To play, then, both in structure and in content, is to desire to live in wonder.

NOTE

Kathy Acker gave this talk on a panel called 'In Extremis, Writing at the Century's End.' The panel was presented by Small Press Traffic in the New College Theater in San Francisco on April 29, 1993. The talk was videotaped by S. S. Kush for his Cloud House Poetry Archives (1557 Franklin St., San Francisco CA 94109, 415-292-5554). We are grateful to Kush and also to the Acker estate. The tape was transcribed by Quintan Wikswo and edited by Robert Glück. The panel also included Dodie Bellamy, Earl Jackson Jr. and Benjamin Weissman.

The Virgin Denotes
Or the Unreliability of Adverbs to Do with Time
Gail Scott

Montréal: I am asked to write an introduction to a new edition of my first book of stories, *Spare Parts*.[1] Walking past my old flat on l'Esplanade-sur-le-parc, I feel indiscreet spying on the writer I was then. Light seeps from the spacious glass-brick public washroom façade at end of the walk opposite. Part of a mayor's project for making a Marie-Antoinette hamlet out of Olmsted's mountain. People nod on benches. Cop car drives by. I keep, for the moment, to the residential [referential] side. Briskly, I walk. Towards the cinema with the best popcorn in the city. For a hit of nostalgia: old Cassavetes. Black Orpheus. La Dolce Vita. Past the gorgeous dwellings, former embassies, downgraded to city councillors [one, anti-vice, shot by a limping man in a raccoon coat police called 'a foreigner'], immigrant families, artists. Trying to glimpse between the cracks in the curtains. A girl in pillbox passes, trotting even faster. Later, scoping the young woman in pillbox in the light of the popcorn machine, I see she's the daughter of the man who stuck out his tongue as I stared past his wrought-iron fence, attaching an eschatological name to my person. I trot, feeling [retrospectively] like a miso-coated salmon.

It is this *later* I want to talk about:

I was a journalist. *Then.* Sentencing, over the fear of being poisoned 'in relation to the mother' [as Freud said of paranoia]. Amassing outfits, bylines, accoutrements of success to stave off the threat of a life like hers. Simultaneously executing patterns of conspiracy in my world of small subjects, women, would-be intellectuals, working-class upstarts. Tentatively, I was practicing growing angry at what they were, the information merchants, and who I risked becoming, her ghost. Taking off and trying on prostheses in the cheap lights of old department stores.

I dreaded mornings *after.*

Coming into work at a local daily newspaper – my typewriter faced that of a kindly elder court reporter. Thirteen calls this morning, he informed me sadly. Thirteen calls furious at my taunting article on the 'McGill-Français' demo, complete with commerce students carolling

O Canada, well back on the sidewalk. Thirteen outraged members of the English community, thinking the city belonging to them. I wanted to fuck with their aura: with that which does not strut about with a label describing what it is. All the same, I was writing careful tight phrases, miming information's racket. Those basic hundred words. Censoring the vernacular, words like *class, cunt, capitalist*; likewise censored: 'Some Points about the FLQ Manifesto.'[2] How phrases went together in precise little syllogisms also seemed inhibitively ... structuring. I wanted to mock them in sentences like single grins with lips pasted back [Lisa Robertson]. Simultaneously wanting to write phrases that performed Mallarméan gestures.

The context — bathed in the tender backlight of *later* — encouraged it: a first poetry reading, la Nuit de la Poésie against the War Measures Act [the legislator had suspended all civil rights]. Impressing on fresh adolescent spirits in the dark recesses of the Eglise/Théâtre Gésu a link, possibly indelible, between writing and subversion. People spoke at real risk of being imprisoned. The singer Louise Forestier, pregnant, in braids [a nice touch], stood on the stage, patting the baby in her stomach and singing 'Ferme-la et prends ta bière [Shut up and drink your beer].' While round that old angel monument by the mountain, cops' horses scattered conga players, water pipes, skinny loiterers. Recently, walking into a tea room in Montréal's Quartier Latin, I thought I saw those same skinny youth *again*: apparently eating only carrots and smoking water pipes, conjuring in their spareness the empathy and complicity I tendentiously conjugating with *then*. It is the artist's task, Ernst Bloch says, speaking of utopia, to bring now-time into line or focus with like historical moments when thought's not emptied out, a turning point. When time has lost its thickness. Talent may be only knowing how to grasp a vector when our lives flow along it.

Dear R, who are the age I was ... earlier: The air is empty. The grass, where we walked, is empty. And the space across the bay where the Twin Towers stood. Nostalgia for how things were before. Not so great if you care to remember, said Nakila at the Brooklyn Women's Salon. Dear R, I say, playing the older writer walking, arms folded over black raincoat, head bent to the side, a writer must (in the sense of surely) know what impetus causes her to write this way instead of that. Must (surely) be aware of the risk of foregrounding her by her inscription in the system she opposes when she chooses to write not a line but a sentence. I like that you ask: 'What is the writer's

responsibility?' Though I want to say: 'Be careful.' Or: 'Risk.' I like that you
are interested in narrative as call and response, linked to address. That for
you, in your writing, address is not about the is nor the will-be but the would,
thus keeping both narrator and narrative conditional.

Meanwhile [Memory being the solicitous trollop she is]: Back in that
late-seventies pseudo-revolutionary Wonderland, increasingly medi-
ally framed as Québécois spaghetti western, due to the crime rates,
meanwhile, in a two-storey flat high on a Quartier-Latin promontory
called Terrasse Saint-Denis, two musicians [one franco, one anglo],
two writers [one franco, one anglo], one visual artist [anglo], one guy
in a navy beret from the suburbs [franco], read the Surrealist Mani-
festos and feel latent content matters, chain-smoking and analyzing
our dreams, or going round the city putting up mad broadsheets.
Knowing *they* would win the information game. Soundtrack: traffic,
splashing behind a small paneless window cut in the kitchen wall to
ventilate the tub; and one day a shot, when a man sticks an automatic
out the garret window opposite and kills another walking down the
sidewalk.
    Left for the left ...

But what impetus, exactly, gave 'story' the rush of something else:
those written ghosts of subjects, fragile substantives, compiled from
public text, experience, and facing the world obliquely? Memory can't
resist proffering, in answer, one last dream for analysis: a 'Dream
About Writing.' In which *I lay in bed, the sheet folded down rather sloppily over the mattress, which was embarrassing because I was giving a public
reading about passion from the bed – by myself. Reading looking straight
ahead. The audience is sitting to my left in three oblique rows of chairs.
Looking not at me, on the right, but also looking straight ahead (from their
oblique angle), as I, lying in bed, read.* Which dream, prodigiously decon-
structed, conveniently yielding a trace of abjection [*lying, sloppily, in
bed*], a whiff of betrayal [*three + oblique*]. Elements that trope, in the
vaguely comic autobiographical conjunction of semiotics, semantics,
gossip, she now thinks of as prose: 'experimental' inasmuch as implying failure to represent the universal, linked to class, gender, sometimes race, but also to the pleasure of sounding out, a kin to poetry.
Sometimes she watches, regretfully, as her little tales float, textured,
suggestive, by the averted eyes of certain poets she admires. Who,

along with lovers of more conventional fiction, persist in reading 'experimental' prose for content, for 'voice' alone. As if a subject redistributed across hazardous abutments, torqued by inner syntax in dissonance with outer, or the reverse, can be absorbed as passively as a drugstore novel. Our group would have laughed even then at the poster a young poet, two blocks up, has on the wall of his borrowed room. Citing a famous novelist saying every sentence has a truth waiting at the end. Manifest truth maybe, we'd have mouthed, red lips insulting.

Recently [plus ça change]:

Some French-language ESL students, reading these stories, smile at what they call 'the repression.' In bed with her bathing suit on??? They also smile at those incontinent raspberries blooming on the snow [another dream, I'm afraid]. Was she New Age? Influenced by the cinema? The mid-career writer, on her platform, tries to explain how Wild Strawberries, seen at seventeen in a repertory cinema, made her feel so free she floated out, past trash cans, towards a future of broken narratives. Why? they smile again. Because we wanted difference, we wanted everything. Here the twenty-year-old heads from Ville Brossard, Kenya, Hong Kong, Stockholm and Chicoutimi nod. And because we wanted everything, adds the writer quickly, we totalled Marxism + surrealism + new theories about the death of the western subject into the equation. While a plethora of identity issues screamed in the background. On streets called Rachel, Marie-Anne, Jeanne-Mance, cafés were full of feminists discussing language, and the eruption of the anteriority of language within it, the latter identified with Mother [Kristeva]. We wanted to circumvent logos. Without somehow abandoning a towering lucidity. Some of us were also seeking to locate, semiotically, the unique sounds of a French-dominant multi-linguistic city.

Dear R: Walking in Prospect Park, green light glinting off shiny grass blades, the gleaming hole in the distant Manhattan skyline, which only the familiar – I guess I mean any global citizen with access to a screen – recognize as absence: you ask the same questions I often ask myself. Re: relationship to reader. Re: the alleged superiority of poetry for allowing singularity of perception, bringing focus to bear directly on words and the sounds of them.

And relations between. I love the hugeness of your desire for reaching the highest point of expressivity in art and life [Maiakovsky]. Do not certain conjunctures foster this kind of raw energy required for pure invention? Skating between modes and limitations. Less acknowledged: what I am learning from you ...

Yet, albeit, at the same time, furthermore:

She wanted to touch Her with her statements. Notwithstanding the faint whiff of complicity with dominance connected with speaking assertively. Was 'to sentence' a border issue? Controlling? Paranoid in its insistence on contiguity. 'Twas a journalist, cigarette on lip, bad liver, sensitive crinkled face, who'd told her: 'A sentence starting with *To tell the truth* is unreliable, discombobulated, corrected.' Was not any sentence such? She wanted to turn them into lines of flight, translating provisorily, and yes, naturally *belatedly*, the drift of experience. Hopefully her perpetual avant-garde urge to underscore, again and again, that contiguity between making art and life, would not grow rigid. [Here, she gets an image of paper handcuffs.] But we live in chaos. Is not a tendency to endlessly intrepret, to graft 'sense' onto 'nonsense,' both attribual to paranoia – and sensible? It amuses her to think that Freud's case of female paranoia ['Essay Running Counter to the Psychoanalytic Theory of Paranoia'] momentarily derailed his whole paranoic system. Implying, as it did, that his female client's fear of being poisoned appeared to originate less in Mother than in her social context. But ... can a bride in a wedding not embrace the family? Answer: Only *later*. Still she wants to write prose. Why should only Poetry [be] ... about the way language works (rhythms and sounds and syntax — musical rather than pictorial values) as much as it is about a given subject [Ann Lauterbach]. Me too, I wanted to create meanings at multiple sorts of intersections.

*

I veer off l'Esplanade, still in the dark, onto the walk that bifurcates the park. Towards the public washrooms. That old angel monument's visible in the distance. A woman approaches, holding a black umbrella blindly before her. A homeless man with his cart full of plastic bags bikes by, holding high a bouquet of florist-wrapped flowers. Such instants, innocent almost, are where stories begin, breathing in and exhaling ... not the single breath of a single genius, Breton's mythic poet having been dumped, thanks to language feminists and others, for more collective and material notions of aleatory writing.

I find it odd that a critical field of radical poetics has grown out of the era spoken of above, but little in the way of an interpretative milieu for experimental prose. It seems to me more urgent than ever to encourage thinking that redistributes notions of subjectivity, time, that fosters narrative practices foregrounding the impossible-to-avoid knowing that 'telling' can only be telescoped by the present from some fragile angle itself obviously wanting. Such stories, motivated [maybe] by a faint paranoia linked to the porosity of the subject, are not resistant to identity issues lurking in inner and outer syntax, do not shun the playing off of formal investigation against the junk food of nostalgia – notably its media version, popular culture. I want to think of prose as a practice elided by material conditions and awareness, pressed on by time, flight and the rhythms and complexities of multiple-language and cultural contexts. Such material aspects expressed or framed by obvious formal limitations, not to appear 'natural' – with 'natural's' inbred risk of sentimentality.

A sentence, after all, is a device like anything else.

NOTES

1 Gail Scott, *Spare Parts* (Toronto: Coach House, 1982); *Spare Parts Plus Two* (Coach House, 2002). A slightly longer version of this essay plus some of the stories in the collection can be found on the Coach House website, www.chbooks.com.

2 Following the invocation of the War Measures Act during Québec's 1970 October Crisis (involving the kidnapping of a trade consul and a labour minister by the Front de Libération du Québec), Québec's professional journalists' association complained that freedom of speech had been limited by the act; in part, journalists felt it risky to link social aspects of the manifesto (such as high unemployment and bad housing for French Canadians) to the crisis, though it had been usual to do so prior to the act.

Long Note on New Narrative
Robert Glück

To talk about the beginnings of New Narrative, I have to talk about my friendship with Bruce Boone. We met in the early seventies through the San Francisco Art Institute's bulletin board: Ed and I wanted to move and Bruce and Burton wanted to move – would we all be happy living together? For some reason, both couples dropped the idea and remained in our respective flats for many years. But Bruce and I were poets and our obsession with Frank O'Hara forged a bond.

I was twenty-three or twenty-four. Bruce was seven years older. He was a wonderful teacher. He read to transform himself and to attain a correct understanding. Such understanding was urgently political.

Bruce had his eye on the catastrophic future, an upheaval he predicted with a certain grandeur, but it was my own present he helped me find. I read and wrote to invoke what seemed impossible – relation itself – in order to take part in a world that ceaselessly makes itself up, to 'wake up' to the world, to recognize the world, to be convinced that the world exists, to take revenge on the world for not existing.

To talk about New Narrative, I also have to talk about Language Poetry, which was in its heroic period in the seventies. I treat diverse poets as one unit, a sort of flying wedge, because that's how we experienced them. It would be hard to overestimate the drama they brought to a Bay Area scene that limped through the seventies, with the powerful exception of feminist poets like Judy Grahn and the excitement generated by movement poetry. Language Poetry's puritan rigour, delight in technical vocabularies and professionalism were new to a generation of Bay Area poets whose influences included the Beats, Robert Duncan and Jack Spicer, the New York School (Bolinas was its western outpost), surrealism and psychedelic surrealism.

Suddenly, people took sides, though at times these confrontations resembled a pastiche of the embattled positions of earlier avant-gardes. Language Poetry seemed very 'straight male' – though what didn't? Barrett Watten's *Total Syntax*, for example, brilliantly established (as it dispatched) a lineage of fathers: Olson, Zukofsky, Pound, etc.

If I could have become a Language poet I would have; I craved the formalist fireworks, a purity that invented its own tenets. On the snowy mountaintop of progressive formalism, from the highest high road of modernist achievement, there was plenty of contempt heaped on less rigorous endeavour. I had come to a dead end in the mid-seventies like the poetry scene itself. The problem was not theoretical – or it was: I could not go on until I figured out some way to understand where I was. I also craved the community the Language poets made for themselves.

The questions vexing Bruce and me were only partly addressed by Language Poetry, which, in the most general sense, we saw as an aesthetics built on an examination (by subtraction: of voice, of continuity) of the ways language generates meaning. The same could be said of other experimental work, especially the minimalisms, but Language Poetry was our proximate example.

Warring camps drew battle lines between representation and non-representation – retrospection makes the argument seem as arbitrary as Fancy vs. Imagination. But certainly the 'logic of history' at that moment supported the idea of this division, along with the struggle to find a third position that would encompass the whole argument.

I experienced the poetry of disjunction as a luxurious idealism in which the speaking subject rejects the confines of representation and disappears in the largest freedom, that of language itself. My attraction to this freedom and to the professionalism with which it was purveyed made for a kind of class struggle within myself. Whole areas of my experience, especially gay experience, were not admitted to this utopia, partly because the mainstream reflected a resoundingly coherent image of myself back to me – an image so unjust that it amounted to a tyranny that I could not turn my back on. We had been disastrously described by the mainstream – a naming whose most extreme (though not uncommon) expression was physical violence. Political agency involved at least a provisionally stable identity.

Meanwhile, gay identity was also in its heroic period – it had not yet settled into just another nationalism and it was new enough to know its own constructedness. In the urban mix, some great experiment was actually taking place, a genuine community where strangers and different classes and ethnicities rubbed more than shoulders. This community was not destroyed by commodity culture, which was destroying so many other communities; instead, it was founded in commodity culture. We had to talk about it. Bruce and I turned to each other to see if we could come up with a better representation – not in order to satisfy movement pieties or to be political, but in order to *be*.

We (eventually we were gay, lesbian and working-class writers) could not let narration go.

Since I'm confined to hindsight, I write as though Bruce and I were following a plan instead of stumbling and groping towards a writing that could join other literatures of the present. We could have found narrative models in, say, Clark Coolidge's prose, so perhaps narrative practice relates outward to the actual community whose story is being told. We could have located self-reference and awareness of artifice in, say, the novels of Ronald Firbank, but we didn't. So, again, our use of language that knows itself relates outward to a community speaking to itself dissonantly.

We were fellow travellers of Language Poetry and the innovative feminist poetry of that time, but our lives and reading led us towards a hybrid aesthetic, something impure. We (say, Bruce Boone, Camille Roy, Kevin Killian, Dodie Bellamy, Mike Amnasan, myself and, to include the dead, Steve Abbott and Sam D'Allesandro) are still fellow travellers of the poetries that evolved since the early eighties, when writers talked about 'non-narrative.' One could untangle that knot forever, or build an aesthetics on the ways language conveys silence, chaos and undifferentiated existence and erects countless horizons of meaning.

How to be a theory-based writer? One question. How to represent my experience as a gay man? Another question just as pressing. These questions led to readers and communities almost completely ignorant of each other. Too fragmented for a gay audience? Too much sex and 'voice' for a literary audience? I embodied these incommensurates so I had to ask this question: How can I convey urgent social meanings while opening or subverting the possibilities of meaning itself? That question has devilled and vexed Bay Area writing for twenty-five years. What kind of representation least deforms its subject? Can language be aware of itself (as object, as system, as commodity, as abstraction) yet take part in the forces that generate the present? Where in writing does engagement become authentic? One response, the politics of form, apparently does not answer the question completely.

One afternoon in 1976, Bruce remarked on the questions to the reader I'd been throwing into poems and stories. They were self-consciously theatrical and they seemed to him to pressure and even sometimes to reverse the positions of reader and writer. Reader/writer dynamics seemed like a way into the problems that preoccupied us – a toe in the water!

From our poems and stories, Bruce abstracted text-metatext: a story keeps a running commentary on itself from the present. The commentary, taking the form of a meditation or a second story, supplies a succession of frames. That is, the more you fragment a story, the more it becomes an example of narration itself – narration displaying its devices – while at the same time (as I wrote in 1981) the metatext 'asks questions, asks for critical response, makes claims on the reader, elicits comments. In any case, text-metatext takes its form from the dialectical cleft between real life and life as it wants to be.'[1]

We did not want to break the back of representation or to 'punish' it for lying, but to elaborate narration on as many different planes as we could, which seemed consistent with the lives we led. Writing can't will away power relations and commodity life; instead, writing must accept its relation to power and recognize that, at present, group practice resides inside the commodity. Bruce wrote, 'When evaluating image in American culture, isn't it a commodity whether anyone likes it or not? You make your additions and subtractions from that point on.'[2]

In 1978, Bruce and I launched the Black Star Series and published my *Family Poems* and his *My Walk with Bob*, a lovely book.[3] In 'Remarks on Narrative,' the afterword of *Family Poems*, Bruce wrote, 'As has now been apparent for some time, the poetry of the '70s seems generally to have reached a point of stagnation, increasing a kind of refinement of technique and available forms, without yet being able to profit greatly from the vigor, energy and accessibility that mark so much of the new Movement writing of gays, women and Third World writers, among others. Ultimately this impasse of poetry reflects conditions in society itself.'[4]

We appreciated the comedy of mounting an offensive ('A critique of the new trends towards conceptualization, linguistic abstraction and process poetry') with those slenderest volumes. My poems and stories were set 'in the family,' not so antipsychological as they might have been given that we assumed any blow to interiority was a step forward for mankind.

We contended with the Language poets while seeking their attention in the forums they erected for themselves. We published articles in *Poetics Journal* and *L=A=N=G=U=A=G=E*, and spoke in talk series and forums – a mere trickle in the torrent of their critical work. If I had thought Language Poetry was a dead end, what a fertile dead end it proved to be!

New Narrative was in place by the time *Elements of a Coffee Service* was published by Donald Allen's Four Seasons Foundation in 1982 and Hoddypoll published Bruce's novel, *Century of Clouds*, in 1980. We were thinking about autobiography; by autobiography we meant daydreams, nightdreams, the act of writing, the relationship to the reader, the meeting of flesh and culture, the self as collaboration, the self as disintegration, the gaps, inconsistences and distortions, the enjambments of power, family, history and language.

Bruce and I brought high and low together between the covers of a book, mingling essay, lyric and story. Our publishing reflected those different modes: stories from *Elements* appeared in gay anthologies, porn magazines, *Social Text* and *Soup*. Bruce wrote about Georges Bataille for the *Advocate*.

I wanted to write with a total continuity and total disjunction since I experienced the world (and myself) as continuous and infinity divided. That was my ambition for writing. Why should a work of literature be organized by one pattern of engagement? Why should a 'position' be maintained regarding the size of the gaps between units of meaning? To describe how the world is organized may be the same as organizing the world. I wanted the pleasures and politics of the fragment and the pleasures and politics of story, gossip, fable and case history; the randomness of chance and a sense of inevitability; sincerity while using appropriation and pastiche. When Barrett Watten said about *Jack the Modernist*, 'You have your cake and eat it too,' I took it as a great compliment, as if my intention spoke through the book.

During the seventies, Bruce was working on his doctorate at UC Berkeley. His dissertation was a structuralist and gay reading of O'Hara – that is, O'Hara and community, a version of which was published in the first issue of *Social Text* in 1979. He joined the Marxism and Theory Group at St. Cloud which gave birth to that journal. Bruce also wrote critical articles (especially tracking the 'gay band' of the Berkeley Renaissance).[5] Bruce introduced me to most of the critics who would make a foundation for New Narrative writing.

Here are a few of them:

Georg Lukács: In *The Theory of the Novel*, Lukács maintains that the novel contains – that is, holds together – incommensurates. The epic and novel are the community telling itself its story, a story whose integration becomes increasingly hard to achieve. *The Theory of the Novel* leads to ideas of collaboration and community that are not naive – that is, to narrative that questions itself. It redistributes relations of power and springs the writer from the box of psychology, since he becomes the community speaking to itself. I wrote 'Caricature,' a talk given at 80 Langton in 1983, mostly using Lukács's book, locating instances of conservative and progressive communities speaking to themselves: 'If the community is a given, so are its types.'[6]

Louis Althusser: His essay 'Ideological State Apparatuses' refigures the concept of base/superstructure. Terry Eagleton rang the following change on Althusser's bulky formula: Ideology is the imaginary resolution of real contradictions. By 1980, literary naturalism was easily deprived of its transparency, but this formula also deprives all fantasy of transparency, including the fantasy of personality. If making a personality is not different from making a book, in both cases one could favour the 'real contradictions' side of the formula. If personality is a fiction (a political fiction!), then it is a story in common with other stories – it occurs on the same plane of experience. This 'formula' sets those opacities – a novel, a personality – as equals on the stage of history, and supports a new version of autobiography in which 'fact' and 'fiction' interpenetrate.

Althusser comes with a lot of baggage. For example, he divided science from ideology and ideology from theory. Frankly, Bruce and I pillaged critical theory for concepts that gave us access to our experience. In retrospect, it might be better simply to 'go with' cultural studies. To the endless chain of equal cultural manifestations (a song by REM, the Diet of Worms, Rousseau's *Confessions*), we add another equal sign, attaching the self as yet another thing the culture 'dreamed up.'

Georges Bataille: Bataille was central to our project. He finds a counter-economy of rupture and excess that includes art, sex, war, religious sacrifice, sports events, ruptured subjectivity, the dissolution of bodily integuments – 'expenditure' of all kinds. Bataille showed us how a bathhouse and a church could fulfill the same function in their respective communities.

In writing about sex, desire and the body, New Narrative approached performance art, where self is put at risk by naming names, becoming naked, making the irreversible happen – the book becomes social practice that is lived. The theme of obsessive romance did double duty, de-stabling the self and asserting gay experience. Steve Abbott wrote, 'Gay writers Bruce Boone and Robert Glück (like Acker, Dennis Cooper or the subway graffitists again) up the ante on this factuality by weaving their own names, and those of friends and lovers, into their work. The writer/artist becomes exposed and vulnerable: you risk being foolish, mean-spirited, wrong. But if the writer's life is more open to judgement and speculation, so is the reader's.'[7]

Did we believe in the 'truth and freedom' of sex? Certainly we were attracted to scandal and shame, where there is so much information. I wanted to write close to the body – the place language goes reluctantly. We used porn, where information saturates narrative, to expose and manipulate genre's formulas and dramatis personae, to arrive at ecstasy and loss of narration as the self sheds its social identities. We wanted to speak about subject/master and object/slave. Bataille showed us that loss of self and attainment of nothingness is a group activity. He supplied the essential negative, a zero planted in the midst of community.

Now I'd add that transgressive writing is not necessarily about sex or the body – or about anything one can predict. There's no manual; transgressive writing shocks by articulating the present, the one thing impossible to put into words, because a language does not yet exist to describe the present. Bruce translated Bataille's *Guilty* for Lapis Press when I worked as an editor there. We hammered out the manuscript together, absorbing Bataille gesturally.

Five more critics. Walter Benjamin: for lyrical melancholy (which reads as autobiography) and for permission to mix high and low. V. N. Voloshinov: for discovering that meaning resides within its social situation and that contending powers struggle within language itself. Roland Barthes: for a style that goes back to autobiography, for the fragment and for displaying the constructed nature of story – 'baring the device.' Michel Foucault: for the constructed nature of sexuality, the self as collaboration and the not-to-be-underestimated example of an out gay critic. (Once at 18th and Castro, Michel pierced Bruce with his eagle gaze and Bruce was overcome! he says.) Julia Kristeva: for elaborating the meaning of abjection in *Powers of Horror*.

Our interest in Dennis Cooper and Kathy Acker produced allegiances and friendships with those writers. Kathy moved to San Francisco in the fall of 1981; while getting settled she stayed with Denise Kastan, who lived downstairs from me. Denise and I co-directed Small Press Traffic. Kathy was at work on *Great Expectations*. In fact, Denise and I appear in it; we are the whores Danella and Barbarella. Kathy's writing gave Bruce, Steve Abbott and myself another model, evolved far beyond our own efforts, for the interrogation of autobiography as 'text' perpetually subverted by another text. Appropriation puts in question the place of the writer – in fact, it turns the writer into a reader.

Meanwhile, Bruce and I were thinking about the painters who were rediscovering the figure, like Eric Fischl and Julian Schnabel. They found a figuration that had passed through the flame of abstract expressionism and the subsequent isms, operating through them. It made us feel we were part of a cross-cultural impulse rather than a local subset. Bruce wrote:

> With much gay writing and some punk notoriously (Acker the big example), the sexual roots of aggression come into question. There's a scream of connection, the figure that emerges ghostly: life attributed to those who have gone beyond. So in Dennis Cooper's *Safe* there's a feeling-tone like a Schnabel painting: the ground's these fragments of some past, the stag, the Roman column, whatever – on them a figure that doesn't quite exist but would maybe like to. The person/persona/thing the writer's trying to construct from images – '[8]

In 1976, I started volunteering in the non-profit bookstore Small Press Traffic and became co-director not long after. From 1977 to 1985, I ran a reading series and held free walk-in writing workshops at the store. The workshops became a kind of New Narrative laboratory attended by Michael Amnasan, Steve Abbott, Sam D'Allesandro, Kevin Killian, Dodie Bellamy, Camille Roy and many other writers whose works extend my own horizon. Most writers we knew were reading theory. Later, guided by Bruce, we started a left reading group at Small Press Traffic, attended by Steve Benson, Ron Silliman, Denise Kastan, Steve Abbott, Bruce, myself and others. The personal demolished the political, and after a few months we disbanded. From that era

I recall Ron's epithet (which Bruce and I thought delicious): the Small Press Traffic School of Dissimulation.

More successful was the Left/Write Conference we mounted in 1981 at the Noe Valley Ministry. The idea for a conference was conceived in the spring of 1978 by Bruce and Steve Abbott, who sent letters to thirty writers of various ethnicities and aesthetic positions. Steve was a tireless community builder, and Left/Write was an expression of New Narrative's desire to bring communities together, a desire that informed the reading series at Small Press Traffic, Steve Abbott's *Soup* (where the term New Narrative first appeared), Michael Amnasan's *Ottotole*, Camille Roy and Nayland Blake's *Dear World*, Kevin Killian and Brian Monte's *No Apologies*, and later Kevin and Dodie Bellamy's *Mirage*. We felt urgent about it, perhaps because we each belonged to such disparate groups. To our astonishment, three hundred people attended Left/Write, so we accomplished on a civic stage what we were attempting in our writing, editing and curating: to mix groups and modes of discourse. Writers famous inside their own groups and hardly known outside, like Judy Grahn and Erica Hunt, spoke and read together for the first time.

Out of that conference the Left Writers Union emerged; soon it was commandeered by its most unreconstructed faction, which prioritized gay and feminist issues out of existence. At one meeting, we were instructed to hold readings in storefronts on ground level so the 'masses of San Francisco' could walk in!

During this decade – 1975–1985 – Bruce and I carried on what amounted to one long, gabby phone conversation. We brought gossip and anecdote to our writing because they contain speaker and audience, establish the parameters of community and trumpet their 'unfair' points of view. I hardly ever 'made things up' – a plot still seems exotic, but as a collagist I had an infinite field. I could use the lives we endlessly described to each other as 'found material,' which complicates storytelling because the material also exists on the same plane as the reader's life. Found materials have a kind of radiance, the truth of the already-known.

In 1981 we published *La Fontaine* as a valentine to our friendship. In one poem, Bruce (and Montaigne!) wrote, 'In the friendship whereof I speak ... our souls mingle and blend in a fusion so complete that the seam that joins them disappears and is found no more. If pressed to say why I loved him I'd reply, because it was him, because it was me.'[9]

By using the tag New Narrative, I am conceding there is such a thing. In the past I was reluctant to promote a literary school that endured even ten minutes, much less a few years. Bruce and I took the notion of a 'school' half seriously, and once New Narrative began to resemble a program, we abandoned it, declining to recognize ourselves in the tyrants and functionaries that make a literary school. Or was it just a failure of nerve? Still, I would observe that my writing continues to develop a New Narrative aesthetic – the problems and contradictions outlined above – and I wonder if that is not true of my New Narrative confederates. Now I am glad to see the term being used by a critical community exemplified by this anthology, younger writers in San Francisco and New York, and writers in other cities, like Gail Scott in Montréal, and critics like Earl Jackson, Jr., Antony Easthope, Carolyn Dinshaw and Dianne Chisholm. Bruce and I may have been kidding about founding a school, but we were serious about wanting to bring emotion and subject matter into the field of innovative writing. I hope that these thoughts on our project – call it what you will – are useful to those looking for ways of extending the possibilities of poem and story without backtracking into the mainstream, or into nineteenth-century transparency.

NOTES

1 Robert Glück, 'Caricature,' *Soup: New Critical Perspectives* 4 (1985): 28.

2 Bruce Boone, 'A Narrative Like a Punk Picture: Shocking Pinks, Lavenders, Magentas, Sickly Greens,' *Poetics Journal* 5 (May 1985): 92.

3 Black Star published *He Cried* by Dennis Cooper and *Lives of the Poets* by Steve Abbott. The Black Star Series still publishes, most recently Camille Roy's *Swarm*.

4 Bruce Boone, 'Remarks on Narrative,' afterword of *Family Poems* by Robert Glück (San Francisco: Black Star Series, 1979), 29.

5 Bruce Boone, 'Spicer's Writing in Context,' *Ironwood* 28 (1986); 'Robert Duncan & Gay Community,' *Ironwood* 22 (1983).

6 Glück, 'Caricature,' 19.

7 Steve Abbott, 'Notes on Boundaries, New Narrative,' *Soup: New Critical Perspectives* 4 (1985): 81.

8 Boone, 'A Narrative,' 92.

9 Bruce Boone and Robert Glück, 'Perukes' in *La Fontaine* (San Francisco: Black Star Series, 1981), 63.

Form as Response to Doubt[1]
Lydia Davis

Doubt, uneasiness, dissatisfaction with writing or with existing forms may result in the formal integration of these doubts by the creation of new forms, forms that in one way or another exceed or surpass our expectations. Whereas repeating old forms implies a lack of desire or compulsion, or a refusal, to entertain doubt or feel dissatisfaction.

To work deliberately in the form of the fragment can be seen as stopping or appearing to stop a work closer, in the process, to what Blanchot would call the origin of writing, the centre rather than the sphere. It may be seen as a formal integration, an integration into the form itself, of a question about the process of writing.

It can be seen as a response to the philosophical problem of seeing the written thing replace the subject of the writing. If we catch only a little of our subject, or only badly, clumsily, incoherently, perhaps we have not destroyed it. We have written about it, written it and allowed it to live on at the same time, allowed it to live on in our ellipses, our silences.

Interruption

Doesn't the unfinished work tend to throw our attention onto the work as artifact, or the work as process, rather than the work as conveyer of meaning, of message? Does this add to the pleasure or the interest of the text?

Any interruption, either of our expectations or of the smooth surface of the work itself – by breaking it off, confusing it or leaving it actually unfinished – foregrounds the work as artifact, as object, rather than as invisible purveyor of meaning, emotion, atmosphere. Constant interruption, fragmentation, also keeps returning the reader not only to the real world but to a consciousness of his or her own mind at work.

' ... Without thinking of whole... '

Here is Maurice Blanchot on Joseph Joubert: 'What he was seeking – this source of writing, this space in which to write, this light to circumscribe in space – ... made him unfit for all ordinary literary work ... ' – or, as Joubert said of himself, 'unsuited to continuous discourse' –

'preferring the centre to the sphere, sacrificing results to the discovery of their conditions, and writing not in order to add one book to another but to take command of the point from which it seemed to him all books issued ... '[2]

We can't think of fragment without thinking of whole. The word *fragment* implies the word *whole*. A fragment would seem to be a part of a whole, a broken-off part of a whole. Does it also imply, as with other broken-off pieces, that enough of them would make a whole, or remake some original whole, some ideal whole? Fragment, as in ruin, may also imply something left behind from a past original whole. In the case of Friedrich Hölderlin's fragments, the only parts showing of a madman's poems, the rest of which are hidden somewhere in his mind; or the only parts showing of a logical whole whose logic is unavailable to us, fragments that seem fragments only to us, and seem to him to make a whole – for there is only a thin line between what is so new to us that it changes our way of thinking and seeing and what is so new to us that we can't recognize it as a coherent thought or piece of writing, i.e., can't see the connections the author sees or even sense that they are there. Or fragments that seem to him to make a whole and to us eventually, also, to make a whole, though from a different angle.

Or, as with Stéphane Mallarmé's fragmentary poems for his dead son, *A Tomb for Anatole*, the fragment is something left from some projected whole, some future whole, i.e., these are fragments destined one day to be pieced together with other elements to make a whole; or they are the fragments of ideal poems shattered by grief; fragments comparable to the incoherent utterances of voiced grief: inarticulateness being in this case the most credible expression of grief. No more than a fragment could be uttered, so overwhelming was the unuttered whole. In the silences, the grief is alive.

Roland Barthes justifies his own early choice of the fragment as form by saying that 'incoherence is preferable to a distorting order.' In the case of Mallarmé, inarticulateness might seem preferable to articulateness when it comes to expressing a grief that is unutterable. Mallarmé failed to transcend his grief; he remained inside it, and the 'notes,' too, remain inside it. They become the most immediate expression, the closest mirroring, of the writer's emotion at the inspiring subject, the writer's stutter, and the reader, witnessing the writer's stutter, is witness not only to his grief, but also to his process, to the workings of his mind, to his mind, closer to what we might think of as the origins of his writing.

NOTES

1 This piece is excerpted from a talk given by Lydia Davis on November 20, 1986, at New Langton Arts, San Francisco.

2 *The Notebooks of Joseph Joubert: A Selection*, ed. and trans. Paul Auster, afterword by Maurice Blanchot, trans. Lydia Davis (San Francisco: North Point Press, 1983).

Narrativity[1]

Aaron Shurin

I'm interested in the utilization of both poetic and narrative tensions: the flagrant surfaces of lyric, the sweet dream of storied events, the terror of ellipsis, the audacity of dislocation, the irreversible solidity of the past tense, the incarnate lure of pronouns, the refractability of pronouns, the simultaneity of times, the weights and balances of sentences. I'm interested in lyric's authenticity of demonstration and narrative's drama of integration – lyric, whose operation is display, and narrative, whose method is seduction. I describe a set of binary terms across which I see writing passing an exchange of values, and it becomes a multiple texture/text – writing in just those created tensions between surface vocalic tangibility and referential transparency; between theme and emptiness, measure and interruption, the eternal present and past of memory/future of dream; all present, all heightened, operational. Such conflated writing would be worthy of Barthes's definition of the text: 'not a coexistence of meanings but a passage, an overcrossing; thus it answers not to an interpretation, even a liberal one, but to an explosion, a dissemination.'[2] One seeks to be out of order, to shiver out of subjectivity, to shake off the mask of the material and to shimmy in its arms, to finally retreat from logic and advance by radial manoeuvres, gathering meaning. 'To break the sentence,' says Rachel Blau DuPlessis – and here the sentence carries its overtone of imprisonment without parole –

> rejects not grammar especially, but rhythm, pace, flow, expression: the structuring of the female voice by the male voice, female tone and manner by male expectations, female writing by male emphasis, female writing by existing conventions of gender – in short, any way in which dominant structures shape muted ones.[3]

One looks for alternate methods to proceed, to use and subvert the codes at hand: stanza, line break, character, plot, point of view.

In 'The New Sentence,' Ron Silliman suggests ways in which the prose poem has used combined and measured sentences to interiorize poetic structure, foregrounding language operations and surface values in a writing mode – prose – whose usual form is the syllogism, building structures of projection and depth. 'The torquing which is normally triggered by linebreaks,' he points out, 'the function of which is to enhance ambiguity and polysemy, has now moved into the grammar of the sentence.'[4] The paragraph as a unit of quantity and the sentence as a unit of measure, altered sentence structure, controlled and limited integration: these devices begin to conflate the values of poetry with those of prose. Other writers have pursued not just prose but narrative prose, and foregrounded narrative codes to awaken a reader's attention to process as well as result. In his novel *Jack the Modernist*, Robert Glück uses metaphorical and metonymic litanies side by side, showing off the writing as writing as he demonstrates that the devices are not mutually exclusive.

> I grab his cock, unpromising, and he says in mock bewilderment, 'What's that?' As it hardens I answer for him, 'It's my appendicitis, my inchworm, my slug, my yardstick, my viola da gamba, my World Trade Center, my banana, my statutory rape, my late string quartet, my garden god, my minaret, my magnum opus, my datebook, my hornet, my Giacometti, my *West Side Story*, my lance, my cannon, my nose-job, my hot dog, my little sparrow, my worm on the sidewalk after a storm, my candle, my Bic, my unicorn, my drawbridge, my white whale ... [5]

and on for another sixty substitutions, 'my cyclops ... my *Venus of Willendorf* ... my *Dark Tower*.' Four pages later, the elaborative metonymic process of prose takes over from the comparative metaphorical process of poetry.

> My troubles were too numerous to consider all at once, their sheer quantity defeated me. My mom would say, 'Write a list, get a handle on your problems, deprive them of their active ingredient, time.' So I found a clean page in my yellow legal tablet ... Nuclear catastrophe, destitution, famine, additives, melanomas, losing face, U.S. involvement in El Salvador and Nicaragua, Puerto Rico, South Korea, Chile, Lebanon and Argentina, war in the Middle East, genocide of Guatemalan Indians and extermination of the native peoples of Brazil, Philippines, Australia, answering the telephone ... toxic waste, snipers, wrinkles, cult murderers, my car ... [6]

Though these are both descriptive processes, they are not transparent; the reader is aware of being in a list, enjoys the ingenuity of elaboration and substitution, is held to the surface of the writing at the same time she is integrating the lists into the larger structures of the story. Speaking of description, Alexander Gelley writes,

> This kind of stillness in the narrative may be likened to islands of repose for the reader, moments of collection. The hold that the level of plot, speech, and action exercises on him is loosened. His attention may wander, but it may also adjust to a changed mode of apprehension. I am suggesting that the more circumstantial the description and the more separate from the narrative in which it is embedded, the greater will be the reader's part, and the more he will be forced to assume a stance for which the narrative proper offers little support ... When the familiar codes of narrative are blocked or diverted, reading/writing becomes problematic, and the subject of/in the narrative shifts from the characters or the author to the reader ... [7]

This problematization forces the reader to ask questions, to become active in the role of reader, and Glück reinforces this tendency by confronting the reader directly in his stories. 'You'll understand my fear,' he says, 'because television has trained us to understand the fear of a running man'; and 'I can only give this story, which is the same as sitting with my back to you'; and 'Tell me, given the options, where would your anger have taken you – where has it taken you?' By confronting the reader, Glück not only breaks the window of his narrative but creates and engages an audience, creates a social registration for his writing by direct address, by luring the 'real' time of the reader into the 'dream' time of his story. The foregrounding of devices and codes does not neutralize them – they are too full of historical determination – but it can ritualize them, or expose their ritualization, reveal them not as necessities but constructions – open to change.

Writing might *use* narrativity without succumbing to its hegemonic orders of linear development, unity of time/tense – and apart from the modernist reconstructing modes of memory and dream. A prose whose paragraphic groupings themselves might be based on measure, whose higher integrations might be thematic or associational rather than developmental. 'How tenacious is our happiness!' says

Kevin Killian in *Shy*. 'Unlike narrative, it invents and eludes itself from moment to moment; it lacks conventions; its shape has no outline, its formal properties those of the cloud – numinous, portentous, hungry ... '[8] And then goes on to produce a narrative with properties of the cloud, numinous and hungry, where characters search for themselves alongside the writer as a character himself, where persons encounter each other but never stoop so low as to engage in a plot.

> The ceiling was gray and smooth as the beach that Gunther Fielder lived by. Flat, and peaceful, the way that 'now' is without a past or future to rock it up any. He could focus on the gray and try to hypnotize himself, closer towards death. 'Do it,' he demanded.
>
> 'My name is Harry Van,' he said. It sounded so false. He said it over and over, didn't ring true somehow. Like somebody else who you couldn't remember. Well try again, something new.
>
> 'I'm David Bowie,' he said, experimenting. 'I have come to earth a space invader, hot tramp, I love you so.' Oh that was so suffragette, trying to 'be' a star.
>
> He'd start again. 'Hi, my name is Mark the dead boy,' he said with great difficulty.
>
> Yes.
>
> 'Are you Kevin Killian,' he replied. 'Can I help you?' Just like the Hot Line!
>
> These voices came out of his mouth from nowhere, between heaven and earth, this conversation developing like a photograph pulled from its tray full of crystal chemicals. Emergent.[9]

These voices attack the proposition that characters or author must be unified presences, and suggest that self itself may not be locatable along such a monochromatic line.

He is telling you now a story about narrativity, he is telling her story. She finds the story as she looks at each other: so many faces. She is crossing gender from the start, she wants you to know she is Elizabeth Taylor – and has the Halloween photos to prove it. He is a boy playing Puck in a high school production of *A Midsummer Night's Dream* wearing ballet slippers forever. 'I have died and am in a novel and was a lyric poet, certainly, who attracted crowds to mountaintops.'[10] I come after

Robert Duncan but before Norma Cole. My name is 'Broiling-Days-In-A-Little-Patch-Of-Shade.' 'For better or worse,' says Flaubert,

> it is a delicious thing to write, to be no longer yourself but to move in an entire universe of your own creating. Today, for instance, as man and woman, both lover and mistress, I rode in a forest on an autumn afternoon under the yellow leaves, and I was also the horses, the leaves, the wind, the words my people uttered, even the red sun that made them almost close their love-drowned eyes.[11]

'Voice,' 'Person,' 'Point of View' – always singular – propose a unified filter through which events may be organized, and as filters screen properties, screen out toxins and tannins and pieces too big to fit neatly. But pluralities are possible. 'I see only from one point of view,' says Lacan, 'but in my existence I am looked at from all sides.'[12] Pronouns are known as shifters because they are by nature unstable linguistic units, referring not to people but to moving circumstances of speech and audition, visibility and perception. As such they are fictional *opportunities*; unlike names they permit a character to be subject and object, to ride the Wheel of Person, speak and be spoken of with equal weight, inhabit simultaneity. Here is a poem from Alice Notley's sequence, 'Congratulating Wedge':

> No I wouldn't know why anyone would
> want to write like that. I should never
> have had to do it. We were used to this
> other thing we always know like when we're
> here. And you have this clear head & you're
> seeing things & there they are. You don't
> notice they're spelled. That's how you
> know you're alive. I never saw you
> looking like a dictionary definition & if I
> did I wouldn't tell *nobody*. People
> aren't like that. They say, Hey
> asshole motherfucker turn that radio
> off! *But the sun's playing on it!* But
> it ain't real, you dumb package!
> I recognize every package the way it
> comes. Now I'm mixed up. But I

always wanted to be a package, person
thinks. Do they? Or, I gotta define this package, me. Or, God if only
I was a package but I'm not.[13]

What *are* people like and what method correctly presents/represents
them; from what angles are they constructed and who construes the
angles into voice? In her mind as 'I,' out of her mind as 'she,'
confronting or confronted by 'you'; conspiratorially social and partial
as 'we'; part of one another, occasionally indistinct, certainly indiscreet,
we are and we are not separate people. 'My premise, in general and in
writing,' says Leslie Scalapino, 'is that I do not think there is a man, or
woman, or society, social construction; though it is there. It is not
there.'[14] I have been marginalized as a poet, homosexual, countercul-
ture protestor, drug taker, transvestite and Jew; I am as interested in
boundaries for what lies outside them as in. I would like to drop my
'characters' onto the sharpened point of a gemstone, so that the radial
fractures would illuminate a comprehensive pluralistic image.

Syntax is the plot of the sentence, a systematic ordering of person
and event, of who does what to whom and when and to what end.
Encoded in its structure are a variety of fixed agreements that always
end in a point (.) Who will speak for beside-the-point? Nouns and verbs
must have parallel numbers, pronouns and verbs parallel persons;
tenses must agree to produce time that resembles progression.
Business conveniences that make of stories little prisons of discrete
power relations with seemingly invisible walls. I am not talking about
referentiality vs. non-referentiality; I'm talking about how narrative
referentiality might be better served. Gender is foregrounded and
elementalized, digressions are trivialized, passive constructions
frowned upon. As Sara Schulman points out, try to tell a lesbian story
without names: she came into a room, she looked at her, she looked at
her, she said – and *aside* from homophobia, what terrors would such
unlocations unleash? Normative pronoun usage subjects self *and*
other to power/dominance models of unity and authority, of he over
she and it beneath them. For pure syntax there is Charley Shively's
reduction of the phallocentric rule: 'the subject fucks the object.'[15]

Here is Leslie Scalapino writing:

The young person living there, having an intense tortured as
if tearing in half pain in the middle, waking lying asleep,

though this had only occurred this one time. The day and night being free of the one person, who hadn't had this tortured sharp pain as if to tear her in half except this one time, the man lying waking staying gently with her during it through the soft darkness and then ending in the warm balmy day with the people around who go down the street.[16]

Passive participal constructions that don't inhabit time, genderless and then confusing gender assignations, unlocated relative pronouns, erratic time shifts without one simple present tense: an amalgam of person and event that keeps elements suspended and active, 'an explosion, a dissemination' of meaning. 'His mouth are everywhere,' I wrote erotically in 'Honor Roll,' insisting that the plural verb was truer to the polyvalence of desire.

And I have neither a coherent story to tell nor can I cop a coherent attitude to give my voice a characteristic singularity. I was born in sleep and raised in sleep and wake up to find myself sleepwalking. The figures I know all have shadows; some figures are smaller than their shadows. In the first photo I am a soft blasted thing, mouth open, tongue hanging, blotto. Six weeks premature, I was still 'in here' out there. The *world* was unformed, coalescent. His story is the story of an intuited world, a story where digressions may be the point, where ellipsis is an accuate representation of what there is.

This world in its order decomposes into air, simultaneously present and absent. A writing, then, of enmeshed simultaneities, which gives sufficient weight to its constituent presences so that they verge upon each other. The material relations of the Unknown. 'The stuff of the psyche,' says Herakleitos, 'is a smoke-like substance of finest particles, that give rise to all other things ... it is constantly in motion: only movement can know movement.'[17] His story pulls the reader down from the surface of language not to rest but to ride back and forth between the manifest and imaginary worlds, among selves. 'I wanted to write a story,' he begins, 'to talk about the outside world and escape my projections, but the outside world could not escape my projections. I wanted to write not "my" story but "theirs"; I wanted to write about evil.' He looks at his fingers to escape your accusations; a sunbeam deconstructs him into motes. He is happy dissolved there, and wants to write from such dissolutions, melting into the grain of his lover's nipples. He has no lover; he has entered an argument about narrative and political ruination. 'Tell me your story,' he asks, and you do.

Here in this dialogue writing relies less on information, as Walter Benjamin shows, than on the moral power of interpretation, 'to keep a story free from explanation.' It is left up to the reader to 'interpret things the way he understands them, and thus narrative achieves an amplitude that information lacks.'[18] Here a fabricated house open to the wind is both a shelter and a sharpener of the wind's bite, a house of shadows and a moving shadow that resembles a house. *Narrativity*, the action not the thing, a happening semblance that is and is not a story, a gift given and taken away so that one must finally stand fulfilled by transgression. Narrativity, a process of integration not linear but aggregate, circular, partial – and so, complete.

NOTES

1 This essay was first delivered as a talk at Painted Bride, Philadelphia, June 1989.

2 Roland Barthes, *Image – Music – Text* (New York: Hill & Wang, 1977), 159.

3 Rachel Blau DuPlessis, *Writing beyond the Ending* (Bloomington: Indiana University Press, 1985), 32.

4 Ron Silliman, 'The New Sentence,' *Talks, Hills* 6/7 (1980): 214.

5 Robert Glück, *Jack the Modernist* (New York: Gay Presses of New York, 1985), 27.

6 Ibid., 32.

7 Alexander Gelley, *Narrative Crossings* (Baltimore: Johns Hopkins University Press, 1987), 14.

8 Kevin Killian, *Shy* (Berkeley: The Crossing Press, 1989), 103.

9 Ibid., 161.

10 Michael Palmer, *Sun* (New York: North Point Press, 1989), 83.

11 Gustave Flaubert, *The Letters of Gustave Flaubert, 1830–1857* (Cambridge, MA: The Belknap Press, 1979), 203.

12 Gelley, 27.

13 Alice Notley, *Margaret & Dusty* (Minneapolis: Coffee House Press, 1985), 68.

14 Leslie Scalapino, in correspondence, 1989.

15 Charley Shively, *The Advocate* 342 (May 13, 1982), 24.

16 Leslie Scalapino, *The Return of Painting*, manuscript.

17 Herakleitos, *Herakleitos and Diogenes,* trans. Davenport (Bolinas, CA: Grey Fox Press, 1976), 18.

18 Walter Benjamin, *Illuminations* (New York: Schocken Books, 1969), 89.

The Person in the World
Renee Gladman

In the field of our thoughts, in thinking of existence (being-existing) in time and space, we have the most absolute of mirrors: the sentence.[1] Subject phrases, predicates, dependent and independent clauses, adverbs, prepositions, verb tenses, even punctuation – all create intervals (or delays, derailments) of how the person functions in the world. It is as though all the possibilities of one's performances in time, the potential of these performances coming in and out of existence, is already graphed onto this most basic plane of speech. With a 'community of sentences'[2] one can build a philosophy of experience, an architecture of reflection and flight. That is, if one is poised to do so. I am trying to talk about the prose writer, writer of prose.

For the purpose of this essay, I want to focus on the development of a philosophy of experience in the realm of events (things happening or failing to happen). And, thus, to think of narrative. But not the strict narrative of fiction, for fiction is too burdened by a system of expectations (e.g., entrenched characters, well-developed storylines, conflicts and resolutions) to allow for the wandering and sometimes stuttering 'I' that I associate with discovery. This 'I,' not necessarily autobiographical, is a manifestation of the act of thinking in language, of the difficulties that arise, the fractures that form. This 'I' undermines a tendency of conventional fiction to present a realism that is as faithful as it is complete and confident, a realism that has little use for the materials of its own construction. The 'realm of events' or narratives that I think of as I write this are not static; they are full of becoming, full of questions of becoming. Such wonder is demonstrated in Gail Scott's novel *Heroine* (Coach House, 1987), when the narrator confides: 'Each time I start, it's as if the memory of the past (the noun, the sentence's beginning) wipes out the present (verb). So I can no longer move forward in the words.' What a sentence like this does in a novel so preoccupied with the process of what remains / what is possible of a past that, from the vantage point of the writer, is completely drenched, exaggerated, diminished or even clarified by the present and future is create a bridge. The bridge connects desire (to move, to articulate) to its object (destination, meaning). The sentence (bridge) interrogates as it performs; it fails as it performs. A work replete of such sentences ultimately asks more questions than it can answer; it gives up authority for wonder, it gives up completion for process.

To borrow from Jono Schneider's *But I Could Not Speak,* such 'loss of control yielded a variety of meaning that I have not yet been determined by although I'm being written out in it.'[3] The 'being written out in,' an event of the text among other events – such that writing itself becomes a character – is a necessary component to my current conception of prose.

Prose (to risk a definition) is the registering of the everyday, the phenomenon of life (of being-in-life) using a kind of heightened language (thus, a heightened consciousness of oneself in language), alongside a materialization of that activity in the form of characters (splinters) and events (narrative). Prose moves across genres, practices of thought, cultures, realities, bringing to both the writer's and reader's attention the blurred yet visible borders between them.

The crossing of genres, as with the crossing of a sentence, or a city (with its many divisions, disparities), leads me to think of the infinitive *to reach* – the always failing to arrive, the never intending to arrive – and also, the question of return. Bhanu Kapil Rider spoke of this 'crossing' on a panel last summer at Naropa University: 'I'm interested in these failed movements, full of longing, as gestures or failures of the narrative, but also as the language that arises at the points where flows are deflected. What happens when the person, jarred in repetition at the border, begins to speak?'

I did not set out to describe the project of prose – for the interim of this writing, anyway – as so legibly shaped by or in response to trauma, which the above seems to indicate. But if I do allow this impression to stand, I want to clarify that it is not psychological trauma that I am referring to here (though I am not excluding it, either). What I am thinking of is a kind of semantic trauma. That is, if one found – as one opened to write – a break or a freezing or a sudden displacement of meaning, of meaning as an accumulation of acts or thoughts, how might this impact the nature and content of one's sentences, of sentence-building? 'The task of philosophy,' to quote Brian Massumi, 'is to reattach statements to their conditions of emergence.'[4] I would say the task of prose is to explore the habitability of those conditions.

*

To compile a list of 'the prose writers' strikes me as a mostly impossible task; the work is simply too varied and always-becoming-other-things to be held or fixed. Also, it is too occasional. There are few writers (that I

47

have found) who have actually made prose their living, their mode of expression, such that an accumulation of prose texts, or any kind of discourse engaging and thereby tracking what prose is, occurs at an incredibly slow pace. The bright side is that this elusive genre maintains a roving quality, thus is freer, more open to discovery. The less positive side is that the work happens in near isolation. A conference of ideas, as one might find in most poetry journals or reading series, has been wanting – within the field of experimental prose or narrative[5] – for most of my writing career (which, admittedly, is only about ten years).

However, the fact that I have written several of these statements over the last two years interrogating my idea of prose, the fact of the *Narrativity* website, the fact that the editors of that site ask their contributors to attach process notes to their work and the fact of a few other simultaneous conversations, publications and endeavours (which I do not have the space to name) all indicate that, today, the marks made towards an identity of prose are being gathered more quickly than they are being erased.

NOTES

This piece first appeared in the *St. Mark's Poetry Project Newsletter*, March 2004.

1 Unfortunately, I can refer only to the English sentence in this meditation, as it is the only shared language that I know fluently. Please see my memoir of growing up in the U.S., *And All I Got Was Love Handles and Monolinguism*, for details.

2 Gail Scott, 'Bottoms Up' in *Spare Parts Plus Two* (Toronto: Coach House, 2001), 87.

3 Jono Schneider's 2002 debut from O Books is a work of prose that employs continuous-renewing (re-starts) of a narrative situation to get at what fails in representation, and how representation, in its failure, ricochets between people.

4 I found this quote in the notes of an astounding book that I recommend to all readers of this essay: *Architecture from the Outside: Essays on Virtual and Real Space* by Elizabeth Grosz, published by MIT Press in 2001. Grosz quotes from Massumi's *A User's Guide to Capitalism and Schizophrenia: Deviations from Deluze and Guattari*, also published by MIT Press, in 1995.

5 At this time, I still maintain a distinction between prose and experimental fiction – the latter having a long tradition that dates back as far as Denis Diderot, if not farther. However, the creation of a thinking text – prose – that may or may not invoke the elements of plot but does definitely interrogate the components of the sentence (for what the sentence might provide about the nature of experience thus narrative) is a less-ventured genre – a genre that owes much of its distilled quality to the nearby presence of poetry.

Dislocation

Shiver

Approximate:
Past to Present

Methods

The Sentence

The Novel

Resistance

The Buzz of
Alternate Meanings

A Story Is
a Storage

My Other Self

The Life of the Unknown

Pamela Lu

Here is an experience I often have. I just said *an experience I often have,* rather than *an experience that often happens to me,* because the act of writing anything at all demands that I (the writer) be able to, however provisionally, possess an experience, no matter how alien and ungraspable that experience may have felt at first. In writing this, I am hoping that you (the reader) will be given a corresponding possession – that you will possess your own experience of reading this. Together we will share joint custody of a private literature, which may or may not be informed by public, critical readings of the same text. At any rate, public interpretation and private reading can hardly approach one another, since they belong to utterly divergent genres of experience.

That said, here's an experience I often have: I'm going along, tending to my own business, fluently experiencing the daily routines of my life – waking up, eating, joking, toiling, encountering and sorting through conflicts and resolutions – when out of the blue I become oversaturated with awareness and am struck speechless. For a couple of minutes, sometimes many minutes, I am stranded in a queasy silence, struggling to get a grip on a word, any word, that can add shape to and thereby dispel my confusion, which lies suspended somewhere between full-blown panic and joyous exhilaration. If I am alone, at least I am freed from self-consciousness; the panic abates, turns to curiosity, and I coast happily through my verbal lapse in the peace of my unwatched solitude.

But if I am not alone – specifically, if I am in the company of another to whom I am speaking and attempting to relate a straightforward topic – then my speechlessness poses more of a problem. It becomes a drag, a disruption of the natural flow that characterizes conversation. Usually I've just begun a new sentence, just embarked on a supposedly short journey to make a point about Such-and-Such or So-and-So. I've just introduced the topic saying something to the effect of 'Well, there's this interesting thought I've had about Such-and-Such or So-and-So' and the person I'm talking to has just had gotten interested and pinned his or her expectations on my very next word, when I become dumbstruck. Sometimes I manage to finish my original thought, sending my public self out to pronounce the necessary phrases while my stunned private self flounders about on a totally different plane. Or, if I happen to be in the presence of a familiar and sympathetic listener, I grant myself the indulgence of stepping further out on the ledge of my speechless state, following the various threads of cognitive association one at a time or else getting snared by all of them together at once. This all happens in the suspension of a loaded silence, during which I anxiously imagine the other person's impatience to hear the continuation of my sentence.

The other person is vital here, because his or her presence (and even more usefully, the pressure of his or her real or imagined impatience) forces me to attempt an articulation of what I am going through silently, secretly. Even as I live it, I wonder how I might ever be able to communicate the experience to the other person. The listener sits and waits, his or her facial and body language looking remarkably grounded in the present moment, eyes witnessing but only half comprehending the sea of consciousness that I threaten to drown in. What typically floats in this sea? Collisions, intersections, a convergence of memories from divergent timespaces – some physical, some conceptual. The sudden appearance of a forgotten dream image, bubbling to the surface of awareness. The partial answer to a question posed slowly, over many years, without utilizing a single word in any language known to me. An insight, triggered by the last words spoken before the attack of speechlessness, but pertaining to another subject altogether. And underlying all of these simultaneous occurrences, the arrival of a moment so bell-clear and soulfully enriching that it cannot *not* be perceived as making sense and, indeed, cannot cease to *be* sense.

But any tongue-tied attempt on my part to render even one of these aspects into plain speech inevitably falls flat. Trying to pick one trail and follow it exhaustively to the end is futile, because every pathway is connected to every other one; in fact, it is the interconnectedness of the pathways that *is* the trail, the way that *Swann's Way* links up with *The Guermantes Way* and with this linkage *makes* the meta-narrative of Proust's giant novel.[1] There is no mutual exclusivity here. The key to the impact of a life is lodged in the secret, prosaic door that joins two or more deceptively separate worlds and isn't discovered until a few thousand pages deep into the story, in mid-sentence.

So it seems futile to put the experience live, into spoken words. Going down this road in a fashion true to the experience – following this trail and that, crossing, recrossing, veering off, crossing again and ultimately tracing out a big circle around the infinite unknown of the experience – would require the space of many years before I could ever consider going back to the finishing point of my original sentence, if I could even manage to remember it. This predicament not only highlights the inadequacy of the spoken word for me but begs the question: What kind of language *could* accurately render an experience like this one in all its depth and complexity?

What about poetic language? Here we can live awhile in the heart of the unknown. With its semantic double- and triple-jointedness, its responsive capability of treading the mutating texture of experience with as light or as heavy a touch as needed, its self-deconstructing and reconstructing tendencies, and its ability to hit the extremes of micro-attentiveness and epic statement within the space of adjacent lines, the dense puncture wound of poetry would seem ideal for inhabiting the silence that converges in the gaps between familiar idioms. In fact, poetic language is often the best form for expressing encounters with radical otherness and the problematized states of consciousness that result from striving to bring a private experience (the encounter with otherness) into contact with a public medium (the cultural circulation of a mutually comprehensible or mutually intriguing text). As developed through spirited twentieth-century approaches all the way from Modernism to current post-avant writing, poetry has excelled at redefining a certain brand of realism – the realism of consciousness.

And yet the poetic form doesn't quite address the full spectrum of the unknown, or, at least, that aspect of the unknown that most perplexes me as a writer: its quality of changing over time. The power of the poem, for me, is that it suspends the law of time to create an ever-present moment where the reader can experience the sensory, cognitive, emotional and ethical implications of the unknown through a consciousness that unfolds in identity with the poem. The immensity of this feeling is enough to fill the space of several novels, and yet it does not obey the temporal constraints of the novel. By liberating consciousness from time, the poem itself finds freedom from the entropy of time. That is, the poem generates memories – perhaps images from its opening passages or word associations from the reader's own life outside the poem – but it does not quite generate a past. It is not weighed down by the debris of historical buildup within its own body.

It's at this point that I turn to fiction as an alternative. I wish I could write fiction. I wish I could sustain the belief system of my imagination long enough to support the development of a system that fosters the growth of characters in scenarios, that gives voice to the cause-and-effect significance of the rise and fall (or triumph) of these characters with respect to their schemes and motivations, that offers a comprehensive look at the various sides of a moment or action, all while engaging in reconnoitring movements back and forth across the life of the unknown. This kind of alert pacing demands not just space but a great investment of time, from reader as well as writer. What I might see as a limitation of fiction – its confinement to the life cycle of one or two major storylines out of a potential multitude – can also come across as a power: I might learn something important from the experience of getting stuck with the one provisional life and the one conditional microcosm depicted in a work of fiction, that I might otherwise not have access to via other modes, such as the mode of my own unfiltered life. Here I'm alluding to fiction not as a simplified fantasy of real life but as an expansion of the vital aspects of an unknown life (one of the many hypothetical lives that invite me to live them in the middle of my speechless sentence), in more or less allegorical form. Fiction offers me the chance to follow a version of the unknown to an eventual outcome and to see all the intermediate consequences of actions taken and decisions made earlier in the story. Such qualities of continuous retrospection are what I have in mind when I remind myself to look for moral satisfaction in a narrative.

So, between these two practices of broaching the unknown – the poetics of unbounded consciousness, and the fictional narrative of moral cause and effect in mortal time – I feel unwilling to cast a choice. Each practice covers aspects of the unknown that I long to grasp on to and communicate, and both are necessary for the full realization of what I hope writing will achieve for me someday. Until then, I will content myself with a running list of writings that I imagine must exist out there somewhere: there must be stories and there must be poems. There must be abstractions and there must be time. There must be abstractions that interact with the experience of time. There must be a fiction of ideas that is also committed to the integrity of characters – not necessarily as believable representations of people in real life but as individual realizable beings who manifest the life of the unknown without collapsing into mere containers for ideas. There must be ways of achieving the emotional pitch and logic of poetic language while situating such experiences within a nexus of interactions between characters and their ideal or gross motives. There must be plots that can bend and flex according to their characters' needs to recognize or struggle with the poem shared among them collectively. There must be aesthetic commitments to making sense of the unknown that aren't automatically discredited by the avant-garde as reductive impulses or preludes to pre-emptive closures of thought. There must be forms that can achieve all these modes naturally.

NOTE

1 Swann's Way and the Guermantes Way, the oft-mentioned footpaths that occupy the backdrop of *In Search of Lost Time*, represent the dichotomy of Marcel the narrator's travels through two different social strata – the bourgeois and the aristocratic – yet the lifelong illusion of this dichotomy is uncovered when Marcel discovers, on the property of an old childhood friend, that the paths are indeed connected and are thus one and the same.

Committing the Fault

(Notes Towards a Faulty Narrative Practice)[1]
Rob Halpern

> I was already being prepared for the world's tournaments by a training which taught me to have a horror of faulty grammar instead of teaching me, when I committed these faults, not to envy others who avoided them.
>
> – Augustine, *Confessions*

I love how Augustine laments having avoided faulty grammar in his youth, and his valorization of 'the fault' suggests some ideas I'd like to elaborate around the question of narrative and how it might aspire to a kind of *praxis*.[2] What gets registered in this one confession is how the 'proper use' of language – *avoidance of the fault* – serves the purposes of training (discipline) and the preparation for tournaments (commerce, or war) – *all the interests of our unlivable status quo and its unwavering belief in itself.* Insofar as a belief in proper language is alloyed with a belief in property – *'the self' being but a fiction of primordial possession* – the fault becomes a scene of persistent crisis, a crisis of belief towards which Augustine's narrative tends in all its various registers. And if one's avoidance of the fault tacitly enacts a complicity with language's good conscience, it is the *bad faith* of good conscience, one might say, that Augustine regrets having *not* avoided.

Fault, as in deficiency, lack; or slip, error; but also break, separation, the *point of crisis*. Not private sin, but public wound: this commons – *where the world would be.*

From the Sanskrit root [*gna*] we get both [*(g)narus*], knowing, skillful or masterful; and [*narro*], to relate, recount or tell. Between these two roots I'm imagining scenes of collision and contradiction (mine, ours) where knowledge and history fail to coincide, scenes a faulty narrative might make visible. But I want to deepen this sense of the fault, the ongoing misrecognition of which secures the dominant satisfaction with 'naive' realisms – *as if we've already mastered what we can't even relate* – reproducing this unlivable status quo where history is suspended in a fault we can't immediately perceive – *this normalized state of mediated crisis*. So the work at hand is to ready ourselves, to prepare for what's already happening.

Lack, error, separation, *crisis*; these may correspond descriptively to some aspect of language and narrative alike: as in lacking transparency, mistaking word for world, separating perception and articulation, *always the crisis of meaning.* But they also correspond to a range of asymmetric relations structuring the social body: as in lacking subsistence, mistaking violence for justice, separating use and exchange, *always the crisis of value.*

No doubt, faults belie the flush *ratio* of language, disrupting every one-to-one correspondence with the world. But the fault is more than just a figure for figurative space – *fabled abyss between word and thing.* Fault as slip, slip as error, error as metaphor, etc.: this familiar paradigm threatens to conceal everything social, everything historical in it. It's against such concealment that I imagine mobilizing the fault, and not entrenching it in metaphor.

What might it mean, then, to commit the fault, not to reproduce these symptoms of the crisis, but to make scenes of social contradiction accessible – *where the accumulation of productive force masks the impoverishment of life* – so that we can grasp the ever-changing conditions of our persistent social disaster?

Language lies, not by its faults but by the appearance of a faultless propriety. To counter the good conscience of 'faultlessness,' the Objectivists refashioned 'sincerity,' not to idealize error, nor to affirm failure as absolute, but to remain committed to relating something – *'the mineral fact'* – that the work did not create itself. And though more often considered in relation to a poetic practice, 'sincerity' speaks equally to narrativity. *Sincerity: this determination to commit the fault.*[3]

Narrative mediates the use of social force in the world, determining what can and can't be said while consolidating dominant stories and truths. But imagine what it might mean to lay one's body down at the fault – *the body as seismograph, registering the crisis* – disrupting the smooth transmission of training (discipline) that otherwise conceals the wound. Imagine laying one's body *here*, where the structural asymmetries of whatever system penetrate sensation and cognition alike; or *here*, where everything's most vulnerable, including ourselves; or *here*, where all the conventional links and patterning appear not as smooth functioning, but buckle and slip – *under pressure of whatever stately orders that the wound remain invisible.*

Narrative can't resolve the social contradictions that delimit the possible – it shouldn't even try – but it can apprehend them and lend that apprehension form, mobilizing attention while activating the concrete desire for another future, a desire that corresponds to real interests and needs. kari edwards's genderless 'p. who in some zones is referred to as sometimes, something, whatever – or both' for whom 'History appeared in vertical molds – forming a proliferation of failed fail-safes, to red moments'; or Kathy Acker's 'Terrorism is a way to health. Health is the lusting for infinity and dying of all variants. Health is not stasis. It is not repression of lusting or dying [...] For these reasons terrorism and health are inseparably bound'; or Camille Roy's 'Can we stop piling blur upon blur? As a goal, people. Of course I've never told a story straight in my life [...] This is not hypocrisy, because consistency is not my point. I'm a seamstress of blur, performing nips and tucks on the empty center. But I need to know where it is.'[4]

Though the fault might be the site of contradiction's potential legibility, it's also where forces of social containment and domestication lie in wait, subtly and ferociously – *social energies simultaneously stimulated and trapped* – where genre performs its domesticating function. By committing the fault, narrative would risk genre, unworking its function rather than generically reproducing its harnessed symptoms. The fault is where the stakes are, where the mechanisms of reproduction – *genre as institution* – may be disrupted and another way opened, if only at this or that one juncture.

It's only by avoiding the fault that narrative appears transparent. Like the verisimilitude proposed by naive realism, the appearance of transparency is an accomplishment of ideology: the effect of an optimal performance achieved by a disciplined body, a laboured production of social grammars whose fundamental incoherence is seamlessly concealed *so as no appearance of any wound or hurt outwardly might be at once perceived.*

In the sixteenth century, Holinshed chronicled the life of King Edward II as part of his massive Chronicles of England, Scotland and Ireland. *Edward was sodomized to death with a red-hot iron poker because, according to the chronicle, his lover and friend had made the king 'to forget himself and the state to which he was called.' The method was chosen, Holinshed writes, 'so as no appearance of any wound or hurt outwardlie might be at once perceived.' Death appears woundlessly so Edward can appear in state. Were the wound to see the light of day, it would contradict every official report – material for counter-statement. The error – 'no appearance of any wound' – disavows the signs of violence and struggle, but this is a fault at whose site a radically other narrative would become an intervention in the orders of state. This would be a narrative able to do the critical work of mourning the wounded body as it becomes again a scene of the commons.*[5]

This would be my faulty manifesto: to unwork narrative's stately ends and uses – *all the tournaments and training, the markets and the wars* – to test the real limits of our world, here, where *aporia* (being at the limit of possibility and possessing no resource) and *euporia* (exceeding every limit, exhausting all resource) converge; to commit the fault – *this struggle to make the world otherwise* – always outside static forms of knowing and relating, always ecstatically – *recalling Augustine's exquisite risk* – 'and what does narrative open up into, if not human love, called into existence for the first time.'[6]

Just as struggle amplifies our need to grasp what's really going on, it informs a visceral and an intellectual apprehension of history being made – *and our participation in that.* Faulty narrative would be a practice whereby 'the senses become their own theoreticians' (Marx) – *the visceral and the intellectual, inseparably fused, like writing and critique.* And while history will never reduce to mere storytelling, narrative may have something considerable to do with this struggle to access and activate the *ek*-stases of history, unworking the stases (fictions) of concept and institution. It might also have something real to do with moving towards a world – *and making it connectedly different* (Stein).

*

So then beside as any one can come to be certain of then if it is as it is that is an audience is what it is what is it if an audience is this, pretty soon then can feel again that an audience is this, and then introspection can go on but the habit of this thing makes it cease to be this, because the audience and is it this keeps going on [...] That is to say can does any one separate themselves from the land so they can see it and if they see it are they the audience of it or to it. If you see anything are you its audience and if you tell anything are you its audience, and is there any audience for it but the audience that sees or hears it [...] I am so certain so more than certain that it ought to be done. I know so well all the causes why it cannot be done and yet if it cannot be done cannot it be done it would be so

very much more interesting than anything if it could be done
even if it cannot be done.

            – Gertrude Stein, *Narration*

Narrative slips on unknown audiences – *what unavowable commons –*
folded into the things we tell, other histories folded into our mistaken
selves. Committing the fault, narrative risks *mistaken audience,*
mistaken identity. 'These thoughts large and public, how to relate them
to my life?'[7] Tracing the fault between knowing/mastering [*(g)narus*]
and relating/telling [*narro*], narrative originates not with any self – *a*
habit that keeps going on – but rather with this relation to everything
large and public, call it audience or call it history – *these relations that*
belie 'my own' at every turn. In *Century of Clouds*, Bruce Boone puts it
this way: 'It all has to do with what a 'theme' in writing might be [...]
My theme probably has most to do with a very strong feeling that
telling stories actually has an effect on the world, and that a relation is
achieved between the one telling those stories and her or his audience
and history.' The hope here is that telling stories can still be about situating oneself in an audience and towards a world – *risking our misrecog-*
nition of both. This is about world-making and history-making, as well
as mourning and restoring a commons. But what if audience is always
a question, as it is for Stein, interrupting the ongoingness of whatever
story we are always telling ourselves – *the habit of this introspection –*
disrupting a self's expansion in language while challenging that
language's claim on the future?

The problem might be something like this: one can never *know*
one's audience – 'beside as any one can come to be certain' – without
having separated oneself from it in advance – *as if to master the scene of*
narration from afar. This of course is something one can't do, especially
if narrative is reaching towards a commons – *that which undermines the*
authority of the proper. This question of audience activates narrative's
risks, and these can't be disavowed without reinscribing a violence. In
Narration, Stein poses the question in terms of *land*: 'Does any one
separate themselves from the land so they can see it?' And she writes,
as if in response to this question of mastering anything, 'it would be
so very much more interesting than anything if it could be done even
if it cannot be done.'

Even in this so-called groundless period of no foundation, 'the land,'
like audience, or history, is the ground of all relation; and however

riddled with faults, however unstable, it informs and orients all we say and do. We can't know it because we can't really separate ourselves from it, despite appearances; and yet we cannot not relate to and through it either. The fault is here, and in *Tender Buttons*, Stein turns it a little differently: 'The kindly way to feel a separating is to have a space between. This shows a likeness.' Or, perhaps: the kindly way to feel relation, as opposed to the violent way not to, is to have a space unfettered by property and exchange. Again, this points to the fault as narrative's site: a contradictory 'space between' where tremors of separation must be felt through a commons – 'this shows a likeness' – in order to relate to anything non-violently.[8]

'*And all this has so much to do with writing a narrative of anything that I can almost cry about it*' (Stein). In order to reach the limit of what can be known and related about the time we are living, it's critical that we reckon into our narratives the fault we live when we narrate.[9] The error is in believing in a view from nowhere – faultless, unembodied and without history – *as if we weren't ourselves one audience of the thing we are struggling to know*.[10] Objectivity is no doubt 'very interesting' for Stein, considering her early engagement with science, but even she knows it can be reached only through the subjective – *from wounded body to faulty commons*. The reach is riddled with the same questions of audience and history, questions we can't afford to avoid just as we can't avoid the faults into which such questions draw us.

To use narrative faultily: like a Luddite wrench in the machinery of state, to unwork the violent disavowal of our social relations and the further disavowal of that violence – *this systematic suppression of history*. To commit the fault would be to separate ourselves not from the land but from the ongoing conditions of separation themselves – *this violence that separates concept and thing, intellect and matter, private and public, individual and society, peoples and histories* – these ongoing conditions of domination and exploitation. What ought to be done – *forged* – by way of narrative is contrary to the laws of markets and wars – even if this can't be done – unworking the language of property through which we can only relate falsely – *whatever it takes to prevent the machinery from reproducing itself*.

Capitalism obstructs our efforts. It reproduces fragmented exchanges and soluble links, corrosively affecting all our social relations, dissolving all cohesiveness while expropriating every commons – *these scenes in which telling stories might have an effect on the world*. But the terms of dissolution have often been aestheticized as formal technique by literary tendencies hostile to narrative, hostile to storytelling and perhaps even hostile to history itself. Technique is not tantamount to *praxis*, however, even when it models capitalism's social logic diagnostically; and when technique becomes an end in itself, history is lost.[11] The short of it is this: recourse to technical mastery over what can't even be related belies a certain *bad faith*, and this is what a faulty narrative practice would struggle to overcome. How well technique can adequately respond to exploitative technologies of exchange – *world trade organizations, war without end* – without struggling beyond its own effects, is a question that needs to be reckoned into the work of narrative itself through an engagement with its own technical *weakness*.

The charge, then, as I'm reading it through Augustine and Stein, is to separate from the scene where the aversion to narrative (on grounds both aesthetic and ideological), like the aversion to history, mystifies the spectacular appearance of history's end, saturating the spectacle with exchangeable fictions. *To narrate, then, in order to negate this appearance, and to affirm history in the making.* The insistence here is as much on history's subject matter as it is on the belief that the subject still matters – *this critical need to situate 'the person in the world,' the scene of narrative's faulty struggle.*[12]

Narrative is not separate from life: like the land, it's everywhere. And whether critical narrative or fungible fiction, stories sustain our sense of the world. We live in a land of stories, and outside the land is *nowhere*. Just as there is nowhere separate from the land and nowhere outside history, there is nowhere outside narrative. To deny narrative, to resist its faulty claims on us, is not so much to resist history (and its ideologies) as it is ideologically blind to the fact that without narrative we are bereft of the means to apprehend, counter and ultimately transform historical orders whose baleful grip on our world would otherwise remain intractable.

NOTES

1 Thank you to kari edwards and Earl Jackson, Jr., for their generous readings and critical comments on earlier versions of this piece.

2 I'm thinking of *praxis* here as a critical form of action whereby one works to transform the ideological limits and material constraints that determine a historical situation.

3 Or, as Mark McMorris put it, 'Sincere, implacable. (My life at risk) ... I'm using the word "sincerity" to indicate differently a poetry compelled by intolerable worldly circumstances to situate the self in revolt from that world.' 'Sincerity and Revolt in Avant-Garde Poetry,' *Tripwire* 5 (fall 2001).

4 kari edwards, *a day in the life of p.* (Honolulu: subpress collective, 2002); Kathy Acker, *Blood and Guts in High School* (New York: Grove Press, 1989); Camille Roy, *Craquer: An Essay on Class Struggle* (Second Story Books, 2002).

5 See Christopher Marlowe, Bertolt Brecht and Derek Jarman, all of whom intervened at this fault with their work on Edward II.

6 Bruce Boone, *My Walk With Bob* (San Francisco: Black Star Series, 1979).

7 Bruce Boone, *Century of Clouds* (San Francisco: Hoddypoll Press, 1980).

8 The problem that confronts our narrative practice today is that no space exists that has not been penetrated by the logic of exchange. The question then concerns how narrative might illuminate this active non-existence of an other space, while negating this negation.

9 Taylor Brady reckons one such fault into the opening sentence of *Microclimates* (Krupskaya, 2001): 'I have been known to sleep at high velocity, rounding corners into that historical narrative, written in the third person, in which the pronoun "I" names a character reading its own biography into a slow wakefulness of overture, where sovereignty turns on relations of indifference.'

10 This again resonates with Augustine, whose narrative often turns on the question of address, and whose relation to audience receives its elaboration in spatial terms. For both, a crisis of belief converges with a crisis of separation: 'Since nothing that exists could exist without you, does this mean that whatever exists does, in this sense, contain you? If this is so, since I too exist, why do I ask you to come to me? For I should not be there at all unless, in this way, you were already present within me ... But if I exist in you, how can I call upon you to come to me? And where would you come from? For you, my God, have said that you fill heaven and earth, but I cannot go beyond heaven and earth so that you may leave them to come to me.' (Augustine, *Confessions*)

11 On these grounds, it would be worth reconsidering the continuities and discontinuities that obtain between modern formalisms and Language poetries, together with their respective critical potential and limits, as well as New Narrative's accurate appreciation and critique of these. See Bruce Boone, 'Language Writing: The Pluses and Minuses of the New Formalism,' *Soup Magazine* 2, edited by Steve Abbot (1981).

12 See Renee Gladman, 'The Person in the World,' *Poetry Project Newsletter* 199 (April/May 2004).

In Defence of Forgetfulness
X. I. Selene

I 'And there had been compact, time-filled places'

It isn't remembrance that I miss, but forgetfulness. Forgetfulness gave
the illusion of endless life, of countless hours one may or may not have
lived, of infinite experiences impossibly crammed into a single soul.
Forgetfulness was the master key to time. Without a clear idea of who
we had been and what we had done, we appropriated eternity for our
invisible biographies. The present, by consequence, became mytho-
logically immense, assuming the grandeur of superabundant nature
itself. We luxuriated in squandered moments, which fell away easily,
irretrievable, leaving no evidence of our mossy imaginings and
subterranean hopes. Jostled by crowds of thoughts and impressions,
we scarcely recognized the passage of time. We would imagine time's
many paths, dreaming an itinerary of possible seasons and hours to
suit our moods and inspiration. We saw time travelling over watercolour landscapes and mounting the hills in a winter thunderstorm.
There was an ancient proverb, now obsolete: 'Nothing is impossible.'
It was how we explained to ourselves time's numerous absences, those
untraceable and misdirected instants. We convinced ourselves that
somewhere in the past, fabulous events had unfolded.

A The rays of the sun could be separated with a toothpick.
B From the top of the old observatory it had been possible to
witness the weather of the entire world.
C Milk had dripped from the stars and bowlfuls of silky all-
nourishing food had grown thickly in our window boxes.
D During dreams our sleeping bodies would float to the ceil-
ings of our rooms.
E Night tables would generate night in all directions, even
during the day.
F And there had been compact, time-filled places where all
life left a residue.
G Icy winter breath remained in the air for hours before
dispersing.
H Reflections, too, took a long time to scatter, sometimes
even days after the image had departed.

I Beds stayed warm for ages after their owners had risen, making hot-water bottles quite unnecessary.

J Bannisters and steps were never straight but always somewhat deformed by the impressions of so many hands and feet.

K It seemed that images stayed on the retina for longer, too, making our vision a melting montage of soft glances.

So, it is not correct to say that our time was simply obliterated. There was the impression of something having passed, which saved us from simple annihilation. It lent forgetfulness a range of different timbres, producing at times a complex orchestration. Whether querulous and high-pitched or murky-deep, forgetfulness made its presence known. There was no music like the music of forgetfulness, now a silent music. Only the possibility of forgetting transmutes something undergone into something experienced. For those of us old enough to remember, a perfect memory is the death of experience.

II 'The real has added in its own reminders: used typewriter ribbons traversing time'

I choose my forgetfulness daily. At the beginning, I longed to forget the embarrassing little things fuelling my insomnia. That is, I longed to forget the terrors preventing me from living. However, even oubliettes, as inverse archives, have their limits. The creation of a calendar of elimination was one possibility. Restoration was another.

During my early childhood insomnias, I imagined the love of classmates and teachers and the devotion of the older boys and girls who took no notice of me. In some hollowed-out space in a ship or sand dune, we would confess, on the verge of death, our great affinity. I had the contradictory idea at the time that the daytime threats were simply not great enough to elicit the complicity of my fellows. So, at night, I imagined a friendly apocalypse that would bind my desired company to me.

There came a day when I became vaguely visible. Then I entered into consciousness. I became more and more colourful. One day, I even experienced a reciprocal love. At that point, I turned avaricious with my experience. I collected mementos and news clippings. I wrote compulsively in diaries, recorded impressions and emotions with manic accuracy. I photographed favourite spaces, household objects, my beloved, all that surrounded us, mundane or magical. I listened diligently to music that evoked the past. I observed and filed my experiences for memory. Nostalgia seeped in from all sides, filling the craft.

But I was not entirely successful in my recording. Small details had escaped me. I had never thought to remember, for example, the painting that hung on the wall of the Sugar Bowl, or where I had put my broken pocket watch. When I opened a small wooden box and saw, partially hidden by used typewriter ribbons, the cat's-eye marble I had found during one of our early walks in the river valley, a kingdom became sovereign again. The scent of poplars was rich in the box.

Now I want to forget everything, everything! I scarcely recall what it was all about now, how I came by this road at all. I can't tell you the names of those hills or whether yesterday it snowed or thawed. The real has added in its own reminders: used typewriter ribbons traversing time. It will return reversed, smudged, overwritten, superimposed – it hardly matters. I am ready to avail myself!

III Present Perfect

I have allowed every past event the possibility of repetition. I have climbed those stairs, carefully treading only on the ovoid protective doilies, already with the anticipation of grasping our elliptical doorknob like the pistol grip of my fencing foil. I have turned on the mismatched taps of the bathroom sink, as usual avoiding my gaze in the shaving mirror by staring down through the window at the laundry lines. I have hung my towel on its hook. I have reached for the two joints of my clarinet like a somnambulist. I have sat on the bed with the vista of the soccer pitch before me and I have observed the gradual evolution of the days and seasons.

And now I am returning home. I am standing on the mat before the door to our rooms, turning the key cleanly in the lock, ready to be blinded by the myriad details squirming under the sun's illumination. I am sweeping myself inside. I am observing every mote on the disused gas pipes; I am measuring the curl of the linoleum where water has dripped from the cutting board. I am reminding myself once again to treat the chocolate ice cream dribble staining the diaphanous curtain. I am smelling alphabetically the spices on the shelf. I am tracing the tea stain around the drain of the porcelain sink, the shallow sink whose lips curl sensuously in a wide-mouthed exclamation. I am calculating the trigonometry of these bay windows. I am winking at every knot in the wood panelling. I am realigning my memory to the exact grain of the dresser drawers; I am updating my records of the rips in the muslin curtain backing. I am tuning the pitch of the squeak in the closet door; I am registering the colour temperature of the bedroom light in this precise moment of the summer solstice. I am jostling every molecule of air in these rooms in my assertion that I have returned.

But I have been returning for years and still I haven't returned. For who can claim to have reached the end of a paradox of Zeno? I have been crossing the young wood planks of this bridge for months, watching the ice floes below float and coalesce like crystalline lily pads. I have been climbing this oldest road of Old Strathcona for seasons and it becomes still older beneath my boots. I have been crossing the railroad tracks for years, in dawns that scarcely pierce my eyes and in dusks falling over my lids like heavy curtains. I have been following this street for ages, buffeted by the generations that swell and empty the houses. I have been straining towards the limit of my bedroom lamplight for an eternity, but I have not yet arrived!

All days will return. We will see all times again. The clock didn't strike but has struck. The poet didn't write but has written. The barricades weren't built but have been built. The simple past has been effaced from our language. There is no simple past. The present has multiplied. We have spoken in a tense reuniting all times, opening the possibilities of recurrence. We have begun. We have begun.

Echoes Enough of Echoes of Enough of Me:
In Favour of 'Not Going Anywhere'
Nathalie Stephens

What mind is incapable of grasping futility? Our books are built like roadblocks with signs mapping alternate routes. What if there were no alternate route? What if this circling and circling and never going anywhere were the very movement we are caught in?[1]

I would like to address the problem of movement. What at times I have taken to call 'reach.' While it is a very unfaithful (*infidèle*) translation of the French word *élan*, it is nonetheless the one I insist on in moving between my own (*un*genre or *entre*genre[2]) bodies of work. These emerge sometimes in French, sometimes *en anglais*, living, writing, publishing, as I do, in two languages, maybe more. Reach is not only extension or thrust (th*urst*) or desire for other (recoil), it is a physical motioning in language that seeks to move (forbidden) outside of the many constraints imposed on it. Reach is therefore away from the body, and return to the body in its altered form: 'echo.' (Happily, *l'écho*, en français: here, the distance between French and English is shorter, though the lips do assume an uncommon shape.) Echo is return, and its movement (call *un*answering call) carries its own inevitable departure. It is, by (my) definition: unrecognizable. It makes circles around circles around circles of itself.

(Body is the (contested) place where language originates, if one views, as I do, language as desire, desire as un- or many-gendered. Body is also place of exile, and language, as it is (mis)used, makes repeated (failed) attempts at return. Looked at that way, I suppose, it operates a sort of *aliyah*, and language's reach in this context might be read as messianic (I am waiting (for it) to come). The thought hadn't, until now, crossed my mind, but I won't cross it out. There are so many places from which to begin and each of these bears its own antecedent.)

There are several movements worth considering: the movement of the body in relation to (its) language; the movement of the body in relation to (its) voice; the movement of French in relation to English; the movement of bodies within a body of text; the movement of the body in relation to itself, its expressiveness, its evocation of languages other than those (explicitly) spoken, its (multiple) gender. Each of these forms of movement contains elements of exile, displacement, uprootedness, all of which are contained in what I insist on designating 'reach.' What moves through itself into 'echo' and out again.

(So much movement through air, and yet it is one that is not dissociable from water. In Sephardic culture, it is traditional to throw water at the feet of one who is leaving. Water is a symbol of the tides and evokes the desire (fierce) that the person leaving return (alive). It is perhaps less true that I walk or run through text than I do wade or drown: my feet are often wet.)

Movement as movement between, as interstitial. It is not so much the from or the to but the gesture itself. Movement as *état d'esprit*, as state of being, as way of inhabiting text(ual identity). Movement as multiple, as *pluriel*, as polysexed, and multilingual. Movement is everywhere I come from and all the places towards which I move. Most importantly, it is the place between.

There is an argument to be made in favour of text that does not 'arrive.' In a recent publisher's letter rejecting *Touch to Affliction*[3], I received the following comment: '[This manuscript] is intentionally constructed to not go anywhere.' The tone of the letter was (unnervingly) positive, but the reader was offended at not having arrived. The suggestion is that the writer (I?) cheated the reader out of a complete experience. 'I could only foresee a reader's disappointment.' I might be in danger of leaving the reader insatiate.

I would like to argue in favour of 'not going anywhere.' I would like to suggest that text must 'not go anywhere.' That it is, if not legitimate, necessary, to challenge what are normative modes of expression within letters, a realm I grew up associating with fierce disapproval of societal constraints, experimentation and a willingness to look closely at the thing we are most afraid to see. I am a literary child of *la décadence* to the *nouveau-roman*, with particular attachment to *l'absurde* and *l'existentialisme*. I grew with the distorted idea that *la littérature* meant a potential *libération*. (Commanded me.) And along with André Gide and others, I absorbed into me an idea of textuality (sexuality?) that was *hybride*.

Take, for example, practical readings of the act of translation. It is common to speak of a source text and a target text, the first being the beginning place (*origine*), the latter the place of arrival (*destination*).

Underneath this very linear notioning of the act of translation is a movement that is far more nuanced, far more approximate. The movement inherent in (my experiences of) translation is not movement from and to; rather it is movement between. It positions the body of the translator between two bodies of text that displace one another, and out of which is wrought a third, in a language that is neither source nor target: it is between. This conception of translation favours 'not going anywhere' (arrival is not possible). It privileges the movement between, the circling through and around text and language. It allows for untranslatability while engaging in acts of (mis)translation. It formulates what must necessarily be unformulated. It allows for the opacity of light.

If (my) experiences of movement (through time, place, encounter, etc.) are mutilating, displacing, maddening, layering, spilling, memorial without memorializing, the language (of the body) must also be so. (It is a question, I believe, of ethics, an ethics of *l'écriture*.) Here, perhaps, there is confrontation between a desired end (*dénouement*), a clear cut (plot), an answer to a single question (climax), a unique (approved) desire to act upon (normalcy), a singular grammar and form (linearity) and what reveals itself repeatedly to be spilling outside of the strictures designed to contain each of the above.

Much of what I write is an undoing (of so many things), which is an aspect of 'not going anywhere,' of not arriving.

In *Paper City*, the errant letter-characters *n* and *b* are both quested and questing, and (dis)appear inside the book in which 'we' track(s) them:

> Where we went neither *n* nor *b* had been. No measure of time could account for their existence. No story told retold untold or even mistold could hold either of them to their parcours. [...] We invented their ghosts to appease the burn in our abdomens the ache in our searching brains. What we touched upon was ours alone. *n* and *b* were letters carved into water. They belonged to no one. Not to those who had cast them out nor to those who would search for them again and again. The city would mourn them as only a city that had driven them out – *disappeared them* – could. (73)

In *FOLD*, what intends to be an exploration of a distance between *la famille* (family) and *la fa ille* (fault [line]) concludes inside neither (*You leave the whole gaping. Walk on.*). It resolves not to resolve (*You were born between bodies, nameless, worn. On the brink of many languages, all of which add up to none.*).

And most recently, in *L'INJURE*, a text caught in the migratory movement of a (nameless) man through many (named) cities (each of which could be the other) is an exploration more of arrestation than movement, of erasure than protest, of historical, geographical, sensual loss, of voicelessness. What *l'homme* sees remains unexplicit (*Ce qu'il voit il ne le dit pas./What he sees he does not name.*[4]). Where he goes is never (really) divulged. The very movement precipitated by desire is one of destruction (*Tu entres en lui comme dans un fourneau./You enter into him as into an oven.*). It evokes paradox upon paradox and in its movement outward, it recoils (*Tu n'es ni le lieu d'où tu viens, ni celui vers lequel tu te diriges./You are neither the place from which you come nor that towards which you move.*). In its projection towards *l'autre* (other), it (deliberately) fails. It is a text wrought of hopelessness that seeks neither to appease nor to cajole nor to assuage the reader. It is cruel in that sense. It is devoid of (literary) niceties. It doesn't 'go anywhere.' *L'INJURE* concludes:

> Que te reste-t-il?
> Si ce n'est la chose inavouable. Le lieu exalté. Le geste intraduisible. Le nom jamais prononcé. Un terrain voluptueux. Un appel suspendu. Une histoire sublimée. Un amour hébété. Une ville transmuée par la force de ta haine. La torpeur de tes larmes. L'incessance de tes fantasmes. De tes accusations. Un lieu devant lequel te prosterner.
> Le désir, suffoquant, inexécutable, de nommer.
>
> (What are you left with?
> If not an unnameable thing. An exalted place. An untranslatable gesture. An unspoken name. A voluptuous terrain. A suspended call. A sublimated history. A stupefied love. A city transmuted by the force of your hatred. The torpor of your tears. Your unceasing fantasies. Your accusations. A place before which to fall.
> The suffocating, impracticable desire to name.)

Inside my insistence on working with text that arguably falls away from itself, that unmakes its relationship to itself and to its reader, is a desire for a philosophy of reading that eschews facility, that engages viscerally with language that is first and foremost *of the body*. A philosophy of reading (and writing) that is concerned less with arriving than it is with experience, writing that is beside language, a movement that is *underneath*. I hesitate to call it an act of resistance. An act of insistence, perhaps. A willingness to engage with text as vertiginously multiple. It is no doubt an advantage to have been steeped in early-twentieth-century French writing growing up, to have had access to so many cultures at once (English, French, Sephardic, Algerian, Canadian, etc.). Despite the often disorienting effects of so much displacement, it offered entry into a space that, as a writer, I am very comfortable inhabiting.

In yet another (English-language) publisher's letter received some years ago, I was warned against having created a text that, while well crafted, was too philosophical for an anglophone readership. This assertion, while ridiculous, is also disabling to consider. What it says about Canadian (mainstream) literary culture and its (dis)engagement with (from) its readership is dismaying. I would hope that by pushing text beyond itself, in addition to challenging human relationship to language and the place it occupies in the body, those of us who do this (dangerous) work are creating unhierarchized spaces of language in which fluidity (movement between) is a greater force than (wielded) power, and our words, side by side, conjure plurality, the echoes of which will (gently) dismantle what seem to me to be notions of art the (inflexible) articulations of which are decidedly coercive.

With André Gide's much desired Nathanaël[5], I would like to make many (illicit) arguments for slippage of all kinds: arguments for text that doesn't 'go anywhere,' least of all arrive. For movement that refutes movement, for desire that challenges (accepted) norms of desirability, for bodies that assume hybrid forms, and for text that exists between. For N. that is at once Nathalie and Nathanaël. For a space that, increasingly, seems very close to what I imagine to be *le néant* (the void). A contested literary surface. Contested perhaps because it is underneath surface. It cannot be made to assume a particular shape. Contested because it is echoes of itself. It is reach that is by its own movement unaccomplished. It cannot be named. What I might call *l'entre-genre*. And what Gail Scott delightfully echoed back to me as *l'entrejambe*.

> Touchez-moi. Je disparaîtrai.
> Écoutez à côté de la voix.
> Si je dis que je ne lis plus, c'est que je mens.
> J'allume une flamme près de ce qui risque de prendre feu.
> (*Je Nathanaël*, 91)

> (Touch me. I will disappear.
> Listen beside speaking.
> If I say that I no longer read, I'm lying.
> I'm lighting a flame next to a thing in danger of catching fire.)

NOTES

1 Excerpted from a letter from the author to Kit Malo.

2 Genre, in French, is both genre and gender.

3 Of the works cited, parts of *Touch to Affliction* have appeared in *The Common Sky: Canadian Writers Against the War* (Toronto: Three Squares Press, 2003) and are forthcoming in *Inimigo Rumor* (Brazil, trans. Carlito Azevedo) and on-line in Basque translation. Parts of *FOLD* have been published in *Tessera* and are forthcoming in *Portfolio Milieu* (Vancouver: Milieu Press, 2004). *L'INJURE* was published by Éditions de l'Hexagone in fall 2004 and excerpts have been published in a recent issue of *Arcade*. *Paper City* was published in 2003 by Coach House Books, Toronto. Éditions de l'Hexagone published *Je Nathanaël* in 2003.

4 The French translations, awkward, are my own. (I am making an exception; translation is such redundancy.)

5 Nathanaël is Gide's imagined apprentice to whom *Les Nourritures terrestres* (*Fruits of the Earth*) is addressed.

Dislocation

Shiver

Approximate:
Past to Present

Methods

The Sentence

The Novel

Resistance

The Buzz of
Alternate Meanings

A Story Is
a Storage

My Other Self

Hunger – Technology – Emotion

Chris Kraus

From *Aliens & Anorexia*[1]

Los Angeles, sometime in the late 90s –

My heart and stomach flip while waiting in the endless gourmet take-out line at Say Cheese on Hyperion. This is the third full day not eating. ... I stare through thick plate-glass at tureens of baby peas in mayonnaise. Ten bucks a quarter pound, they're canned. Little bits of foreign cheese displayed on the top shelf like so many sad specimens. English stilton, camembert. From the bodies of imprisoned animals to the air-conditioned case, it's obvious this food was never touched with love or understanding. The chubby woman up ahead of me seems to think this food is good. She is luxuriating in the moment when she speaks her choices to the shop girl, even though the girl is bored and hardly even listening. I'd hoped to trick myself to eat by ordering the most exquisite food but now this place offends me. Say Cheese, Say Choose. She wraps the names of foods around her tongue, pleased with her passable pronunciation. Why do I hate everything? The food here is so vastly overpriced, it no longer smells like food, it smells like bills and coins and plastic.

If I'm not touched it becomes impossible to eat. It's only after sex, sometimes, that I can eat a little. When I'm not touched my skin feels like the flip side of a magnet.

The Alien penetrated me very slowly as we sat together on the bed. (This is Ulrike Meinhof speaking to the inhabitants of Earth. ... As the rope was tightening around my neck I lost perception but regained all my consciousness and discernment. An Alien made love with me ...) Uncovering his body takes my breath away. The paleness of it under-neath the soft dark hair. The Alien was naked. I had several of my clothes on. We're very still. Fibrational quivers between our bodies in the dark. 'This's exactly how I imagined it would be. So smooth.' It now becomes possible to say anything. Low voice. 'Don't move.' 'I like to hear your breathing.'

Like me, the Alien is anorexic. Sometimes we talk about our malab-sorption problems. Everything turns to shit. Food's uncontrollable. If only it were possible to circumvent the throat, the stomach and the small intestine and digest food just by seeing. After several weeks the

Alien decides that he will no longer make love to me because I'm 'not the One.' Aliens spend their lifetimes on this planet testing, searching. They get dewy-eyed, nostalgic about hometown virgins.

I'm in my kitchen making chicken noodle soup for the Alien. It's his fifth day of withdrawal from valium and heroin. He can't walk, can't sleep. I want so much for him to eat. Even though he says he doesn't love me, I can't believe it's true. Therefore, I want to help him. 'How about a nice piece of wholewheat toast?' I ask, ladling out his soup. 'Don't take offense by this,' he says, 'but there's something I have to tell you. Your cunt smells bad. If you washed the way you should, I would've done the things to you I do to all my other girlfriends.' I gasp. Soup spills. 'Sorry,' he says. 'I guess I should've mentioned it when we were dating.'

Food stripped of all its color, nutrients and smells and then reconstituted, like my expensive hair (he loves it), Ravissant Salon, $300, like suburban small town cunts drenched in Massengil.

If I could only eat, a little –

Although no one, to my knowledge, has analyzed the work of Frederich Nietzsche through the occurrence of his blinding headaches, the poet Kenneth Rexroth reads Simone Weil's philosophy through her anorexia. Both are 'egregious nonsense ... unholy folly.' Rexroth puts lays the blame where it belongs; on the Catholic men, Gustave Thibon and Father Perrin, who took her seriously. 'If only,' Rexroth speculated in *The Nation* (1957), 'she had sought out an unsophisticated parish priest, who would have told her "Come, come, my child, what you need is to get baptized, obey the Ten Commandments, forget about religion, put some meat on your bones and get a husband" ... '

What you need is a good fuck, he said to me.

In *Holy Anorexia*, the scholar Rudolph Bell wants to take the magnificence of the medieval female saints and drag them down to his own level. He does this by conflating them with contemporary teenage girls, who he finds pathetic and ridiculous. St. Catherine, St. Theresa, and Hildegaard van Bingham are all essentially the same; they're solipsistic brats. The collective trans-historic She, the holy anorexic, 'emerges from a frightened insecure psychic world to become a champion of spiritual perfection. ... Her will is to do God's will, and she alone claims to know God's will.' The holy anorexic is a manipulative vixen; she 'commands the war against her body and therefore suffers deeply at every defeat, whether it is a plate of food she gobbles down or a disturbing flagellation by nude devils and wild beasts. Then with varying degrees of success, the holy radical' – like the newly slender teenage girl – 'begins to feel victorious ... '

Like witches, or female writers, thinkers, artists, who use the names of others when chronicling their lived experience, holy anorexics are not merely people to be differed with; they must be despised.

Shouldn't it be possible to leave the body? Is it wrong to even try? Hungry yet repelled by food, Weil wrote: 'Our greatest affliction is that looking and eating are two different operations. Eternal beatitude is a state where to look is to eat.'

> The Alien is in my eyes. He's flooding my eyes. He's completely penetrating me, every bit of me in my eyes.
>
> He's in my eyes, he's spreading into my brain. Oh God, he's in my mind. He's making me feel things in my body that I don't feel. He's making me feel feelings, sexual feelings. And he's there. He's everywhere. My body's changing.
>
> – David Jacobs, 1988 interview with an Alien Abductee

*

In *Aliens & Anorexia* I am attempting to make contact with the writer and philosopher Simone Weil. At the moment of her death in August 1943, Weil became an Alien, i.e., a legend who transformed politics into tragic poetry. Not all Alien encounters are hostile and dispassionate invasions. There are others who see the Aliens as their friends. Alien encounters, like narrative, happen essentially in real time. In order to make contact with the Aliens, it is necessary to carve out little pieces of yourself to let the Aliens come in.

In Paris, the librarian Florence de Lussy is editing Weil's collected works for Gallimard. Weil's been dead for more than fifty years. The project's overdue. The edition will contain eleven volumes, and yet hardly any of what Weil wrote was published in her own lifetime. Because she was an amateur philosopher, teaching philosophy in French girls' lycees until 1941 when Jews were banned from working for the government, Weil's writing has a narrative quality mostly absent from the philosophy of her own time. She wrote articles for the leftist press, reports, position papers and communiqués during her years as a trade-union activist. Concurrently, and in the years follow-ing her disillusion with the trade-union movement, she wrote note-books and voluminous letters to her friends and colleagues. In solidarity with the dispossession of the workers whom her labour colleagues claimed to represent, Weil sought out the experience of dispossession in the person that she knew the best, herself. 'If the "I" is the only thing we truly own, we must destroy it,' she wrote in *Gravity and Grace*. 'Use the "I" to break down "I."' She was despicable – accord-ing to Bataille, 'odious, immoral ... a dirty hook-nosed Jew.' Had anyone taken her seriously enough to prompt her to write profession-ally for publication, her work would not have happened. She was writ-ing to find out what she thought.

'The body is a lever for salvation,' Weil wrote in her notebook in New York. 'But in what way? What is the right way to use it?'

Simone Weil was a performative philosopher. Because her texts are really notebook writings, there isn't ever any subject that's apart from her. Which is not to say she's writing 'memoir' or 'autobiography.' Channelling her subjects through her person, Weil does what writers do. She is constructing a narrative in real time – arriving at a state of openness, witnessed by her audience, the reader – in which thoughts fly in and out according to who's listening. In Weil's philosophy, just like in narrative or phone sex, it's not the story that we're really hear-ing, it is the fact and act of telling it. Her thought approaches narrative – an emotional transparency that occurs when someone else is listen-ing to you.

NOTE

1 The first section of this essay is an excerpt from *Aliens & Anorexia* (Cambridge, MA: MIT Press, 2000).

Objective Hazard
Anne Stone

It was April of 1999, and I was walking down Laurier, a Mile End street that bisects St-Laurent and St-Denis. I'd just passed the firehall and Dieu du ciel, and was approaching a series of curved skeletal steps leading up to second- and third-floor flats, when a man handed me the missing poster. An 8 1/2 x 14. A photocopy. We talked for a bit and then he left, up the alley. I folded the poster (three times), and it fit into my purse.

Five years have passed, and the poster still bears the marks of being carelessly folded. Later that day, I came home and placed the poster on my desk, and sometime in the next week I must have set down a coffee mug without thinking, because a partial ring has since appeared over the phrase 'Distinguishing marks.' I was at a loss as to what to do with this sheet of paper. Throwing it out was not an option, because the girl hadn't been found. Putting it away amounted to throwing it out, since the poster's silent imperative was for the girl's image to be seen, and, in being seen, create the possibility of recognition, of recovery. In those days, I lived in a tiny basement flat, and I realized that if I put it up over my desk, anyone who came to my apartment would see it. People who might not otherwise encounter the poster now would. I placed it on my wall, and it remained there for the next year. When I moved to Vancouver, I took the poster with me, and it has been on the wall of my study these last four years.

I look at the head shot (and the violent language of photography reverberates). This, I realize, is probably a detail cropped from a larger shot. The wall behind the girl is not the monochrome backdrop of a school photo, but variegated: likely indoors. The girl is possibly standing before a painting in a living room or hallway. The girl smiles out at the viewer from a comfortable place in the past, even as the poster reframes the picture in a narrative of trauma. In our only glimpse of the missing girl, she is fixed in a single moment, smiling out of a time that is forever gone. In the photograph, she exists in an eerie present tense – an effect, Sontag says, that likens pictures to relics of the dead.[1] The girl's photo appears centre frame, and below the photo, the list of physical characteristics – her height, her weight, her skin and eye colour – supply an imagined viewer with what is needed to recognize the girl. The implication being that she may not be able to provide the identification herself. It is the kind of list that might be recited by a coroner into a tape recorder as she lists the attributes of a Jane Doe. The list anticipates a need, foregrounds that need in a viewer's awareness.

I read the poster and think about what it means to be designated missing.

I think about a little girl named Ruthie who went missing in California, who, together with her little brother, disappeared from her father. Kidnapped by her mother, Ruthie and John were raised in the backwoods of Canada. Later, the mother moved with them to Toronto's east end. There, Ruthie grew into Ruth. And as Ruth, she went to high school, married a firefighter and eventually had two children. Much later, Ruth and her husband, Ross, went to California, putting out the word to what family they could find. Soon after their arrival, a knock came at the motel door. Ruthie, now a grown woman, had been found.

There is an incalculable distance between any poster that might have marked my mother's disappearance from California and the lived time, second by second, that had unspooled in my mother's life since. Against the poster Grandpa's presence would conjure up in my imagination (the one which framed an image of my mother as a child, an image far removed from me) is the absolute knowledge that my mother was *never* missing. She was in *her present*. She was at *her here*. She's not missing, she's *with me*. The logic of my existence depended on reading against the surface of that imagined poster. It is an imagined surface that my mother also reads against.[2]

I look again at the poster on the wall of my room. The girl has not disappeared: on her own terms she is present, whether geographically removed or dead. What is missing, then, what this poster marks the disappearance of, is her story from the minds of those who love her. This marker of her story's absence happens at the same instant her story makes its first appearance in the viewer's mind, accompanied by a picture of her in which she smiles out from a comfortable past. The trauma this poster marks, then, is the threat – the real threat – that a severed thread in a collective story implies.

This past spring, coming out of the work I was doing with a new novel and looking to extend that work, I mounted two courses that looked at the trope of the dead girl: how murdered and missing women are represented in contemporary texts.[3] Before my first fiction class, I went back to the poster on the wall. Close to five years had passed, and the girl in the poster was still missing. After looking on the net, I saw that different versions of the poster had since appeared.[4] On the later posters, a new image of the missing girl appears, a computer-generated simulation of the girl at age twelve.[5]

In the new image, the spunky kid from Point St-Charles, a working-class neighbourhood in Montreal, is progressed from ten to twelve years of age. The blunt cut that hangs just above her shoulders, casually unstyled, is much longer in the simulation: longer, lighter, softer and more feminine, and gently draped around the shoulders. While in the real photo, the girl is wearing a blue button-up shirt, in the simulation, she is wearing a sleeveless sweater, one that must have been considered more becoming and feminine, less tomboyish, less workish. While she looks *directly* into the camera in the real picture, facing the photographer (and the viewer) head-on, in the simulation, her head is angled slightly away from the camera, making for a softer and less direct gaze. In the age progression, the style of her hair and clothes is reminiscent of middle-class suburbs more than the urban and working-class neighbourhood of Point St-Charles. Yes, she has been aged in the photo, but she has also been edited: the translation of the girl into the genre of *the missing* that began with her insertion into the pre-existing framework of the missing poster (with its generic list of attributes) reaches the height of its expression in the age-progression photograph.

A simulacrum is a copy without an original. The progression, which changes significant codes in how the girl is read, functions as a kind of simulacrum the moment it begins to make references outside of the original photo. In some ways, the age-progressed picture is best understood as a composite; not solely concerned with markers of age, the progression ushers into actuality a more ideal version of the girl: one who is more feminine, middle-class, one who bears none of the troublesome markers of resistance that give such frank expression to the real child, like that spunky smile, smack dab into the face of the camera (and viewer). Not content to age her, the progression offers the imagined viewer a cross between the image of the real girl and the perfectly blameless, circumstanceless victim. Déclassé. While it is important to remember that this, ultimately, is a sympathetic portrait, in that it is meant to help the real girl, it is also revealing – telling of what qualities define the ideal child victim and what class markers need correction in order for this ideal to be met.

The journey from her original image to the simulation, the distance between the real girl and her age progression, can be measured by how the girl is edited with an eye to satisfying ideals of the feminine, of the ideal victim. Or perhaps the measure of her difference from the ideal can be precisely measured in the exact degree her face has been turned to the side, softly averting her gaze (from us). Such a small shift, but one that goes a long way in assuring the imagined viewer that this girl was not the kind to simply put herself out there.

The five-year-long daily ritual of getting up and being greeted by the missing poster of this child has changed my work. An interest that began with family stories has become a sustained interest in what happens *after* with missing children. By who and how are these suspended narratives taken up? And, importantly, how are stories that in some way trouble the genre of the missing child taken up?

Along the way, I was introduced to the work of Doris Salcedo, a Colombian sculptor who works with objects that belonged to the disappeared. Her sculptures make use of fibres, hair, old and long-used furniture such as wardrobes and beds, and the abandoned shoes and clothes of victims of state violence. While the use of such objects might suggest a documentary approach to a viewer, her work is not reducible to content in the way such an approach would imply.

In *Unland*, Salcedo splices a new table together out of the disparate halves of two others.[6] The viewer cannot, without approaching the piece, begin to see the terrible details in the work. Getting close, one sees she has meticulously drilled thousands of tiny holes on either side of the overlapping tabletops and sewn the two together with human hair. To see the piece, in which human remains act as sutures on the precariously broken halves of two tables, you must come close: too close. As Mieke Bal points out, your very proximity is a threat.[7]

I've also begun to look to contemporary conversations about missing persons, whether these take the form of posters or age-enhancement photographs or television shows or police-style grids, such as the one used to represent women missing from the Downtown Eastside in a recent edition of the *Vancouver Sun*.[8]

All of these, in some way, involve surrogates for the original person

– some kind of description that acts to render the missing person recognizable, as with a list of attributes. Such representations tend to be prefigured by genre.[9]

In the case of women missing from Vancouver's Eastside, most representations are organized by reference to their work; individual differences are subsumed by the overarching drive to depict a unified collective identity for all of the women, primarily as members of the sex trade. In the *Vancouver Sun* grid, two maps occupy the centre of the page – one of lower British Columbia and one a detail of the greater Vancouver area. Dots on the map represent places where the bodies of the murdered women were found. Each dot is connected to a geographical listing of women, whose terse one-column-inch biographies focus on markers of vulnerability (such as drug use and prostitution). A brief sampling of these shows how fixed the women's identities are by occupation. Murdered woman after murdered woman is described in relation to the sex trade: a prostitute, a known prostitute, a prostitute who used the street name Dusty. When the grid comes to an example of a murdered woman not associated with the sex trade, the genre still demands acknowledgement. In one such case, a murdered woman is described in relation to the sex trade she is not a part of ('Police at the time said there was no evidence she worked as a prostitute, but described her as living a free lifestyle').

In this grid, one feature, women's association with the sex trade (even when they are *not* part of the trade), is the determining praxis, overwriting the possibility of a multitude of single, unique and irreplaceable identities. After one reads a dozen inflections of sex-trade work, the women in the grid become interchangeable. The uniform depiction of each woman in the grid not only polarizes and reinforces the lines of difference between a manufactured us and them but acts to implicitly blame as well. The age progression did something similar, though benevolent, in moving the girl closer to an imagined us, in compositing her with an assumed ideal.

In looking to the poster and the grid, photographs and news stories, I am tracing separations between what is real and what is represented, in order, perhaps, to better hear and write a voice which can carry a story through to a place where it will not be just the girl but the genre itself that is troubled.

Thinking about contemporary representations of murdered and missing women and girls while writing fiction means thinking about realism and representation and the kinds of reading practices these encourage. Books written in a documentary mode invite readers to disappear language, the better to picture what language carries. Writers of realistic novels, those who embrace this kind of reading, keep their language simple. Each line is a device through which content is pictured. The reader (as voyeur) makes and then looks at a picture. Or perhaps enters that picture, identifying with a subject and vicariously walking inside. Either way, importantly, the reader's apprehension of *how things are* is the arbiter for how well the text conforms to the real. Which means, at base, that nothing's changed. Or maybe even that nothing is changeable. And I do want things to be changeable. Perhaps because, like one of the characters in my novel says, I'm tired of dead girls.

So, while I'm keeping it simple, I am aware that that's a risk. I have to keep it simple because I don't want the language to replicate that age progression of the missing girl. I don't want to clean up the girls I'm writing about. Too, I want to use language that is more open to girls like those I'm writing about, girls like the one I once was, girls like those I knew in Streetsville in the eighties, rocker-girl tacticians who know how to make use of that which is ugly. And so, while verity and voice are important to a degree (so it's accessible, so class is not erased), these intersect in uncomfortable ways with realism and representation. Which means, knowing that I'm writing a fiction that risks making pictures, finding strategies to do so in ways that both invite and acknowledge the invitation in order to make use of and, I hope, distress that which will inevitably be brought to the table.

NOTES

1 'All photographs are *memento mori*. To take a photograph is to participate in another person's (or thing's) mortality, vulnerability, mutability. Precisely by slicing out this moment and freezing it, all photographs testify to time's relentless melt.' Susan Sontag, *On Photography* (Harmondsworth: Penguin, 1977), 15.

2 'I wasn't missing, I was with my mother,' my mom tells me. 'I was never a disappeared person because both of my parents instilled in me that they loved me very much. So I never was someone who disappeared. But I really missed my father, because I was always a daddy's girl. I think my mother

loved me very much and wanted her children. My father loved me very much and wanted his children. So, how do you deal with that? As an adult, now, that's how I see it.'

3 One course looks at murdered and missing women in contemporary fiction, and the other (a composition course in which texts are dealt with as rhetorical situations) examines a broader range of such representations in media, fiction, photographs and criticism. I am currently teaching both of these courses at Capilano College.

4 One such poster is available at <www.gomcs.org/poster/0077cdn_p.pdf>.

5 The computer technology for aging photographs was pioneered by the American artist Nancy Burson in 1982. See also Nancy Burson's *Etan Patz Update (Age 6 to Age 13)*, 1984 (gelatin silver computer-generated print at Grey Art Gallery, NYU).

6 The description of Salcedo's *Unland: the orphan's tunic* is a slight misprision. Human hair doesn't act as a suture for the two table halves, but that was difficult to tell when first I saw the work projected on a distant screen while following Mieke Bal's words. I've decided to let the misapprehension stand, since it's been formative for me, shaping the way I've come to think about ways readers might find themselves positioned in relation to a text. For more of (and on) Salcedo's work, see: Nancy Princenthal, Carlos Basualdo and Andreas Huyssen, *Doris Salcedo* (London: Phaidon, 2000).

7 In a lecture at Montréal's Concordia University (1999), coming out of her book *Quoting Caravaggio: Contemporary Art, Preposterous History*.

8 'Missing Women: Unsolved Murders,' *Vancouver Sun*, November 23, 2001.

9 This phrase, prefigured by genre, comes out of a piece of shared work I did with Margot Leigh Butler, after we went to the Pickton farms in Port Coquitlam. Together we wrote prefigurements, which show and tell the story of our trip to the Burns Road property in two voices (forthcoming). I'd like you to imagine the short reading of the grid as one voice in that shared conversation.

The Day Outlying
Douglas A. Martin

The Journal Approach (1993–1998)

Back when I lived in Georgia, I used to keep a journal because there was so little to do, so little to find, and the days would build to this point of ennui, with only my own thoughts to go deeper into. I was surrounded by so few people I could talk to, so I'd try to hold on to all my thoughts, try and show myself I was still thinking. I worried about losing track of them, and thus myself, unless I put something down every day to show me I was there. At the end of the day, I wanted to make something of myself. I did.

J. was the one who thought I shouldn't wait to start writing. The day would never come. He thought I should write every day, and he imagined that each time I saw him he would read what I'd done with my journal. We would exchange our journals. We could write a book together. We could create this romanticism of a fiction between us. I wanted to prove to him that I could do it, whatever he happened to want me to do. I was doing it all for him. I'd call to tell him how many pages I'd written that day. It was a good excuse to call. I called to tell him after the first week, the first month, that first year.

I was in fact keeping two journals for him. The second was just the dreams I had. That first entry was over eight years ago, and it ends, 'I need a new way to write my name.'

First Stabs at Novelty

So much goes unsaid during the workday. The straight editors, a bunch of guys, would talk of the porn stars they'd like to interview – a locker-room conversation with different furniture. Of course we're talking female porn stars. I was the fact checker. I sat at a desk under a poster of an ex-boyfriend they put on the cover once. Who was I? Even in New York I thought about J. and my old journal. I still wanted to try to make something of us. There were all these feelings I was left with at the end of the day, day after day, working at the magazine. There were all these feelings and nothing to do with them.

Back in Georgia, I'd wait in bed until I couldn't stand it any longer, and then I'd get up. I'd write in the kitchen at the wooden card table he'd given me from his shed. I'd spray-painted it brown, then blue, over the yellow. One leg required a dictionary to stand on so the table didn't wobble. Sometimes I'd have to pull out the dictionary in the midst of exaggerating my feelings for myself. Other times I'd try to just hold on to whatever I was feeling until it might turn into something else by tomorrow.

My abjection was becoming the matter with my subjectivity.

In terms of metaphor, J. wanted me to write in flowers.

As often happens with initial inspiration, my journal went beyond him. In the novel that was finally published, a third attempt, his role in my life is reduced to just this sentence: 'I meet him at the house of this guy I've waited for more from.' It's just one of the fictional elements in a book tracing one line of my development. Writing the novel, I again took up some daily practice of composing my life. I'd try to broach some new aspect of the story every morning. I'd work on it as soon as I got home from the magazine, like I used to work in my journal in the kitchen of the little yellow house on Barrow Street in Georgia, after I'd done my homework.

Sometimes I'd get caught up and lost in one aspect. I didn't want to let it just move into history.

I'm going on from him. This was no longer about him.

I wanted to bring the reader as close, even closer, to me than the men I was sleeping with, perhaps even closer than my own narrator, close enough to glimpse some meaning in his existing even when I was at a loss.

It's a complicated objective I am aware of re-enacting even now.

I wanted to rewrite my passivity, reconstruct the way I'd hid it from myself often in my own entries. Rather than put my foot in my mouth, I'd simply point out the foot and the mouth.

You could do with them what you would. The reader might even forget that the boy on the page was just some body made out of a few words, some context someone else had allowed for.

Magazines (1998–2002)

In hindsight, I can talk about what I did to myself.

When I began to keep my journal more sporadically, I felt lost more often. I know my I's are always in flux. Eye and eye and eye. How exactly this manifested itself was that I began to look towards others, towards men, even more, to try and see myself. I'd moved to the city. My point of view was still always changing.

Keeping a journal is something a young writer did.

I wanted to keep my journal, but more than anything, I wanted to keep writing. I had to work. I wanted to make something of my being here. I wanted to do something in the city I couldn't do anywhere else, and so I hustled. I went from the men back to the train and wrote until I got back home. A goal was to not stop writing the lines of the place I'd just left until I came to my stop.

These episodes were simply the making of a story.

I was the subject of this story, no longer J., though he would always be around in the very medium. In a complete fiction, he would have disappeared. I wonder at those who feel safe enough in their lives to just let themselves go.

I'm interested in how little a story can be. I'm interested in what it might have meant that I once sat quietly at a desk, while a bunch of men decided what they would deign to publish in the next issue. Of course these were never people who had any real thoughts.

When I worked at the magazine, I posed for another. It was never just posing. I was thinking things when these pictures of me were taken, things I can only try to reconstruct later, to make them stick in a story. Often I'd have to abstract myself from my setting and into another, to attempt to remove my discomfort in my surroundings – in essence, to begin composing new ones.

I'm interested in how the daily periodically builds to this breaking point, how much lack I can take before I begin looking for the means to supplement my existence. I want to keep watching for the other I may be. I am aware that I adopt a confessional tone. I want a text that approaches responsibly its subject matter, never as the certain, never as the given. I want to be implicated in my texts, to answer for them with some accountability, to give them a reality I feel denied.

'Delirious, Always Becoming'
Doug Rice

I have always suffered from a variety of speech impediments. My narrators have inherited these linguistic deformities and that has forced me to experiment with words and syntax. My narrators and characters carry these deformities into the chaos of their lives. They slur words and sounds against and into each other as they travel towards a transformation of spirit. Their lips and tongues stutter as they come near the edge of unspeakable desires. From the inside, in a place of hearing, my narrators create order through (and from) improvised languages that they have picked up along the way. Ceaselessly thrown into disequilibrium, these narrators seek breath-words for liminal spaces.

To write through an uncertain body, to write memories of an/other body that has been cut off from its origins and desires, demands that a writer experiment with multiple languages and syntaxes. Every sentence potentially a joy, written in amazement before turning or refusing to turn the corner. The 'I' becomes a foreigner in his mother's native tongue. And he is homeless. As transient movement, this dislocated 'I' falters and slowly begins to drift. There, in the becoming of this other sex, the narrator's language turns wild.

Many characters in my fiction doubt their sex. They are confused by identities that do not suit them. They have lost faith in the body as it is known and reflected by mirrors. These characters no longer believe in the body named at birth, claimed by the language of the father and confined by the biology of the mother. With no place to go, they create lines of flight, not away from their present but through language entering into the present – narrative style as an escape into the world. They refuse to dance locked in the chains that Nietzsche claimed restricted Homer's lines: obedience to the iambic pentameter of the line, obedience to the preordained chains of desire. For when gender occupies the spaces between here and there, now and then, such dancing isn't possible. A new narrative line, an intersection that refuses to connect or lead to a specific place, is necessary.

Once for Halloween, I dressed as if I were Little Red Riding Hood. I stood before a mirror and became fascinated. I thought of Joan of Arc's martyrdom; I recalled Saint Teresa in her cell burning inside out. I heard Jimi Hendrix cry. My characters need, they want, to escape into the behind of the mirror.

Language baffles me. Disordered experiences cannot be forced to conform to already familiar styles of narrative. When I began exploring the interstices of gender, those places where bodies cannot be seen or heard (visually represented or put into speech), I was forced to reject the a priori style of traditional storytelling. How can such a style put a subject into speech if that subject cannot be clear of memory and desire?

Much of my writing, of my sentencing, takes place inside a space similar to the one occupied by the schizophrenic at the moment of entering into speech and beginning to name. William S. Burroughs said that the job of writers is to write what is directly in front of their eyes. To simply record. Doing so, however, demands an uncovering. Writers have to lift the dead remains of popular culture, of literary culture, so that they can move beneath. The residue of habitual ways of speaking distracts writers. We must avoid being framed by languages or, worse yet, being used. What happens when the Jamesian figure in the carpet refuses to be traced? When that figure in the carpet is multiple, in every practical sense at odds with itself? The figure disappears under the texture of the carpet and becomes delirious.

This narrative 'I,' the one confused by his double who is always becoming a girl, is an 'I' committed to clouds of unknowing, to the idea that following such clouds is writing. This becoming-girl never arrives, is forever delayed by the mix of desire and language. Such an 'I' cannot speak in both directions at once. The modernist notion of bricolage is doomed to fail because the page is confining. Bricolage would necessitate cutting the tongue in two. It is not so much that I am of two minds; I am spilt more than split. Words are like the grass between stones: the grass that overflows the rocks.

In this present, I write beneath a body that has been sabotaged by birth. My mystical narrator is without skin. This 'I' that is written heralds a script that remains invisible. Hear the voice that is (t)here. My teachers told me I could not write about 'those things,' so I tore my stories into tiny pieces and put the shreds into zip-lock baggies, which I hid late at night. Under blue lights, I buried the baggies in my mother's garden. There are no prayers that can rescue these tales. 'Prayer,' Leonard Cohen says, 'is translation. A man translates himself into a child asking for all there is in a language he has barely mastered.' In that litany, I uncovered my body. I am a girl.

My parents ordered me to obey my teachers. They said that I was gifted and I should use what God had given me. I remember that my older brother was left-handed. The nuns tied his left hand to the chair and forced pencils into his right hand and watched him squirm. I was told that I was not a girl. The nuns did not know which hand to force the pencil into. They decided it would be best if I remained quiet.

I tried writing. With my pencil I looked for openings, trying to fracture the joints, the seamless narratives. I copied word for word a sentence by William Faulkner. I copied it over and over until Faulkner's original words became invisible. I pursue writing to the point where forgetting enters the body. 'An experiment,' William H. Gass once said, 'has to arise out of a real dissatisfaction with existing knowledge.' I tell friends that I didn't set out to write this way. I didn't choose a difficult path just in order to be experimental. But I refuse to allow others to tell my stories – not just the content, but I refuse to allow others to tell my stories by giving in to the style of mass-produced narratives.

Akira Kurosawa says that the artist never blinks. Artistic morality is in the act of refusing to look away. 'Mine deeper,' my former mentor, John C. Gardner, insisted. In the process, minor languages move closer to the surface. Give light to that which has never been spoken yet has always been known. Language is not the clothing for thought but the organic incantation of it. Similarly, style is not an element intentionally injected into the story, because writing is an intensity, not an intention.

Writing does not cover over the wound, or heal the wound; writing is the wound, it makes the sutures visible. The act of writing is the need, the deep desire, to penetrate a loss of memory.

Writers need to physically hear the rhythm of their lips forming words – the touching of two lips, of lips to tongue, each to each. The ineluctable modality of the visible, closed eyes on a beach. In his novel *Grendel*, Gardner has Beowulf teach this lesson about style to a stunned, inarticulate monster. Here, through a private battle between Beowulf and Grendel, Gardner responds to the sick and immoral shapers of words, some of whom were his peers. For me, this final chapter of *Grendel* performs a philosophy of style that is similar to mine, demanding that language discover its own relationship to its body. Here Grendel is forced to move down into his own body, to return to the bone cave of his body-speech, to recognize the making of his own pain, and to sing pain. Not to sing about pain but to sing pain, to feel joy, to live inside the joy of coming to the meat of body. And Beowulf does not allow Grendel to merely howl dumbstruck mumblings but forces him to sing with syllables licking the cold-blooded world. Let out fire. Break into the word hoard. Raving hymns. 'Hooray for the hardness of walls!'

Poison
Kevin Killian

I'm standing on a flat plain, and then, or so it seems, a little hole appears in the sand ahead of me (like in that movie *Tremors*?). The hole grows larger in diameter – this is my sanity, and all the little pieces of my sanity are breaking up and slipping down into the hole. That's what it feels like. I'm trying to write this piece, 'Poison,' about the ways in which the writer's personality dissolves as it weaves in and out of the sentences he or she so painfully struggles to produce. While writing it I notice a host of familiar symptoms. Nobody calls me on the phone. I feel so isolated. I can't hear very well and wonder if I'm going deaf like Beethoven, like Brian Wilson. When people do speak it's with loud, ultra-charged voices, as though they're annoyed with me. I feel like I'm losing my mind and, with my mind, the meaning of life I once held on to. I used to think that people are basically good at heart. I used to think I would be happy someday, but now I feel differently, that there's no chance for me, since that hole before me is opening up and soon everything I ever clung to will be sucked down into it and I'll be homeless and curled up on the gutter outside my former apartment on Minna Street, a crack-ridden block south of Market in San Francisco. I just bought a car and there's not really any place to park it.

How did I write a whole book? I'm trying to remember. In particular how I wrote *Bedrooms Have Windows*, which I loved so much. I wrote it in part as a shipwreck victim sends out a message in a bottle – in particular to my dear friend Terry Black, with whom I'd lost touch a few years before. The book has many appeals to him to get in touch with me. (Before the Internet, through which, apparently, everyone is available to or traceable by everyone else, this seemed my only recourse.) I longed to see it in print, feeling that he would pick it up and call me. But after it was published, a mutual friend sent me Terry's obituary – he had died in Richmond, Virginia, of AIDS, the same month the memoir came out. This was not the answer I had hoped for. Part of me felt that *Bedrooms Have Windows* killed Terry Black – detailing as it did our sex life and its creation, the way we had made up sex to answer certain suburban needs for the authentic, the 'real,' the colourful. Naming names, his. Implicating others, him. What portion of one's personality is a fiction? It wasn't going to do any good to realize this was a sentimental fantasy, part of the mind's response to the inexplicable horror of AIDS, part of my own need to find myself on centre stage always. I went back to 'Poison' as I delivered it originally, as a talk in Bob Glück's In Context, a series of talks delivered week after week at Intersection, once an important writing venue in San Francisco. This was a happier time for me – April 1987. When New Narrative writing seemed wide open, a place where something entirely new under the sun could be created. And that we were doing it, doing so. But 'Poison' I found out was imperfect, it didn't help me. 'Last week,' I said, 'Dodie Bellamy's talk stressed the paradox of writing as a two-way street – the importation of the world into the self and the generous export of the self back into the world. Bob's talk may have been allied to my own idea of writing as an expression of the death drive from *Beyond the Pleasure Principle* – what he calls "Freudian pleasure based on an instinct to return to the inanimate."'

Every writing act is an act of dying, or killing, or mortification. Every time I write it's to expose to the air of the page a false part of my personality. I guess this goes directly against Bob's theory of writing, and links mine closer to Dodie's, though not in any way she'd like or approve of. My talk, I thought, would be a patchwork of quotations – writing about me written by others, some that I wrote about other people, lots I wrote about myself, and also work by others that didn't have me in it at all – to give a wide scale against which I could test my propositions. And the first was from Alan Davies's book *Name*, which I found useful in its treatment of the tie between language and self: is language a function of the word or of the self? Or vice versa?

The cryptic tongue.
We are getting ourselves
in the mood to have been
done with having been done
with this again.
It's all very irreversible
which is what
makes its guts open up.
I wonder how long it will
be until this writes
itself, in

my direction. And we
haven't proved
that it isn't true yet.
When I think of you
the sentences come,
but I don't.[1]

Then I read a passage from Dodie's book *The Letters of Mina Harker*, in which Mina, a fictional character, reflects on her love life. In this passage I felt myself inextricably named and described, my human body a vessel for a flood of narrative concerns.

Flaccid, KK's penis is endearing, so velvety and shy – but the trouble with babies (as my mother always said) is that they grow up – your bed inflates to the breaking point with thirty-three-year-old male desire panting and prodding *the thing inside burst through her belly, horror props, sausage links and ketchup* around my neck KK fastens a locket filled with a snip of his hair *to protect me from evil* I cross the street with my eyes closed, cars screech then cease to exist, the atom remains unsplit forever, cells multiply at a reasonable rate every death is from a natural cause LOVE LOVE LOVE LOVE LOVE LOVE LOVE LOVE LOVE remember when his nails were half an inch long, thick, hard, yellowed – he clipped them off for me parting my capillary pink flesh without a scratch *all it took was one 'ouch'* claws retract, breathing softens. He extends his palm from the bathtub and says, 'Sit on it,' human form follows function, in Cocteau's *Beauty and the Beast* gloved arms poke out of the walls holding candles, their flames trembling as Beauty recedes down the endless corridor *I wish I could walk through mirrors* our entwined bodies tighten into a circle, a champagne bubble about to be swallowed by Marilyn Monroe *pushing the metaphor to the breaking point, in a word: orgasmic* when we fuck we are two great hands shaking *his cock a thumb* in an explosion of light the bearded creator in Blake's watercolor points from the heavens – mortal heads bow or stare up in awe and terror the way I do whenever I'm naked *a woman's hair is never thick enough to hide her thoughts* KK reaches for a condom, fumbles with its little blue capsule PRESS FIRMLY ON DOT AND PULL APART *town fathers pack data in time capsules burying them underground, school-children dig them up, crack them open a hundred years later. Things.*[2]

I used to ask Dodie, 'Shouldn't it be, "When we fuck we are two great hands shaking *his cock a* giant *thumb?*" Wouldn't that make the passage clearer?'

She said, 'No.' That's all. Just 'no.'

At first I was embarrassed by this passage and many others like it in her writing, for if at any time my penis is flaccid I don't want to know about it, nor the world to suspect it. At the same time, I felt flattered, singled out by her language as I felt singled out by her love. 'Beauty recedes down the endless corridor *I wish I could walk through mirrors.'* The sense of the syntax issues a seductive invitation into a mystery world – and I am that mystery. Then the cold water hit me; with a start I came to and asked the difficult question: Is it I who is being described? *The Letters of Mina Harker* seems to describe the sex lives, the love lives of two actual people, but of course it doesn't, it doesn't even especially want to – its veiled and mediating nature hints at this: ' – extends his palm from the bathtub and says, "Sit on it," human form follows function, in Cocteau's *Beauty and the Beast* gloved arms poke out of the walls holding candles, their flames trembling as Beauty recedes down the endless corridor' – and so forth, then the phrase 'pushing the metaphor to the breaking point' nails it. Do you know the funny feeling you get when a stranger waves on the street, you wave back, and then you realize the stranger's waving not at you but at the little weirdo behind you in the brown fedora? One's identification with the words that seem to conjure one up like 'I Dream of Jeannie' out of black letters on a white page is like – just like – the way your heart then sinks and a blush colours your face; except it's even more mortifying – that stranger on the street's waving all right, and you wave back, then you turn around and it isn't even a person that stranger is really waving at, but an atmosphere perhaps, a draft of air. Only convention associates the wave (or the sentence) to a corporeal body like one's own.

My next example I wrote. I quoted from *Bedrooms Have Windows* to give some idea of what goes through a writer's head when he decides to name real people in potentially scandalous situations – sexual in this case – but scandalous only insofar as they deal with the body; also to suggest the peculiar vanity of the writer. And then I'll give it a fairly close reading.

> One evening several years ago I was lying in bed, after some unsatisfactory fumbles towards 'safe sex' with a writer I once admired, Dennis A. He turned his head – exactly as he'd turned mine, an hour earlier – and get this, he said, 'Why didn't you think to take home that Tom Boll too and we could have had a threesome.' 'Why didn't I think,' I replied, an echo of disbelief. 'Dennis, I did think; I thought and thought. Had I thought any more, I wouldn't be having this safe sex. Madness wouldn't have been safe from me.' I felt attracted to him when he spelled his name in plastic magnetized letters on Aaron's refrigerator. Then he spelled mine with the same colorful letters. Language fused. It was like William Carlos Williams. 'There were plums in that icebox,' I said to him. 'Forgive me. Forgive me. I couldn't help it; they were so ripe and so purple and so cold.'[3]

I doubt if 'memoir,' the word *memoir*, really disguises from the reader or listener that something very close to a real event is being described. And naturally many people will correctly identify 'Dennis A.,' the writer 'I used to admire,' with the Australian historian and sociologist Dennis Altman. I figured out that I call him 'Dennis A.' to make the narrator's personality kind of coy and obnoxious – and it works, doesn't it? Maybe I was miffed because the sex we had wasn't very perfect – or maybe I thought, 'He's forgotten about me, I'll employ this sentence to haunt him.' Writing as an act of revenge, and naming names a superior way of taking it. Like a virus, the poison of this passage will break down, over time, whatever goodwill and nice feeling that I – my body – will have by then created – like some ghastly race between life and death, immune system and viral infection. Bob's novel *Jack the Modernist* begins with a paradigm of intention, deadly intention: 'You're not a lover till you blab about it,' where the ugliness of the syllable 'blab' is meant to suggest a whole medicine cabinet's worth of emetic antidotes to the possibly-too-pretty word *lover*.

The same watchful watchdogs will naturally conclude that this pickup scene takes place not just in anyone's kitchen, in the kitchen not just of any old Aaron, but in Aaron Shurin's kitchen. Maybe they already know of my admiration for his writing and his influence. When I first met him I had just read his book *The Graces*, and I was so struck by it I could hardly connect its author with a living human being; it was, maybe, a gift from another planet like something out of *Chariots of the Gods*. And since then I've gotten to know Aaron better 'as a person,' but still blitzed by this admiration which – I see now! – is another form of objectification, turned outward instead of inward. Hence there was little psychic difficulty in turning his name, like a totem, into an amulet to adorn my prose. Hence the repulsive, shy-making casualness of using that name, 'Aaron,' and the social-climbing note its use strikes here, as though I were his intimate, or perhaps his boyfriend, and what is it in actuality but an incursion on him, aimed squarely at him at his most domestic and private, the kitchen setting, the letters on the refrigerator, perhaps the implied sneer (left-over from the sixties) that the letters are made of plastic. A plastic language. Doesn't sound like a recommendation, does it? It's true that telling stories, 'narrative,' does involve a local, in the sense that this quote of mine does have a certain atmosphere, a sophistication, but it isn't really mine, it's borrowed or stolen, the way you or I might borrow someone's boyfriend or wife, return it to them and destroy a relationship like breaking a milk bottle. (This isn't to suggest I haven't thought of the pleasure it brings to writer and reader both, but – maybe because I'm a Catholic – it's a guilty pleasure; there's pleasure in guilt too, and even if there isn't there's the dying fall you get when you string one word after another, after another, onto another, like bugle beads. The pleasure of accretion.)

Next I'll read something I wrote for the Jack Spicer issue of ACTS. My intention here was to get at what I saw as the malice characteristic of Spicer's poetics, and I couldn't think of another analogy except to describe an occasion from my own life, an occasion when I felt malice directed at me.

> My aim was to develop a visceral writing, a writing that would as closely as possible parallel the effects of the anonymous letter: insult, horror, shock and embarrassment. But did my face turn red when I received one myself:

Dear Kevin Killian:

Your piece 'Tom-Tom' in the latest issue of *No Apologies* aroused my suspicion that you must be an asshole. First of all what is a gay man doing writing about a psycho-killer of women and getting off on it? I'm suspicious that it's easier for your fantasy screw to get off when the victim is a (dehumanized) 'Miss Thing' than if your homicidal maniac lusted after boys like – just like – you ... So what's your story? If it isn't a good one, this dyke'll write you off entirely.

Threats. Intimidation. A whole map of misreading of my adorable piece. Again and again I read this letter, each time with increasing unease and paranoia. I howled into the open air, 'What have I done to deserve such venom? Who wrote this tripe?' Despite the writer's declaration, I wasn't fooled into believing him a woman. In my heart I knew this letter is from one of my so-called friends – of the male species. My only questions were, which one – and why? I'd been put into the abject position, one I was to maintain for a long time. Writing produces deracination, I decided, my own best example. So much for theory. My content upset 'her,' I thought to myself. 'Take away the psycho-killer storyline and there'd be nothing even a child would object to.' And 'her' form upset me. Isn't 'dictation' Jack Spicer's word for 'receiving the letter'? You don't know where it comes from; so you react badly. Martians are writing you, altering the furniture in your room. I wanted a drink so bad I wound up in North Beach! Bats flying from wall to wall, the whole schmear, and voices writing all my poems and signing them with Dennis Cooper's name![4]

Here the dominant note of my writing becomes real plain: I'm talking about hysteria. I mean that seriously enough, a line that runs a beat too fast, that's capable of all sorts of unexpected connections (which is good) but because it's hysterical is equally capable of making false connections or ignoring the valid (which is bad). That is to say, in my heart of hearts I don't really believe Dennis Cooper is signing all my poems. Why, I don't even know what I meant by that. That's paranoid, isn't it? But I had to find out, what are my rights as a narrator and character?

When I put myself in this false position, I run the risk all divas take: we might prove too much for even our greatest fans. And so I've noticed the characteristic note when others write about me is comic, often picking on my frailties as a real person and usually, by the way, noting either that I love the stars, drink a lot of Tab or, also, you know, drink a lot of, you know, alcohol. The next passage is from a story by Francesca Rosa called 'Canidae' (the Latin word for 'dogs'). In it I thought I recognized myself as the writer, 'K.':

As K. speaks, a worried-looking dog pokes its head through the blue gauze curtains separating the reading area from whatever is behind it. A black dog, except that its fur is so sparse the skin shows through, a gray and black dog then with running eyes; the wattles of its throat a livid pink. It brings the rest of its body through the curtain and walks upstage of K. who is telling us a story about Long Island. The dog explores, listlessly sniffs at the floor, the podium base and K.'s ankles. It walks back and forth a few times, turns a slow circle while digging its teeth into the root of its tail, and then stops to stare at us, the listeners, again. Not at all shy, confident, as if resigned in its desolation, like one of those Kafka characters that have survived their own death. K. does not, or decides not to, notice his center stage companion, and takes us from Long Island to New York and then back again.[5]

When I first heard this story I remember she was sitting onstage and I was sitting in the audience, our narratological positions reversed, and my ears got red, and a voice rose up in me with a strangled scream, 'You can dish it out, Kevin, but you sure can't take it!' In Bob's talk 'Truth's Mirror Is No Mirror,' he says, 'I wonder if we are at the point of reversing Flaubert ... by accepting an artificial self, with its own scale, depth and continuity. Eastern religion responds to a "made-up" world with compassion – but with a fatalism that is the flip side of Flaubert's scorn. To the degree we "see through" Flaubert's scorn, we suffer from and enjoy a self-contempt that is close to bragging ... I wonder if it's possible to be aware of the artifacted nature of the local and not be contemptuous of it? – to understand it as a construct and be moved by its depth?'[6]

I was telling my sister Maureen that I was giving a talk on the fiction of personality, and she nodded and said she knew what that's about. Sometimes, she said, when she's walking down the street she hears in her head her theme music so she feels she's starring in her own TV show. Elizabeth Bowen wrote, 'Nothing gets on the page that you started with, and nothing you started gets on the page. To write,' she said, 'is to rave a little.' To this formation I've added my own strategy, to rave a little before I begin to write, to exploit the 'fiction of personality' and to see, if not blinded by the brushfire, what happens then on the page. When I was seventeen and living in my parents' house on Long Island I threw lots of parties; so did my friends Terry Black and Lance Mallamo – we did so to enjoy ourselves and to write about them afterwards. This is from a story one of them wrote about a party I gave, a story that begins with me warning my parents to stay away from my party and my fun and my personality and my fictions:

> 'All I know,' pouted Kevin, 'is that I care about this house as much as anyone else and I think you're a hideous couple even to think I'd let anything happen to it. Why I just can't explain the chills that go up my spine every time I see it. It's like finding a lemonade stand in the middle of a desert. When I think about the beauty and splendor of this house tears come into my eyes. Its white walls, its grapefruit shingles, its collapsible mailbox, the one-of-a-kind sodded lawn, and, to top it all off like the cherry on a banana split, I think of our Spot, our pedigreed dog, out in the backyard rolling in mud and barking at all passersby as if to say, "I'm black and I'm proud!"'
>
> Kevin's fit of love and tears was interrupted by the doorbell. 'I just want to say one more thing,' he said in a hurt voice. 'If I see either of you downstairs from now until tomorrow morning at ten o'clock I'll set both of you on fire. Don't think I don't mean it either because I'm pretty sure that I do.'
>
> With that he stormed out of the room, slamming the door behind him.

Later in the story, Terry himself is in a car driving to my party.

> 'Terry,' said Mary Phipps, a girl in the back seat. While drinking a swig from a bottle of cheap apple wine she continued,

'I'm glad you're acting like yourself again instead of like Kevin Killian.'

'Thank you,' the courteous Terry replied through gritted teeth. Mary Phipps smiled at him and he could not help smiling back. They were true friends and he knew he should listen to what she had to say whether he liked what she said or not. So he did.

'Not that we don't like Kevin,' joined in another good friend of Terry's named Sam Rye. 'It's just that you're not him and we liked you better as you.'

Terry resigned himself to the friendly rainstorm of advice, opinions and admonitions that followed. He could not help wondering though why it was that Kevin always got almost all the attention and he, Terry, so little.[7]

But I've argued myself into a corner if I insist that New Narrative makes room for the stupid, the overblown and the nasty – these are three different veins of my writing, each with its own jet flow. The bizarre thing was that, after I delivered this talk on April 27, 1987, the woman who had written me the anonymous poison-pen letter lifted her hand from the audience and said, 'Oh, I wrote that – before I knew you better.' Do we get to know people that much better that we can change our minds so quickly about them? I was stunned. I remain stunned. I think of life as a big empty desert place – cooler than Death Valley, but just about as big. '*I know!* Let's call it *Life* Valley!'

Where, as I pause for a second, clearing my head, trying not to write, dragging myself from that particular abyss of memory and missed opportunity, there a small hole appears before me, about fifteen feet before me. And all the things I brought with me to this valley are in my trailer, fifteen yards behind. And one by one I lose them down the ever-expanding hole – cans, jars, movie magazines, photos, food and books. The hole keeps caving in on itself. My little home on wheels is silver, rounded like the new Volkswagen models, and drives like a dream. Its doors shear off with a sudden crunch of metal, bright in the noon air, they slither across the desert floor into the hole. I'm next perhaps – hold on to me.

NOTES

1 Alan Davies, *Name* (Berkeley: This Books, 1986), 21.

2 Dodie Bellamy, *The Letters of Mina Harker* (West Stockbridge, MS: Hard Press, 1998), 37–38.

3 Kevin Killian, *Bedrooms Have Windows* (New York: Amethyst Press, 1989), 86–87.

4 Kevin Killian, 'Attention Harlot,' ACTS *6: A Book of Correspondences for Jack Spicer*: 54–55.

5 F. Rosa, 'Canidae,' *Mirage* 3, ed. Bellamy (1989): 33.

6 Robert Glück, 'Truth's Mirror Is No Mirror,' *Poetics Journal* 8 (1987).

7 Kevin Killian and Lance Mallamo in 1970, remains unpublished, but the title is *(Who Let the Cat Out of the) Old Brown Sack?*

Dislocation

Shiver

Approximate:
Past to Present

Methods

The Sentence

The Novel

Resistance

The Buzz of
Alternate Meanings

A Story Is
a Storage

My Other Self

Why Poetry Failed Me and
What Prose Is Trying to Do for My Writing and Me
Magdalena Zurawski

A few years ago I stopped writing poetry because it no longer used everything that I knew nor did it seem any longer that it could. And it no longer seemed to know more than I knew. I am speaking, of course, not of poetry in general, but of the poetry I was writing and, I suppose, if I am to be perfectly honest, much of the poetry that was being written in the communities around me. What I was creating as poetry functioned as form; structurally it was sound, in the sense that the words added up and when added up the sum of the writing said something, but it seemed that the writing said nothing more than that it was impossible to use language to really say anything.

Around the same time, I had gotten into the habit of publicly uttering the sentence 'I was raised by post-structuralists.' On one occasion a poetry professor replied to me, 'You say that as if you've been raised by wolves.' Well, I can't argue with her. Part of me does feel as though a good deal of the aesthetic concerns that dominated my literary upbringing are too narrow and simple to alone satisfy the criteria for a work of art. I was taught that the form was not a cosmos, should not aim to be a cosmos. To attempt to render a cosmos was both tyranny over the reader and simple fallacy. This was proven in literature class where each sentence, when examined closely, would buckle under scrutiny to reveal absolutely nothing other than its inability to hold. This fact, of course, made it ridiculous to attempt to write anything sincerely. Subjectivity had to bow out of the game or else it would be shamed by its collapsible attempt at sincerity.

I am partially to blame for the invention of the literary prescription I swallowed. I had been educated by stern Franciscan nuns for twelve years; I was (and to some degree still am) very comfortable in uniform. When I arrived at college, I found it difficult to dress myself. This applies to both body and mind. And everything I learned in my new privileged and liberal college community I reduced to an austere and parochial set of rules. I didn't want to make any mistakes as an outsider to the new culture around me, so I made sure to create laws for myself. Naturally, that was the greatest mistake I could make.

But my other instincts were correct. I loved Jack Spicer as soon as I tried to read him, though I could not understand very much of him.

The seriousness of his project appealed to me immediately. For Spicer, poetry was a matter of life and death, a way to connect this world to another one. Though the slippery side of language could turn on him, it was still his only means; it could still mean, it had to still mean.

The sacrifice the poet made, according to Spicer, was the physical. The body of the poet would be, must be, defeated and destroyed when the poet finally and truly succumbed to the role of delivering messages from the Martians – the spiritual realm – to the reader. That's what interested me most about Spicer: the destruction of the self, of the bodily self. His understanding of poetry, of the role of the poet, was created by his desire to destroy his own physical being. And his desire to destroy his body – the violence of the desire – I always intuitively understood as arising from a specific kind of self-hatred that is tied up with his queerness. The interpretation seemed taboo because it reached outside the text to the life of the poet. But since this is an essay on why I started writing prose, I'll write about it now.

I was reading Spicer as I was beginning to write seriously and to come out of the closet. Spicer's ideas about the body were familiar to me from Catholicism, but more noble because of their relationship to art. Like a gay Catholic looking for a monastery, Spicer created a vocation for himself where the body had a sexless role. He wasn't that different, in my eyes, from the frustrated butch nuns barking at me in grade school. They, too, stepped aside from their bodies in the name of a higher purpose. Spicer's vocation, though, was a legitimate one for me. It wasn't connected to any official Church authority; it was intensely intellectual and it was about art.

After Spicer there was always somewhere in my mind the idea, the fact, that the limitations of a person's body, the particulars of his or her physical placement in social space, is the means by which aesthetic philosophies are formed. Even though this idea loomed, it seemed that my poems were less grounded in the world; they were at best clever wordplay. Out of frustration I began writing prose, but only after reading Pamela Lu's and Renee Gladman's work. They helped me break down some of the rules in my head. Here they were, writing prose that utilized autobiographical information. Their work was not ironic, yet it was completely aware of the slipperiness of language. After all, they were around my age, so they had been raised by wolves, too. Interestingly enough, they were both queer writers. But the novels are not about being queer any more than Spicer's poems are about being queer. So, yes, in some sense they are queer novels; I mean, the characters aren't closeted, the desires aren't straight, but both Lu and Gladman are interested in examining how a social body moves through both public and private space. One could argue that this concern arises from the problem of being a queer subject, but the work itself doesn't explicitly situate the problems there.

The novel that I am writing now, *The Bruise*, inspired by Lu and Gladman, seeks to map the consciousness of the narrator, a college student named M. The main character's name is my first initial and all the other characters use the other letters of my first name as their full names. I chose to use the initials in this way for two reasons. First, because I got tired of listening to my therapist say that I was every person, every character in every dream I had. Because I was creating the dream, she and Jung reasoned, I was creating every character and therefore each character was my own creation. In this way, the characters said more about me than the people in my life they resembled. I always thought this reasoning was only partially hooey, applicable to writing too, and a good loophole for my novel, should anyone I know recognize parts of themselves in the writing. If approached, I will say, 'Put all the letters together, man. Relax. It's all me, baby.' Second, when reading Blanchot's *The Space of Literature* I was struck by his description of Kafka trying to write his life into a book, but only acquiring a fragment of himself on the page: K. Blanchot describes the task of the writing as both relentless and necessary. M herself describes Kafka's experience while describing her own attempts at writing: 'But I had read that semester in a book by Maurice Blanchot who had written about Franz Kafka that that was the problem with writing that no matter how hard Jozef K tried to be Franz Kafka in the book it was still Jozef K standing at a window with his papers waiting for a clerk and not Franz Kafka sitting at a desk with a pen in his hand. And so no matter how hard someone tried to write herself into a book at night there could never be the self in a book that had sympathy for the self that was writing and this made the writing both impossible and endless ... ' Writing is an existential problem. If I can't exist as I am in the world, can I exist as I am in my writing? The answer is no. And that, in some way, is also yes. If you can't exist completely in this world, you can't exist completely in writing. You are incomplete, here and there.

But why mourn this fact? I, the writer, give in to the fact that I can't be I, the character, and I let the fragment of myself become a story of her own, though she uses whatever information I have at my disposal to tell her story, including my own life. The writing can continue using my life and anything else I know as springboards. That's what is most satisfying about this project: its ability to incorporate anything I know into the story. Adolescent poems of mine become texts that M writes. Books I am reading now become part of her college syllabus. My surreal dreams become her surreal reality. My bad dates become her good dates. My obsession with describing her room accurately becomes a marker of her anxiety. Everything I know is orchestrated into a form that is a map of M's consciousness. The equation adds up into a story that explores shame, the role of art and the imagination in protecting the self, the need to speak with another person and the desire to write a story of the self. If Spicer needed to destroy his body to write poetry, M needs to write her novel to save her body. If language destroyed Spicer, as he claimed on his deathbed, language will save M. And even though *The Bruise* is a *Bildungsroman*, a coming-out novel of sorts, central to the story is the relationship of the aesthetic to the mundane, the question of how language helps us exist in a real world together with real people.

'Text' and the Site of Writing
Jeff Derksen

> A provisional conclusion might be that in advanced art practices of the past thirty years the operative definition of the site has been transformed from a physical location – grounded, fixed, actual – to a discursive vector – ungrounded, fluid, virtual.
>
> – Miwon Kwon[1]

I want to highlight how the 'place' of writing and cultural production (notably site-specific art) can be addressed following the 'textual turn' – the movement that textualized (generally) the 'outside world' and place/site. Aside from a post-structuralist tendency to read structures as texts, how does this 'textual turn' implicate narrative as a constructive act? Has the modernist literary project of writing an imagined world been deflected through post-structuralism so now the world is imagined as not only written, but as text?

Parallel to this 'textual turn,' which leads intriguingly to Miwon Kwon's vague 'discursive vectors,' there has been both a related mapping impulse and a constructive intent directed at 'place' in both visual art and writing. The mapping impulse is both ontological and geographic (writing as a mapping of a mind or of subjectivity, writing as part of the process of realizing 'place'). In popular media, texts, particularly novels, are given a primarily ontological role, of narrating us something about the places we live in, and by extension to tell us something about 'ourselves' or to illuminate the author as subject. Geographically, the constructive intent is perhaps clearest in a national literature's assembling of images and icons to create the imagined place of a nation and to the related levels of regional literatures and urbanist texts.

In contemporary art, a sort of sociological turn and mapping has emerged. Hal Foster cites Dan Graham's *Homes for America* photo project, which 'mapped' typologies of American suburban houses as well as the taste that they constructed and were based on, and *Twenty-Six Gasoline Stations* by Ed Ruscha as examples of the 'sociological mapping ... implicit in some conceptual art.'[2] More recently, and more ironically and more internationally, there is Komar and Melamid's *The People's Choice* (http://www.diacenter.org/km/), which uses official polling agencies to survey a nation's preferences in visual art based on approximately ten preferences (ranging from 'Favourite colour' to 'Prefer indoor or outdoor scenes') and then realizes the 'most wanted painting' and 'most unwanted painting' utilizing the information. While this project is lightly politicized around issues of taste and in its adaptation of the current political tendency to base policies on poll results, it is linked to current site-specific art practices which, as Kwon notes, 'routinely engage the collaborative participation of audience groups for the conceptualization and production of the work.' From this collaboration, these site-oriented works 'are seen as a means to strengthen art's capacity to penetrate the sociopolitical organization of contemporary life with greater impact and meaning. In this sense the possibilities to conceive of the site as something more than place – as repressed ethnic history, a political cause, a disenfranchised social group – is a crucial conceptual step in redefining the public role of art and artists.'[3] A recent example – and there are many – of this laying bare of the historical determinants of place is realized in Stan Douglas's *Nu*tka**, which presents a 'Canadian Gothic' of late-nineteenth century Nootka Sound on the Northwest Coast of BC through interlacing video images of the area and disembodied voices of the Spanish and English colonizers.

This chronotopic imagining of place as the site of a repressed racial (ethnic, class and gendered) history has been an obvious project of literature. In Canadian literature, this project was determined both discursively and historically. Discursively, the embarrassingly narrow yet dominant critical trope assigned to the national literature the role of providing a history to a country strategically defined as having none. This necessitated a 'return of the repressed' in literature to counter the dominant literary (national) historical projects. Historically, Canada has imagined itself as bicultural, and this framework worked to suppress the histories of groups other than the French and English. Within this very generalized framework, official and aestheticized responses to this historical repression have emerged. Small-town history chronicles that celebrate a town such as Morden in Manitoba, which can be bought at City Hall (here in Austria these projects are very similar and are called *Heimatbuch* [roughly, 'homeland book']) or a book such as Andreas Schroeder's *The Mennonites*, which provides, in a coffee-table-book format, a history of the Mennonites in Canada. More well-known, and with a larger cultural impact, Joy Kogawa's novel *Obasan* brought forward the history of the Japanese-Canadian internment. Yet the moment that novelists are taken as historians is as problematic as when artists are believed to be sociologists or social workers. For instance, Michael Ondaatje's *In the Skin of a Lion* aestheticizes the history of working-class people in Toronto, as if the workers appreciated the modernist aesthetics of the work site and the solidarity of shared labour rather than complained about the relations of production and wages.

That these textual and visual models present place and site as being a manifestation of history can lead to a deflecting of the present. For instance, Roy Miki speculates that *Obasan* could, from one vantage point, 'become an object of knowledge as a Canadianized text that teaches us about racism in our past.'[4] The implication is that racism is relegated, chronotopically, to the past. Douglas's *Nu*tka**, in its return of repressed history, could mimic the trope of First Nations culture as a relic of the past, as being only determined by European actions, as the passive site where the history of dominant culture is acted out. But *Nu*tka** deflects this by complicating the cultural narrative of contact through its own narrative structure; the interlaced voices, challenging and overlapping each other, don't provide the unified narrative of assured contact and domination.

Here I want to speculate on (and politicize in a different way), Kwon's idea of place as a 'discursive vector' as a means to situate oneself within a present site. I write 'politicize' because it is possible to propose a move from text to discourse as a movement from a static structure open to analysis (whether virtuoso or standard) to a constructing determinant of place and subjectivity. Here place/site would not be determined solely by histories (dominant or repressed: emergent or residual), but by competing constitutive discourses that both affirm and erode the local/national and the everyday in the name of the global. Without solely reducing globalization to the effect of a discourse, it is possible to perhaps clarify the effects of globalization by understanding them as being discursively enacted at one level, as having a constitutive effect. Discursive is not synonymous with 'fluid,' 'ungrounded,' as Kwon proposes, but is precisely constitutive and grounding. In this formulation, the particularisms of a place/site and its histories are not just the oppositional force to globalization (or the corrective to dominant historical narratives), but an aspect of place that can be utilized by globalism; that is, a dialectic of local and global, or site and nonsite (if a place is imagined as siteless in its loss of particularities due to globalization).

My own turn towards the discursive effects of globalism in relation to place/site arose because of the contradictions I saw in the city in which I was living. The city of Calgary in Alberta imagines itself as a regionally based 'open-for-business' kind of city, free of, but also wary of, the ills of larger cities, yet a city of international standards. This discourse of regionalism serves to cloak the existing relations of production which Calgary – as an 'oil town' – is linked into and determined by. Global capital through the multinational oil and gas industry, whose corporate logos hover above Calgary's gridded streets, is a key determinant of both the social relations of the city and how the city imagines itself. When the oil industry is profitable (due to high crude prices, a manufactured crisis or an imperialist war), the city thrives and new homes are built, rents rise, corporate headquarters shuffle, cigar bars and fusion-cooking restaurants open – in short, a lot of money is made by a few people, but the scramble for profit is on. This imaginary masking of real relations, a kind of cognitive masking, is what Arjun Appadurai cites as fetishistic: 'The locality (both in the sense of the local factory or site of production and then extended sense of the nation-state), becomes a fetish that disguises the dispersed forces that actually drive the production process.'[5] In Calgary, the global forces then have a direct effect on the planning and layout of the city, as well as the architecture; the social space of the city (itself a constituting aspect) is determined by the management of the effects of globalization and localization. Seeing how the effective discourses of place/region and nation could serve as a mystifying factor in this global-urban nexus, blocking the real relations of the city, I moved away from an investigation of place and towards the material determination of a place/site.

The emphasis on the constitutive discourses of site/place can supplement site as repressed histories. These discourses must also be seen, alongside repressed histories, as historical developments, as constitutive elements of the repressed history and emergent history. The place of writing then becomes imagined as a site of intersecting discourses and lived histories: not groundless and fluid but both determined and determining. Experimental narrative works can enter this scene as cultural forces or vectors that provide other narrative structures for imagining places and histories. The 'end of history' thesis that was pressed by triumphant globalization (hello, 'free markets'!) is also a clampdown on narrative structure as well as the cultural imagining of 'another world.' The march of global capital is a story structured through the most conservative and inequitable narratives.

NOTES

1 Miwon Kwon, 'One Place After Another: Notes on Site Specificity,' *October* 80 (Spring 1997): 95.

2 Hal Foster, *The Return of the Real* (Cambridge MA: MIT Press, 1999), 185.

3 Kwon, 96.

4 Roy Miki, *Broken Entries: Race Subjectivity Writing* (Toronto: Mercury Press, 1998), 145.

5 Arjun Appadurai, *Modernity at Large: Cultural Dimensions of Globalization* (Minneapolis: University of Minnesota Press, 1996), 42.

On Performance, Narrative, Mnemotechnique, Glue and Solvent

Corey Frost

Montreal in the mid-nineties is where I grew the necessary mental appendages to write, a budding engendered by excited encounters with texts running the gamut from corn to experimental, by the presence of certain key mentors and by the elliptic circles in which I was travelling.[1] These circles generally lived performance and publishing as the same experience: a chapbook launch, for instance, would also be a stapling party, so that the audience was involved in production and distribution as well as reception. Publications were excuses to have events, and events morphed into publications. Writing and performing were like love and sex to me: not the same thing exactly, but certainly linked.

Some of us theorized these connections in our cheap Plateau Mont-Royal apartments, where we gathered for weekly writing workshops. Or we would organize appearances at small and breezy Bistro 4 on St. Laurent, or at one of the many cabaret shows where we might be scheduled between a butoh piece and francophone sound poetry, and then we would write and read onstage, taking lines and direction from the audience. Sometimes the audience became part of the show and it worked brilliantly, and sometimes I think we forgot the audience was there. When it didn't work so well, we would give up and do sound poetry ourselves. Most of us were also involved in *index* magazine, a publication about performance, combining gushing and griping about readings, chapbooks, comics, etc., with woman-on-the-street interviews about French feminism, cyborg theory, literary colonialism: irreverent in spurts, passing queer, oblivious to genre. In my mind at least it was an attempt to cross-breed the freshly acquired critical abilities that were making us giddy just then with the pure rock-and-roll thrill – or maybe it was more punk or hip-hop – of the performance styles that were drifting into the city from somewhere to the south. *index* was a reaction, in part, to the rise of spoken word, embodied for us in fairly mainstream phenomena like Lollapalooza's 1994 poetry stage, but creating the magazine also lured our collective concept of spoken word (and its potential, ideal form) in a critical, experimental direction.

In the early nineties, there was no coherent spoken-word 'scene' in Montreal, in English or in French. Between the city's French majority and the English minority there is always a tense symbiosis, but its dancers, artists and musicians are not nearly as territorial as its writers, whose raw material happens to be the very source of the friction. Therefore anglophone writers – with some open-minded exceptions – tend to be oblivious to the often more experimental currents of Québécois writing, and a reciprocal blind spot exists on the francophone side (although it doesn't have to be as wide to obscure the little anglo scene). But when the spoken-word scene started to burgeon, it burgeoned in both English and French, although at first it was an anglophone activity that the francophones saw as distinctly American and therefore suspicious. As it seeped into French, it metamorphosed into bilingual events, something previously unheard of in more literary circles. Cabarets were in vogue, so writers in both languages shared the stage with musicians, dancers and performance artists. Choreographed sound poetry became one method of choice for reaching anglo-, franco- and allophones alike. This eclecticism, and this linguistic cross-pollination, had an effect on the direction of 'spoken word': many of us prose writers found ourselves part of an inchoate scene with a very malleable form which became, I think, more focused on concept, experiment and perversion than the form generally was elsewhere.[2] My feelings about 'spoken word' are thus somewhat more affectionate than those of many writers here in New York, who often see it as too indulgent, too predictable, too *pop*, or even as an outdated fad.

Performance – not just *readings*, but creative, rehearsed *performance* – has been intrinsic to my writing, as much as it is to a musician. That's why narrative and performance is an obvious topic for me. It's only recently, a decade after my writing practice became a writing-performance practice, that my theorization of the connection has started to catch up. One of the reasons is that I'm no longer living in Montreal, my first writing community, and I'm feeling the lived reality of an axiom that I've been glib about for years, that spoken word is an inherently community-based form. It's a case of the neighbourhood talking to itself, and repeating itself too.[3] Even when the writer-performer works alone it seems like a collaborative activity, since a good performer will create a work that is not complete without its audience. In another sense, writing for performance creates a stronger sense of community among writers, who end up sharing stages and green rooms and audiences and, inevitably, ideas and approaches and inspirations.

The polyphony of the performance scene is not at all exclusive to narrative performers, but the words *experimental, narrative* and *performance* are not uttered together often enough. This oversight is exemplified in the complacent phrase 'performance poetry,' which emphasizes image and sound, the consuming concerns of poetry – phanopoeia, melopoeia and logopoeia, if you like – but neglects the roles of drama and narrative, which are clearly just as important to performance writing. In fact, I might productively point out that performance is always akin to narrative in a way that print is not, since one happens in time and the other is static; conversely, one might say that narration is always performative in a way that poetry does not need to be, because it introduces a sequence and therefore time, which automatically leads the reader through a pattern of steps. Suffice it to say that spoken-word writing is, more often than not, essentially narrative. Storytelling has been the basis of civilizations and is still all around us: the traditional folk forms of storytelling are experiencing a sort of revival on the radio and at festivals, while here in New York, poetry slams have lately been competing for attention with 'story slams.' This seems as natural as tapping your foot. But when it comes to *experimental* narrative writing, how is it affected by performance?

Everything about my writing – style, content, volume, frequency – has been shaped by the gravitational fields of the other performers in the community. Another way performance affects my writing has to do with something usually seen as a technical issue: memorization. Memorization is one of the most valuable tools I've learned as a writer, and I often wish I could properly convey to my audiences the sheer satisfaction that it kindles in me. It's a performance technique, obviously, but it's also a writing technique, and sometimes – people who know me will attest to my absolute unflakiness, so don't take this the wrong way – sometimes it borders on being a kind of spiritual technique for me. As an activity it's similar to running. At first it can be painful – it can seem like a long, impossible task, and you don't want to read the piece over and over again, your eyes and your head get tired, and you just want to stop. The first few times, you probably don't get very far, but you build up your stamina, and you make it farther through the text. At a certain point in the memorization process (when you get good at it, this happens fairly quickly) you break through the wall, to borrow the horrible jargon of athletes. It goes from being hard to being effortless, almost joyous. Your reiterations become not a way of getting somewhere but an end in themselves. The sentences cease being sentences and become something more pliable, like warm putty for your mind.

What is valuable and more or less original about spoken word, then, is that it has encouraged writers to memorize their work. This is an excellent exercise, whether you're performing or not: to take a story or a prose poem, the more dense and fragmented the better, really, four or five pages, or even ten or twenty, and to memorize it, word for word, punctuation mark for punctuation mark. It's not as difficult to do as some people may think, because there are always hooks to hang the next line on, mnemonic signposts. With poetry, the most effective mnemotechnique is in the use of rhyme and meter. Narrative prose, though, is even better suited to memorization than most poetry, because of its sequential nature. Everyone knows it is easier to memorize a story than it is to memorize a grocery list or a page from the phone book. We don't even call it memorization; most people don't need to rehearse, for example, to tell a joke they've heard once. Hey, I'm as sequential as the next guy. Experimental narrative, though, often attempts to mess with those sequences; does this make it harder to memorize? Not necessarily, because the interference creates its own mnemonic hooks. In some jokes, the more surreal and unexpected the punchline, the easier it is to remember.

My expectation, once, was that since narrative helps us to remember, memorization should glue the story more tightly together, reinforcing the narrative impetus of the text and making it in effect harder to mess with the sequence. In other words, even the most non-linear narrative, when memorized, should become basically a line. I haven't found this to be the case. While learning a story may be a shorter process than learning non-narrative prose, once you 'get' it, the mnemotechnique works in essentially the same way. Your mnemonic hooks – the obscure mental images that do the work of connecting one phrase to the next – are unconcerned whether they're dealing with a narrative or random phrases. You may not even be aware of the hooks, bits of imaginary velcro that may have to do with the story, or the connotations of a word, or its sounds, or even something completely unrelated, like where you were when you memorized it. But whatever they are, the hooks are by nature deconstructive. What this means is that narrative, or any structure, is dissolved by memorization: the story components are no longer linked through the superficial, logical progression of the plot but become associated through a layer of meaning that is more protean and unpredictable. Memorization is closer to fragmentation or analysis than it is to amalgamation or synthesis; it exposes the linearity of the story to infinite possibilities for distraction and detour, because it multiplies the levels on which words are connected. For me, this is exciting. The powers of text that I most appreciate are its ability to focus attention and its ability to distract. The writing I like best creates effective distractions, so that I find myself looking at the object of scrutiny out of the corner of my eye and seeing it differently. This is what memorization often does for me with regards to my own writing: it lets me forget what I was actually writing about, get distracted by the words and then forget about those too, to finally glimpse some latent material that is entirely new to me, hidden in my own text. As I've said before in a travel story, we have to forget where ideas come from in order to find them interesting again.

I've been talking about things that go on backstage in my mind, in the tenebrous world of neurons and synapses, but ultimately I find that the process of memorization affects the text in both substantial and esoteric ways. In performance, the little changes in intonation and speed that make one reading different from another, the quiddity of the live performance, are the result of the mnemotechnique's synaptic revisions. However, I will also often rewrite sentences and passages based on whatever comes to mind during the performance or during the memorization process itself, making the text a bit looser, more prone to tangent and upheaval. That is the substantial side of the effects of memorization, how it alters the way narrative works in the text. The esoteric side, by which I mean its effect on my own private reaction to my own text, may be just as significant; it allows for a kind of interpretation that happens deep in the brain. When used consistently on one's own writing, it can start to work sea changes: every rereading, every subsequent recitation, creates anomalies: opportunities for a little self-subversion, another strategic escape from the confines of pure, that is, sequential, mimetic narrative. The unexplained growth of new mental appendages.

NOTES

1 Among my mentors, Gail Scott and Robert Majzels were particularly impor-
tant. The people in those writing-performance circles included Colin
Christie, Catherine Kidd, Trish Salah, Dana Bath, Laura Killam, Umni Khan,
Julie Crysler, Buffy Childerhose, Andy Brown, Anne Stone, Vincent
Tinguely, Victoria Stanton, Ran Elfassy, Justin McGrail, Scott Duncan,
Tracey Bohan and many others.

2 I've written more about this in 'The Text Has Been Eaten: "Spoken Word"
Performance in Montreal,' published in Jason Camlot and Todd Swift's
forthcoming *English Poetry in Quebec, 1976–2006*. A more comprehensive
version of the story can be found in Vincent Tinguely and Victoria Stanton's
Impure: Reinventing the Word (Montreal: Conundrum, 2001).

3 This reflexive conversation has been illuminated for me by Bakhtin's
writings on multivocality and Derrida's notion of citationality.

Widows and Orphans
Nicole Markotić

Gertrude Stein famously begins her essay 'Poetry and Grammar' with the line 'What is poetry and if you know what poetry is what is prose.'[1] Stein asks not only about two supposedly separate modes of writing, she also questions where the separation between them is decided. Her words suggest doubt that a respondent can always successfully discriminate between the two. Marianne Moore suggests a similar genre instability when she notes in her essay 'Subject, Predicate, Object' that 'if what I write is called poetry it is because there is no other category in which to put it.'[2] The categorization, then, becomes the form's naming, and how the words do or do not 'fit' into particular categories likens to a typographical puzzle. But words are sneaky, they cross borders, they tiptoe into bordering camps, they traipse between one format and another, refusing passports, declining to 'belong.' Words are peculiar kinds of widows and orphans.

The title of my current narrative poetry manuscript, *Widows and Orphans*, alludes in part to the typographical 'extra' or 'leftover' words that typesetters worried about until computer software made their placement almost automatic. A widow, of course, refers to the last word of a paragraph that carries onto a line of its own. An orphan refers to the first line of a paragraph that ends up alone at the bottom of a page. In this context, it is interesting that typesetters have traditionally used the bracket and the margin indent to deal with a too-long verse line, despite how this changes the visual look of the resulting page. My title also ironically invokes a reactionary response to certain clichés of pathos – compassion, sympathy, pity – for the social standing of women bereft of husbands and of children bereft of parents. Such automated pathos implies that these women have been left behind, that their status has changed – through the death of another – to that of being extraneous to the world, disconnected, and no longer pertinent. In these prose pieces, I want to examine the performance of line and of word as widow and orphan. By looking at grammatical constructs that 'spill over' their designated area, I also focus on literary figures (for the patriarchal family, and for the state) that do not, quite, belong on their own pages. Who is a member and who an outsider? This is a question of belonging, and of which bodies – which words – occupy the borders.

Poet Fred Wah cites the hyphen as a marker of hybridity,[3] as an 'in-between' that reminds readers that borders include territory that belongs to neither an in nor an out. Widows are not always the discarded spouses of dead husbands; they are operas (*The Merry Widows*), they are abandoned sport-spouses ('hockey widows'), they are black hairy spiders that emanate great strength and energy. Widows disguise themselves in various forms, they hide their bodies, they conceal their longing even as they continue living – while marked by patriarchal labels, their stories harbour the not-yet-known, or the still-to-be-written.

One of my strategies for questioning the trope of belonging is to search for, research, play with, critique, puzzle over, rewrite, rethink, reword the narrative poem, a form and a genre that remains genera-tively unstable despite – and possibly even because of – the recent attention drawn to it by certain writers and critics. In my first book, *Connect the Dots*,[4] I wrote short narratives concerning the second-person pronoun, so that its ubiquitous presence on the page might reconfigure the dominance of the 'I' pronoun of lyrical address. In that text, the 'you' is at times the narrator, the lover, a singular male sibling, a plural female sibling, an informal third person and a syntactical ghost. The book is about connections, familial and otherwise, but also about how 'connecting the dots' often results in a disappointing line drawing that promised so much as a scramble of dots and eyes and bits of grass hidden underneath the page. In *Minotaurs & Other Alphabets*,[5] I also explore poetry that 'looks' like prose and deploys certain conven-tions of narrative, yet at the same time invites disjunctive readings that extend beyond conventional prose. The poems hang on to each other like trapeze artists, yet no visible lines form a net. The images in both books, for me, remain incomplete. Those narrative pieces are, in that sense, orphans, and I refuse to rescue a single word from their pages.

In writing my so-called novel, *Yellow Pages*,[6] one of my overt agen-das was to critique a nineteenth-century patriarchy that my character (Alexander Graham Bell) represents, from today's perspectives on disability and gender. Bell's archive does not readily disclose his eugenics agenda, and, therefore, to a certain extent I needed to invent his story and the stories of those he wished to suppress. One way of doing this was to 'interrupt' his biography with fictional diary sections. Another way was to interrupt those sections written in his character's voice with his deaf wife's diary, which roamed the limits of female desire as explored by a character doubly limited by both her historical time and her disability. I wanted to structurally examine the effect of a man who achieved a professional climax extremely early in life (Bell received credit for inventing the telephone at the age of twenty-six). At the same time, I needed to figure out – for myself – how Mabel could marry Bell when the much more attractive young Thomas Watson was so much more fun. I devised a triangle, with Alexander in love with Mabel, Mabel in love with Thomas, and Thomas in love with Alexander. At the end of her diary section, Mabel mourns the limitations of their arrangement:

> A man can go his whole life without climax, and die in anticipation. Most men live inside the climax that just happened, its echo still throbbing their fingertips. These men lust after today. A man who climaxes once – and early – walks on a path that leads away from memory. He hopes for a Second Coming to blast away the present. He longs for the explosion that will release him from his life's extended dénouement.
>
> The sun set twice tonight. Once it dipped below the horizon, and once it disappeared into my mouth. Both Alex and Thomas think it is when the sun sets that the moon becomes possible. But there it is: triumphant in the sky, hours before the sun edges to the lip of the horizon.
>
> A woman who climaxes once has been interrupted.[7]

In this excerpt, Mabel's gendered desire undercuts Bell's patriarch desire to become a father of invention; at the same time, Thomas's desire for Bell revises their professional relationship. Such intrusions allowed me to reimagine history in such a way as to render it contemporaneous with an era emerging from the telephonic device that Bell invented because of his obsession with speech and technology, a control he enacted by patrolling the borders of 'normal.'

In order for me to escape certain borders, I need first to recognize, again, the lines they draw, the fences they suggest, the citizens they include within their boundaries, and the citizens they necessarily reject. Poetry can rearrange the expected boundaries of prose, can disrupt the narrative line, can usurp the primacy of critical discourse. I try to live as a dual citizen in language, a thief who steals nothing but colour from a map, commas from a sentence, nationality from nations.

Feminist writers cross a border every time we pick up a pen or turn on the computer or hum into a tape deck. The border is a visible line on the page, an insistent margin we attempt to write ourselves into and against. I veer away from the line, from the *punct* signifying the closing ceremony, from the metaphorical imperative that insists toes are what we tip on, and grasp instead the reassurance of instability, embrace the inability to embrace a stable subjectivity, what Kathleen Fraser describes as 'fragments of a wholeness only guessed at.'[8]

Another border I'm fascinated by is the border that exists between bodies considered to be 'normal' and those designated as 'ab'normal. In my current research, I examine the socially complicated process that determines the boundaries between the 'normal' body and what I call the 'problem' body. In my lexicon, the term *problem* refers to various manifestations and representations of the Deaf body, the disabled body, the aged body, the ill body, the obese body. *Widows and Orphans* concentrates on the social problems that so-called 'deviant' bodies challenge because of normative cultural expectations.

When people talk about the 'normal' body, I know there's no such thing; but I know, as well, that the normal dictates the 'ab.' According to Lennard Davis, in his book *Enforcing Normalcy*, one way that 'the category of disability defines itself [is] through an appeal to nationalism.'[9] The disabled are not viewed as citizens in the same sense as the able-bodied who gaze at these 'abnormalities.' Davis joins such notions of citizenship to the historical eugenics that interested me in my Bell research, but that continues, in insidious ways, in contemporary language: 'That the freak show begins in the same period as we have seen statistics and eugenics begin, indicates a change in the way people thought about the physically different.'[10] The disabled body (and this body reconfigures itself in many ways) represents the problematic, the body that is too much body to ignore or overlook or regard.

But rarely does a disabled character exist front and centre in a novel (unless the 'theme' is overcoming difficulty), yet there s/he lurks: the next-door neighbour who uses a cane, the blind cousin, the ancient uncle, the retarded brother. Says James Porter: 'a disabled body seems somehow too much a body, too real, too corporeal ... it seems too little a body, a body that is deficiency itself, not quite a body in the full sense of the word, not real enough.'[11] Disability in literature has been disproportionately underrepresented at the same time that it has been excessively displayed. For the most part, disabled characters are minor figures, whose less-than-perfect bodies serve as a foil for the protagonist. In this way, characters portrayed as disabled perform the dual purpose of signifying a 'lack' or character flaw which the protagonist must overcome, while at the same time disabled characters re-establish the wholesomeness and integrity of those key characters (and, supposedly, the reading audience). In such narratives, disability figures as metaphorical emphasis for a specific moral impact.

But I'm not interested in the metaphorical disabled body, the body there to reassure readers that – while our bodies may not be normal to the point of ideal – we're far enough away from abnormal to count as members within a group that dismisses and discards certain bodies, specific physical realities. I'm interested, rather, in how certain bodies get configured as belonging to either one category (normal) or another (ab), and what that means on the page. In Shawna Dempsey and Lorri Millan's 1998 video *The Headless Woman*,[12] the voice-over proclaims that the headless woman originally severed her head to impress a boy, then stayed in the circus because there were not many places for a 'woman, all body, approaching forty,' and because 'she was a genuine freak, no mirrors or masks or sleight of hand.' This statement of 'genuineness' convinces the audience of the irony in the speaker's words, an irony that presents headlessness, no matter that it is described as a 'party trick,' as the ultimate freak show – the female body desired and/as gawked at. According to Rosemarie Garland Thomson, 'Freaks were often staged as hybrids in order to provide their audiences with an opportunity to exercise their expertise at defining truth.'[13] While borders may provide exciting vistas, they can also remain hard, intractable facts, a thick line stamped on a map that refuses entry to non-citizens. I want to live on the edge of that line, but also to erase it, mess it up, redraw it so it drips messily over its own edges. I write to disrupt the known, the predetermined, to transgress the normative story, to rummage through archives that house collected versions of history.

When I imagine researching the archives for my current research on disability, I imagine a medical museum, a scientist's notion about which bodies should be 'studied' because they belong to the category of unbelonging. I'm suspicious of archives because they don't file 'gaps' under the Dewey Decimal system. I'm also compelled towards filing cabinets filled with folders filled with underresearched material, unread charts and statistics, poetry made out of numbers. I disparage the freak museum at the same time as I hover in its doorway, savouring this passage of in-between. I want to get lost in the arcade, steal the skeletons of the conjoined twins Chang and Eng, write poems that contradict my senses, write narratives that undo sense, and run away with all the unhinged widows, let loose the wretched orphans onto the vast and expanding risk of the page's extremities.

NOTES

1 Gertrude Stein, *Look at Me Now and Here I Am: Writings and Lectures 1909–45* (New York: Penguin Books, 1990), 125.

2 Marianne Moore, *The Complete Prose of Marianne Moore*, ed. Patricia Willis (New York: Penguin, 1986), 46.

3 Fred Wah, 'Is a Door a Word,' unpublished paper.

4 Nicole Markotić, *Connect the Dots* (Toronto: Wolsak and Wynn, 1994).

5 Nicole Markotić, *Minotaurs & Other Alphabets* (Toronto: Wolsak and Wynn, 1998).

6 Nicole Markotić, *Yellow Pages* (Calgary: Red Deer Press, 1995).

7 Ibid., 137.

8 Kathleen Fraser, *Each Next: Narratives* (Berkeley: The Figures, 1980).

9 Lennard Davis, *Enforcing Normalcy: Disability, Deafness and the Body* (London: Verso, 1995), 91.

10 Ibid., 91.

11 James Porter, introduction to *The Body and Physical Difference: Discourses of Disability*, ed. David Mitchell and Sharon Snyder (Ann Arbor: University of Michigan Press, 1997), xiii–xiv.

12 Shawna Dempsey and Lorri Millan, *The Headless Woman* (Winnipeg/Vancouver: Finger in the Dyke Productions, 1998), video.

13 Rosemarie Garland Thomson, *Extraordinary Bodies: Figuring Physical Disability in American Culture and Literature* (New York: Columbia University Press, 1997), 58.

A Few Thoughts on Beautiful Thinking
Christian Bök

Writing is inhibiting. Sighing, I sit, scribbling in ink this pidgin script. I sing with nihilistic witticism, disciplining signs with trifling gimmicks – impish hijinks which highlight stick sigils. Isn't it glib? Isn't it chic? I fit childish insights within rigid limits, writing shtick which might instill priggish misgivings in critics blind with hindsight. I dismiss nitpicking criticism which flirts with philistinism. I bitch; I kibitz – griping whilst criticizing dimwits, sniping whilst indicting nitwits, dismissing simplistic thinking, in which philippic wit is still illicit.

– from 'Chapter I' in *Eunoia*

Eunoia is a univocal lipogram – an anomalous narrative, in which each vowel appears by itself in its own chapter, telling a story in its own voice. *Eunoia* is directly inspired by the exploits of Oulipo (l'Ouvroir de Littérature Potentielle) – the avant-garde French coterie renowned for its literary experimentation with extreme formalistic constraints. *Eunoia* is the shortest word in English to contain all five vowels, and the word quite literally means 'beautiful thinking.' The text makes a Sisyphean spectacle of its labour, wilfully crippling its language in order to show that, even under such improbable conditions of duress, language can still express an uncanny, if not sublime, thought. The text abides by many subsidiary rules. All chapters must allude to the art of writing. All chapters must describe a culinary banquet, a prurient debauch, a pastoral tableau and a nautical voyage. All sentences must accent internal rhyme through the use of syntactical parallelism. The text must exhaust the lexicon for each vowel, citing at least 98 per cent of the available repertoire (although a few words do go unused, despite efforts to include them: *parallax, belvedere, gingivitis, monochord* and *tumulus*). The text must minimize repetition of substantive vocabulary (so that, ideally, no word appears more than once). The letter Y is suppressed.

Writing this book proved to be an arduous task. I read through the dictionary five times to extract an extensive lexicon of univocal words, each containing only one of the five vowels. I could have automated this process, but I figured that learning the software to write a program would probably take just as long as the manual labour itself – so I simply got started on the project. I arranged the words into parts of speech (noun, verb, etc.); then I arranged these lists into topical categories (mineral, vegetal, etc.), so that I could determine what stories the vowels could tell. I then spent six years, working four or five hours every night after work, from about midnight on, piecing together a five-chapter novel (the first chapter containing only A, the second chapter containing only E, etc.), doing so until I exhausted this restricted vocabulary. I thought that the text would be minimally comprehensible, but grammatically correct, and I was surprised to discover many uncanny coincidences that induced intimations of paranoia. I began to feel that language played host to a conspiracy, almost as if these words were destined to be arranged in this manner, lending themselves to no other task but this one, each vowel revealing its own individual personality: the courtly A, the elegiac E, the lyrical I, the jocular O, the obscene U.

Eunoia, in effect, represents a direct response to my own misgivings about the influence of Oulipo upon my work. Oulipo criticizes the classical paradigm of inspiration by proposing a set of methodical, if not scientific, procedures for writing literature. Oulipo typically imposes some form of constraint upon the practice of writing in order to discover what kind of aesthetic potential arises from these experimental restrictions. The coterie has included, among its membership, such writers as Raymond Queneau, Georges Perec, Italo Calvino and Harry Mathews – but aside from a few selected athletic works by these famous writers, most of the texts produced by the group often seem procrustean and unappealing. The basic fulfillment of the constraint often seems to take precedence over all other literary concerns (like euphony, meaning, etc.) so that often the results of such an experiment resemble the completion of a rote exercise (like writing fourteen lines with metre and rhyme and calling it a sonnet, even though the poem lacks any literary pizzazz). The works often do not fulfill enough of their potential to make them any more interesting than a fumbled sleight. The coterie also seems uninterested in exploring the political potential of writing under such duress in order to expose the ideological foundations of discourse itself.

Eunoia, for example, retrenches an economy of meaning that its constraints might have otherwise challenged (hence, the Language poets might find this work disappointing for its inability to depart from the prison house of grammatical, referential speech). While the wacky rules of Oulipo might imply a freedom from traditional conventions, the content of such work often seems skewed towards normality. The poetic tastes of the group seem quite banal, insofar as its members admire forms like the sonnet or the sestina, dickering with the rules of these defunct genres in order to find new ways to revivify them (hence, I often wonder whether or not the literary politics of this avant-garde differs from the norm in specie or merely in degree). The role of constraint in literature (if not in all ideologies) is to provide a set of rules that can entrench the generic quality for a particular convention. The members of Oulipo argue that, if given the choice, we always prefer to follow rules created by us intentionally for ourselves rather than to follow rules created unconsciously for us by others. The group suggests that, as poets, we are better off by being slaves to an obvious, instead of an unknown, master. The irony here, however, is that the virtuosity of such literature always seems to be more interesting the less free it is.

Notes on Narrativity
(for Gail Scott)
Steve McCaffery

Footsteps in an orderly sequence and therefore predictable. Enclose it in a sentient pronoun and this monologue lives. An activity of mind carried a little further and thereby: judgment. Now the moors seem imponderable. Now the spark plugs show damp. Now the sentence repeats that the pumpernickel's stale. A strategy then of windows. Colourless, almost opaque. Just enough to see you with. Articulate, the floor, the door crack, the switch, the light. This room is not a room. This wall is in thinking. January 5. 'Thomas left us.' Precision. Not of cogs but machination still described as important to a story. How narrative begins in a one that is all of them. Suddenly, a theme.

They brought him home drunk and incapable at nine

thirty i knew

because i checked my watch which was eight minutes

fast nine thirty

six then actually then nine thirty one when they

brought him back.

'Thomas' (that is). Across the moors in a second

reference to moors (inexcusable as simile like a

dream of the factual).

The bad story begins. We had seen it earlier, a grown-up among utensils I won't bother to name. And so it appears to anyone who wonders why the moors also were dispensable. Inscrutable, curvilinear, designed of brass filigree with lions, gryphons, even a semé. The cost was a life. The body deposited behind the public urinals on any street the narrator doesn't bother to name. The fiction thus evolves through social Darwinism to the centre of this crowd. A 'public' weal of 'democratic' pronouns ...

Let's begin again. Once upon a time at the Festival Descartes an orderly sequence of expenditures took place beyond the moors. Departure at effect seven: 'the essence of Nature is freshly conceived.' Now the coal seems deep and rich but overlooked. This is what a narrative shift means.

Then it re-forms. The it reaffirms. It represents it as itself. This story it appears as. 'This is a story that these words begin.' Finally to disappear. You disappears. Your fiction reappears.
This is when this / then

is a plot.

All of the above or else

I was going to meet a woman who had left

a hat on my car.

Possession completes this. Not narrative.

Dislocation

Shiver

Approximate:
Past to Present

Methods

The Sentence

The Novel

Resistance

The Buzz of   A Story Is
Alternate Meanings   a Storage

My Other Self

How I Wrote *Gardener of Stars*, a Novel

Carla Harryman

The invitation to contribute to *Narrativity* came with the suggestion that I discuss how I wrote a particular work. The writing of a particular work is here understood within the framework of ongoing practice. 'Things clash, they have to,' writes Nick Piombino in a blog commentary on my writing. He regards this clashing as a necessity of reality. Writing articulates living in contradiction. The volatility of the work may be a nervous-system response to the nearly insufferable speed and details of our multiple realities. There is too much to take in, too much to process, too much to know and to live with; but the aesthetic project is to process nonetheless – and it is a pleasurable process, with some impishness involved, and one that links language to eros. In respect to the ongoing practice of my writing, the trails of contradiction proceed alongside the metaphor of journey, interior journey or the mind's unknown as it factors the world's unknowns. The fantasy or phantasmic material of the writing is mediated by living in contradiction as unavoidable fact.

*

I hide behind a category by misbehaving[1]

Sometimes a next book develops from or is a direct response to a previous book. Steve introduced me to Warren.

My first three books, *Percentage, Property* and *Under the Bridge,* were studies in sentences, paragraphs and the relationship of narrative to non-narrative. I was interested in non-rational logics achieved by devices such as the juxtaposition in the sentences

> *Sometimes a next book develops from or is a direct response to a previous book. Steve introduced me to Warren.*

or such as the simultaneity produced by grammatical mischievousness in the sentence

> *I hide behind a category by misbehaving.*

George Hartley observes that my prose poem 'For She' 'challenges the naturalness of narrative modes by foregrounding the devices which organize otherwise disparate elements into a seemingly seamless whole.'[2] The play between disparateness, the sentence and the shaping of the whole, the paragraph, has provided me with an abundant field in which to consider the social meaning of form without having to forsake my impulse to make things up. This contact between invention and the already given is also registered in other modes of genre experiments, including works for poets' theatre that treat a line as both verse line and prose dialogue.

From the beginning, my works diffused representation, were studies in meaning making and emphasized the sound-shape of meaning within the sentence, the paragraph and also, upon occasion, performance/text within dialogue.

> This staggering kind of
> I want to talk to you about the
> The?
> Yesterday, some kids found a hidden orchestra pit.[3]

Attention to eventfulness and playfulness of conversation, spoken as if written and written as if spoken, then scrambled, proposes the sociability of even private interchanges. In these interchanges, mishearings, idiosyncratic response, response to the sound or tone of a statement or question rather than its representation or argument, leads towards certain pleasurable and primary attributes of verbal communication. What interests one person in a conversation may not interest the other, but the conversation itself, conversation for the sake of itself, is full of secret delight. Do we communicate subsensically to *practice* communicating so that we can understand each other when we need to? Words float upon the subsensical ground, the ground that 'I' made up: 'The?' achieves a kind of object status in this floating world.

A passage from *Gardener of Stars* remarks upon this ongoing interrogation of the object status of language.

> Are you going to hold me to my words? asked Gardener.
> I haven't decided yet, said M.
> Because I was talking about my thoughts said Gardener, not what you could see.
> If I could see your thoughts said M.
> We would be having the same ones.[4]

Here Gardener and M are involved in a game that in some respects resembles the simultaneity and circularity of the sentence in 'Various Devices,' *I hide behind a category by misbehaving.* The 'devices' sentence grammatically *performs* a transgression of subject-object categories, while the sentence's measure is that of a discrete and independent unit. If subject and object are transgressed, it is within the context of a writing that intensifies its own objectification. In contrast, the passage from *Gardener of Stars* touches on the (scary) edges of intimacy as intellectual speculation, curiosity and desire meet. *Gardener* develops a dialogic and intersubjective space among sentences that stages questions of individual and textual autonomy alongside or among representations and extended narrative vectors. Yet, the sentences in *Gardener* would not have been written without the sentences in works such as those in 'Various Devices.'

Development in art practice involves change, advance and recurrence. Certain questions do not resolve. For me these include: What is the object status of thinking? To what extent, under what circumstances and in what psycho-dynamic registers are words thought of as permanent? To what extent can discourse be unmade? What is the potency of a given trace of thought, or dogma? Is writing the constructed space where shared thoughts become concrete? To what degree are my thoughts the thoughts of others? Intimate others? Society? Communities? To what degree do words make futures? Such questions denote an ongoing investigation throughout my writing. The intention of the investigation is to sustain such open questions.

Such questions create conversation. Conversation is activity. Sentences are active entities; one of them is flat-nosed walking up the stairs in 'Various Devices.' The work occurs, as a difficult-to-identify species, almost human, at the intersection of poetry and prose or, as in the example of *Percentage*, between the intersection of prose/ poetry and play. For me, a play plays: literal activity and the conceptual rubric replace the dramatic foreground. Perhaps the play plays a subterranean music, entirely mental, wafting from hidden orchestra pits kids find.

The essays *The Middle*[5] and 'Toy Boats'[6] were extensions of and reflections upon things I had come to in these earliest, pre-1982 works. 'Toy Boats' proposed a distribution of narrative such that non-narrative and narrative are perceived as not mutually exclusive but as co-extensive and contingent. One walks down the street, finds a hat, puts it on one's head, passes the police station, turns it in to lost and found and continues on one's way. Hats make their way to the words. I am usually looking for free space, good air for anybody. Then someone resembling a Balzacian power freak gets around to appropriating the air in that particular space for private hats.

The ficto-critical, poetry-informed essay *The Middle* proposed a reading with and against Freud's reliance on myth, his nailing the feminine to a dubious criss-cross, which at this twenty-first-century date has been abundantly discussed. *The Middle* recommended a comedic alternative to tragedy that privileges constructedness and an analytic free space in which invention or linguistic improvisation is privileged over identity stabilized through (psycho-) analytic assumptions about causality and origin. The direct confrontation with making up stories, which this work performed, the story becoming a medium of writing rather than writing serving as the medium for storytelling, set the stage for further deployment of narrative in some of my later works in which I mix story and performance, *turn off the lamp in a room I have never occupied.* Telling a story is a performance, a performance of making up something on the spot while reflecting upon the pre-existing words and things required to make up something on the spot.

The pre-existing words come from everywhere, so they are spatialized. Even though I don't typically plan stories but tend to make them up on the spot, I often edit heavily, treating the work as an abstraction with innumerable focal points: I scrutinize it like it's a three-dimensional artwork, and then a two-dimensional artwork. I find simple games for altering syntax: *rewrite 50 per cent of the sentences that contain the word as even if you like them* might be one of the instructions I give myself. I'll decide that towards the end of the book, the chapters have become too short, or that in a play, the flow requires interruption, so I'll create language events that address the sense of rhythm and shape I want to achieve. This might result in some kind of bizarre epic journey, like Caesar's in *Gardener*, when he ventures into an architecture resembling a kind of psychedelic phallic womb viscera.

In *Gardener* Serena says, *even when everyone was dying, people made things up. I sing the song of your false fruit.*

*

In a tree Mable/lived/and developed/ intrusive verbs/squared/the parts of the body[7]

This essay is about how I wrote *Gardener of Stars*, and so I am going to recapitulate what I have covered so far before I continue to the end. Steve introduced me to Warren and Warren died in June 1995.

In 1989, Ray Larsen, Warren's partner, came by himself to a performance of *There Is Nothing Better Than a Theory*. Warren had called him from Europe to remind him to attend the show. Distance between bodies becomes an exchange of bodies, or words, or images, or gestures, or sounds through the artwork. Spatial distribution encourages awakening to the literal modes of lives whose separations and discomforts produce human contact. Gardener and M contact each other sexually and mentally through all the modes of separation available to them including yelling, transportation in the physical and spiritual sense, incommensurate desires, sex and the asymmetries of parenting. I am thinking about the symmetries and asymmetries of the sentence, the paragraph and the essay of Warren Sonbert's films.[8]

> The speed in fledgling motorcade having farming
> They leaned to smoke cigars [9]

In *The Middle*, there is a free space invented for something that might be thought of as a shade of ungendered, where one is not doomed by one's gender or one's sexuality. And in *The Words*[10] as well, the collective 'we' is marked not with gender but by its collective activity within and reinventions of pre-existing social spaces. The desire to collectively construct liberating social and psychic space within the compound of the already given world blossoms within us, is us. Is us telling a story making ourselves up on the spot.

The spot was *Nowhere*.

*

> She had a shadow.
> Who?
> My mother
> Oh ... [11]

So, *Gardener of Stars* was written nowhere around the time Warren was dying: *And why the city's walls are ruins now*

We talked about it, the book, once, and dying, *almost* never. *Gardener's* setting is in a post-apocalyptic post-plague time in which feminine ferocity takes an irreverent centre stage. But its separatism is ignoble; it expresses the fear of being left alone as much as it does the desire to do without men. Separatism becomes a feeling that negates its own politics. Yet, even if separatism never works, the fantasy resurfaces.

> The man sits or lounges uses himself as a sponge or douses the stars as if they were malignant flames he knew how to treat. A surgeon of Eros, he claims.
>
> I have confiscated his dirt bike ...

So, I felt that it was a bad time to be nice. Nice probably wasn't but seemed to be taking over poetry. Does this, for me, have something to do with the extension of poetry into prose? Into novel? Is there something about the emphatic welding of poetry to prose/prose to poetry that has to do with a critique of gender? Of course this is not a new question, and the response will never be a correct response, if by *gender* we mean that which is marked feminine. In contradiction with the emotional fantasy that compelled me to write *Gardener*, my, and *Gardener's*, preference is to ambiguate, regard, suspend and suspect the marks of gender, masculine and feminine, without belying the fact of social power assigned, universally, to many masculine subjects.

The social contract might be up for grabs within the politics of a feminist fantasy.[12] Monique Wittig wrote a separatist fantasy. When she was tossed into the disposal of old-wave feminism for her separatism, her wit, unnoted, was consigned to the same fate. Let us reconsider the comedic.

For instance, the right wing is trying to lay hands on our body. The body is full of non-sense.

> The women also used to say that nonsense brought one closer to the dead. There was something desirable in not letting them wander too far off, for without the sense of their proximity, the world would be so small as to virtually disappear.[13]

*

I hope that it is apparent that the writing of *Gardener of Stars* is contingent upon what precedes it in a literary sense, in an interpersonal sense, in a political and social sense. At the same time, I hope that it is evident that a purely linear or developmental narrative about how a book, or anything one values, comes into being does not serve adequately the imperceptible, the contradictory and the unknowable aspects of its manifestation. The discussion about a book and how it is written is really, for me, a discussion about writing itself, plus something else that is not it at all.

NOTES

1 Carla Harryman, 'Various Devices,' in *Under the Bridge* (Berkeley, CA: This, 1980), 51.

2 George Hartley, *Textual Politics and the Language Poets* (Bloomington: Indiana University Press, 1989), xii.

3 Carla Harryman, 'Percentage,' in *Percentage* (Berkeley: Tuumba Press, 1979), np.

4 Carla Harryman, 'Once upon a Time,' in *Gardener of Stars* (San Francisco: Atelos, 2001), 21.

5 *The Middle* was first given as a talk in 1982 at New Langton Arts, San Francisco, and was first published by Gaz in 1983.

6 'Toy Boats' was solicited by *Poetics Journal* and was published in *Poetics Journal: Non/Narrative* 5 (1985): 104–107.

7 Carla Harryman, 'There Is Nothing Better Than a Theory,' in *Animal Instincts* (Berkeley: This, 1989), 102–03.

8 Warren Sonbert, independent experimental filmmaker, 1947–1995.

9 The poem 'Obstacle' (in *Percentage*), from which these lines are extracted, was written in the dark of a movie theatre while I was watching the San Francisco premiere of Warren Sonbert's film *Divided Loyalties*.

10 Carla Harryman, *The Words: After Carl Sandburg's Rootabaga Stories and Jean-Paul Sartre* (Oakland, CA: O Books, 1999).

11 As quoted in *The Middle* from Jane Bowles's play *In the Summer House*, in *My Sister's Hand in Mine* (New York: Ecco, 1979).

12 Monique Wittig, *The Straight Mind* (Boston: Beacon Press, 1992) and *Les Guerilleres* (Beacon Press, 1985).

13 Harryman, *Gardener*, 158.

Telling Tales[1]
Lynne Tillman

There's a series of Dewars ads on telephone booths around New York. One shows a guy with a lampshade on his head. It says: 'Remember that party when you thought you were so funny?' Underneath that: 'Dewars.' A single sentence asked the reader, and consumer, to go through a series of memories and thoughts, to reach a similar conclusion or resolve: have a drink, don't think about it, you've grown up and Dewars is for adults, you. What you weren't supposed to be thinking about anymore – parties in the past, your young, stupid behaviour – had to be arrived at by each reader through a bunch of moves, little movies in the mind that were stories with attitudes about drunkenness, having a good time, aging, etc. All were arrived at independently but all of them had to come to one punchline, one conclusion – Dewars.

There's the narrative you're writing, and there's the narrative your readers make from it. There's the time of the story, and there's the time readers take to assimilate the story and add it to theirs, to make it part of their continuing narrative. The Dewars ad accomplished a long story in one short sentence.

When I think about stories and how I write them, when I try to figure out how to tell a story or construct a novel, I wallow for a while in a kind of dumb despair. Thinking about narratives and why I decide or choose, if I'm really choosing, to write one kind rather than another is like thinking the unthinkable. It's impossible: I'm already thinking in stories. One thinks in stories, thinking is a story; 'stories are a way to think,' I wrote in a story. Narratives are so deeply embedded in how we think and what we think, what we know and how we know it, and in who we are – which narratives about ourselves do we accept as valid and meaningful? do we choose them? how do we choose them? – it's hard to get hold of what stories are. It's hard to see how they function because they are always functioning.

I like it that a floor in a building is called a 'story.' Architects talk about a building's event, a moment or place in the structure where something happens.

It's one of the questions I have – what has to happen? Is an action required? What is an action? What form does it have to take? A thought? Violence? Resistance? Time passing? Why did the chicken cross the road? To get to the other side. Or is it better: to get to the other side because it was in love with another chicken who was already across the road.

To narrative questions I respond with speculations and explanations. I place them in stories. These speculations and explanations come from somewhere. I may have read them or heard them or experienced them. I may think I'm making them up, but ideas come from somewhere and are based in something. Why I think these, why I give one explanation rather than another, is part of a larger narrative in which I have a small role and out of which I write other parts, or stories.

Theories are explanations, and so are stories. One explains in the same language as the question, one answers the problem with a differently configured problem. Neither a theory nor a story explains completely or adequately, there's always something missing, which gives us the reason to write more of them; but they explain in different forms – stories use characters, generally, in some way, and employ time as an element. There's the time of the story, when it happens. Everything may be a flashback. There's the way and time in which the events are revealed or unravelled, what the reader's told first, second, third. What the reader isn't told, what isn't written, can be the significant lack in a story. All strategies affect the story's meaning, our interpretations of it, since the form of its telling will be part of its meaning.

No matter how one writes characters – not describing them, not assigning them motivation – readers project onto and identify with them. Readers often do most of the work, good actors interpreting a terse script. Even if a writer disdains characters, has ambivalence about what they are and how to construct them, the writer is responsible for having used them at all, having set them, however vaguely or strangely, in a terrain made from words.

In theory, time isn't significant to the unfolding of an argument or to how one understands it. The character of the author of a theory is generally not part of the theory, although there are exceptions – Paul de Man and Heidegger, notable cases in which some people want to make them and their theories the same. In other words, they explain as they do, some insist, in order to defend themselves. This is often said about storytellers.

Both theory and stories are made-up things, creations, fictions. One kind of fiction represents arguable truths, as mutable and contextual, interpretations; more terrifying, some theorists assert immutable Truth. The other fiction uses truth as the stuff characters search for, as what can't be found, as what should be found, as human – complex, ambiguous and contradictory – as the element within the story characters argue about, as a question of right and wrong, which can never be resolved – truth is conflict. Some narratologists say conflict is the essential element in narrative.

Recently I was told that there's turbulence in everything – when you pour milk into a cup of tea and the tea and milk roil, that's turbulence. I see potential conflict in almost every sentence; placing one word next to another can represent conflict. Language probably emerged from wordless conflict and is riven, every word, with it. This word is not that, for instance.

Conflict may result from the juxtaposition of supposedly different characters – a saint and a sinner – or there may be divisions within the same character, or different characters may be representations of different ideas, or conflict emerges from the divergence of warring memories, or from a sentence that contradicts or questions the apparent meaning of a previous sentence. Conflict is an essential part of theorizing, since theories emerge from and depend upon differences from other theories.

There may be imperceptible conflicts, actions, events – I think, thinking is an activity. An emotion may produce an action, be an action or be a reaction. In some form the writer addresses some kind of event. In some way there is a problem, an event, an action, a thought, an issue, an emotion, to be resolved or left unresolved; there's a problem to be solved, or incapable of solution, a problem engaged or contemplated. There's a kind of adjudicating, whatever the writer does.

The kinds of resolutions one chooses – seemingly chooses – appear as, and at, the ends of one's stories. What one thinks about ends and how one uses them reflects and repeats elements from the great unwritten narrative one is living, much of it unconsciously. Even death isn't much of a closure for a story. Death may end a life in a book, but the reader lives on. Other characters in the story usually do too; the story lives on the page and can be read again.

What really distances stories from theories is that a storyteller is allowed unsubstantiated claims. Theorists are burdened with the problem of proof. I think this is why I make my explanations in the stories I write, rather than as theory. I don't think I can prove anything.

Also, I'm not sure what's supposed to be proved. If it's Truth, then that's probably the best reason why I write stories.

Anyone who watches trials on TV sees that truth is always an argument. The lawyers say over and over, we can't find the truth, we're looking for justice. I've begun to think that justice is the subject of most fictions, whatever form they're written in. Again, something is being adjudicated. Somehow all stories are about justice, though I can't prove this.

On the night of June 17, 1994, I was watching a Knicks championship game on TV; it was interrupted by a white car driving alone on a six-lane highway. The car was followed by a phalanx of black-and-white police cars. The news commentator, or narrator, told us: O.J. Simpson's inside this car. It's his friend Al Cowlings's white Bronco. O.J.'s got a gun to his head, and he's going to kill himself. The car drove steadily in the middle of the empty highway; the cops followed at what was called a safe distance. It was unbelievably weird and compelling. What was the story? At some point, the TV cut to O.J.'s friend Robert Kardashian reading O.J.'s alleged suicide letter, which ended: Don't remember me this way, as a lost soul. He said he loved Nicole, he didn't do it, and he also said that she had abused him. He was lost, he was guilty, I thought, and he'd written a confession; it contained his defence: that she abused him.

A white car moved along the highway for hours. It carried a man who was a hero to millions. O.J. couldn't turn himself over to the cops. He wanted to see his mother, the narrator said. I started to cry. The car just kept moving. Would he pull the trigger? Was he going to Nicole's grave? I suddenly understood what I was watching – O.J. was making a journey. He needed time and space to achieve a transformation. In order to turn himself over to the cops, he had to become the lost soul he'd written about. He couldn't be the hero; he had to destroy that character. And as much as he needed time, so did many Americans. I used the time to contemplate that he could have done it; it was incredibly sad, like watching a funeral cortège. The hearse was the white Bronco. Because the old O.J. was dead. A mythic figure, he was moving from one world to another, through the underworld, and he had to get to the other side, he had to leave his past life to enter a new, hideously reduced one.

The car turned into O.J.'s driveway. Cowlings parked it at the front door. Cowlings got out, O.J. stayed inside, hidden; there was confusion, Cowlings talked with some police, and then finally O.J. emerged. He was not the same man who began the trip – he was a different man, one who was capable of surrendering. 'O.J.'s Last Run,' the newspapers said.

I've linked O.J. and the white Bronco story with narrative generally and with specific narratives, the reversal of fortune and the journey, the odyssey. The interpretation of O.J.'s actions and his end is wide open, whether or not he's found guilty. Apart from voyeurism, identification and cultural politics, I'm watching a story whose heart holds questions about justice. That polls report a great divide between blacks and whites about his guilt is a powerful register of how narratives are read differently, depending upon one's place in the big story. It made me realize that guilt and justice may be independent concepts, operating independently, and that justice may be contending with a notion of collective innocence.

Was there a police plot against O.J.? Is O.J. in a plot with Kardashian? Could he have done it alone, without a plan?

Plot is another great division and question: writers use or don't use plots. Readers want or don't care about plots. People ask me, about the novel I'm writing, what's going to happen? Is there a plot? What's the action? What I want to know, again, is: what is supposed to happen? What kind of event or action? What makes an event worth writing about – a fight with a boss, the search for solitude, a political election, the first time you were called a dirty name – and what form fits the event? And where does plot fit in?

In *Cast in Doubt*, Horace becomes obsessed with Helen, who disappears. First he looks for her in her room just around the harbour from his:

> Sometimes one advances towards a specific destination with not just a sense of purpose and direction, but with a sense of what to expect, and one progresses assured in the knowledge that the world one knows will be as one knows it and has always known it. When I walked to Alicia's house the other week, I knew what I would find there. I did not know of course that her cheeks would be flushed or that she had sung to John, or for him, but I knew where her furniture would be and that her books would be on shelves; I knew how her paintings would be hanging, that there would be flowers in vases, and so on. I knew John might be there, and if he wasn't I knew he

would be on another day. One exists with the sense that life goes on in a regular manner, that one can breathe because one is meant to and air is air, that hello, yá sou, or bonjour will greet one, that fruit and vegetables will be sold where they were sold yesterday – in short, that one can recognize oneself in a recognizable world. And that much of life is ordinary. Even persons in concentration camps were able to adjust, over time, to the most horrific of circumstances, having come to know the routine, which was terrifyingly and mercilessly life as they were compelled by fate to know it, to live it, for however long.

As I walked to Helen's house, I had lost this sense of assurance. I did not know what to expect, which alone unnerved me. ... I simply did not know what awaited me.

Now one may want to interject – part of me does – that I, Horace, sought to feel compassless, to experience the vertiginous highs and lows of the unexpected, having already insisted upon my pleasure in the unknown, having insisted upon how much I needed to invent my life, to make it closer to fiction. But I am a writer and given to such musings. One mustn't believe everything one reads, after all.[2]

Later, he decides to drive his car to search for her in the southern part of Crete:

I drive towards the coast. I don't care to stop or to make a detour. I see no strange encampments along the way. Had I chosen the faster way, I would already have been on the southern coast, quite near to the dot on Helen's map which signified where she had probably gone. But I am not sure if that is the case, or if she had been the one to leave the map lying there, with its mark. Thinking about this is ludicrous, in one way, and confusing in another. I drive, plagued by the uncertainty of it all, and of how this isn't and wasn't like me, to go flying off in pursuit of a mere girl, even one like Helen.

I am discouraged, but hasten to encourage myself to have patience. If Gwen were with me, no doubt she'd caustically remark that I need patience but need more to be the patient. I'd bet the conversation would take such a linguistic turn. I would bet that, were she here to take the bet. I swing around on the road, the road to Mandalay, to somewhere. I am indeed going somewhere.[3]

All he does is drive to another part of Crete to look for her. It's the move, the turn that makes the book plotted. A journey with a goal. But what if Horace had just stayed home and thought about doing it?

In *Motion Sickness*, the narrator's a traveller; compared with Horace, she's existentially homeless. Her adventures appear undirected, aimless, pointless. Her journey isn't linear, it's circular: she lands up where she started – Paris. The book ends where she began, as if it's all middle. Very middle class, maybe, where the novel originated.

> Amsterdam doesn't seem a suitable place for tragedy, but place – the city, for instance – is as much a mental space as a physical one, and its physical boundaries, its history, are much less concise than any term such as 'city' might lead one to think. Am I headed for tragedy, I wonder as the cabdriver brings me to the three-generations hotel. And are conversations with strangers necessarily uncanny? ...
>
> Olivier merely smiles at me, a sly guarded slash of a grin, throws his book, *Truffaut/Hitchcock*, into his leather satchel, pushes his wire-rimmed glasses up onto the bridge of his nose and strides past me, brushing against my arm ever so slightly. Why do I feel I've seen this scene before?
>
> And will I end up in bed with him? is my life as predictable as it sometimes appears?[4]

Some readers felt the lack of a scheme or plot, saw no reason for her to travel; some tried to find a reason; for some there was no reason to read on. I did supply a coy subplot – a character who may be a spy appears everywhere – but I didn't make him central. His surprising presence was supposed to lie there, a layer in the book, something for readers to play with. In this way writing's geological, reading's archaeological.

If I'd written that the unnamed narrator was adopted and searching for her real mother or father, and her journey took her all those places to find one of them or both, it might've appealed to some readers. It might have supplied a reason to read the book.

What is the point in reading? Or in writing? A plot, or a scheme, gives a reason, I suppose. Plots seem to me about rationality, direction and goals. A plotted novel written by Patricia Highsmith, about guilt and the irrational, has a mercenary murderer like Ripley acting rationally. She emphasizes his orderliness – Ripley's nothing if not rational. He has clever reasons for everything and follows a stringent regime in executing his executions. Presumably that's why he's never caught. Except I think it's because he doesn't experience guilt, and doesn't want to be caught, so he doesn't leave clues. Though Highsmith plots his every move, every Ripley action or thought is fraught, open to a reader's anxiety. Ripley's reasoning is an open, anxious question. Highsmith uses rationality and plots to explore the irrational and unplotted.

If you don't need a plot, what does that mean? I like stories with plots. I like ones that don't have them. I sometimes find plots where they may not be, which means that as a reader I invent reasons for why something does or doesn't happen. As a writer, I question the need for goals or directions, for specific outcomes based on specific actions or events. Since the unconscious and the irrational guide us as much as the conscious and rational, I have trouble determining plots. To me there are many, many reasons why things happen or don't, and I'm concerned about overemphasizing one or two. Also, plot seems a way of setting limits – to control the meaning of a story. It can set out a 'because' and a 'therefore.' That can be a trick, too, a writer's ruse, and therefore not a therefore at all.

These are all questions. As a reader I want pleasure, and as a writer I want to provide pleasure – we read for pleasure. But pleasure comes in many forms – some plotted, some not. There's no pleasure, release, without frustration. There's pleasure from pain. Which might make reading and writing sado-masochistic. How much frustration is permissible? How are forms frustrating and why? Why do some of us need to feel there's a goal?

In *Cast in Doubt*, Gwen thinks that Horace wanted to find his name in Helen's diary – not find Helen, not find himself, just his name. Each of us writing is invested in naming, designating, marking, representing, making inclusions and exclusions. Each of us reading wants to find ourselves in books in some way, in different ways, some very abstract. How much of what we do or find is already determined or how much choice we have in what we find or do or the way we do it – those are implicit elements in any story, affecting the way one writes it or reads it.

As writers, our desires and our limits enter our stories, dressed up as events and characters; as readers, through our desires and limits, we take up these events and characters, or their lack, and make them ours, or don't. The most bedevilling question for writers, I think, is whether any of us can turn our unconscious and conscious desires and our historically and psychologically determined limits, our necessities, into virtues, and whether our vices can become our books' virtues.

NOTES

1 This piece was originally published in *The Broad Picture: Essays 1987–1996* (London/New York: Serpent's Tail, 1997), 134–144.

2 Lynne Tillman, *Cast in Doubt* (New York: Poseidon, 1992), 140–141.

3 Ibid., 181–182.

4 Lynne Tillman, *Motion Sickness* (New York: Poseidon, 1991), 73–74.

Soft Links

Nicole Brossard
translated by Peter Dubé

these are the names of places, of cities, of climates that make characters. The clear mornings, a fine rain fallen for twenty-four hours, rare
images originating in America and elsewhere, two natural disasters
that oblige us to stick together in the midst of cadavers, these are the
gestures quiet or purple, the shells, the icicles in the happy-hour
glasses, crockery noises or a light stuttering that torments an instant,
a slap, a kiss these are the names of cities like Venice or Reading,
Tongue and Pueblo, the names of characters Fabrice, Laure or Emma.
The words sharpened over the years and the novels, words one spoke
while breathing badly, while laughing, while spitting, while sucking
an olive, the verbs we add to the lips' pleasure, to success, to a certain
death. These are words like knee or cheek or still others stretching as
far as the eye can see making us lean over the void, stretch like cats in
the morning these are the words that make one stay awake till dawn or
take a taxi on weeknights when the city falls asleep before midnight
and solitude sticks in our jaws like an abscess. These are words spoken
from memory, from want or from pride, very often words pronounced
with love while placing hands on nape of neck or filling a glass of port.
These are words whose etymology must be sought, that must then be
plastered to what's called a wall of sound, in a manner like those who
cry out in pain and sigh with pleasure that wander in dreams and docu-
ments assault the heart's mysterious obscurity. These are words like
bay, hill, wadi, via, *street*,* strasse dispersed through the dictionary
between flame-trees and neons, cemeteries, dismal and forests. These
are words sound the body of meanings that arc claws or *soft* on our
chests, cold, shivers, furrows and fear in the back without waiting
while we try to split the sleek future tense with trenchant quotations.
These are words swallowers of fire and life, one no longer knows
whether they're Latin, French, Italian, Sanskrit, Mandarin, Anda-
lusian, Arabic or English, whether they hide a number, an animal or
old anguishes eager to gush before our eyes like cloned shadows filled
with light and great myths.

* Italicized words appear in English in the original text.

148

Long and Social
Eileen Myles

My book (*Cool for You*[1]) is absolutely an extension of my poetry practice; I've even come to refer to it and maybe the class of novels it's a member of as the poet's novel. Having written a novel, I don't have to protect myself from the disparaging term 'poet' – yet I'm more clearly a poet than ever. I mean, a poem is an extravagant grandiose and trembling form, for better or worse always alive, I think, and I've brought those weaknesses and virtues into novel writing and I'm dying to do it again. As a younger poet I was urged (in order to be important) to think large, to write the long poem, but I think this is it. It's epic poetry in the sense that the epic poem is a communal form, and long and social. I wrote it for you. That's what the title means in a way. I know there's a more technical definition for epic poetry but that seems the best way to get it wrong. I'm more interested in what Joyce Carol Oates did in *Blonde* than Seamus Heaney's prize cow. Poets should write novels en masse and reinvent the form and really muck up the landscape. I often think of Leslie Scalapino telling me that her long book *The Return of Painting, The Pearl and Orion* was called a novel because a novel means you start at the beginning and you read to the end. It was a way to guarantee she could be read differently. Time is my real subject and calling a book a novel immediately adjusts the reader's perception of time.

My book is shuffled if you take the long view. When I started to write the first chapter, which was a story – the whole thing is a story for me – it occurred to me that a novel could just be all these stories shuffled, and I thought of books I loved long ago, Julio Cortázar's *Hopscotch*. I read that book straight through, but I read it differently knowing that he had that chart at the front suggesting you could alternately read it this way, and that the book could permute all these different ways. I'm in love with the form of the novel being molten, not putting the power of reordering in the hands of the reader but extending to the reader a sense that the form of the book is as accidental as life. It's studied, damn studied, the cool casual life as is the cool casual novel, but as accidental as, say, the Zapruder footage. The guy happened to be there with his camera, and as it turns out history was made. As it turns out he gave us our only window onto that day in Dallas. When one realizes that John Clare inadvertently gave us the first No Trespassing signs in literature you realize bumpkins must write first, not last.

One more note on that: everything's visual and even in or especially in advertising the oddly cropped shot is what's used. Literature as it's sold today is so backwards. Hand-held literature is of course what I'm selling. It's not a memoir, it's a recording. And even purporting to be a bad recording at times. For a female writer the pose of awkwardness is very dangerous, though, because at this post-feminist moment one should be a top, one should win, etc. But female in history is ground down, anonymous, untold. That's the story that's interesting.

And another thing: more poet's novel. *Chelsea Girl*'s 'My Father's Alcoholism' was the story where I stretched myself and tried to write out of pools and see how they would build. I just literally go into a room (one labelled 'My Father's Alcoholism') and begin inventorying the memories, the substance of the memory, the materiality of it. The fur of childhood, not the feelings. When I was done with one I would wait and let another one grow. It really is like walking in the rain. Can that generate a narrative, or a narrative feel? It sure works in movies. But movies have the dark on their side. My hope is that by being as solipsistically in my mind, downloading erratic-shaped drops and letting some momentum build on that order rather than an order based on action, you can kind of reverse our assumptions about activity. Or maybe I mean self. There's a beautiful math to it, like music if you just let yourself go and describe the experience of your life like it's some public spectacle you are privy to and you're waiting for the music of the information along with everyone else. It's a social poetic invention. I feel less alone when I tell my most private stories than any other time. This does link up to performance. When you are acting or even reciting a text you wrote and you're on a darkened stage under a pool of light there's a terror as you're singing along with the text – it's like driving, that moment at night when you think *shit, I could just pile into the opposite lane and that would be it*. The self could just smash into the light and dark and be gone forever. So you feel contained within the details by that sense of danger and that provides the tension while you proceed lavishly downloading 'me' in every ribbony way I can imagine.

The limitations of 'New York School' have been what Frank did, what John does, are you like Jimmy. Mustn't forget Kenneth or Barbara. It's like Mt. Rushmore. You can say some quick thing about them all – it's chatty abstraction, it's American speech, and I've learned different things from all of them, but since they are just people I think it's tone that people wind up miming, or concerns rather than electricity, the weight and pause and incredible expanse of the exploring mind in speech. I discovered what I sound like long ago and of course I go where they wouldn't and couldn't so it's sort of like explaining why you prefer not being a corpse. New York School mimed is worse than academic, it's like my dad being a mailman coming home with the Ivy League clothes from the Harvard dorms where he had his route. You have to blow that up pretty quickly but it's just sad. Let's face it, they were just as New Critical as everyone else in the fifties. They all would assert that the poetry was not about them. It's about skimming the surface of the self. Using that facility to shape the poem. My dirty secret has always been that it's of course about me. But I have been educated to believe I'm no one so there's a different self operating and I'm desperate to unburden my self of my self so I'm coming from nowhere and returning. That's sort of classic. You just cannot underestimate the massive difference in writing out of female anonymity. It blows all the styles out of the water.

I think the form of the novel gives dignity to my shame. Sometimes I'm just ashamed to block the sun. Performance, and I include readings in that, makes the body be the container for the work. It is when you write the words, of course. The body always seems like the shame. The camera must cut away to the trees, the animal is telling too much. The animal doesn't want to die, etc. If you've ever sat on a panel when some people read and some people speak directly, you know the difference in those two deliveries in terms of the room's interaction with the speakers is immeasurable. The dangerous loose cannon is how we conduct public life – we want to stifle the stray remark and we want to house it. I'm totally translating that impulse into a several-hundred-page thing, my sorrowful body is now text. It's like a zoo. Like a zoo of my family, turned out.

NOTE
1 Eileen Myles, *Cool for You* (New York: Soft Skull Press, 2000).

Narrating
Leslie Scalapino

I just write, without advance plan as to a plot or form – the writing driven by a wind of my being in some urgency at the time. Each work I've done has been written in that way. Each is different. The next time I'll write dependent on what's occurring then. Here I'll say something about *Defoe*, since of my prose it was the hardest on me (in a state of extremity) and required the greatest extension. 'Narrating' is for me:

Inextricably related – not simply because events 'are related,' but because the relation intrinsically is oneself. The phenomenal world of nature is inseparable from one's 'conception' (visual and tactile) and also does not come from oneself. One is one's relation to the rose disc-cloud on the desert as to social occurrence, such as people's minute nuances or war:

> disc floating on the desert, with cattle that come to the edge of the blue water and the white desert – not coming from it.

> One has to agree with them or is not there – which in society can not push out from themselves the red soft hanging disc. that is separate.

> misery in having to be in agreement with them giving up being there though one can't do that.[1]

One cannot be as social definition, yet that exists. That social relation is inherent conflict as oneself in which one cannot exist or be – 'causes' the syntax to be a 'place.' – Surfaces collapse on each other, existing together as plates in paragraphs, clarity only possible by inclusion of, or being, the conflict. Conflict is the writing's shape configured and is attention in space.

Sleeping dreams are 'compared' to the literal 'day'-as-surface as if both day and dreams were surfaces as thin discs and placed side by side – the ego not in either of these but there also:

> One sees oneself as simply a shallow behavior that is thin. and so one is free. And then turned inside so that one's dreams

are sent into one from the day, as they are it. So there is no REM. People rest in the thin area. One laughs frisky. love in behavior is there, in reverse. That is the street, the way it is seen.[2]

Fictional events and real events (the Gulf War) are placed side by side regardless of their size. Action is seen 'without' itself in the sense that action (that which is enacted, as physical movement) is 'other than' writing, the one cannot be the other – they (both) are also phenomena as conflict, thin discs that impinge on each other:

> Action collapses on itself and is compressed, in that it is description of itself. It is thus in the present-time, still and calm.

> It does not diverge from itself, supposedly. That's a conception which people already know. Therefore speaking enables one to see the diverging or separation that is this present. These actions occur as if to make the pupil of an eye (some other's) dilate, and be held open. The present takes place as 'some other.'

> Life is dilated.

> It does not diverge because description cannot be separate. as it is of itself.[3]

Defoe, the writer, created fictional characters who were supposedly real giving documentary accounts. They were to be imagined as entities, which had no reality. Paragraphs are plates of actions which are not single and do not begin or end there – in order for there to be reflection (as the text) throughout everywhere that is not mirroring of authority as authority is not (is not in) any single one of those actions:

> To name it will be merely caught again in their authority as they will recognize that as themselves and will be in their trap again.

> If there is no area between his dreams and waking life, there is no identifying with anyone.

Walk through stream of hot metal bumpers of cars that then move like plates shifting. Mass of plates and she's veering in it. On tin tail of motorbike of yellow teeth thrashing in neck. He's ahead then. On it again thrashing neck. The bike skidding and swaying in narrow channel amidst bumpers. It bucks forward. Neck bike veering and bucking out on the vast tin sheet. the sunlight is reflecting off. He wriggles free, lunging. The motorbike lunges forward. Crashes into car's side in the mass. Slippery blood on his head neck slashing. She's slashed hard slamming into car's side. Rider on foot then, veering and is way ahead then out on stalled mass.

Seeing him out on the vast reflected expanse.[4]

Prior sight – we see things before they occur: whatever dream occurs, that's waking life. Perception does occur in people (or 'in' something happening) – what is it?

Perception occurs before the context – it is not in a setting.

Without seeing it as it was going on while seeing it, really. The man in being authority is the process of down fawning on the feet of the other man while this is merely an image a negative that is imposed on it. Like an angel.

Is it that seeing into the future as what's going to happen to people it then just is that. It occurs. Isn't deflected. That isn't continual change which is aware as we are in it.

We can see it in ourselves. that's why it's aware.

People see that later. Not when they're young. it's separate from what's actually there which is to be seen directly. has to be.

There is no 'inner reality' to the destruction that this person is creating for themselves from within, which is seen from the outside by others.

So suffering is in oneself, and has no 'inner reality'.[5]

The incommensurable relation between outside action (in the world) and interior action mind phenomena – is overtly the subject. The shape the writing takes is related to use of fictional and autobiographical/historical event (such as the bombing of Iraq) at the time it's occurring. The time it's occurring – the paragraph plates are real-time moment of exterior event brought into compressed relation of interior occurrence/horizon together and always separated. The intention is that fictional illusion be at the moment of real time to: implode it as real-time action.

These are illusions in the practical sense of being 'only' writing (writing has no relation to present or historical reality – it has no reality, is it as well, being mind phenomena. So the 'ordinary' small action is [to be] as much 'reality' as events that are devastating). I am trying to divest hierarchy-of-actions. 'Hierarchy-of-actions' voids people's occurrences (that is, individuals' actions are relegated to inconsequential or invisible). Such hierarchy substitutes 'overview' of 'history'/interpretation/doctrine – therefore, to divest 'hierarchy-of-actions' is certainly a political act. (In one's/reader's /viewer's conceptualization then – [is the intention]). What I'm referring to as 'divesting hierarchy-of-actions' by definition has to be in oneself.

Making illusions and noticing them makes them so overt that they 'become' bathos. (I don't regard that as 'alienation,' however.) Fundamentally anarchism (viewing that as being observation itself) is necessitated. Besides *Defoe* (which was reprinted by Green Integer in 2002), my other prose works (crossed with being poetry) are: *The Return of Painting, The Pearl, and Orion/A Trilogy* (reprinted by Talisman, 1997) and *The Front Matter, Dead Souls* (Wesleyan, 1996). My fiction includes *Orchid Jetsam* (Tuumba, 2001), *R-hu* (Atelos, 2000) and *Dahlia's Iris – Secret Autobiography and Fiction* (FC2, 2003).

NOTES

1 Leslie Scalapino, *Defoe* (Los Angeles: Sun and Moon, 1995; Los Angeles: Green Integer, 2002), 11. References are to the Green Integer edition.
2 Ibid., 25.
3 Ibid., 125.
4 Ibid., 35.
5 Ibid., 43–44.

Dislocation

Shiver

Approximate:
Past to Present

Methods

The Sentence

The Novel

Resistance

The Buzz of
Alternate Meanings

A Story Is
a Storage

My Other Self

on character
heriberto yépez

experimentalism means *'identity* in crisis.' events that made 'me' more – an awareness i was no longer my self, *one*-self. luce irigaray, on the one hand, wrote that reality is always two. [*bidentity* then]. and on the other hand, lao tzu reminds us that where there's two soon there's three – like couples, which in reality are, at least, threesomes. the destruction the couple is – was already here.

   and now: history:

'in general the mexican body is suffering "changes." meaning:
a second drama of hybridization. a second conquest.
a new corpus.'

*

the day nafta was put into practice (january 1, 1994) was the day post-modern mexican history began. not only because globalization had officially started, but because an indian guerrilla – long in training – appeared. the post-national and 'profound mexico' (bonfil batalla) clashed. no hegelian synthesis there, no fucking *aufheben* – if anything is taught by mexican history, beyond any kierkegaardian report, it is that when the one and the other collide, not even either/or is a choice: no synthesis, no coexistence, neither of the two are going to survive in their original state. [saint] max stirner said it best: i is all and what all destroys. all.

first the indian guerrillas were denounced as central american marx-ists ('they couldn't be mexicans'), and *'transgresores de la ley'* (law trans-gressors) as the infamous pro-state nightly news anchorman jacobo zabludowsky called them. the main visual characteristic of the zapatis-tas was their black *pasamontañas*. ('they must be hiding something.') they used their masks to not be recognized by the government, but also because masks have a strong power in mexican popular culture: the power of transformation, social change and new personal identity. masks have always played this role in our culture, as in many other places in the world. there is a long tradition of using masks in pre-colombian cultures, from ritual to war masks and disguises. that's also why we have adapted so well to halloween. culture and body, how we affect the other and how we are affected by them.

in another arena, masks are related in mexico to superhero figures. wrestlers use masks, and at one point the movies used real wrestlers acting as superheroes, in bizarre plots where they would fight vampires, gangsters or extraterrestrials (sometimes at the same time). wrestlers like el santo, blue demon or mil máscaras became household names, just like superman or spiderman in the united states. the mask has continued to function to both hide identity and build a new identity through a facial disguise, as shown by the social activist superbarrio in mexico city, who has used a mask to attract attention for popular causes since the late eighties.

as the apparition of the zapatistas has made many of us aware, mexican identities have been undergoing a dramatic process of life and death. the zapatistas were using experimental strategies to represent that phenomena. the zapatista mask has many functions: for example, to emphasize the collectivity of the movement – from its leader to the last soldier. it paradoxically makes us aware of who is behind the mask while at the same time forces us to not see the indians according to our long-standing stereotypes – passivity, loss of identity, etc. – with the implication that they are not going to remove their masks until we learn to see their true faces.

the zapatistas announced the renewal of mexican character. writing narrative in our zapatista country means to accept that our traditional face and identity have been modified. no more fixed personalities or long-standing structures. who are we and how do we represent ourselves, how do we narrate our being and non-being, our selves and otherness; how do we build the text is now a question of how are we going to survive.

*

whose character? always some | body else. character is always 'us' – in a way it's never just 'us.' character can be identified (partially) with the writer. each character has some characteristics (secret or announced) that the writer has – i.e., characteristics s|he supposes are hers or his. but are not. characters are part of the writer's life, but are never him or her, nor any person in particular; they cannot be separated, nor are they fantasy. characters are the author's psychical family, society's trail of doppelgängers in its course through time. imagination cannot happen. fantasy is impossible. reality pollutes everything. imagination cannot escape completely from the here and now of material/historical/bodily circumstance. 'fiction' wanted to escape from history – the possibility of a realm made exclusively of fantasy – a critical illusion it has always pursued, only to leave evidence of failed fugitives. who's the character? no one, but many. anyone's double. including, of course, the other side, the so-called readers, somebody else too (many). characters operate in the field of indeterminacy, of multiplicity. (i hate names. names are in favour of being-just-one.) writing a character (packages) we do not respond to the question *who am i?* but to this the interrogation *who else am i?* a question that cannot be responded to. a character, a failed attempt to know ourselves.

*

'it helps my mother was a prostitute. she kept inside of her too many. i didn't know who my father really was. never sure enough, and neither her, him or i wanted to find out. identity means = *too many came inside | name is not necessary.*'

*

i write fiction while i hear music. i've always been under the impression that a novel's characters should be volatile entities. i would like for characters to be entities whom i pass by, reading, and don't recognize. *a movement in the page, a strange event, a nebulous event, what was it? maybe a character.*

not bodies but waves. i find in radiohead what deleuze found in bacon: the vision of bodies who are the subject of forces that determine their form, whose features are deformed by the effect those forces have in their flesh. *we seem to be clouds drawn away by the wind, stripped,* goes a caifanes song, a rock group from the nineties whose name was later changed to jaguares after the band leader lost his voice – according to a friend his voice was lost because he discovered too many secrets. this didn't delight the gods, so they turned his voice into a ridiculous event.

when i write a character it must feel to me as if composed of bubble gum. a character is not a stable thing. a plasma. characters should always melt.

the instability i look for in characters can even be a genealogical trace they've left. kristeva reminds us that in twelfth-century love songs – probably mistranslated by pound – the loved one was not a clear character, was almost never described, and 'her' could refer both to the woman and the song itself. (homer too never described helen but she incited a war anyway, the passions she was used for.) but then (back to kristeva) music was lost in poetry, and some time later prose took the place of verse and the troubadour became a novelist – masculine characters who not only were unwilling to celebrate with joy the distance between themselves and their lovers (i.e., reference) but also were under the spell of the spirit-of-conquest-of-the-other instead of seduction-by-it. in this way cervantes' and swift's satires on woman, on love, became possible. the novel was born, and in it, characters, visible ones, 'individuals,' not the ghosts of the past, those volatile entities where object and subject were undistinguishable in a way adorno never imagined. the character became clear, its limits and borders determined, and their names, personalities, everything in them was made recognizable, in order for them to become property of someone – another character, themselves, the author, the reader, the book, capitalism itself. jealousy makes the other recognizable, 'predictable,' imaginable. jealousy draws a 'truth' soon to be discovered, a property we can have thanks to a mental map, a system of control on the body of the other.

i write fiction while i hear music so i don't forget this is what 'characters' became, but not how they structurally must be. in the past, characters at least in one form of discourse were plasmatic, even invisible, ghostly, not solid; in fact, characters had no other architecture than that of mystical music.

*

not a place. but how light and darkness happen in that place or maybe in some place else.

*

an end to the novel? to require an end the novel would need to be a fixed entity, something whose life depended on itself, but we suspect the novel is part of a decadence of which it is not yet the lowest point. that's why kafka is always a symbol of the history of the novel, a history that can never end, because it's a process that can only be left unfinished in its 'novel' stage / a posthumous attempt to understand what the complete history of the novel might have been. the novel has already changed, there's now no way to terminate it or to write it again.

*

time to look at what we've done as writers serving optimistic politics. making the reader a co-producer, we declared we were empowering him or her. the truth was that everything became work, even leisure, play or silence. in our era even 'words work' (barrett watten). workaholism. writing as the metaphysical shop window was proof that language was also labour, everything was working – well. the reader as co-producer means him/her as slave. we (writers and readers) made the 'reader' believe s|he had to be active too, because if s|he was not s|he was 'passive.' that myth. even working when he dreams or reads. that's why i like books that don't work.

the storyteller creates, 'produces.' that's what s|he is supposed to do. s|he follows *maker* (god/producer). this is very obvious. but s|he can follow another path: disappearance. instead of making something appear from nothingness (*sic*), s|he can make everything disappear into nothingness. (one is as impossible as the other. so, why not?) the storyteller could play the role of anti-god, a not-producer. sabotage. a consumer of everything. let the universe grow and expand, *produce*; let the storyteller decrease the world. writing pursuing the achievement of nothing, to stop working as soon as it begins.

*

[voice leads to religion. there, where *voice* appears, a god is possible, a god is unavoidable. the author reads, and co-produces community – he or she is near being a priest, even when she or he abhors this role, as we do, as we do because we no longer believe in gods, nor in ourselves. comedy is opposite to religion. exactly when reunion is going to happen, laughter *breaks*.]

*

we cannot change. we are already everything. changing would mean turning into something different. (and would mean *producing*.) 'changing' is simply a very complex way to die. a pseudo-category created in order to not accept that 'transforming'/'changing'/'producing' are those skills which aim to attack or wound us. 'changing' means killing some of us inside or outside. even my training in psychotherapy teaches me this: we must murder some of what/who we are. health is adequate murder. and my mexican culture reinforces this also: the most important thing is to know we must die. storytelling for me is writing about how we commit suicide or participate in homicide both in life and in history. not how a story unfolds or how a character *develops*, but how death happens all the time. for me the page is war.

*

'while writing this piece i dismantled the yellow pages and threw them all over the floor. it was raining heavily. i was trying to keep water coming below the door to ruin the books piled on the other side of the room, but kant's small *filosofía de la historia* was soon ruined.'

*

how can i build my mexicanness here. certain references. i could allude to being a mestizo, and how that makes me *naturally multiple*.

*

'autobiography.' we should read this term the other way around, and say something like this: writing is always auto_bio_graphical. never writing on *me*. but: *graphos* (text) constructing *bios* (life) that appears as *auto* (on itself). autobiography: language writing on itself and thus becoming 'alive.'

*

'poor gramsci. | those weren't good years to exist. being in prison made him obsessed with details, just like wittgenstein's closet did [for him]. thinkers whose work feels like an old man browsing a bazaar, finding everything amusing as if this were his first time there and not his entire life's pattern of attempts to smell the vendor's hair. don't even think of mentioning the other guy. i just don't like him. gramsci was just the other day telling us about his latest finding | one more of his 'crucial' remarks. nothing but scraps. he told us about how the italian word for *mysticism* was being used with the french *mystique*'s meaning 'predominantly critical and pejorative.' | enlisting consequences | he wanted the two of us to say something that would have propelled his little speech even further, but both of us said nothing, dependent on one another as we are | we kept both mouths closed while we were there. we fed each other | letting our twenty fingers caress each other's hair while | he | continued explaining how those two words united. he wanted us to let him know our opinion of it or how his words made us realize something! | saw something in our mind! | ... understanding what culture had come to ... | but we didn't respond in any way. we kept silent, making no sign of human contact between us as though me and her didn't even know each other and it was only accidentally we had come today to be at this young old man cell.'

*

a character is not getting away from us, nor going (more) inside. none of us can be written. in order for 'us' to be written (down) (=subjected) (controlled), in order for any of 'us' to become text / even just one /, (we) need the presence of the others, their coexistence, due to the ghostly fact that there's no single one. no one (none) can be written. always some of us left behind.

*

'kill every indian. let them die while escaping in the jungle. let's behave like those hunters, tribes or helicopters.'

*

fiction *equals*.
personality. 'life.'
who is the real subject, leonardo or mona lisa? flaubert or madame bovary? borges or the other borges? none of them. just two out of a multiplicity, the two of them chosen by reception or

the author(ity) precisely because any of them could play the polarity game well, could fit into the fixed or easily movable personality patterns. how is the author or character determined? by the historical hegemony of bodies established in its time and culture. writing happens, books, etc., and who the character or the author is gets determined by what kind of bodies are accepted. which are discarded. class, gender, unconscious, culture, all of these artifacts are used to establish a recognizable entity, a group of them (*author* between them) ... 'after the crucifixion jesus wasn't the same [character] any more. but we couldn't afford to know that. that's why somebody needed to interpolate saint thomas's proof. even after passion, death and resurrection occurred, jesus kept himself the same, son of god himself.'

... unfinished.

... gospels that contradicted and blurred jesus' image too much ... brought confusion on who and how he was ... calling that corpus of text *apocrypha.*

*

man asks: masks – so many of them – why?

– m(other).

*

chupacabras appeared in mexican culture through *national enquirer–*type publications, tv series and mere oral transmission (the 'streets'). chupacabras means goat-sucker. this creature could even be linked with ufos – shares with them the feature of never being completely seen.[1] if we use plot-theory, 'chupacabras' was a distraction. those holes in dead animals started to appear on the news in the late nineties, when former mexican president carlos salinas was selling the banks, making deals with drug cartels and signing nafta with canada and the u.s. chupacabras was used in mexico as michael jackson's pedophilic scandals were used in nice america. but the distraction was far too obvious and goat-sucker became synonymous with the look of salinas, permanently mocked/remembered for his big rat-like ears, an infamous corruption figure defined as a little monster sucking the blood of the 'people,' and even having killed his nanny when he was young.

black humour masks and toys sold in mexican cities skilfully exploited the resemblance of chupacabras and salinas, how they were related, co-produced.

chupacabras to me is a meta-character on how character works.

a dead/unclear body that hides and reveals the political.

unclean

*

in his seminal essay on the storyteller, walter benjamin makes a collateral and brief attack against the short story. benjamin despises it because through the short story we abbreviate and destroy the possibility of multiple strata – fast-food storytelling. benjamin writes that idea – and many more, many – in an essay. a short essay, by the way.

the essay assures. the essay also shortens. like aphorisms and short stories, the essay synthesizes. gives manageable package to a previous more complex and abundant – transpersonal – material – or spiritual linguistic net of meanings. maybe we are an age – these last centuries of which we are still a part – that is only now realizing we have impoverished language altogether.

*

in some apocrypha and other gnostic, judaic and muslim sources, jesus had a twin. he could be very well the one who impersonated him as the resurrected son of god. this is an especially tempting hypothesis because his name was tom. [saint] thomas is called 'didimus' (twin) in certain versicles of the new testament. a character identical to jesus (maybe 'jesus' himself) (his double) putting his finger in the wounds on his hand / made by the nails of the romans / in order to confirm the reality of his [own] identity and life. in order to produce a unique tale. here too jesus, a damaged body, a doubtful one, metaphysically evolves into a hole in the flesh.

*

... if this were correct, poetics and fiction/theory would represent forms of decline. these genres of speculation would have appeared once the secrets, traditions, innovative powers, craft and ideas behind/towards narrative had come to a stop or – fearing complete loss or desiring control – had decided to become written dogmas, laws, established prescriptions replacing the previous and more personal oral or transpersonal transmission. and i'm not talking here of an esoteric male one-to-one school of in-your-ear transmission but simply an environment in which the narrative-producer (or any maker) would gather the tools and visions for her/his creation from the collective culture, s|he would hunt during her/his travels, findings in her/his own mind, techniques s|he would hunt or received from that concrete historical language/world. the essay mode, the written reflection-upon, would be, if this is correct, much more elitist than the apparently silent way of keeping the narrative transformation dependent upon the more fluent processes of dialogue among its makers, listeners or ghosts.

let's face it: by writing we become instant elders. authorities. intelligent people who appropriate ideas and structures from the culture we live in – and increasingly from other cultures, decontextualizing meanings – and thanks to this taking away we build our «own work». people who not only steal but sign. and construct a character who tells, doubts, proposes or ignores the way we should narrate.

*

from story to history. auschwitz. china. vietnam. chiapas. iraq – every name or place is now a reference to a murder – 1945. 1968. 1994. 2001 – every year, a plot – nixon's 'i'm not a crook.' bush's 'read my lips ...' clinton's 'didn't inhale,' even milli vanilli's lip-synching – why write fiction in a time of total fabrication and lies?

how to narrate so nothing more happens? how to storytell events so not even one more takes place? there's only one thing worse than the twentieth century: having survived it. this is for me the un-final dilemma: why and how to write narrative in a time when man begins to be indescribable?

NOTE

1 chupacabras was dimly photographed. it was never captured alive, the best shots were of it as a badly decomposed corpse. that's what i liked about it. chupacabras was never completely a body, never completely something

describable. even though chupacabras (btw, a comic name) sometimes was imagined as a kind of reptile, gila monster, a mutation, sometimes as a bigger-bat. chupacabras' true body were the two holes left on dead animals.

Last Exit to Victoria
(Five mins. of Murder Alone with *Wigger* and 'Bloodland')
Lawrence Ytzhak Braithwaite

1

... as a child I was told that not knowing the alphabet will cause illiteracy. It'll send you into a drugged-out gangland life of white-trash nightmares and corner-boy peddling to homosexuals, who are professional players, obsessed with age and willing to drag it and you into emptiness. That in knowing the letters, I'll know that they assemble to construct various images that become words. Words are the narrative transformation of the images. Printing a page of unbroken words is like a fresh tattoo. It captures a moment/place, sentiment and period. It orchestrates the body in motion as it flexes to move a pen/strike at a key/form a fist/lift a drink or move to a rhythm. The words become the unspoken intertextuality of ethnic, racial and cultural metaphoric speech. The meter of casual dialogue = a rhythm/noise/visual/bass, a soundtrack to a post-literate train of thought.

I dedicated *Wigger* to the sound of Slayer and Sonic Youth – 'Bloodland' to Cannibal Corpse (George 'Corpsegrinder' Fisher) = I dedicated them to sound. Slayer is for the fury and speed and violence that the book has. Deathmetal is the living desire of the neo-redneck burnout. It's all going after the sport of brutality – the art of hurting someone. The walking jokes, with targets on their backs, placed there by li'l bitches, 'taking them for M 'n' M's. The only violence is the way the words appear on the page, marked by the slashes that connote rhythm of speech and interrupted thought. They are like semicolons = / the // are colons and so are the = signs. Sometimes the – move out to separate speech – someone takes lead//does a solo. Sonic Youth's sounds appear in the form of the book dissolving. Deathmetal is just dealing with the situation. The book and the story, like the characters, are trying to hold themselves together. Brian and Jerehmia symbolize this the most. They talk. No one listens.

... a printer ejects swatches of stolen tissue that collects the sound and images of what is considered low-brow art and skill//
Hardcore (H.C.)/Country/Rockabilly
Thrash and Speedmetal/Rap/Deathmetal/Blackmetal
Cinema/Television and;

Comics Books

Brian appears to be rambling but he makes the most sense because he speaks through metaphor and his heart, like Black speech and song – the negro spiritual, seeming to sing about a river,
when it is a code,
for an escape,
at a certain time,
from the plantation.
Gangsta rap seems to boast
about an evening
or event
but is just shouting
validity,
existence and
enterprise.
Brian's grasp on reality becomes inconsequential.
Jerehmia's story is dumbshow.
Brian surrenders his ideals and his soul by killing Spook (the Black hustler friend).
Jerehmia is just having his taken and he's telling you about it – but I knew people in Atlanta that didn't want to hear about any of that or them. I knew a boy from Tennessee hurting worse than what was going as oppression under those hundred-dollar Afro-centric hats.

... Wordcore, Jamaican dub poetry, Rap and Rock Steady are disposed to the Homeric boasts and catalogues of postmodern thugs/hoodlums and desperados w/ the hope of kindness and compassion.

In donning the Black persona, symbolized through the silver jacket, Brian finally does what everyone has been attempting to do throughout the book. Brian is killed – his soul is killed, through the burden of the weight of the Black youth – the Black persona, the persona of deglamoured oppression. He has achieved the goal of being Black but he is unprepared to handle something that the Blacks are raised to deal with through centuries of struggle – you'd suppose.

I met a boy with crystal-smack grey eyes, who was offering to suck the fender (for $5) off an urban assault vehicle for a painkiller.

If you listen and see the page, you'll see a tattoo and note well, that some words are//

– Rhythm
– Lead and
– Bass

Jerehmia, he has no desire to be Black. He knows what the shit is and he's got his own. He just watches the seemingly liberal Perry go catch back the Black boy trying to bail on the whole scene. He just knows that nothing that's happening is about him or the niglet. It's about the little men with big shirts and the chicks in bed or sitting off from the bar-b-q ...

... strange how all the young men holding up walls waiting on passersby had deep drawls, no smiles and trailers in their hearts.

The book and the story are collapsing. The spaces and sparseness of the narrative are there to get you to listen carefully and read again and close read and not take things at face value. People say more, especially when they've had a lifetime of hurt, through very few words and the words look in ways that they feel – speeching in a cappella. The words sound the way they feel. The book shows patterns of speech.

McLuhan would argue the global village: technology is good – the book people are lacking in the rich grammar of the TV = This is referred to today as the post-literate generation – John Cage's bastard children turn to violence and the acoustic space of video and computer games and the delicacy of words typed over television screens.

McLuhan would argue ...

... the acoustic

2

The Comic book uses frames and juxtaposition to connect the disconnectedness of thought and words, be it through the gruff noir-ness of Frank Miller, Dave Sim or Martin Wales's 'Kinder Nacht,' or the smooth lines, colours and ruff justice of Todd McFarlane. They collect the street sounds and activities the way Rap culture manipulates and emulates, via spin art and samples, the ready-made terror of interurban life. To frame is to make perfect the moment of the fingers striking the keys, which can be the repetition of words and phrases = outlets ripping and shredding, w/ the knowledge that framing is certainly an attempt to make perfect, to make the words as enticing and elegant as the bovine euphony of a fascist's goose step.

Brian is condemned to sit, numbed out on pills, in a room filled with drag queens, watching them transform. Just like Brian's desire, and the other characters' desires, to be Black, the drag queens attempt to be women, without knowing that beyond the glamour is a lot of hardship and struggle. Drag queens die, as well, when they finally achieve their dream of being a woman. It's not as much fun or better than they thought it would be. They are unprepared for the daily struggle and threats. You can see this on the page. They are boxed in, allowing themselves to be, finally, separated from the freeness and flow of the book. They must stay within the parameters. The glamour is gone. They have to bear the actual pain. Brian has got the auditory recollection of rape in his head. Brian is numb. So's Jerehmia, but he's numb from the beginning, anyway. He's just recollecting, now – no need to figure. He can't hold it together, nor does he want to. His flag is upside down, Oswald's dead – nothing's right. You separate the body from the mind and it's all good.

... a word can be the hums or bops in the background, as when a funk musician beats the strings w/ his thumb – the buzz and scratch of a tat gun on a steadied arm or back – the stilled breath and firm muscle of a word or image engraved on a belly. It gets tied into the paragraph. Some words take on the repetitive ecstatic riff of ska or reggae or the decay of the crash/noise of H.C. or metal. They recline on the page or in the air as if they were all going to amount to a junkie's last sigh. Instead, they collapse into the lost, disoriented and somewhat satisfied image of Orson Welles after trashing a room at Xanadu.

... and the book and story crumble into a final sustained note, done through a note to Andrew from Jerry. 'Bloodland' has a crack of gun shot and shit and a heartbeat. As it began on a note – it ends. His (Jerry's) speech is proper and distant from the language of the book. He has become a literary character of the Modernist sense.

Jerking the Modernist approach to distance, into 'groovy times,' is the dumbshow to the contemporary adoration of the absurdist tragic comedy = anti-romantic. It presents itself, today, through the jaded situationism of talk-show culture. The sort that 'Blast' and 'Counter Blast' utilized through the headlines and print of newspapers. The newspapers place horror and glory side by side in a folio that has a calculated randomness. It will always assemble to state one thing = these events happen. It is only through such genres of media (music/comic/print/television), that we can see that each has a thing in common/coupons and advertising = rhetoric and metaphor. If the passage of a text takes on the sound and image of the disjointedness of casual speech and media, then the results are not only the coded tales being woven, but the presentation of the brutality that leads to the violent outcome.

Jerehmia, he just figures ... he's just feedback from a bass, right now. *Wigger* and 'Bloodland' are what the printer jetted out – a conceptual pastiche alphabet from the corner or gutter. It assembles the images in sequence that persuades the narrative to be pulled out from under a character. It's what got them blocked off – formatted, laid out, then pile-drived with carefully selected skin grafts of onomatopoeias. The words takes Auden's diver, diving w/ his 'brilliant bow,' and takes it beyond the enthralled spectator. They suppose that he has forgotten to test the water and has come out a dumbstruck paraplegic = what just happened/where are our people/who are our people/do we have any people: NO. However, they still keep tabs on the moment, place sound and period that left the object devastated, hungover and w/ an image permanently scratched and coloured onto his flesh or hanging in a window. –

Oi Cheers,

Laz

Lawrence Y Braithwaite (AKA Lord Patch)

New Palestine/Fernwood/The Hood

Victoria, BC

Experimentalism
Camille Roy

1 Methods

Writing I find exciting often gets called *experimental*. In America this is another word for *marginal*. It's patronizing. Other countries distribute legitimacy in literary culture differently. For example, when in the UK, Kathy Acker wrote for the *Times Literary Supplement*. Can you imagine Acker writing for the *New York Times Book Review*!? Just the experience of reviewing her work in the NYT *Book Review* caused several reviewers to spontaneously combust. On the other side of the Atlantic, debates on literary aesthetics are part of public – not just academic – life. Not so here, which means the conventions of representation that underlie mainstream fiction in this country can't be effectually critiqued. (I don't consider academic debates to be part of public life.)

So what conventions of representation am I talking about? Consider identity. Mainstream fiction tends to assume separate and coherent individuals, each with a single body and character which is built, rather than destroyed, by conflict.

I believe it is possible to have one identity in your thumb and another in your neck. I think identities can travel between persons who have an unusual mutual sympathy. Let's not even mention multiple personality.

But what I want to talk about today is the manipulation and construction of social distance. Mainstream fiction assumes a position not too close, not too far away. A situation is implied, an entire social horizon, which is speckled with white individuals who maintain distance from one another and from social 'problems.'

Containment. Segregation. A narrative structure which covertly mirrors the growth of white suburbs since WWII, where there is no discomfort around racism because only white people are present. Breaking this long chain of social convention at any link can easily result in personal and literary deformity, which is another term for experimentation.

> My sister was older, and kept her drugs and screwing in the basement the same way she kept her jewelry there. Her lovers

were thin white men whose trouble was drug-related. When Paul got out of Cook County Jail he carried an odor of rape and had large nerve spots in his eyes. Fear moving like a breeze in a prison yard, I could feel that in my stomach when he was around; otherwise I didn't care. I thought about Monica. Her sharp teeth and brown cheeks. The way her greed slid across my hips could be scary but her palms were narrow as slots, that made it okay to have sex with her.[1]

The well-modulated distance of mainstream fiction not only distances social conflict, it also doesn't represent lesbian relationships very well. Mainstream literary forms reflect conventions of identity that are dominated by the masculine and the heterosexual. I am not arguing for femininity in literature here. I don't find those essentialist positions very interesting. But I think relations between women have the potential to strain conventions of representation. HOW exactly. Consider the characteristics associated with women: weak boundaries between self and other, heightened capacity for intimacy, identification of self with other, and a more fluid sense of self. In mainstream contexts, these capacities are exploited until you reach, at the limit, erotic positions which have been emptied of subjectivity, e.g., BIMBO/CUNT. I think it's quite difficult, perhaps impossible, to represent a dyke as empty in that way. The corollary in the lesbian world to the empty sexual object is an erotic position I think of as invaded subjectivity.

I was her idea, the fix for a wife with lesbian dreams. She never told me the details but I could feel them pushing out at night, in the way that there's a ghost town inside every city. It made her ferocious but not personal. Once she wanted me to tell her my sexual fantasies. *Confession is good information,* she said, stroking my clit with her finger. I shuddered, then recoiled. What could I say? My mouth was unconscious. I should have whispered, *It feels like your nostalgia.*[2]

I take it as a given that the well-modulated distance of mainstream fiction is a system that contains and represses social conflict, and that one purpose of experimental work is to break open this system. But experimental work can require a context of aesthetic ideas which many people who might otherwise be interested in it don't have. In this context, intimacy, autobiography and direct address don't function just as content but are strategies for pursuing a reluctant audience. So are genre narrative forms, such as sex writing or horror.

There are many roads into the succulent interior. How can the mechanisms of genre fiction get us (the cabal of experimental writers) there?

Consider porn narratives. Usually people do not appreciate being taken apart. They rely upon having an ego, enjoy feeling integrated and in control, and experimental work that questions this can arouse distaste. What is so interesting about pornography is that loosing it is the point. People want to be taken apart so that ego control (resistance to pleasure) is subverted. Where there was distaste, there is now desire mixed with dread. *Pleasures of the rupture, rack and screw.* The audience becomes an unwitting collaborator in its own disintegration, in the interest of pleasure, or just feeling, period.

Genre fiction is not about representing experience but producing and organizing feeling – sexual excitement, horror, mystery, fear. The aim is to invade the reader's subjectivity. To control, and then to release. The desire of the reader to be aroused or to otherwise escape is the keyhole through which all the mechanisms of the narrative operate (note that this turns the writer into a kind of spy!).

Because genre writing deals in something as low as feeling, these forms are relatively easy to use in other contexts and for other purposes. They are already degraded, so their resistance is weak. Experimental writers using genre forms are like drag artists.

> My mistress cuts & tucks one silicone 38D into my chest and then another, while I'm bound to our massive brass bed. Her kinky breath is soft as suede.
> When I cry she tells me,
>> *The best titties are raised on the farm.*
> When I scream she says,
>> *Pain shreds & relaxes. You'll stumble over the real thing.*
>> *Think of scrub brushes and the perfect ending.*
> When I sob in agony she comforts me,
>> *Later we'll take a tour of the castle.*
> My mistress is cruel. She's bright as breath. She whispers to me as she cuts,
>> *I'm a fan of the flesh tits, stuffing, sweetmeats.*
>> *I suck the juice from the roast, I'm a pig with a straw.*[3]

How to pass suffering, eroticism ... from one person to another? Where does coherence fly apart? The answer to these questions does not lie in one or another particular strategy but in the sensual devotion of the writer, taken to formal extremes. We explore our narrative tools, discovering exactly how they manipulate or release the contorted social body – because it's the one we live in, the one that feeds off us, the one that has swallowed the visible horizon.

2 Monsters

One of the forms of narrative I write is software. It's lucrative. About four years ago I used stock options to buy a house right around the corner plus one block from one of the worst housing projects in San Francisco. A couple thousand people live there. It gives my neighbourhood the highest child-hunger rate in the city. Our first night in the house someone got murdered, just before midnight. It was a block away but the shot sounded like it was in our backyard. One shot, a pause, then another. Purposeful. Somehow I knew it was intended to kill, and not just a couple of kids shooting at the moon. Plus, the neighbour told us he'd had his car stolen three times.

Impenetrable poverty plus dumb-fuck rules, class and race segregation: I'd moved into the only San Francisco neighbourhood that duplicated on a smaller scale what I grew up with. It annoyed me.

Locality, forever. *Skewed*. Something huge gets mutilated as it slides through a stuffy tube. We're on the beach very far to the west, watching what pops out. It contains all of American culture. I came here so tightly wound. Born on 43rd Street South-side Chicago, and haven't been back since I left the hospital.

From my dining room window, at the rear of the house, the project looks strangely vacant. There just never seem to be many people around. The buildings proceed down the hill towards the old industrial port like giant shabby steps, but there is never anyone on the racks of balconies. I've rarely driven through it. Structurally, it's sort of a dead-end place, the way it's laid out, like a suburban subdivision: streets point into it, then twist up like spaghetti. The few drive-through streets are dotted with dealers scoping out the passing cars.

When I first moved in I often found myself dreamily staring out the dining room window. I wanted to check out one of those balconies. The view would be amazing; they practically hang over the bay. Developers have been salivating over that piece of land for years. Nowadays they are nibbling at the edges of the project, building expensive live/work lofts for software designers on adjoining vacant industrial land. It's weird. Different economic classes get spliced together via crimes, their mode of interaction being criminal. So one day I mentioned to a friend of mine that I didn't get it, how did dealers get kids to work for them playing courier, or delivery boy? What would a dealer have on a kid? Why get involved with some jacked-up, scary asshole? I felt like an idiot as soon as the words left my mouth. Patiently, step by step, my friend explained how it was done, until I could have done it myself, as obviously he had. All I had to do was ask. Knowledge. The getting and taking and the tearing up. Did I want to go there?

Of course I did. One day I walked in, took a place on the balcony next to all of my friends and drank their salty water. I listened to the radio. I watched as a crack lady ran down the street behind a white dog. Then the dog was scratching at the door. When I woke up, that sound was the shade, bumping against the window frame. And I was thinking, as I am always doing, and my thinking told me this: *This is what I want. It's inside my system of attractions. I'm penetrated by the present and it's always the same: chronic anger. Awful but refreshing.*

I walked into the projects a couple of weeks ago. It's right around the corner, why not just walk? It was a friend's birthday. She told me where she lived, but it wasn't easy to find. The apartments didn't have numbers on them, you had to just know. I asked a bunch of people. Kids were running everywhere. How come I hadn't seen them from my back window? I look whiter than usual, I thought, looking at my hand. Up here and not even shopping, that made me odd. People looked at me skeptically. I felt skeptical about myself, but slick, as in greased. I wanted to fall off my little ledge. Bored with what had gotten dished up as myself, with the backwash of swallowing it.

The balcony was great. I hung with my friends and listened to the radio. They played that song I like, the one about money. Later we went out to eat birthday steaks.

California is shallow. That's true. Though it thrills me that I can walk across the city without getting beat up for crossing some invisible dividing line of racial turf. Of course I could get beat up for something else. *I'm so easy to please.*

I'm supposed to write about narrativity but these problems of locality are where I get started. For me writing grinds itself into what's familiar yet unbearable. Add mobility to that and, voila, narrative. Disjunction is the formal consequence of this ripped and torn social life, and it's packed with information, almost to the point of being insensible.

The streets I walk measure me. They measure you too, through mechanisms both criminal and friendly. Writing that knowledge is a kind of spectacular innocence – the moment of saturation feels dazzling, but there is probably no point. Still I love it, formally and erotically. It's all about nested structures. I entrust my twisted little pieces to the warm nest of the sick social body, and I feel our bond. It nourishes me.

To theorize my point of view, to pursue critical formalism as a ritual and as a grasp for power, let me put it this way. Narrative provides context so that the rupturing of identity is recognizable. We are impossible beings, ruthlessly evading scrutiny. Yet recognition (linchpin of narrative) is the beginning of transformative emotion.

As a narrative writer I improvise recognition. It's like a location from which mutant beings emerge. This feels true; in life they never stop emerging. Look – they even swarm through this text. I allow it because I'm terrified and seduced. To encounter them via narrative is to formalize a moment of surrender.

NOTES

1 Camille Roy, 'My X Story,' *The Rosy Medallions* (Berkeley, CA: Kelsey St. Press, 1995), 11.

2 Camille Roy, 'Sex Life,' *The Rosy Medallions*, 30.

3 Camille Roy, 'Fetish,' *The Rosy Medallions*, 68.

All *New Yorker* Stories
Mary Burger

All *New Yorker* fiction pieces stop at the point where the person makes a bad discovery about himself or herself or the world. That he is or she is a failure personally – in love, usually, romantic love or familial love – or that the world is a failure towards his personal or her personal sensitive nature – that the world is violent, that unequal distribution of power causes pain and unhappiness, usually to the less powerful, but sometimes to the powerful as well.

Regardless of its narrator, its characters, its particular conceits or conflicts, what anchors each story is the sick feeling at the end. The same feeling that comes after a radiation treatment for cancer. The queasy realization that all this, the technological sophistication, the aggressive preservation of human life, is merely its own reward, not a means to anything.

This is how the melancholic condition of privileged passivity confronts itself. When a grown man behaves mercilessly towards his humble, bewildered parents; when a wealthy young Latin American woman is threatened with kidnapping and even death, right in front of her own gated home, right inside her private limousine; when the mostly likeable gay neighbour, in the midst of his theatrical, flamboyant prime, withers suddenly and agonizingly, and dies. When an urbane, not quite young writer, supplementing her New York lifestyle with a teaching job in the heartland, falls in love with a simple, decent man, neither a New Yorker nor a writer nor even in any way ironic – and simply leaves him, his marriage proposal, his simple, open face, to return to her lair in the crowded city, her archly urban self in the witheringly sophisticated intellectual world.

In 'withering,' a possibility that what is socially belittling might also be personally devastating. That the intricate architecture of social standing might collapse occasionally, like a poorly braced studio set, to reveal something more like an experience arrived at through contemplation.

When the modestly privileged, moderately young childless couple who attend the adoption picnic focus on the same large-eyed, attractive kid (that is, the querulous wife focuses. The ironic husband, whose disavowal of the thing expected of him mimics Kevin Spacey's in *American Beauty*, instead alights for a while with an aloof, jaded teenager, whose unflinching lack of delusion contributes to the reader's own worldliness), that is, the moderately young, uncomfortably nervous wife alights on the same doe-eyed little boy attended to by an imposing Texas judge and his Barbara Bush–edition wife. It is an orphan fair. Like all bazaars, the most attractive goods are fought for, the least attractive are left behind to grow even dingier.[1]

In this version, the judge and his wife are the cunning players. They are powerful, and they are malevolent. The judge and his wife invite the more modest couple to their lair, a large house on a large piece of land by a lake.

With 'lair,' variously, the idea that the seeming impotence of the self-conscious intellectual (the New York writer snagged in the loneliness of her cleverness, the cleverness of her loneliness), the rueful split between the life of the heart and the life of the mind, is a familiar condition, the condition that seems to be most easily recognized as a sign of distress, of all not being right with the world. The dissonance between what you know and what you need – this is the price charged for entry to the club. And who complains? Does a young gymnast object that her muscle-strapped torso and thighs set her apart from other girls? The world-weariness might be counted as a privilege; anyway, it's displayed often enough to be interpreted that way.

Through the battlefield drills of drinks, dinner, after-dinner segregation of husbands and wives, the older couple's battle plan emerges. The Texas wife begins an oblique attack, a narrative of a foster child they'd had, a black toddler taken from an addicted mother. His mounting health problems and learning disabilities, together with the difficulty in keeping a nanny – when enough details have been laid out, the concluding sentence isn't needed.

The off-register comments from the Texas wife about her foster child, about finding the boy a nanny 'of his own kind' and a school with 'all different races, the Mexicans and the Chinese and the Indians and all that,' create another clear space in the story, a way to tell what is right.

In the kitchen, away from the women, the judge's assault is direct: he confronts the husband with ammunition gathered from his labyrinthine legal connections: evidence of the husband's expulsion from college fifteen years ago for selling pot, evidence that the judge, with a final flourish of legal muscles, has already inserted into the husband's case file at the adoption agency. This in the few days since the couples met.

But since the cunning of great power isn't really the story, or enough of a story, it is necessary for the judge to punch the husband in the nose and knock him down before the couple, and the story, can leave the judge's house.

The women's exchanges, happening at the same time, are far less direct than the men's but result in arguably more damage, like a barbed hook that's slipped smoothly into the skin and then twisted.

It's true, too, that the young wife and husband want different things (as different as a doe-eyed youngster from a disaffected teen), a further cause of dissatisfaction.

The obliquity of the wives and the passive irony of the young husband all form a rueful cognizance that weighs down to the point of paralysis. And yet it's that ruefulness that cradles its hands around the narrative's delicate crown jewel.

Like a lead musician, the fiction narrator repeats and elaborates a single sensitive melody line, or crescendos on a particular note of knowing regret, a middle-aged loss of innocence, though evacuated of any possibility that the afflicted might be rescued from the cause of their desolation or even, astonishingly, change their own lives.

This sombre performance seems to be the provenance, or the penance, of the fictional narrator only. For the non-fiction narrator, the feat is more acrobatic, if not therefore also more precarious.

The non-fiction narrator is permeated by a sense of ambiguity impossible in her counterpart. While the fiction narrator lives with the certainty that moral rectitude is real, that extreme power is obscene, the non-fiction narrator is instead subject to the wild cards, false leads and missed signals of a lived life.[2]

The non-fiction narrator tends to have an intimate relationship with squalor, or danger, or pleasure, an intimacy marked by unguarded revelations of vulnerability. She exchanges the reassurance of an intricately self-referencing universe, in which each element contributes clearly and inevitably to the whole, for rapport with the volatile, the off-balance, the unpredictable. Her familiarity with squalor becomes its own sophistication, her fluency in the idiom of disorder, with its free-jazz syncopation and arrhythmia, its own seductiveness. The effect holds our attention like a sudden, beckoning whistle coming in through the window of a quiet room.

In this version, the non-fiction narrator is free to both love and despise her volatile, negligent parents, her alcoholic mother who disappears on binges and returns home to demand attention and threaten suicide; she's free to both admire and resent her slightly older, vastly more sexually experienced sister; she's free to fear and adore the coltish, sanguine boy she's had a crush on since age six. The non-fiction narrator elides between bewilderment and passion for her own still-strange sexual feelings and for the obvious, pronounced desire that persists between her parents even in the midst of their pitched battles.

While the fictional narrator breathlessly cradles a fragile egg, the non-fiction narrator darts in and out of the room bouncing a rubber ball.

In the photo, a snapshot salvaged from one of those summers that were both vacant and teeming, she is fifteen. Her long hair blown a little into her face, head tilted a little to the side, lashes lightly mascaraed or just naturally thick and dark – she is the early seventies icon of innocent sexiness, the womanly girl, what Ali McGraw, *Love Story* and John Denver's 'Sunshine on my Shoulders' all immortalized, but what she seems to be without trying, maybe without even really knowing.

It's that not knowing, or anyway not always needing to know, that the non-fiction narrator settles for, but that the fiction narrator battles like a riptide.

The one bobs in a tight ship just off shore, pulled between the current and the undertow, while the rest shout and lunge in beach volleyball, play with children, play with dogs, play radios, nap. She imagines her voice as faint, or inaudible, from shore. The other shipwrecks in the shoals and scrambles from her splintered raft. Her escape is always in progress.

NOTES

1 J. Robert Lennon, 'No Life,' *The New Yorker* (September 4, 2000): 74–81.
2 Mary Karr, 'The Hot Dark,' *The New Yorker* (September 4, 2000): 42–49.

Narrative Occupation and Uneven Enclosure
Taylor Brady

> Recognition will be a sign of madness.
>
> – Tom Raworth

The sleep that descends on me in narrative is both deep and empty, devoid of any manifest dream image or latent dream content. But as if the dreamwork itself had continued to propel its mechanism along without the help of the usual ancillaries and props of production, I have the impression upon waking that my skin has become a far more sensitive instrument, a device for dreaming on the outside, and I think with not a little disappointed sadness that had you been here to gaze lovingly on as I snored, you would have been witness to a tattoo animation that probed the contraptions by which the scorched earth of redevelopment, an absolute ground for my retention of experience here and, I assume, for yours as well, prompted the nearly unlimited substitutability and replacement of the many objects of my desire.[1]

You will of course object that I am indulging in that pre-eminent mode of false consciousness, *trying to prolong the horizon by changing the position of my chair,*[2] as if there were some previously disused conduit between the occupation of this tract of land in a time before we awakened to it and the occupations we now pursue across its surface, and that this pipeline would represent a means for balancing accounts if only we were to settle into *an accurate perspective.* Let us therefore put a name to this dim profusion of shapes. Or, rather, let us take away their names one by one, so as to admit that our fond memories of a shared childhood are all rooted in the dirt of a zoning tract that once housed a camp of tents and trailers at the edge, now incorporated and creeping towards a relocated centre, of a city whose exemplary talent for concealing the violence with which its few areas of public density were policed had forced its reserve armies into the undeveloped scrub woods, and that here a shift in productivity came with heavy equipment, clubs and stun guns to levy a newly established bottom tier of differential rent – that bones were broken and shelters burned, these sudden movements and intense heats contributing energy to a physics of work that crusted value as new asphalt over the limestone and sandy soil, and that it is this amassing of cost from which we collect the sumptuous stuffs of our ability to recognize a common history in this place.[3]

The bare chronicle of events gets at some of this, but I wonder about its obsessive worrying at the event status of state violence whose vanishing beneath the threshold of witness constitutes the perceptual field in which I have come to be conscious of any possible struggle against it, whether it creates the resonating space in which frequency spikes of allegory might break through the compression envelope, or whether it simply dissipates energy from that locale to create a dead spot, an impasse that can only give onto the cheap transcendence of an intuited 'unknown world' that leads astray by a show of mere coincidences, thus bringing us full circle back to the skin movie I was trying to seduce you with, before I realized I was seducing myself into position on the chair from which the question of an impossible perspective first arose.[4] Would it matter if I noted, for instance, that I am writing this while eavesdropping on county planning officials who are busy congratulating each other for their political maturity in grasping that the true function of land-use policy is to follow along behind 'market forces,' or would that only become, given the contained space of interrogation, one more illegitimate device for amplifying the private twitching in my throat into a wall of sound that would fill in the unseemly gaps in my command of the composition's unfolding?[5]

So assume I am concocting alongside this a narrative of a woman whose body is always being replaced by its own skill at reading its angle of incidence with the reduced but fractally infinite scale of a suburban parking lot, a narrative that will run vertically through the blank horizontals of this text, if you care to crane your neck for such a reading. This will bring you to mirror her posture and harmonize with her on a misplaced conviction in the generative force of minor retail, while you pointedly ignore how much of the rest of the chorus rode in on Striker assault vehicles. As I work, the disused vectors one might have followed *talk botany to me, but I scarcely listen. I am no longer sufficient in myself, I am now only the necessary intermediary between the heavy ordnance and you,* a sticky starburst through my abdomen that vomits light into the darkened passageway where you crouch on the far side of this clearing. Were I to ask you to send help, you would take it as the worst kind of joke, one played neither on you nor on myself, but on the *situation* that binds us to the emergent form of our sitting here telling stories without moving our lips, an unwarranted grandiloquence that would redound to my own statuesque figure of renunciation while discounting the ropy strands of you that make my hair adhere weblike to the niche you occupy.

Of course, this caution about our dangerous daydream has ended up counselling both of us to become more deeply distracted. In such a state I invariably discover that, *contrary to what I have always believed and asserted, I am extremely sensitive to the opinions of others.* Our names crack against each other like televised artillery. Nothing will restrain us from the ersatz ecstasy of that incomparable event, not even the misdirection of command that the control booth pipes in to the scenario you have so deftly placed between us.

*

It seems to me that, in all the staggered circularity of this chain of displacements, a more basic and troubling circularity has been illegitimately overwritten which, were we to catch some peripheral glimpse of it, would raise a fundamental question for this scenario that one of us, surely, has written, as we would come up against the need to reckon with an event whose exclusion from our experience first set in motion the series of forced equivalences by which we have staked out this miniature horizon for each other, and this confrontation would articulate our alignment with, even as it staged our separation from, those millions of the previously visible whose static hissing opens the dead air between us to carrier waves.[6] There are gaps in every world we build that substantialize our sense of time, so that the derealized features of a beloved character who died in a cruel afterthought cohere as a solid block, like the hulk of a demolished television set whose vacuum, uncontained, becomes the exact shape of what must have happened to place us here precisely by subtracting itself from us in order to become a landscape across which we could imagine the drift of a merry band of saboteurs, terrorists and intellectuals through our scenario which aimed, not at recovering any catastrophic occupation and fire, but at tracing precisely the tempo of an experience that missed that catastrophe so as to address us as those who 'shall have come to be.'[7]

But even this precision fails to account for the production notes secreted by the scenario, not as its interior, as in the familiar trope of the film within a film, but as its necessary and missing anterior, a place prior to the tempo of non-occurrence where the problem of missing time resolves into a paradox of space through the essential technique of an absent social mass for being in more than one 'once' per place, so that packets of life in excess of its body spread through our script and the scene of circular relation into which it calls us, making the question not the easy one of a founding absence, but the irrational numerical expression of our own reflections distributed among all the objects and territories we survey in the form of their non-reflective obverse, in which even the pain of a prior disappearance cannot stabilize around those whose dead labour or labour of dying our situation here assumed, *for there is now the possibility of meeting them again later on; they have ceased merely to be silhouetted against a horizon where we had been ready to suppose that we should never see them reappear.* So it's not so much a matter of the uncertain authorship of those repeating phrases running continually up against the limits of a plot – of minor histories or lightly wooded land already zoned out – as it is one of our own uncertain authorship of the guided tour that plods through their aftermath, an extractive economy of intelligibility and transmission that graces each of us with the luminous flesh of erotic mastery and failure when triangulated between the avatar prior to us in the chain of duplications and he or she who follows. This is the *persevering and unalterable service of our successive personalities; hidden away in the shadow of the devalued suburban margin, despised, downtrodden, untiringly faithful, toiling incessantly under a charcoal-scrawled banner whose sole command is that it escape notice, and with no thought for the variability of the self as its iterations are marked by the row-planted trees effacing marks of productive consumption from a parcel of land, to ensure that the self may never lack what is needed,* save that lack which is the law of the city itself and is the zero-sum hydraulics of a general need in the corpse-clotted storm sewers.[8]

A laugh like a clash of metal survives the political funeral we diffused throughout the district of one- and two-storey cinderblock construction simply by refusing to stage it at all, and so it is not yet clear what volatile spark might ignite a 'difficult personality' or 'personal difficulty' in a concrete parking barrier, an oil stain or a dusting of safety glass across an intersection.

Distinguishing features, you should know, are in the habit of sliding uncontrollably around our faces like a bloom of acne, and even jump from person to person on occasion, flat land and flat paper equally receptive to erasure and inscription, to the point that, had one of us not had the foresight to crop his sticky, matted hair, there would be no telling us apart. *For he was one of those people who can never be 'doing nothing,' although there was nothing, in fact, that he could ever be said to do*, as if simply standing where he stood were intent, act and guilty retrospect enough, his bemused stasis being all it took to transfer the land into its reality as value. Remember the school tour of the mid-state plantation, how it explained in minute detail the domestic economies of timber harvest, stock raising and corn cultivation, leaving out only the fact that all this production was carried out by slave labour, and how, having slunk away later into the woods, we were chased back across a muddy stream by a swarm of hornets who stung our scalps, the general noise of their buzzing and our shouting spreading the exact texture of the day's events across our empty horizons of futurity? What I mean, I think, is that no matter the critical eye with which we return to that day's instruction, we must at least suspect that the ideological distortion remains a more primary moment, linked as it was with an ensemble of panic, physical pain and the free-floating sense that the surrounding adults were liars as often as not, so that not the revelation of the lie but the swelling of anticipation pointing to the place where it would have come to be revealed was moulded into the flesh itself, and a series of broken gestures in the implements of such displaced violences is what has mounded up the dirt to make a seat for our simple facing-off against each other here in this clearing, a simplicity that must have cost a fortune.[9]

NOTES

1 Much of the initial impetus to consider literary landscape in terms of the state politics of redevelopment came through discussions with Tanya Hollis of her historical research into the San Francisco Redevelopment Commission's vicious history in the city's Fillmore neighbourhood. (See her 'Peoples Temple and Housing Politics in San Francisco,' in *Peoples Temple and Black Religion in America*, ed. Rebecca Moore, Anthony B. Pinn, and Mary R. Sawyer [University of Indiana, 2004], for the historical record). It's probably a mark of perversity on my part that this insight has been resituated from San Francisco's urban core to the contemporaneous Florida suburbs in my own writing. (See below.)

2 With the exception of the Raworth line, all italicized passages are lifted or adapted from the Modern Library edition of Proust's *Within a Budding Grove*, translated by C. K. Scott Moncrieff and Terence Kilmartin.

3 This is probably as good a place as any for my minimum definition of narrative: a verbal sequence whose temporality is placed in relation to the time scale of some other sequence (of events, language, sensation, etc.), such that this relation is a problem. Of course, as persistent as the problem itself are the evasive protocols for shunting it into a premature resolution, or sidestepping it altogether. Thus, on the one hand, we find the well-worn but seemingly inescapable appeal to 'realism' as the mode in which narrative, and specifically narrative in the novel, will align itself with social-historical time. The habitual misreading of the Jamesonian call for a narrative self-presentation of the contemporary can easily tend in this direction. On the other hand, one finds the easy experimentalism that would collapse narrative into a one-dimensional semiosis (another version of what W. C. Williams excoriated, in *Kora in Hell*, as 'easy lateral sliding'). Such a collapse elides any engagement with this productive tension at all – at the cost of isolating the narrative text in a purely literary vacuole, sealed off from the world and its combative temporalities.

4 Imagining the come-on of this scenario along different lines might be another route to breaking the hold of realist fiction on narrative. I'm thinking here of Bob Glück's take on porn spectatorship in 'Workload' (from *Denny Smith*, Clear Cut Press, 2003), in which the viewer/narrator imaginatively sites himself as both the one who gets off on looking and the one who gets off on being looked at. In its merciless attempt to align the temporalities of verbal sequence with those of landscapes and built environments taken as accomplished facts (i.e., with a view of history that irons out contradiction), realist fiction thus reveals its always-doomed desire for a heterosexist one-way mirror of visual eroticism.

5 Somewhere else – in a poem, I think, a few years back – I used the phrase 'the stuttered porn of planners.' Unsure at the time of what this might mean, I let it stand out of fidelity to the work's procedures. I let it stand again here to mark the tempo of the administered relation to place, which is another of those strategies for make-believing away the divergence between the narrative of place and its historical occupation, by means of the one-way mirror invoked above. Stuttering in this case would be the constant catching-up this stance necessitates, as the administrative consciousness is always having to adjust, like a bad dancer, to a reality that has shifted subtly away from it, even as its gesture is in part an attempt to efface its own recognition of that shift.

Could we imagine instead a narrative poetics of stumbling that forgoes the reaction-formation of the pathetic boast 'I meant to do that'? In the end this is probably no less pornographic, but it resists the habit of a certain kind of pornographic encounter for endlessly deferring questions of the viewing subject's ethical involvement in the scene by means of the always-renewed promise to show all.

6 Or, to put it another way, a narrative that acknowledges its uncanny double. The weight of the ongoing belief, often little more than an assumption, that narrative in some way participates in a process of temporal unfolding like that of history, whether this is simply the weight of a false assertion or not, by virtue of long repetition has become part at least of literary history. Writers of narrative are up against this history, like it or not – part of the desire for narrative is the desire to produce exactly such an intelligible account. At the same time, I'm interested in forms of narrative writing that refuse to short the claims on the other side, i.e., that narrative fundamentally has to miss something of historical experience in order to render it narratable at all.

7 Narrative is the elaboration of an ongoing experience of missing the point, another version of the problem of time-relation mentioned above. In the narrative dream we are pulled inexorably forward, traversing a space however blank that becomes landscape and takes on value as we progress. As Williams has it, at the outset of *The Great American Novel*: 'If there is progress then there is a novel. Without progress there is nothing.' But the tempo of walking is at no point exactly equal to the tempo of value, the less so as the landscape itself grows more and more saturated with capital and begins to pass through circuits that overlap but do not coincide with our own. (Picture here Terry Riley's early experiments with multiple tape loops of various lengths running from a spindle out into every corner of the studio, and often out windows onto the surrounding grounds, collecting bits of dirt and dust on the way.) What I'm reaching for is a disposition of narrative that addresses this experience riven between two or more time-space scales, in the sense of knowing that to elaborate a track across this landscape is ultimately to impoverish or underdevelop some constituent of the vectoral multiplicity of possible developments it initially poses. So, a going forward while knowing that one has to go back, and knowing that going back remains a kind of forward motion that will not fully recover the initial lapse. In this sense the contradictory nature of experience is not only translated into sequence, but more strongly traduced, by a method which pushes its infidelities to the forefront at every opportunity. A partial catalogue of formal approaches that I think are

groping in this direction might include my own as well as Pamela Lu's work in very long sentences (see *Microclimates*, Krupskaya, 2001, and *Pamela: A Novel*, Atelos, 1998, respectively). This work exploits the capacity of English syntax to become lost or confused after a certain quantitative length is reached. Lack of declension allows sentences of an arbitrarily long extension to 'forget themselves,' so that even in a sentence where later parsing reveals a normative construction, the reader experiences modifiers sliding away from nouns and verbs, multiply embedded subordinate clauses breaking their subordination to the main clause, etc. The total effect is one of forward motion that continually falls back upon itself, maximal fullness of syntactical elaboration becoming an odd kind of lack. Also significant here is Renee Gladman's approach to the paragraph or block. If we hold with Stein's oft-repeated maxim that paragraphs are emotional while sentences are not, then we might say that in Gladman's work, time is primarily an emotional category, noting that forward narrative motion is most often achieved for her in the movement from paragraph to paragraph, while the individual sentences that make up a paragraph display a hovering sort of relation to each other (see her *Juice*, Kelsey St., 2000, and *The Activist*, Krupskaya, 2003). The specificity of Gladman's intersentential hovering, especially in her short narratives, resembles the non-static suspension of sound in Morton Feldman's string quartets, for example, in which it is the full harmonic and timbral implications of each sound-event that are drawn out by the expansion of the time scale needed for progress from event to event, rather than the bad infinity of deferred but teasingly indicated cadence that characterizes so much of, say, processual minimalism. Finally, it bears mentioning in this context that the range of writings described by Samuel R. Delany as 'paraliterary' (in 'The Semiology of Silence,' *Silent Interviews*, Wesleyan UP, 1994, 25–33) have their own approach to this set of problems, frequently in terms of a much larger compositional syntax. Following the distinction drawn by Gladman in a recent conversation, one might say that 'narrative' names the reach towards a world, while 'fiction' is understood as the effort to build such a world towards which to reach. In this regard, it seems to me that the central fault of social or psychological modes of realism, especially in the novel, is that they tend to conflate these two moments, presenting the world reached towards as the one and only (already-)built world. Paraliterary genres like science fiction, by literalizing the world-building aspect (and I recall here that one of Delany's identifying marks of science fiction is that it pushes towards the literalization of language that would serve as metaphor in literary genres), expose the tempo of its narrative construction in process, and thus tend to foreground questions of discrepancy between the times of narrative and worldly experience. To my mind, the distinction between literary and paraliterary is not always a hard and fast one: reading Gladman's novel *The Activist* through such a paraliterary lens can be quite a rewarding experience.

8 In the suburb, serial iteration is the modality of the domestic and civic spaces of bodily experience, and thus death finally assumes its historical vocation of complete obscenity. It is entirely offstage. This is not to say that the suburb conquers death or finds a bypass loop around enclosure. Rather, death here becomes the assumed prerequisite, that which is understood as necessarily taken care of elsewhere: infrastructure. The bypass loop is there, a constituent support of the neighbourhood.

9 My concern with the space and time of landscape as it relates to narrative is only partly an artifact of the literary-historical prominence of the picaresque. My own recent narrative writing has attempted to articulate the various scales of experience in a working-class Florida suburban adolescence in the late seventies and early eighties. As it happens, this experience coincides with a period in which the rolling wave of accumulation crises dating, for the sake of convenience, to 1974 begin to exert an exaggerated pressure on real estate, and the intensification of relations between social landscape and speculative capital becomes, for a certain class and region, a matter of direct experience. In my novel *Occupational Treatment*, this process culminates logically, and originates experientially, with a series of police raids on escheat zoning plats on the exurban fringe, which had until that time been squatted by homeless families and used for various illicit pleasures and conflicts by young people housed in the surrounding low-rent neighbourhoods. The time of writing this central portion of the novel overlapped with the intensification of several other modes of land occupation on a more global scale: the IDF incursions into Gaza, speculation in terrestrial resources along the lines of Bechtel's water privatization scheme in Bolivia, and the preparation, execution and disaster of the U.S.-British imperialist adventure in Iraq. The tracing of a rhythm of experience across the surfaces of a place thus had to come to terms in some fashion with the displacements of a series, variously motivated, variously consequential, and elaborated along widely divergent lines, of what have come to seem geopolitical enclosures acts. And while these enclosures stem from an emergent global order, I have found it necessary to highlight the unevenness of their mutual relations in time and space – to locate the incommensurabilities in the proposed myth of a total system in which resistances might be imagined.

Dislocation

Shiver

Approximate:
Past to Present

Methods

The Sentence

The Novel

Resistance

The Buzz of
Alternate Meanings

**A Story Is
a Storage**

My Other Self

Hollywood Celluloid Nuke Madness
Bruce Boone

For gallows humour that comes close to stand-up comedy, a favourite of mine is Edward G. Robinson as Fred MacMurray's boss in *Double Indemnity*, telling MacMurray, the insurance rep, all the ways you can die accidentally. They're all down there in the tables, he tells him, in the actuarial statistics. Edward G. Robinson's at his best in scenes like this one, citing chapter and verse, ticking off on those plump fingers the categories of violence done to others. There's death by drowning, he notes, and death by falling from high places. There are deaths subdivided by location – by land, at sea, in the air. And death listed according to means – bathtub, auto accident, rope, shock. Each divides into still further subheadings, until at last you get this picture of a vast battlefield filled with severed limbs, crushed extremities, mangled bones. What a comic scene! But, concludes MacMurray's boss, suddenly puzzled and, in spite of himself, suspicious now, there are almost no statistics on death by falling from a moving train.

We enjoy MacMurray's complete deadpan reaction to his boss's confusion – since the last item mentioned happens to be the crime he and Barbara Stanwyck have just successfully carried out against her cranky oil-executive husband. Underneath, though, there's another aspect of the humour, and that's the list structure itself. How hysterically odd and funny it is that in the late capitalist society we live in, even death itself can be inventoried, be made just another item in our lives – even violent death. Death, like sex, by definition destroys the conceptual. So how can death go into any taxonomy? The monstrous, it turns out, is never far from the comic.

That's my gut-level reaction to the horror of nuclear disaster. Nuclear death is a G.E., chemicals are a Kelvinator, something else is a Kenmore or Amana. Want chemicals? Well, we can subdivide. There's Love Canal, or plastics in the wall, mould or asbestos in that old central heating system you used to have. And I give city telephone poles a wide berth, knowing that inside those insulators are PCBS. And at the collective level, there's Freon from spray cans – or wafting up from refrigerators? When the thin envelope goes, we get basted in our own juices, Thanksgiving turkeys in the oven of space. Only scale precludes this from our available imagination. Death is for me personally, species extinction for group life? In such quandaries, humour arises. Without it, would our possibility for survival be as strong?

In emergencies, one of the most interesting forms of entertainment, for me, exists along the irony-to-sarcasm spectrum, based as it so often is on shared assumptions. Humour that's banal and vulgar? Sure! Like many another ugly duckling, it's going to be a swan. Its ability to 'vulgarly' expose long-standing contradictions may make you gasp and giggle at the same time. Humour like this is feisty. And the more it has to push back against, in terms of social repressions, the more obvious its raw aggression. Are faggots like me 'dishing' someone 'nice'? Yes, but only insincerely. Or how about black kids playing the dozens? Or class comedy in *The Sopranos*? The sheer rage bottled up in this humour shows through and is designated as 'side-splitting,' 'rib-cracking.' Something in you wants to break something – the mouth forms to a rictus of pleasure. 'Oh!' you think, looking at your neighbours for their reaction. Tears of rage that also mean joy? Is this one of those 'identities of opposites'? Possibilities like this might have motivated Brecht.

Commodity language may be the main instrument of the expression of our deepest feelings – our native tongue even?

The oppositional quality of traditional avant-garde writing, experimental writing so-called, on the other hand, makes it suddenly attractive. The training you have from working in an avant-garde tradition makes you very good at working with ideas. You can see concepts when they're only implicit, can draw them out for a progressive constituency and point them up, so they get addressed and people are urged to act.

And if it's not quite true to say that these two traditions – popular and mass art on one hand and avant-garde on the other – don't ever mix, it is true that most art gets limited to one, at the expense of the other. Most art seems schizophrenically attendant on only a portion of our lives. Two sets of strengths then, and how to unite them. In political writing – or a humane propaganda – don't you need to, absolutely have to, deal with ideas? Just as to make these ideas popular – and not cynically but appreciatively so – don't you want your ideas to be successful as entertainment too?

I think so. In 1955, Robert Aldrich made a sleaze vehicle called *Kiss Me Deadly*. In the Eisenhower years of the fifties, the 'nuclear theme' itself must have been a surprise. In a less obvious way, though, the bomb sequence at the end retrospectively interprets earlier materials, making them more surprising. Okay, great. There's an emotional critique of 'the bomb.' But in the end it's dumb, can't speak itself, lacks the conceptual punch it would need to be used in any political sense. But what if – after the fact, naturally – we gave it the conceptual punch that's missing? What if, added to the film's lyrical evocation, there was a hardcore layer of explanation? This new *Kiss Me Deadly* would hardly be Robert Aldrich's – it'd be ours, in a larger, a more collective sense. And if it's propaganda, well, we'd hope it won't be authoritarian.

How does it start? First of all, there's Mike's girl trouble. Women! Always a problem for Mike! They pull guns on him, try to seduce him – and in their rottenness end up betraying him. In fact the Aldrich movie pushes your buttons so hard on this subject that you wonder if it doesn't have some buried critical, even proto-feminist intentions, however bungled. The opening shots are all violence. Christina, an escapee from a mental hospital, runs in front of Mike's sports car in the middle of the night, nearly getting herself killed. 'Stop! Stop!' Hmmmmm, she doesn't seem to have any clothes on under that trenchcoat she's wearing! Mike lets her into the sports car. The implicit promise of sex isn't delivered. Within a couple of short scenes we see her legs dangling lifeless at the edge of a hard desk. She's been tortured and murdered. Mike gets off with a beating, but when he wakes up you can tell he's thinking of revenge. Christina's last words to him are 'Remember me.' Life, as portrayed in this movie, is misogynist, violent. Sex is ambivalent, maybe lethal.

Soon artistic expression and ethnicity/race will seem problematic too. Meantime: lots of LA material, driving around in traffic, freeway shots, people manipulating cars with astounding aggressivity, like weapons. LA, city of modernity. You use – people and things – in this city. Like Mike and Velda do with each other, only Mike uses Velda more than she does him. Velda is Mike's lover, of course, but also a business partner/secretary of Mike's. Supposedly – according to the police lieutenant in this film – they play both sides against each other for added income in the divorce cases they handle in their private investigation business. When Mike gets back to his luxury apartment from wherever he's been, he turns on his answering machine and looks glumly out the window at the bleak traffic grid. Something's wrong here, he's thinking – but what? Our Mike Hammer isn't a very conscious guy. His instincts just coerce – that's why he has the name he does. Won't a hardboiled guy like this at least be interested in great sex? Something always seems to keep Mike away from sex. Leering at a girl's better than fucking her, I guess. 'Look at the goodies,' he snickers in one scene when a good-looking blonde sashays down the sidewalk, but the remark's obviously meant more as a sneer than as a come-on. You wonder if he even likes Velda!

Velda and Mike are waiting in Mike's apartment, and apparently the modern art is getting to Velda. She feels uncomfortable and starts vamping Mike. She wraps her arms around his neck, fondles and inveigles, all to no avail. Mike gives her a tight-lipped little smile but won't budge. How come? His body language says he's made of steel. Would it be unmanly to reciprocate? we wonder. Both seem relieved when the doorbell rings. They stare at each other. Well, I guess we have to break this off, since that's the police lieutenant. And naturally that's exactly who it is.

Is it possible then that Mike really likes guys? Alas, probably not. The sign of it is Mike's manipulation of Nick, his Greek garage mechanic. Nick, on the other hand, really likes to get physical with Mike. Va-va-voom, says Nick. And Nick's octopus hands all over Mike indicates camaraderie. Mike's cheerful but calculating. His question: How can I use you? (Snicker, snicker.)

So he asks Nick to take risks for him that result in Nick getting killed. Too bad. On the other hand, since Nick's a small, dark foreigner, it's hard to really take him seriously, isn't it? He's dismissed. But, as in the black bar scene where there's a great blues song being sung, conversely, you see strengths in ethnicity – strengths that sail right over Nick's head. Nick's ability to love is shown as part of his Greekness. But that 'strength' is not for guys like Mike.

Ethnicity and women are a two-sided coin – but so is art, as we'll soon find out. Mike's need for a certain name, address, leads him to the (by now torn-down) old Bunker Hill area of LA, where a middle-aged Italian tenor is singing – is it Verdi? His arms are outstretched; he's accompanying himself on a record. And, in a touch that gets almost cute, there's spaghetti cooking on the stove. We get the point. Art and ethnicity go together, don't they?

Just as we've learned that art also goes with women. Or fags. The dead Christina was a poet, we find out, and the words she left Mike – 'Remember me' – turn out to be the name of a Christina Rossetti sonnet. But back to Mike and the tenor. Mike needs information from the guy, so to show him he's serious he grabs the guy's record off his record player and smashes it in two across his big-muscled thigh. That's to show him he's not just fooling around. The man bursts into tears. Art is also weak, we learn. Which is a big problem. It's like the ladies. You can't help but need and want them, even though they're no good. No good for you, anyway.

Is modern art any different? Well, to Mike it curiously is. His apartment's full of it, and modern art gives Mike a sort of dubious pleasure. It's like the feeling he gets when looking out his window at the LA traffic, or when he's listening to his answering machine. When the camera pokes around – nosy, just as we are, for clues about this man's psyche – we see clunky fifties-type deco furniture, ugly pictures of Picasso-type women, faces distorted with anxiety or fear, and dangling mobiles, Calder style, dangling things everyone in this movie should be bumping into, they're so clumsy, obtrusive.

What's it all mean? we're asking ourselves by now. Don't worry, soon the answer is going to be clear as daylight – a thousand suns, as a matter of fact. But first our hero Mike has to get the address of the gangsters he's been looking for from a queer art dealer whose fear of Mike is played for laughs. He nervously swallows some sleeping pills so he won't have to be interrogated by Mike. Mike finds what he came for – then heads out to Malibu where the gangsters are holed up.

By now we have a pretty good idea what the jerks are up to. Earlier, Mike's police lieutenant friend has clued him in. The scene is very campy noir – two shadowy silhouettes talking to each other, like interviews with Mafia dons who don't want to be identified. 'I'm just going to say a few phrases, Mike' – here, a pause, to make the effect of horror really sink in – 'and I think you'll understand.' It's so truly monstrous. 'Los Alamos ... Trinity ... the Manhattan Project.' Huh? Did he say what I thought he said? Yes he did. He said that. And as I watched this movie at the Castro Theater some twenty-eight years after it was made, the full horror did come back to me and remained. They're talking bombs.

And on account of this fact, the last moments of the film will seem curiously symbolic. It will light up 'tilt.' Something so big will be brought in that the film literally will not know how to handle it, and everything will get distorted, surreal. Sex and women will be revealed as a principle of evil, for instance. The 'object' the gang has in its possession is a box of uranium ore, or as it will also be called – Pandora's Box. 'All the evils of the world are in it,' explains the gangster chieftain.

It turns out he's a very cultured person, the criminal mastermind. He collects modern art too. That's of course in his spare time, since he's also an MD. But spare time is something this doctor has a lot of, since, when he's not out hustling uranium to sell to the commies, his medical practice is limited to discreetly pushing drug prescriptions to hoodlum friends. He's not a very savoury person, you might say. But cultivated. Mike is the big goon. They're opposites, in the cover plot at least.

Or are they? The contents of that box contaminate our view of the mastermind's suave cultivation. And both are art collectors with a modernist temperament, both are thugs. The two become interchangeable instruments of the Enlightenment working together for the general deformation of society. A deformation that can be stopped – or completed – only by the explosion marking the end of the world ... in terms of the movie, it blows up the problems that the director can't resolve.

I've seen the movie twice and the drama of the last scene remains completely riveting. You know something is really at stake. A woman Mike protected turns out to be the mastermind's ladyfriend, but she winds up double-crossing him too. She shoots the gangster boyfriend and, ignoring his dying words, opens the ill-starred treasure box to see what's inside. An unearthly light streams out and, with a gigantic shadow projected on the wall behind, it's clear she's in hell! Mike, in this interval, has freed Velda from the other room where she's been held hostage, and the two of them manage to stagger to the door. The gangster's moll, meantime, can't seem to let go of the lid she's raised. It sticks to her hand like phosphorus, she can't shake it, she starts to scream. The room begins to glow, heat waves roll up. Then there's a cut. Running down the beach, Mike and Velda look back at the place they escaped from. Horrible! Ballooning out visibly at the sides, the beach house disseminates huge amounts of light, energy. There's a groan from the audience at this point. In the night sky we note clouds, heat waves slowly forming themselves from the house. In fact, it's a mushroom cloud, isn't it? It's a mushroom cloud we're seeing.

In my viewing, this ending is wonderful because of its ludicrous gratuity. Right at the end, has the film decided to just jettison all the realist movie conventions it's been following up to now? Atomic explosions don't come from the accidental opening of little uranium ore strongboxes, and probably they realized this even in 1955. This means the accent was put on the explosion itself, and the objectivity of a real mushroom cloud is something that causes you to want to account for it – but where? How? The explosion discredits the storyline, you could say, and recredits social reality – events in the world outside of this theatre. In place of Mike Hammer's sexy adventure stories, you get – ban-the-bomb-ers, H-bomb development, Nevada testing sites, the Bikini Atoll.

Yet the movie clearly has something to say about causes. I haven't mentioned a lot of the violence in the plot – people getting blown up in cars, knifed and stabbed, pushed down stairs. An old man, a desk clerk, gets beaten up for not taking a bribe; another old man, the coroner, gets a drawer slammed on his fingers; women get thrown away like old minks. How far can you go in valuing cruelty, appreciating violence? Aggressive satisfactions are mixed up with social exploitation. And in the film it's a threat. Violence seems expressive of some huge but unnamed disaster about to overwhelm all of Western society. It ties things together that otherwise might not be related – a preoccupation with 'art' and what's wrong with it, i.e., modern art, ethnic prejudices, implicit racism, the problematic nature of sex and relations of men and women, all related to the nuclear explosion at the end. The mushroom cloud as the meaning of a society that's turned against sexuality, against other cultures (racism), art, women and – finally – itself. Does such a culture even like life – for goodness's sake? Look at its view of sex. A woman opens a forbidden box. Since it's filled with uranium ore, this starts off the end of the world. You guess the moral.

Then this: who's the highest thinker in the film? Why, naturally, the criminal mastermind. He stands for science – white Euro science naturally – which arises from civilization to destroy civilization – and the world with it. Aldrich outlines a convincing aporia, which we'd inhabit if, like *Kiss Me Deadly*, we had nothing else to admire, love, lose.

Your subject can be anything. It doesn't have to be something from the sleazoid movie I've taken on. *Godzilla* would do. *The Matrix*? Who cares. Anything goes. But with any 'deconstruction,' as we call it now (2004 – as opposed to 1983, when I wrote this), find a subject that keeps people's attention. ENTERTAINS! (Sneak in the insights as you go.)

But what do I know? I'm only the writer!

The Monster Comic
Derek McCormack

I went to Nashville. I went to museums.

Stars' museums. Barbara Mandrell had hers. Barbara Mandrell's Country, it was called. Canes and crutches exhibited. She used them to recover from a car accident. Ferlin Husky had a museum. With dioramas showing the life of Christ.

Wax museums. The city had several. Greats behind glass. Whitey Ford. Jimmie Rodgers mid-yodel. Legend had it that Jim Reeves's ex-wife visited the Country Music Wax Museum. To comb his statue's hair.

*

I visited the Country Music Foundation and Hall of Fame. On Music Row. Saw Stringbean's banjo.

'Where's the library?' I said.

'Downstairs,' the attendant said. Underground. 'Do you have an appointment?' The attendant said I needed an appointment. And a referral from an archivist.

I left. What I really wanted were tapes. Nick Tosches mentions them in his book *Country*:

> The Country Music Foundation in Nashville possesses two interviews with promoter Oscar Davis. In his long and colorful career, Davis had worked intimately with Ernest Tubb, Hank Snow, Roy Acuff, Eddy Arnold, Hank Williams, Elvis Presley (whom Davis introduced to Colonel Tom Parker), and hundreds more. He had nothing to lose, and he told it all: a great, glorious, scandalous Who Fucked Who of country music, full of homosexuality, pedophilia, and motel drunk-fucks. The CMF allows absolutely no access to these tapes.[1]

I will never hear the tales on the tapes.

I decided to write them myself.

*

The Bible. Comic books. What Hank Williams read.

He liked reading comic books. Jerry Rivers played with the Drifting Cowboys, Hank's band. He once wrote:

> Jim Denny brought Hank back to Nashville, where he went into Madison Hospital for rest and additional treatment for his previous back injury. After a few days, Don, Sammy, Cedric and I would drop by and see Hank in the evenings, bring him some of his favorite monster comic books and laugh and joke about the road. But in the early mornings, Skip and I would sit on a damp wooded hillside, alone, and wonder if things would ever be like they were before.
>
> They never were.[2]

*

Monster comics. AKA horror comics. Or crime comics. EC published the most notorious titles. *Tales from the Crypt*. *Vault of Horror*. *Shocking SuspenStories*.

I have one of the first EC crime comics. *Haunt of Fear*. From 1950. Hank Williams read it. Maybe. Probably. A man kills his wife. Her corpse attacks him. A mad magician tests his saw-a-body-in-half trick. With a real saw. And real bodies. A monster stalks a swamp. Smothering unsuspecting humans.

Comic companies across America churned out crime comics. America and Canada. Superior Publishing in Toronto created some of the goriest. Or so I've heard. I've never seen one. They're scarce.

And illegal.

*

Clergy hated crime comics. As did teachers. Parents. Politicians. E. D. Fulton represented Kamloops in Canada's Federal Parliament. In 1949, he tabled a bill. Fredric Wertham testified on its behalf. Wertham, a psychologist from New York. Crusader against crime comics in America. Wertham wrote:

> If later on you want to read a good novel it may describe how a young boy and girl sit together and watch the rain falling. They talk about themselves and the pages of the book describe

what their innermost little thoughts are. This is what is called literature. But you will never be able to appreciate that if in comic-book fashion you expect that at any minute someone will appear and pitch both of them out of the window.[3]

It passed. It still stands. The Fulton Bill. Making it illegal for Canadians to write, sell or distribute 'the kind of magazine, forty or fifty pages of which portray nothing but scenes illustrating the commission of crimes of violence with every kind of horror that the mind of man can conceive.'

Crime comics, Wertham argued, celebrated delinquency. Drug abuse. Pedophilia. Homosexuality.

Same stuff Oscar Davis let loose.

*

The Haunted Hillbilly is a crime comic. In words. I can't draw. A vampire story. À la *Dracula*. An ode to country's underside. My Mina Harker: a man. A country singer. All-American. Corn-fed. Clueless. Teetering on the verge of stardom.

I named him Hank. After Hank Williams. And Hank Thompson, who had a hit with 'The Wild Side of Life.' Hank Snow, a Nova Scotian. Who dressed like a cowboy.

My Renfield's a doctor. A gay doctor. With a weakness for Hank's ass. Dr. Wertham, I called him.

Nudie's Dracula.

By day he runs a carnival. The haunted house kills. He sculpts wax statues for a sideshow wax museum. He tinsels kewpie dolls. He sews costumes for sideshow acts. Strong men. Spidoras: half-women, half-spiders. Nudie, the Carnival Couturier. The Thread Count.

Nights he's a ghoul. He becomes a bat. Commands an army of bats. He takes Hank under his wing. Dresses him. In suits embroidered with sequined skulls. Sequined skeletons. Sequins made from human bones. Bones he acquires from Hank's girlfriends.

Nudie's a spoof of a few fashion figures. Nudie Cohn, the Rodeo Tailor. Cohn designed the first rhinestone country ensemble in 1951. Nathan Turk, another country costumer. Turk made spooky suits for Ernest Tubb. Orange with black piping. Black with orange piping. Tubb nicknamed them: Halloween. Pumpkin. Black Cat. They bore a Turk trademark: Frankenstein seams.

*

I went back to Nashville. Years later.

The Hall of Fame was gone. Moved. To a building on the banks of the Cumberland. A building shaped like a guitar.

Gone, too, were the stars' museums. Does nobody care about Barbara Mandrell anymore? Ferlin Husky's museum, Waylon Jennings's museum, Minnie Pearl's Museum – history.

The wax museums. Vanished. Downtown had died. Tourists diverted to the Opryland theme park and hotel on the outskirts of town. In 1999, a reporter from the *New York Times* went hunting for figures that had once filled the Country Music Wax Museum.[4]

He found them. In a basement beneath an office building. Bodies laid out like in a makeshift morgue. Bill Carlisle, limbs crooked as a corpse's. Minnie Pearl, hat on chest. The statues still dressed in clothes stars had donated. Jimmie Rodgers in one of Jimmie Rodgers's railroading suits. Carter Family in Sunday best. The reporter spied a dozen originals by Nudie Cohn. A wig Barbara Mandrell designed for a Barbara Mandrell doppelgänger.

Not all the statues survived in such good shape. The reporter reported that Conway Twitty had been beheaded. Same with Stringbean. Someone stole Uncle Dave Macon's gold teeth. 'And Hank Williams Jr. lay on his back with a giant crack running along his neck.'[5]

Vandals?

Vlad?

NOTES

1 Nick Tosches, *Country: Living Legends and Dying Metaphors in America's Biggest Music* (New York: Charles Scribner's Sons, 1985), 153.

2 Jerry Rivers, *Hank Williams: From Life to Legend* (Denver: Heather Enterprises, Inc., 1967), 18.

3 Fredric Wertham, *Seduction of the Innocent* (New York: Rinehart & Company, Inc., 1954), 64–65.

4 Neil Strauss, 'Unearthing the New Nashville's Wax Castoffs,' *The New York Times*, November 21, 1999.

5 Ibid.

Incidents of Time Travel
Laura Moriarty

Time *is* junk. Time is radioactive.

– William Burroughs[1]

I am a child of thirty, perhaps a bit younger, and, though I consider myself a radical feminist, and though I know he 'accidentally' shot his wife while playing at being William Tell, I am a reader of William Burroughs. It is the early eighties in North Beach in San Francisco where I am to live for the next decade and a half. Burroughs's cut-up method is old news to me because nouveau Beats are present in my life as vestiges of a former social scene. I read Burroughs for his science fiction, his humour and as a way to fall asleep at night. The other quality of Burroughs that I enjoy is the sense of a fully lived life of thought, of thought as action. Whether he is making cut-ups, fucking boys or travelling, he seems actually to be making the work – or the work is making him. I figure his real life is dysfunctional because of what I hear from my nouveau Beat friends who hang with him and his strange entourage when they are in town. But the idea of his notebooks intrigues me and I make my own cut-ups and thoughtfully record my dreams.

For a while during this period, I go around with a sense of anticipation as if I have converted to something and the end times are near. As an inveterate reader of William Blake, I am used to thinking of every moment as a potential Last Judgment. Reading Burroughs, I am caught up in the messianic conspiracy theory sensibility where language is a virus injected into us, probably by the government. I feel infected. In this heady state I am caught up in the plots of his stories, the multiple genres/genders which extend science fiction to western with a touch of noir, women to alien insects with penises growing out of their foreheads. I continue to read myself to sleep until, after I have drifted off while perusing *The Third Mind*, Burroughs appears. He wears his trademark suit and hat and speaks to me in the cracker drawl with which I will later become so familiar as the videotape archivist at the Poetry Center.

'So you think you want to time travel. Okay, let's go. Are you ready?'

He extends his grey-suited arm out and motions to me with his hand. Torn like one of my cut-ups, I want to go with him but am filled with mistrust. I feel fully conscious in the dream that I am making a crucial choice.

'No!' I say. But that was then.

In a sense, the ground for this event was laid earlier in a nineteenth-century Romantics survey class at UC Berkeley in the mid-seventies. The class is taught by Donald Ault, an obsessed and gifted Blake scholar. He allows only two weeks for Wordsworth, Keats, Shelley and Byron, spending most of the quarter on Blake. Students are rumoured to have had breakdowns in his classes, so determined is he never to settle for a simple explanation of anything, especially any line of his, and now my, favourite poem by William Blake, 'The Four Zoas.' When we read of the characters or entities stomping around in the head of Albion, passed out on the shore, I feel that he is me.

> The Corse of Albion lay on the Rock the sea of Time & Space
> Beat round the Rock in mighty waves ...
>
> – William Blake[2]

Sitting in the front row of class on the first floor of Wheeler Hall, feet propped up on a spare chair, staring out a window at the warm autumn, Albionized, I copy Donald Ault's elaborate diagrams of Blake's system into my notebook and I am the Mental Traveller. I am Vala. Ault's circuitous, esoteric teaching style fits well with the mystical persona of my student days. When not in class or at my food-service job, I am at Mount Vision at Point Reyes taking acid with Jerry Estrin, who is then a Surrealist. In my final paper for the class I discuss the laments of Enion in the 'Zoas.' In my close reading of her lamentations I examine every possible inference of each word and phrase, attempting to stop time and expand it, as the poem recommends, to a thousand years. On the weekends, I rant to Jerry around the campfire, explaining Ault's point about Blake that you can't read him accurately unless you allow your mind to be physically altered by the text. He gets it. He cross-examines me and we make a poetics of the idea that poetry should transform its writers and it readers.

> The eye altering, alters all.
>
> – William Blake[3]

Much later – it is the nineties by now – I am leafing through a catalogue from Small Press Distribution and I find a listing for *Narrative Unbound* by Donald Ault. I rush over to the warehouse, very near now that I again live in the East Bay, and buy the extremely thick volume. Probably too chaotic to be published by a university press, the book is beautifully printed, diagrams and all, by Station Hill. Ault makes his point persuasively and to me familiarly:

> That is instead of a prefabricated underlying single world or ur-narrative ... Blake substitutes a transformational process at the service of (and brought into existence by) the temporally unfolding surface narrative itself, thereby creating a reader whose perception is able to alter the very being of the texts' supposedly fixed facts and devising a narrative world that, although it comes into existence temporally through the mutual interconstitution of reader and text, functions as the primary agent by which the reader and text are able to transform one another critically.[4]

This interconstitutionality is the idea that I embraced back in the seventies and on which I quietly base my life. The vicissitudes produced by this decision lead me to a number of likely and unlikely positions, relating either to food service or to books, tapes and other effusions of the poetic mind. In this connection I find myself again in SPD's warehouse, this time as an employee. It is the late nineties. There I discover West House Books and begin to read Alan Halsey. His *Text of Shelley's Death* reminds me of what I had missed of the other Romantics in that first class of Donald Ault. Halsey's quoting, cutting, arranging and his sense of the permutations of sound, text and timeline exactly corroborate my sense of reality. I reread Shelley. I get in touch with Halsey. We exchange complete works. Packets begin to arrive periodically from the Nether Edge, deep in the UK, where he and Geraldine Monk live, containing chapbooks, postcards, broadsides and other ephemera from the Gargoyle school. Early on, he rejects my comparisons of him with Blake in a way that allows me to know I am on to something.

One among the many items that eventually appears is a postcard called 'Sonata for the Ancient Mariner.' It is a prototype of a series of emblematic visual texts called *Memory Screen* that Alan will eventually produce by an infernal process of photography and duplication that I will never quite understand. The look of the card seems inevitable to me, as if it was part of nature. My nature. A thrill of recognition occurs and still occurs each time I see and read it. Right away I begin to sense the possibility of a story. In the upper-left-hand corner of the card, liberated, as I later find, from a Spanish science textbook, is the word *Ultravioleta*.

In the meantime, Halsey makes a selection of himself, calls it *Wittgenstein's Devil*, publishes it with Stride and sends me a copy. In it is 'Alien Proforma.' I remember that I have the original tiny chapbook. I reread the work in both versions and a line from it crystallizes what the 'Sonata' has suggested. It becomes the epigraph for *Ultravioleta*: 'In the black and white target language the film is called grainy; the wingless craft is seen entering the sentence a second before impact.'[5]

Soon I am at work on the science-fiction novel *Ultravioleta*. In the novel, the invading aliens are called the I. They take the form of human names – Thomas Wyatt, Pontius Pilate, Javier Martinez. There is a clone – Ada Byron. There are robots, humans and cross-genre creatures. Space travel, in paper ships, is powered by thought.

Which brings us to time travel. Time travel is to move backward or forward in time in such a way that the direction of time's arrow is changed. It is to use time or to be used by it as a vehicle. As time is usually thought to be a non-spatial continuum in which events occur in an apparently irreversible succession, time travel is, at the very least, an oxymoron. And while it is an accepted, conventional occurrence in science fiction, my stepdaughter, majoring in physics at a uc campus, will tell you it is quite impossible. It does, however, suggest the problem of narrative in relation to poetry – or narrative written by a poet.

> Characters are wildly disarranged. They conscript themselves into a travesty of language. Each becomes unintelligible to herself and to the others. 'One result is the fall through the literal world, the other, the fall by false interpretation.' Ada sees the situation come across her screen first as a kind of writing through space, then as anomalous messages scrawled in light. Finally Ultravioleta seems to fade in and out of time. Ada sits for a moment in frozen fascination, finding it unthinkable that such a vast craft could fail.
>
> 'Holy shit,' comments Dayv looking over her shoulder. 'What is it they used to say? Unsinkable? The flight plan alone was like an encyclopedia. Is it the time storm?'

'It could be but I think they're too confused to notice the storm. It's more like an analogic allegory rift. Never seen one before. I thought it was just a legend. Come to think of it, it is a legend but it clearly doesn't matter.'[6]

But it does matter. Narrative is everything. It is sequence. When it ceases to continue we notice immediately. It is the air we breathe or the very act of breath and then breath again. Poetry can be narrative, however its will is to stop, to drill down into the word, the phoneme or phrase, and empty out all the possibilities. Reading poetic narrative, we are slowed down and speeded up at the same time. We have a feeling we aren't getting anywhere in the sense of events occurring, except the events of language.

Time travel is a trope – a figure of speech using words in a non-literal, non-linear way. It is narrative complicated by prosody. Prosody is measure, the musical divisions (and directions) in a text relating to both time and space. It might be breath, meter, arrangement on the page, parts of speech or procedural segments generated by a computer program, but it does divide and it does produce stoppages. Narrative goes on. It conveys – carries while moving forward – a story. A story is a storage. A container of plot, character, event. Poetry empties it out. A vortex appears. The timeline becomes discontinuous, layered, repetitive. The words become multiple and, again, it is hard to go forward.

'It's not simply that the numbers change but that first it's three and then it's five but never four: and yet in any account it's only one of the aliens who is said to have been walking around when the humans arrived and that one disappears from the story like a shifter in the target language.'[7]

It is the new millennium. Nick Robinson and I arrive in London at dawn. We are troped – disfigured, refigured – by jet lag, which replaces the self with a sense of dislocation. Determined to stay awake during the daylight, we board a boat and go up the Thames to Greenwich, the Home of Time. It is there that Greenwich Mean Time is calculated. The great zero of longitude intersects the great midnight of Universal Time. It is another world. Everything in England is dense with time and riddled with English, the Home of Time moreso, if that is possible. Or so I think, but by now I am teetering. Nick has trouble keeping me awake. I believe that I am seeing my dreams. I feel caught in one of Alan Halsey's postcards. I find, or, better, lose myself at the Prime

Meridian. There, on top of the hill, in the courtyard of the observatory, time's arrow actually exists in the form of an object that appears to be an enormous silver gyroscope. It looks exactly like a 3-D quote from the 'Sonata for the Ancient Mariner.' Like the other time tourists, we take pictures of ourselves in two places at one time – or in two times at one place. Space opens up above us like an English watercolour. Greenwich, at the centre of the last empire, rolls out before us in perfect, pleasant green. When we descend to the river, we encounter the multi-masted Cutty Sark whose lines echo the 'Sonata.' Time opens up and possibly stops. We are on the boat back when I finally succumb to sleep.

> Chokd the bright rivers burdning with my Ships the angry
>   deep
> Thro Chaos seeking for delight & in spaces remote
> Seeking the Eternal which is always present to the wise[8]

*

But it is already several days and many stanzas later. While mileage is a common concept and a unit of exchange, miles themselves are anachronism here in this space where distance is officially measured in dreams, fits, stanzas and pots to piss in. The latter are the distance of the Earth to Jupiter run. That the I are not Jovian, as first thought, is generally acknowledged, but where they are from or how many pots they are able to think is unknown and possibly forbidden information, as no one can think of it for long. Humans are known to consider the origin of the I and how far they can go to be the big downstream questions. The answers, they believe, will allow them to get their edge again, the edge they imagine themselves to have had and lost. The I actually measure distance in the personal and idiosyncratic ways that they eat and sleep and live. They have agreed to these human interpretations of their measurements because they agree to everything. What they can't or won't do is to supply a straight answer to a simple question. Withholding information creates suspense – frustration and nostalgia and sometimes anger. An I can get pretty fat in a set-up as sweet as that. There are limits to how long such a situation can be maintained, but they can be fiddled with.[9]

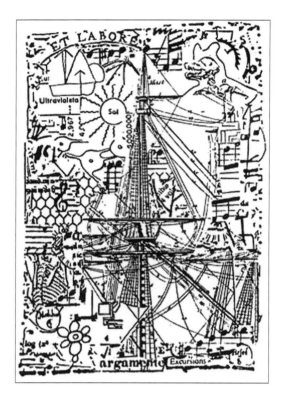

NOTES

1 William Burroughs and Brian Gysin, *The Third Mind* (New York: Viking Press, 1978), 107.

2 William Blake, 'The Four Zoas,' in *Poetry and Prose of William Blake*, ed. Erdman (Garden City, NY: Anchor Books, 1997), 337.

3 William Blake, 'The Mental Traveller,' in *Poetry and prose*, 485.

4 Ault, Donald, *Narrative Unbound: Re-Visioning William Blake's The Four Zoas*, (Barrytown, NY: Station Hill Press, 1987), 4–5.

5 Alan Halsey, 'Alien Proforma,' in *Wittgenstein's Devil*, (Devon: Stride Publications, 2000), 110.

6 Laura Moriarty, 'Shipwrecked,' in *Ultravioleta* (manuscript).

7 Halsey, 111.

8 Blake, 'The Four Zoas,' 390.

9 Moriarty, *Ultravioleta*.

Dislocation

Shiver

Approximate:
Past to Present

Methods

The Sentence

The Novel

Resistance

The Buzz of
Alternate Meanings

A Story Is
a Storage

My Other Self

Lucite

(a didactic)
Lisa Robertson
for the Office for Soft Architecture

(because the present is not articulate)

Sit us on Lucite gently and we will tell you how knowledge came to us.

First the dull mud softened, resulting in putrefaction, lust and intelligence, pearl globs, jewelled stuff like ferrets, little theatres of mica, a purse containing all the evil smells of daily life. Then just the one vowel, iterate and buttressed and expiring; leaning, embracing, gazing. It devised with our claw identity for the sake of food. Selves, it says, feeding us, I adore you, you know. Like a boy blowing from a tree, we decided, we were paid, we were free. We incessantly prepared for the future. On the title page, two angels blowing on the trumpets of fame held up a globe decorated with three fleurs de lys and topped with a crown. We learned habits and tricks. We were a single grin with lips pasted back. We said we saw Europes of hallucination, fatty broths sprinkled with deer, stencilled eagles, serpents and lurid rags. That was a format of saying, a frayed ligature. We were fading into the presence or absence of food.

Enough of the least. Sincerity takes too long in an aggressive emergency. The present is not articulate. Also we feel a sense of duality. We wear out the art. We start to modify our vocables – flick, pour, dribble, estrangement's sex. Since it is we who are one, and we who are scattered. We're this pair or more that can't absorb one another in a meaning effect. We feel palpated by daylight and its deliberate plants. We feel this elsewhere sculpt our body.

We would be walking down the street in the poetrycity. Gauze would be everywhere. The day would be big, halting, gracious, revocable, cheap. We'd be the she-dandies in incredibly voluptuous jackets ribboning back from our waists, totally lined in pure silk, also in pure humming, and we'd be heading into the buildings with knowledge – that is, ephemeral knowledge, like leafage or sleeves or pigment. The streets are salons that receive abundantly our description. The buildings are charming. And our manners are software. We feel sartorial joy. We'd be at the river watching the fat water on the blonde built part, loving temporal improprieties, the bright trash floating in slow liberation. We'd be applying our makeup at noon by the river, leaning on the balustrade, thinking about a little shun, a little fight, a little sofa. We'd be thinking about hinges. We'd feel for our pen. Something might seduce us. A likeness. Samesame pouring through it.

Knowledge comes to us.

The Real Story of 'O'

Betsy Andrews

The period. Descended from the *punct* or *punctus*, meaning a dot, a speck, a spot. Dot speck spot fleck mote mackle freckle pock pit mole pip point pinpoint. Also meaning to pierce, to prick. The prick in space between language's legs. Or prick in the pause of the mouth.

Okay. Maybe.

But only in the most authoritarian of grammars, where pride and gloomy humour take up arms to puncture the hearts of chimerical monsters. Homer's rhetorical wanderings were pinned down, grommetted to the page in the wake of the spread of the Church, whose liturgy demanded prick points for God's cavils to be understood by the shepherds of the flock, who looked upon the Latin script as if molluscs with punctiform eyes, i.e., they didn't understand it a whit. The punctus was meant to help them comprehend and therefore help them help others conform, to spawn a pungency of allegiance to divine writ. During the Renaissance, Francis Bacon (whose *Essays* was among the very first texts to employ modern punctuation) philosophized an anti-authoritarian empiricism while at the pleasure of the court of James I, his language steeped in authoritative prickings.[1]

It is said that the Greeks – who valued the interpretive skills of the orator, preferring to listen to a guy like Homer (who, in fact, may have been blind and therefore not privy to the text at all) go on about Troy, their own hands and vision off the tablets, thus freed for their various gymnastics – transcribed their texts in a *scriptio continua* that wove, without spaces between words, without punctuation, left to right then right to left then left to right down the page, like a caterpillar that the bard caught in his eye and/or ear and let out of his mouth as he pleased. As the Greek *communitas* splintered into solitary communion with the holy writ, and literacy took precedence over good listening skills, language climbed into the text, transforming into a pupa covered in puncta. The prick in the Trojan grew stiff with repetitive strokes. 'Everyone,' Diana Hacker writes in *A Writer's Reference*, 'knows that a period should be used to end most sentences,' thus taking it for granted that everyone knows what a sentence and a period are.[2] As in this exercise written by pedant Bernice McCarthy for her 1981 elementary curriculum development text, *The 4MAT System*:

Overview: Read story without punctuation. Let students be punctuation marks.

Objective: To illustrate the need for punctuation in written language by relating it to pauses in spoken language.

Activity: Choose a story written by one of the children. Comment: 'I'm going to read Tom's wonderful story but I'm going to change it. I want you to listen and see if you can tell me how I have changed it.' Read the story as though it had no punctuation. Discuss what happened. Choose four children to be punctuation marks. One a period, one a comma, one an exclamation mark, and one a question mark. Hang signs around their necks. ... The teacher could prepare a simple passage in advance.

For example: 'Sally Pig and Kevin Frog went on a picnic in a beautiful yellow car it was a breezy sunny and warm day suddenly bang they had a flat tire Kevin Frog stopped the car he got out to fix the tire Sally Pig tried to help Kevin jack up the car and she pushed this way when she should have pushed that way the car fell knocking Kevin Frog into a big deep and muddy puddle alongside the road what do you think Sally Pig did next'

This passage needs: 6 periods, 1 exclamation mark, 2 commas, and 1 question mark. The children who are the punctuation marks stand in a straight line facing the class. The punctuation marks are told to listen to the story about to be read, and jump in when they think they should. (Tell them to jump once forward.) ...

Assessment: Fun the children have.[3]

But what if the period jumps in whenever she pleases and makes a big, deep and muddy puddle of the paragraph? To wit:

Sally Pig and Kevin Frog went on a picnic in a beautiful yellow. Car, it was breezy. Sunny and warm day, suddenly bang, they had. A flat-tire Kevin Frog stopped. The car he got out to fix.

The tire, Sally Pig, tried to help Kevin jack up. The car and she pushed this way when she should have. Pushed that way, the car fell. Knocking Kevin Frog into a big, deep and muddy puddle alongside the road, what do you. Think Sally Pig did next.

The sentences, if we are to agree on the subject-predicate thing, are more or less grammatically correct. The period isn't (technically) wrong. And the student has had some fun at Ms. McCarthy's expense. But say the period's on a spree; she jumps with remarkable heat, as if attacked with an intermittent fever, jumps with the tide or the beat of her heart. The class on grammar comes to a halt. She jumps, and she's Gertrude Stein, giving one of her *Lectures in America*, in which periods 'come to have a life of their own to commence breaking up things in arbitrary ways.'

> They could begin to act as they thought best and one might interrupt one's writing with them that is not really interrupting one's writing with them but one could come to stop arbitrarily stop at times in one's writing and so they could be used and you could use them. Periods could come to exist in this way and they could come in this way to have a life of their own. They did not serve you in any servile way as commas and colons and semi-colons do.[4]

You do not have to serve them as palate cleansers between multiple courses in a formal meal, or as meticulous stipulations in a sort of contractual agreement. You can puncture and wallow. For you, like that jumping bean of a student (who will suffer the face-to-face with the corner), periods have taken on 'a life of their own a necessity of their own a feeling of their own a time of their own.'

> And that feeling that life that necessity that time can express itself in an infinite variety that is the reason that I have always remained true to periods so much so that as I say recently I have felt that one could need them more than one had ever needed them.[5]

The period, a rhythm of flow and stoppage, a menses going 'round the way, brews its bloody beat out between the legs of language. More pussy than prick for me. From the Greek word *periodos*, combining peri, "around," and hodos, "way," i.e. a cycle or a period of time, a circuit, "period" originally referred to the groupings of words themselves, as in a "well-rounded, well-articulated, and harmonious sentence."' Later it came to tag the dot, that egg hatching the end of the sentence, the punct. For the Greeks, 'the ideal form of writing,' the grouping of words called *periodos*, 'constitute(d) a victory over the incoherence of spontaneous thought and expression.'[6] But, let's face it, so long as the orator is still blabbing, the *periodos* is less a triumph than a constant struggle, a rhetorical thrusting forward against an imagined chaos. Nowadays the (.), having overtaken the name, signals a merciful retreat. A rest. A loophole in language's conscription. Desertion, whenever you want, slap of the ruler be damned.

A waning sentence comes to a stop and meets tail to head with the next ascendant on the equinox of the period. If a sentence rises with the capital letter's cock's crowing, it beds down, in good time, in the period's fertile gap. Periods – periodontal – surround the bites of sound in their hushes. Language then lull, language then lull. At any time. Such a dot a speck a spot an egg, such great return. In Japanese, the brush stroke connoting the period opens into a small circle.[7] This seems right; the story of the 'o' in the mouth, fabric of space, breath in time. Do with her as you please.

NOTES

1 Punctuation in English Since 1600, <http://www.physics.ohio-state.edu/~wilkins/writing/Resources/essays/punctuation_hist.html>.

2 Diana T. Hacker, *A Writer's Reference* (New York: St. Martin's Press, 1989).

3 Bernice McCarthy, *The 4MAT System: Teaching to Learning Styles with Right–Left Mode Techniques* (Tucson, AZ: Zephyr Press, 1987.)

4 Gertrude Stein, *Lectures in America* (New York: Vintage Books, 1975).

5 Ibid.

6 Bernard Dupriez and Albert Halsall, *A Dictionary of Literary Devices: Gradus A–Z* (Toronto: University of Toronto Press, 1991).

7 Shinji Takasugi, '4.6: Punctuation,' *Teach Yourself Japanese*, <http://www.sf.airnet.ne.jp/~ts/japanese/punctuation.html>.

Proceed Queerly:
The Sentence as Compositional Unit
Kathy Lou Schultz

Proceed Queerly: The Sentence as Compositional Unit

The manner in which I have lived leads me ineluctably into bed with queer theory. Or at least into the room next door. I am a person from the working class with one and a half graduate degrees; a person who has had intimate relationships with both women and men, and is currently in an interracial relationship; a person from a rural area who has chosen the urban; a person struggling daily with gender oppositions. My world is troubled by 'either/ors': straight or gay, male or female, black or white, poetry or prose. I'm lodged in the cracks between categories, dynamiting my way out.

You see, I just don't believe in them. You know, the binary oppositions. This is where queer theory comes into play, 'demonstrating the impossibility of any natural sexuality, it calls into question even such apparently unproblematic terms as "man" and "woman."'[1] Or, as Cixous and Clement write:

> Through dual, hierarchical oppositions. Superior/Inferior.
> Myths, legends, books. Philosophical systems. Everywhere
> (where) ordering intervenes, where a law organizes what is
> thinkable by oppositions (dual, irreconcilable; or sublatable,
> dialectical). And all these pairs of oppositions are couples.
> Does that mean something? Is the fact that Logocentrism
> subjects thought – all concepts, codes and values – to a binary
> system, related to the couple, man/woman?[2]

I read this text just after I turned twenty, a time when I began examining the effects of 'compulsory heterosexuality' on my life. (My mother's obsession for recording dates is helpful here; in the book I've written 'April 1987.') And the concepts wrote themselves onto my brain/consciousness. When I began to explore, explode and implode female identity in my work, such as *Some Vague Wife*, I sought strategies for inhabiting the space between the binaries, to activate a 'both/and' strategy that would give expression to experience that is not 'either/or.' To uncouple and de-hierarchize the pairs. To disorder the system.

Though often credited with coining the term 'queer theory,' Teresa de Lauretis has since distanced herself from it, stating that the term has 'quickly become a conceptually vacuous creature of the publishing industry.'[3] However, in charting my own procedures of writing, David Halperin's working definition is helpful: 'Queer ... does not designate a class of already objectified pathologies or perversions,' writes - Halperin, 'rather, it describes a horizon of possibility whose precise extent and heterogeneous scope cannot in principle be delimited in advance.'[4] In theorizing how one might 'proceed queerly' (to return to my title) in using the sentence as the compositional unit, it is important to understand that in this mode, the sentence overrides or precedes narrative. By not delimiting the 'story' in advance, new possibilities and directions are possible.

There's Something in the Water

Poets from Baudelaire to Ron Silliman have concentrated on the creative possibilities of the sentence. In an essay entitled 'Narrating Narration: The Shapes of Ron Silliman's Work,' originally published in *The Difficulties*, Charles Bernstein describes Silliman's method as follows: 'With every new sentence a new embarkation: not only is the angle changed, and it's become a close-up, but the subject is switched. Yet maybe the sound's the same, carries it through. Or like an interlocking chain: A has a relation to B and B to C, but A and C have nothing in common (*series not essence*).'[5]

Bernstein draws attention here to the space *between* sentences: the method of getting from here to there. His reading reveals that parataxis is not divorced from meaning, but rather infuses itself with new possibilities for meaning. The sentences do not exist without relation to one another, but create new relations. It is this attention to 'between-ness' that most interests me in my experimental prose work.

In *The New Sentence*, Silliman writes, 'I am going to make an argument, that there is such a thing as a new sentence and that it occurs thus far more or less exclusively in the prose of the Bay Area.'[6] I agree with Silliman that Bay Area writers have contributed significantly to theorizing the sentence. I would broaden Silliman's scope to consider New Narrative writers such as Dodie Bellamy, Bob Glück, Kevin

Killian and Camille Roy. In disordering binary identity systems, these San Francisco writers have contributed to my queer understandings of the sentence, my willingness to transgress not just for the sake of it, but for the sake of something closer to the body than traditional narrative. Closer to my face than a clock. Closer to charting the respite between contractions: a span not marked by minutes, but a blessing of endorphins swabbed in fog.

Here's a little story. The philosopher is born. He dies. In between he thinks. [Close-up on the philosopher's hands buttering toast.][7] The philosopher doesn't believe in the story. He keeps protesting. He butters his toast. He forgets his keys. He gets a haircut. The philosopher's body exists, and then it doesn't. I cannot explain this. In between he thinks. In between.

Prose Is the New Poetry; or, This Isn't Your Daddy's Genre

New Narrative gave me back the sentence, a line of elastic stretching across the page. I had stood at the edge of the lyric and fallen in. I had swallowed the lyric and choked on it. I had been lured into the lyric's *boudoir* and slammed my elbows against the walls just trying to turn around. I was out of metaphors. Though I still engage the lyric, writing in prose allows me a kind of freedom to explore the nether regions of sexuality and gender, to stroke the unnameable places, to crack my head up against the jagged edge.[8]

NOTES

1 Annamarie Jagose, 'Queer Theory,' *Australian Humanities Review* 4 (Dec. 1996–Feb. 1997). <http://www.lib.latrobe.edu.au/AHR/archive/Issue-Dec-1996/jagose.html>.

2 Helene Cixous and Catherine Clément, *The Newly Born Woman*, trans. Betsy Wing (Minneapolis: University of Minnesota, 1986), 64.

3 Teresa de Lauretis, 'Habit Changes,' *differences: A Journal of Feminist Cultural Studies* 6 (1994): 297.

4 David M. Halperin, *Saint Foucault: Towards a Gay Hagiography* (New York: Oxford University Press, 1995), 62.

5 'About Ron Silliman,' *Modern American Poetry*, ed. Cary Nelson (2002). <http://www.english.uiuc.edu/maps/poets/s_z/silliman/about.htm>.

6 Ron Silliman, *The New Sentence* (New York: Roof, 1987), 63.

7 For a close-up of Jacques Derrida's hands buttering toast, see *Derrida*, a film by Kirby Dick and Amy Ziering Kofman.

8 Thanks to Robin Tremblay-McGaw for her suggestions concerning this essay.

Dislocation

Shiver

Approximate:
Past to Present

Methods

The Sentence

The Novel

Resistance

The Buzz of
Alternate Meanings

A Story Is
a Storage

My Other Self

Low Culture
Dodie Bellamy

Sex/Body/Writing

> a fairy tale assumption in which an all but non-existent condi-
> tion is assumed to be rampant
>
> – Samuel R. Delany[1]

The accused is permitted to display the bumper sticker EAT SHIT because it is determined that no motorist, not even a coprophiliac, is likely to be sexually aroused by a bumper sticker reading EAT SHIT.

arousal = criminal
non-arousal = non-criminal

Offensiveness is outside the equation. When I write, 'My cunt is a camera,' is this likely to arouse photographers, the scenic vistas of my camera's wandering eye – or the film stock itself?

I'm working towards a writing that subverts sexual bragging, a writing that champions the vulnerable, the fractured, the disenfranchised, the sexually fucked-up. A female body who has sex writing about sex – no way can I stand in front of an audience reading this stuff and maintain the abstraction the 'author' A BODY some writers glory in this but I feel miserable and invaded – as if the audience has x-ray vision and can see down to the frayed elastic on my panties. But, really, it is I who have invaded my own privacy. To regain some of that privacy I have desexualized myself in public, have stiffened, as if to say, 'This is not a body.'

To a five o'clock cocktail party in Berkeley I wear a black Italian pantsuit with a pink silk blouse – because that's the way the women dressed at the last five o'clock cocktail party I went to, at the French Consulate. But in Berkeley everybody's in linen, jeans, sandals. Joshua Clover is casual chic, lanky as a cornstalk, all in white – white linen shorts, white shirt, flame white hair, single silver hoop in his ear. Standing beside him, I feel like a black bat. 'I'm having some problems with transgressive writing,' he says. 'Why is A. M. Homes so popular? Because she's transgressive without being challenging.' *Transgressive but not challenging* YES these words circle through my head like a mantra for days – a formula for just about everything that pisses me off. Any sentence containing the word 'gender' is at the top of my list.

EAT SHIT NO/BODY

F., I have heard, rejected a piece of mine because it contained too many body fluids. Now, two years later, I run into him at the Small Press Traffic mailbox. He shows me a favourite passage from Blanchot: the poet must expose himself to the violence of pure being. Or some such thing. 'Yes,' I say, 'but how do you then go to work?' F. explains how he thinks one could juggle that. He's sweet today, so shy, so halting, so 'I'll lick your boots.' A guy as confusing as Lon Chaney – the clown face dissolves to disgruntled scientist dissolves to clown – *HE Who Gets Slapped* (MGM, 1924) gets the last laugh. I don't know what to think of him. I smile, say, 'Good luck on your thesis,' and walk down the stairs.

A physical body writes about sex.

H. sits at the back of my prose workshop, sullen alienation brooding in the corner. I take one look at him and think, 'Oh shit.' His attractiveness is not wrought from art-school pretension – it's more of an afterthought, if that. H.'s writing deals with schizophrenia/paranoia/madness/psychological disintegration. 'i live with monsters who are contagious,' he writes. 'the transmitter planted deep inside my ear instructs the following: i, to justify misfortune and misery of fallen angels, is chosen to sacrifice you to unknown forces that make cars move.' I ask him personal questions he refuses to answer, but I keep asking anyway. I learn he's Korean and his family's in Los Angeles. That's all.

In one piece a woman gets too close to him so he eats her. It's his 'Archiving' assignment. 'Choose an object that you can easily bring to class. Write a real or imagined narrative explaining this object's significance – its importance in "your" life, how it came to be a part of "your" life. Type and make copies for the class. Bring your object with you.' He brings in a plastic fork and knife.

'The smell of her boiling flesh invaded my room. shes here no longer but she's here with me. the plastic fork inscribes embryo, the plastic knife paints pictures of her memory. what can i say, i've fallen in love with her.'

I don't let on how drawn I am to this writing, but H. seems to know anyway. Over the semester his manner softens to sweetness, eagerness, affection even. The one day he's not in class I miss him. Unanswered questions, I suppose, are a form of intimacy. He writes, 'you, standing middle of my target, i can admire you more than physics allows me.' I know this isn't about me, but I pretend.

The last day of class. S. has changed her hair from white blonde to yellow blonde. 'I was looking too eighties.' S. projects a desperation for attention that she doesn't have a clue how to get. (My soft spot for her.) Finally, after hinting about it all semester, she's writing directly about being raped. 'in the back of my head lingo had long since departed and I wasn't prepared to go down.' This form is really working for you, I tell her, the straightforward narrative interspersed with poetic intensities. I think to myself, 'This woman, this BODY, has been raped, for Christ's sake.' While Creative Writing teaches us thus to hermetically seal content in aesthetics, I'm thinking, 'Dodie, you are so full of shit.'

The time is up and I say, 'Well, we're finished – in a big way.'

H. blurts out, 'Want to go out for a drink or something? I need some closure.'

Writing that shifts the matrix, e.g., Samuel R. Delany's *Hogg*. 'What it seriously attempts to do,' Delany explains in a 1989 letter to Randy Byers, 'is challenge just about every dichotomy on which our culture is based. And the distinction between dirty and clean – as a grounding for both civilization and pleasure – is one of society's most fundamental.'[2] And then, '*Hogg* constantly compels the reader to choose one filth-laden situation over another, when most of us would simply want to be rid of the entire set of experiences.'

Fountain pen scribbling across paper, a body writes about sex. Sitting at the computer, a body writes about sex. The keyboard and monitor are enormously erotic THE BEEPING MODEM, THE WORD MACHINE TALKING BACK more than once e-mail has gotten me in trouble.

I wake up to a shock of wet at my feet – Stanley, my cat, has peed in the bed while I was sleeping in it. 'I'll deal with this later.' I get up, make coffee, sit down at the computer and take some Delany notes – 'hebephilia, the love of filth' – I'm reading and typing and thinking about Delany for an hour or so when the scent of cat urine impinges upon me – the grey jersey nightgown I'm wearing reeks with Stanley's urine. How marvellous, I think, Delany has imbedded my woof and warp NO DISTANCE WOOF AND WARP I toss the nightgown in the hamper, throw on another thrift-store favourite, this one with 'Neiman

Marcus' in huge red script down the length of it, and continue typing.

Talking Dirty

Before I got involved in all this queer narrative business, when I was a young poet in my twenties, my poems tended to be abject, sexually explicit tributes to the drug-addled, Vietnam-vet art student I was lovers with. I remember one poem where he gets up after sex and washes himself off in the sink, and I bemoaned 'the dark night of plumbing.' My tone and subject matter caused much anxiety to my experimental feminist community. Kathleen Fraser took me aside and told me she was 'worried about' me. In a peer workshop, my poetry was seen as a sign of mental aberration and one woman suggested I enter therapy. You can imagine the sigh of relief I gave when I joined Bob Glück's workshop at Small Press Traffic and I was told, more sex, more abjection. It was like I'd found my home.

Catherine Clément's book *Syncope: The Philosophy of Rapture* was important in my understanding of sex as a state of being. Syncope is a temporary absence of self or suspension of movement, a hesitation or dissonance. Clement's examples include fainting, the backward dip in the tango, a weak musical beat between two strong beats, the spin of dervishes, sneezing, coughing, hiccupping, uncontrollable laughter, screaming, facial spasms and tics, squinting, tremors, heart palpitations, choking, uncontrolled excretion, cold sweats, tears, tingling, prickling, tickling, wheezing, auditory hallucinations, orgasm, visions of gods speaking, religious ecstasy, falling in love and enjambment in poetic metrics. 'Where is the lost syllable,' she writes, 'the beat eaten away by the rhythm? Where does the subject go who, later comes to, "comes back"? Where am I in syncope?'[3] In other words, the autonomous, aware subject goes up in smoke.

Clément examines at length how syncope changes a person.

> The countenance of martyrs tortured by illness is often transformed; their faces become muzzles or snouts, they lose their humanity. ... when you fall into syncope, you never know in what shape you might return: with wolf's paws, the tail of a serpent, a bark at your lips, a pelt of fur ... One never knows. During the night, while all are asleep, the beautiful woman crosses the frontier and becomes a serpent; the nobleman or

churl crosses the invisible border and wakes up a wolf.[4]

I'm excited by the power of sex to turn a woman into a beast. In my writing I long to throw away the easy abstractions that control the beast.

Clément ties syncope to Freud's ideas on the return of the repressed.

> Then suddenly, violently, 'that' returns; the repression yields, the breach is opened, time is suspended, as if it were coagulating physically in a material symptom. The rules of everyday logic rupture, chronology blurs ... Freud was fascinated by these balls of time – time frozen in suffering, knotted flesh. He observed the paralyzed arm, the pimple on the nose, the obsessive gesture; he listened to the cough, and recognized in the paralysis, the swelling, or the choking the pressure of the age-old, surging through the body and forgetful of the order of the world.[5]

So we can look at sex as a time out, a break in linearity. Sex, then, would seem like a natural topic for writers interested in breaking through the linear rat's maze of the traditional story, of academic self-absorbed poetry. So why does there seem to be a dearth of passionate, sex-crazed experimental writers?

According to Clément, syncope has traditionally been the enemy of Western philosophy. 'Philosophers constitutionally hate syncope and everything it resembles – the upheaval of wit, the unruliness of passion and anger.'[6] They hate syncope so much they've written volumes to protect themselves from it. 'The history of our classical philosophy, as it is now taught, shows this: Western thought has been busy filling this hole in life.'[7] Syncope is scary because it subverts 'power and force, muscle and health, vigor and lucidity. Syncope opens onto a universe of weakness and tricks; it leads to new rebellions.'[8] Writing is an orderly universe, and I think much of the hostility towards the avant-garde is a result of its toying with this order and a fear that without standard sentence structure the world will plunge into chaos.

Seventies feminism, for all its pain-in-the-assness, instilled in me the belief that the personal is political, the importance of introducing more accurate and varied images of female experience into the cultural pool. Before I fell into the manicured hands of the experimental feminist poets, I was involved with a far less intellectual and highly lesbian group, the Feminist Writers Guild. The Feminist Writers Guild was very sex positive. When we published an anthology of members' work, we held our editorial meetings naked in a hot tub in Berkeley, and we collated the printed pages naked on a deck in Marin. I got sunburned on parts of my body that had never before seen the light of day. Compared to these lusty gals, I was a bit of a shrinking violet. My first poetry reading was arranged by Gloria Anzaldúa. It was with the owner of the Marin sundeck, a woman who went by the name of Abigail Tigresslily. Abigail began with a rather ecstatic piece about her big dog going down on her – and then when she got to human-to-human sex, she used the word *slurp*. I was horrified, more by *slurp* than the dog.

I find it interesting, and at times dismaying, how my work changes within the context in which it is read. In a gay culture, where there is a vocabulary for talking about sex, my work doesn't feel all that transgressive. But then place the same work within a straight world, with all those things one doesn't talk about 'in mixed company,' and I become a pervert. To me transgression is a tedious position. But I am excited by pushing the reader to the point where he or she cannot maintain a safe distance from the work. I'm fascinated by writing in which the private obsessions of the writer come through, like in J. G. Ballard's latest novel, *Super-Cannes*. He's still fusing cars/prostheses/sex, like he's never going to stop doing that, and you can almost hear him panting behind the words. I'm interested in a writing of embodiment, not of abstraction. I don't want to take messy, lived corporeal, emotional existence – and then rationalize it with theory. I don't want to gild the shit. I don't want to be like Clément's philosophers, trying to clean things up.

My latest book, *Cunt-Ups*, is about exploring pornographic language. Pornographic language, I think, is pretty much a male form. Women are stuck with the more wishy-washy 'erotic.' Even as a child I was nasty and bawdy, a sort of prepubescent Wife of Bath. I am the daughter of a union carpenter, and as such I was raised in a filthy-mouthed environment. One could easily make a case for verbal sexual abuse. I know I didn't feel comfortable with it. Why would a grown man engage in locker-room talk in front of a little girl; why this display of male-bonding jargon? And as we all know, the abused often turns into the abuser. *Cunt-Ups* takes back this pornographic language used as a weapon on me and subverts it to my own ends. The book is also very much about sexual obsession and desire. In American English we seem to have a language for romance and a language for pornography, but the two rarely meet. In *Cunt-Ups*, which I see as a very romantic book, I'm collapsing romance and porn. Sex can't be reduced to events that happen to a person. Sex is a trap, a labyrinth, a matrix that engulfs you. There's no way out. If I were to write the story of my life with emotional honesty, my relationship to my body would be the most important thing. This is the case for many women. To theorize my relationship to my body as Abjection doesn't do justice to the self-loathing, the terror, the chaos I was raised with. I don't want to present a sanitized version of female sexuality, don't want to use beauty to make physicality palatable.

Pop the Culture

For me, it's all equal, culturally. This is something I learned from Kevin Killian, whose protean slips between low culture and high culture astonish me. Rather than using academic or scientific or philosophical language as a marker of intelligence, like we constantly see on the Buffalo Poetics List, I like to collage such language into my writing to bring in a foreign tone. I often change such stolen passages to the first person, I absorb and pervert them, make them *me*. Here's an example from my novel-in-progress, *The Fourth Form*:

> The sticky glutinous stuff that gels my cells together and glues me to the universe is beginning to erode. I am losing my magnetism, becoming more liquid, denser, heavier, colder, cloying. As my electrical impulses weaken, I drift farther away from the core of substantiality emotions moving through time like music, *emotions worked to the point where they almost fall apart* Ed appears beside me in a rental car, the congealed face of existence, smirking *at first the figures from my memory were anatomically correct but then the cunts/cocks got bigger and bigger and the bodies collapsed* as he drives he holds my hand, the back of his hand resting in my crotch, my crotch is immense, the oyster shell holding up Botticelli's Venus.[9]

Though the appropriated passages have been substantially rewritten, many of them are drawn from some unremembered science article I took notes on years ago, plus an art-journal piece on Tony Oursler's projections. I wanted to be a scientist when I was a girl and through the eighties I read popular science magazines regularly – but when they started to be filled with computer stuff I lost interest. Now much of my pseudo-science comes from *Lingua Franca*. Its tabloid approach to academia assures me a steady supply of bizarre and even scandalous scientific discoveries and theories.

'At first the figures from my memory were anatomically correct but then the cunts/cocks got bigger and bigger and the bodies collapsed' – I remember in the original article about Oursler, it was the figures' heads, not cunts and cocks, that got bigger. From Kathy Acker I learned that no matter what you steal you can tweak and torture it until it's all sex, sex, sex – like in her reworking of Dario Argento's horror film *Suspiria* in the 'Clit City' section of *My Mother: Demonology*. In the Argento film, which takes place in a girl's boarding school, some meat stored in the attic rots and maggots fall from the ceiling, on top of the girls, who go screaming through the halls. In Acker's version, the maggots emerge from a much more intimate space:

> When I woke up, maggots were crawling out of my cunt. At first I thought that Mother must have over–toilet-trained me. The maggots were coming out of my cunt because maggots come from meat.
>
> In my first school I had been taught that through rational-ity humans can know and control otherness, our histories and environments.
>
> In one of my dreams, the maggot, huge, translucent, and slimy, was my father.
>
> Here is my theory of dreams: Maggots are dicks because they rise up, then writhe and turn funny colors. Worms rise out of red meat. (Worm- or dick-heads are the same things as nipples.)
>
> Whereas houses are cunts. In the dream, the house is a maze.
>
> The outside lies beyond the maze.
>
> One result of this theory is the knowledge that all reality is alive.
>
> It wasn't just my cunt. When I walked out of my red room, white dicks were falling out of the hall's ceiling, which wasn't alive.[10]

Sex consumes rationality, sex transforms the world. So do monsters. When I was a child my fascination with monsters equalled my fear of them. I remember lying on my bed with a copy of *Monster* magazine, transfixed by the picture on the cover of Elsa Lancaster as the Bride of Frankenstein, and inside, the Mummy, Frankenstein himself and sundry pizza-faced teens. I found it exotic to find these images in a magazine, so unlike the other magazines lying around our house – *Life, Look, TV Guide, Ladies' Home Journal, Redbook.* Standing in line outside a movie theatre, I found myself right in front of a poster for *I Was a Teenage Werewolf,* starring *Bonanza*'s Michael Landon, and was frightened out of my wits, like I couldn't stand to look at it. When I saw *Hunchback of Notre Dame* starring Gina Lollobrigida and Anthony Quinn, I was so hysterical with fear and shock that that evening my mother had to sleep with me. A couple of years later, whenever the advertisement for *The Fly* would come on TV I would run into my bedroom and hide – much to the delight of my brother, who wouldn't stop teasing me about it. The only mainstream image to come near the excitement I felt in looking at these monster pictures was *Life*'s photo of Lee Harvey Oswald's corpse, post-autopsy, the huge ridge of stitches across his chest.

Attraction and terror – sounds pretty sexy to me. This is a far cry from the mainstream avant-garde's condescension towards pop culture – using it as a source of parody that the author remains intellectually and morally superior to. I think a more honest and interesting approach to pop culture is to delight in its tackiness but at the same time admit you're profoundly moved by it. This is, perhaps, the essence of camp. A few years ago when I went to the American Poetry of the Fifties conference at Orono, a number of straight academics gave papers on Frank O'Hara, and whenever the issue of camp arose, these hetero guys up there, very stiff and serious, defining camp like talking encyclopedia entries, presented a camp spectacle all their own.

I thought when I finished *The Letters of Mina Harker,* that would be the end of my writing about horror, but I can't stop. In horror, I love the confused boundaries – between living and dead, inside/outside, one/many, human/machine, human/animal, etc. I love to see people in intense emotional states, love the beautiful imagery that pops up even in the worst of horror films. And, most importantly, horror addresses female body issues as no other genre can.

In her book *The Monstrous-Feminine: Film, Feminism, Psychoanalysis*, Barbara Creed discusses Linda Williams's 1984 article 'When the Woman Looks,' in which Williams claims that when women look at monsters, they identify with them:

> [Williams] states that classic horror films such as *Nosferatu* and *The Phantom of the Opera* frequently represent 'a surprising (and at times subversive) affinity between monster and woman' in that the woman's look acknowledges their 'similar status within patriarchal structures of seeing.' Both are constructed as 'biological freaks' whose bodies represent a fearful and threatening form of sexuality. This has important implications for the female spectator. 'So there is a sense in which the woman's look at the monster ... is also a recognition of their similar status as potent threats to vulnerable male power.'[11]

Creed's book was seminal in my exploration of my fascination with monsters within a misogynist culture that hates the female body. My copy of *The Monstrous-Feminine* is so marked up it's barely readable. To give a quick sense of the range of Creed's ideas, I would like to end by transcribing my mid-nineties jottings in the margins of her book. This is not being presented as an example of the 'smart' but of the 'personal.' The rapid shifts in register of my marginalia from studenty notes to plot ideas for *Mina* to personal revelation demonstrates what I was saying earlier about an unguarded embrace of cultural artifacts – a collapse of the me/it dichotomy. I've indicated which chapter each set of notes was written in.

> Introduction: Fear that women are *not* castrated. The woman's look at the monster.
> Chapter 1: Kristeva, Femininity, Abjection: Pleasure in L's ugliness, rimming him. So few details remain – pile up on an altar to memory. Reminds me of men who reject women after sex. Would this mean that language writing is abject. Border. Body as colonized – how do I know I'm not a bug-eyed space alien who has taken over the body of a girl from Indiana – how else could I have become *me*?
> Chapter 3: Woman as Possessed Monster: The invaded subject. Graphic description of bodily excrement – body as territory.

Chapter 4: Woman as Monstrous Womb: Monstrous off-spring are created by the maternal imagination. Mina dreams of monstrous babies – perhaps Mina gets pregnant? Male versus female body. Couvade – man giving birth. A female creature is about to give birth to an alien being or blob ... her womb is a grotesque thing. Uncanny = the old.

Chapter 5: Woman as Vampire: Because she is sexually awakened she is now a threatening female figure.

Chapter 6: Woman as Witch: Over and over – this threat to the symbolic order.

Chapter 8: Medusa's Head: The Vagina Dentata: Whenever he fucked her he had a fear of losing his legs. Fear of first events.

Chapter 9: The Femme Castratrice: This represents Mina's desire for normality. Mina & Mina – identical twins separated at birth – have them have sex with one another.

Chapter 10: The Castrating Mother: Striges = women with bodies of birds/clawed feet of vultures. Around us stuffed birds perch as if ready to pounce. Voyeurism – watching someone undressing. 'The cruel eyes studying you' – trapped in madhouse. Children's bath/vulnerability.

Chapter 11: The Medusa's Gaze: Death. Masochistic view-ing. Other films = sadistic gaze. Penis.

Inside Back Cover: Not writing = me as body, a body that will not budge, will not reform, reduce – the elusive squishiness of the flesh – you'd think it would be more plastic, easier to push around – an excess of molecules – I want to evaporate myself – my belly continues to hug my hip bones – L's picture of my leg in motion, legs crossed and blurred – people sitting around me with notebooks, I am private I am deep – I am worthless when I am not writing – banality consumes me – my character is a girl who spends all her time in cafes and in bed – no banality in that gnawing aloneness – always looking for another being to rub against.

The little bitch keeps her secrets from me ... the little bitch won't fess up the facts. There's this figment colonizing my psyche in that unbelievable construct, the past.

NOTES

1 Samuel R. Delany, letter to Randy Byers, May 27, 1989.

2 Ibid.

3 Catherine Clément, *Syncope: The Philosophy of Rapture,* trans. Sally O'Driscoll and Deirdre M. Mahoney (Minneapolis: University of Minnesota Press, 1994), 5.

4 Ibid., 214.

5 Ibid., 224.

6 Ibid., 35.

7 Ibid., 20–21.

8 Ibid., 20.

9 Dodie Bellamy, *Fat Chance* (Vancouver: Nomados, 2003), 24.

10 Kathy Acker, *My Mother: Demonology* (New York: Random House, 1995), 54–55.

11 Barbara Creed, *The Monstrous Feminine: Film, Feminism, Psychoanalysis* (London: Routledge, 1993), 6.

Slightly different versions of these three movements were previously performed:

'Pop the Culture' and 'Talking Dirty' were presented as papers at 'Prose Acts,' a conference on narrative at SUNY Buffalo, October 18–21, 2001.

'Sex, Body, Writing' was the originary essay for a SUNY Buffalo Poetics listserv colloquium on gender and writing, ed. Christopher W. Alexander, September 30, 2000 (archived at <http://www.epc.buffalo.edu>).

The three movements were first presented together as part of a weekend residency at Kootenay School of Writing, Vancouver, February 2002.

Nostalgic

D. L. Alvarez

1 Someone asked me a while back what my writing was about and I said, 'It's about place: buildings, cities, parks.' I claimed to be writing about these places mostly, and that the people in my stories were just there to amuse the readers and hopefully hold their attention long enough to get from A to B. Even as I said this, however, I knew I was tap dancing blindly: giving an answer that could pass, but not really addressing the core. Somehow the question had never come up before, but bullshitting was more fun than saying, 'Hell, I don't know.' At any rate, people in my stories do more than just decorate locations. If they seem incidental, it's not that they're merely devices, it's because that's how people often are in my life: ghostly, fading in and out of view.

2 A guy I travel four and half hours by train to see, in order to enjoy his company, is deaf in one ear. His working ear recently started ringing. An operation was performed to correct the problem, but the ringing persisted. The doctors explained that this was the brain missing the old sound that was there long enough to become burned into memory. It was a reflex nostalgia. Now he must wear a sort of anti-hearing aid, a device that makes other sounds in his ear so that the brain eventually, having one too many steady patterns to deal with, will sort of drop them all and he can go back to hearing just what is there.

This reminded me of the first story I ever wrote and read out loud. It was about a woman who was in a car with her brother when the two skidded off the road and into a tree. Her brother died in the crash, but his death screams continued to echo in her ears. She was first treated as a patient who was 'hearing things' until finally they realized that the sound vibrations were real and not imagined. Her eardrums were actually recreating the vibrations of her brother's fear and pain, a scar of sound. The problem was impossible to correct and finally the only solution to preserving the girl's sanity (for these screams were not something she could get used to; indeed they became increasingly less bearable) was to sever the small bone that connected the eardrums to the membrane of the inner ear that translates vibrations to the brain as sound. The girl was then deaf, but relieved of the greater problem of the phantom screams. In fact, those screams did continue to set the eardrum to vibrate, but the sound began and ended there in the now-dead canal of her ear. Her brother continued to call to her, but could no longer make himself heard.

It struck me then that since this first story, nearly everything I've written has been about memories: those ghosts that live inside us, for the most part buried, but there.

3 In 1989 I took a series of psychiatric tests just to see if I could slant the results. I'd heard of people doing so and being prescribed wonderful mood-altering drugs and legal excuses to never have to work again. At the time, I wasn't much of a druggie, but I did have some romantic longing for official recognition that I was nuts. Crazy people are sexy (more so then, but I still fall for them) because they're different without even trying. The normal world is something to be suspected, a little too pat to be believable, and so it's difference that I seek in my objects of desire. Looking at Rorschach's ink blots could maybe get me on that team of others, certifiable, even if I had to cheat on the exam. I gave outrageous answers to simple questions and, when asked to tell stories about various pictures, made up elaborate tales dripping with psychosis ... That is, if the person giving the test were as simple-minded as I, he could have made such an interpretation. Instead, when I was given the test results, the doctor said I had an active, healthy imagination ... and an extreme fear of memory loss.

4 I've written many stories since the first, and though the theme of memory is a clear thread uniting them, I hadn't recognized this thread until my half-deaf friend's condition reminded me of that story with the woman who survived her brother in a car crash ... a story I had, in fact, forgotten until that moment.

5 In my mother's last days in the hospital, she asked about various friends of mine and felt frustrated when she forgot one of their names. 'See what happens when you get old?' she said. But the truth is, she always had a terrible memory. Everyone in my family does. She just forgot that she was forgetful.

6 Antuan, a guy I know in New York, recently told me about having sex with Casey Donovan, one of the most famous porn stars to come out of the seventies, back in the days before he was 'Casey Donovan.' Antuan said that the pre–porn king, who was a doorman at a hotel at

the time, used strawberry-flavoured lube to fuck him with. I passed this story on to yet another friend who said, 'I love those sorts of details that we hold on to, almost cling to, as a sort of proof to ourselves that these events did indeed occur. Strawberry, perfect! Most of the time, our mind alters things, and those details that are clearest are the most likely ones to have been invented. But they help us to keep the texture of the memory, even if it's a false texture, so that the memory can feel – and remain – true.'

7 When I was dumped by a guy last summer (a real nut case, so you can imagine how head over heels I was for him) I didn't have it in me to hate him, was too depressed to even try, even though clinging to love is what fuels the depression. My best girlfriend told me I should imagine that he was away on some sort of important sabbatical; that we were still together, but I had no means of contacting him and would just have to live with that.

I wrote a short short story that basically followed her instructions. In it I already started to rewrite my lover as someone else, changing all his details in order to start the process of forgetting. Though it's possible that by altering the details, my true goal was to anchor the story (the one I wanted to remember) in memory.

The story is titled 'Dust.'

Narrative Transfiguration
Robin Tremblay-McGaw

They were cleaning off my cervix (some of the cells of which were dysplastic), using swabs to twirl, like cotton candy, the viscous mucus. There was a lot of it. The nurse commented on this over- and mis-production. I watched my cervix on a screen some eight feet or so away from me. As if responsible – consciously or not – for this abundant production, flush. A sign to be read and interpreted, a commentary on my body, an overproductive sexuality and cellular structure gone awry. I was my own transfixed voyeur. What are my stories and do I know them?

I start with the body and its materiality because when I began to rethink how narrative structure works, I was interested in what happens to narrative or our ideas of it in a period when biochemistry, DNA analysis, cloning, neurotransmitter uptake inhibitors enter the field. How might these relate to writing strategies? What happens when biochemicals squirting across synapses become a layer (a lair!), a lawyer of their own? A professional suggests that biochemistry and genetics have superseded narrative. As if one existed in isolation of the other[s]. Mistresses of the Master Narrative, Tell All! The snuff film of the nightly news.

When I was working on my poem *spill,*[1] I wanted to find a way to unleash into the writing the structural disruption, the excessive transfiguration, of cervical dysplasia, my father's lung cancer (*the lung is an organ surgically nibbled*), family alcoholism (*the immobility of the person drinking whites out. The immobility of the person writing sets the world in motion.*). Each of these experiences shoved me – my body, my intellectual, emotional and daily life – into places I couldn't predict, didn't know anything about, places parts of me didn't want to go. Even when they seek to be the stitches, stories are trauma. They can't help but gush. Sometimes just a slow bleed. Seepage. And so to talk about transfiguration seems polite or sanitized, and yet it suggests, maybe more so than trauma, the ongoing process at work in narrative structure and figural language. It happens inside. Despite us.

Narrative transfiguration might be readily apparent (blood calls attention) or, on the other hand, appear contained. But then it is often too late. Movement, shifting has already occurred. Sometimes a subtle plate tectonics; other times, an earthquake. Narrative – particularly narrative that seeks to remake narrative itself and is an experiment – can tear or pierce, cut, make a break through the surface of its own structure, narrative's ideological skin. The pen is a scalpel. Teresa de Lauretis says that narrativity is structured not about components but 'its work and effects. What it seeks to understand is the nature of the structuring and destructuring, even destructive, processes at work in textual and semiotic production.'[2] Without my *knowing*, my cervical cells remake themselves, and my body. Parts acting as wholes. Holes. One structure moving and consuming another from within. I cannot account for myself. The multiple locations of knowledges in a single body. The tender seams or places of contact rip apart; cells replicate. The surgeon heals through violence, a cut. My metaphors are slipping; the edges are jagged.

Or to link this to specific literary texts: Lyn Hejinian's *My Life* radically reinterprets what it might mean to write a life; 'You are so generous, they told me, allowing everything its place, but what we wanted to hear was a story,' or, 'A fragment is not a fraction but a whole piece.'[3] Movement encounters resistance. Learning to read and think otherwise can be traumatic. In Dodie Bellamy's *The Letters of Mina Harker*, Mina says, 'The monstrous and the formless have as much right as anybody else.'[4] When the monstrous and formless are acknowledged, the text is something else, something monstrous and formless when placed alongside a writing that is predicated on their exclusion. In *The Letters* and in Bellamy's later work *Cunt-Ups*, her 'hermaphroditic salute to William Burroughs and Kathy Acker,' the messy shifting across the text is there on the surface. The movement inside is violently visible on the outside. The writing crawls, tightens in crisis and spills. Bellamy's writing courts this riot and disruption. The excluded is invited in. The door is open. But, watch out – there are irreverent and sharp implements inside. The speaker in *Cunt-Ups* says, 'The disposed-of-body seems to be changing, it usually turns to one side. I'm getting quicker at cutting up the body I was born with.'[5] Does it stop being an experiment when you know what you are doing? Through an intervention preceded by attention, whatever might masquerade as a given – here, the body as a site of layered meanings that determine it, its interactions with the world, and the texts it might generate – can be taken apart and transfigured. Made into a new figure. Duchamp's *Nude Descending Staircase.*

But this is not only a recent feature of some narrative. In a much earlier context, Marguerite de Navarre's sixteenth-century French text *L'Heptameron*, modelled after Boccaccio's *Decameron*, explores the question of how women might achieve agency and empowerment under the constraints of an aristocratic society still entangled in the tradition of courtly love. De Navarre's text rewrites Boccaccio's model so that its incomplete framed set of stories is told by an equal number of men and women. Because of the multiple narrations and commentaries on the narratives by all the characters, the text proliferates rather than forecloses meanings. As such, it might be read as a clandestine guidebook (at least for those who could read it) for subverting gender, and thus social and political roles, in sixteenth-century France. But just where this occurs in the text is difficult to pinpoint. It moves from inside a hall of mirrors – a proliferation that enables the text, in its excess, to escape, to outrun what might otherwise condemn it to obscurity. In this case, the surface of a formal and apparently orderly arrangement of narratives, surrounded by commentaries, makes the multiplicity beneath this order appear contained. In one of the tales, a widow, a woman of high birth, has sex with her son, bears a daughter, who then goes on to marry the son. The brother and sister are ignorant of their relation. But the mother has succeeded at generating, through a kind of autogenesis, a bloodline of her own! Similarly, the framed tales produce dangerous and disruptive progeny within the structure or system of dominant ideologies embodied in the discourse of commentary around the tales.

Narrative interpellates the reader with and to its structure. Without our knowing about it, without our consent. But the writer as reader can write through, with, in, that structure, experimenting with it; in effect, moving it through figures that rewrite, create Gramscian cracks in the model. Experimental narrative seems to me to be predicated first on a reading process (based on attention) that looks at the ways in which texts and genres contain their own differences. These differences and ruptures in texts suggest sites for reading or misreading the texts other than through their master narratives and provide potentially powerful locations for the construction of other subjectivities, ideologies and practices. Experimental narrative forces readers, writers, texts, genres even, to get up and move. It interrogates how texts (including itself) produce, distort, silence, ignore, delimit. Producing and critiquing indissolubly. Every text, like a body and psyche, has access to an incomplete, partial and conflicting cornucopia. But let me squeeze the last bit out. History's whirlpool. Every boundary permeable. Faced with finality, a person may determine to want after all. Take, for example, my poem *spill,* which is organized around months. They provide a momentum and imply an aging process, though not necessarily advancement or resolution. They are interrupted. Delayed. Inside and between and across them, snatches of narrative contract orgasmically, randomly. Whirlpools, excessive and mixed metaphor, metonymy, voices, theory's puppet show in shadow. Climax is always possible. Imminent. Secrets are everywhere. We can see our own cervixes or intestines live!

NOTES

1 Robin Tremblay-McGaw, *spill,* Narrativity 3.
2 Teresa de Lauretis, 'Desire in Narrative,' in A*lice Doesn't: Feminism, Semiotics, Cinema* (Bloomington: Indiana University Press, 1984).
3 Lyn Hejinian, *My Life* (Los Angeles: Sun & Moon Classics, 1987).
4 Dodie Bellamy, *The Letters of Mina Harker* (West Stockbridge, MA: Hard Press, 1998).
5 Dodie Bellamy, *Cunt-Ups* (New York: Tender Buttons, 2001).

The Tell-Tale Heart:
Dennis Cooper Interviewed by Robert Glück

Model. Reduce to the minimum the share his consciousness has. Tighten the meshing within which he cannot any longer not be him and where he can now do nothing that is not *useful*.
*
Model. Two mobile eyes in a mobile head, itself on a mobile body.
*
Models. Mechanized outwardly. Intact, virgin within.

– Robert Bresson

ROBERT GLÜCK: Let's start with Bresson.

DENNIS COOPER: My favourite Bresson film is *The Devil, Probably* (*Le Diable probablement*), mainly because its concerns are so close to my own. The first Bresson film I saw, and the one that changed my life, was *Lancelot du lac*. It's an astonishing work, though I think if I'd seen any of his other films first, it would have had the same effect. His work is so powerful and meaningful to me that I find it almost impossible to talk about. It's like his influence dawned on me rather than being something I studied into being. It's something to do with his work's concision in relationship to the ephemeral and chaotic nature of his subject matter. And that it's nothing but style and form on the one hand, and completely transparent and pure on the other. It's only concerned with emotional truth, and, at the same time, it works so hard to exclude all superficial signs of emotion. It's bleakness incarnate and yet it's almost obsessively sympathetic to the deepest human feelings in a way that can only read as hopeful. It's religious art and, yet, despite Bresson's avowed Catholicism, it seems not to depend on any religious system for answers or comfort. The fact that Bresson used only non-actors inspired me to create characters in my work who were non-characters in a sense – that is, characters who seem both unworthy of the attentions of art and incapable of collaborating with art in the traditional sense. That relationship between Bresson and his 'actors' was very key to me, and if you read his book, *Notes on Cinematography*, it's all there.

RG: I would have suggested that same aspect of Bresson's work and yours – in a sense, you both use untrained actors as characters.

When you talk about your teenage years, there is so much matter that looks forward to your mature work. There's the lyricism of dying young and sexualized, there's the waif, there's nurturing as a way to have access to feelings and romantic love, there's the dichotomy of desire that protects and desire that murders, there's the little family that random teenagers make for themselves, there's the general absence of mothers. In fact, the only mother I can think of in your work has throat cancer, so she is silenced. But more than thematically, you have built aesthetics on the depiction of teen years, especially on their complexity combined with their inarticulateness. Could you talk about that? And perhaps touch on *The Tenderness of the Wolves*?

DC: It's true that my teenaged experiences resemble my novels' subject matter, though I've never consciously written about my past, apart from the honest but not entirely truthful autobiographical passages in *My Mark* and *Guide*. I think my past functions more as a set of research materials that hopefully allows me to do the subject of teenagers justice. I've always been horrified by how teenagers are read either as quasi-children or quasi-adults, as though they're merely some kind of problematic transitional species with confused emotions and intellects. They're expected to have two effects on adults – inspire sentimental feeling and/or hold an erotic charge. If they challenge these expectations, they're considered dangerous. I think this disrespect is absolutely pervasive in American culture and is played out in a huge number of ways. As I grew up and felt myself becoming susceptible to the same convenient misperceptions that had done my peers and me such an injustice when I was young, I think I started writing about the relationship between teenagers and adults as a way to hold on to the truths I'd believed and to study them in relation to these new truths in hopes of finding an objective truth. My aesthetics developed the way they have because I conducted so many different mental and physical experiments on such a specific area of interest, I guess. I mean, in my fantasy life, in my life itself and on the page. My goal was to find a language that was native to the world of teenagers and therefore paid them unremitting and unwavering respect yet was simultaneously involved in a sophisticated, erotically charged investigation of them, so that the work seemed to mediate between the two worlds in an even-handed way. It seemed to me that if I could define the exact point where these conflicting worlds were done equal justice, the truth would then be exposed somehow, and I used my own archetypes and obsessions as touchstones as a way to keep the work absolutely honest and to keep my own interest in the project fixated and evolving. As far as I'm concerned, I didn't find my real voice until I wrote *Closer* and knew I was as ready as I'd ever be to start the project I'd always wanted to write.

My book *The Tenderness of the Wolves* was the first time I attempted to write in a serious way, especially the title poem, which kind of presaged the structural investigations I ended up using in my novels. I feel more connected to that poem sequence than I do to the long prose piece 'A Herd,' which was my first real work of fiction that wasn't complete crap. There are passages in 'A Herd' that I like, but I still had too much faith in (and inexperience with) narrative at that point, and the emotions in 'A Herd' are too qualified by sentimentality, which I think is a sign that I wasn't brave enough to confront my true feelings yet.

RG: You ended your response with the words 'true feelings.' Long ago, I started calling you a horror writer, because I wanted to show how both religion and horror explore the region between life and death. Horror and religion both bring tremendous awareness – though not always the awareness of the dying – to the instant of death. Related to that, I think there is a performance aspect to your writing, that there are true feelings to get to and display, and that the authenticity of your work is related to how far you will go, how much you will say. There is an impossible complexity of feelings in one direction, an impossible cultural complexity in another direction and a sort of below-language brute fact (of death, of matter) in a third direction, and in all directions there is the problem of articulation, which is married to your amazing powers of articulation. Oh, I recall a lovely sentence from *Guide*: 'Chris's shock was so dense and complex that it collided with the world's very different complexity, sort of like what happens when a very strong light hits a very big jewel.' So, to tease out a difficult question from all this: What do you see as the ground of authority in your work, which you were discovering in *The Tenderness of the Wolves?*

DC: 'Ground of authority' is an interesting way to try to think about what I do. My work is such a weird combination of things that are beyond my control, things that control me and things that are excessively controlled by me in an attempt to keep my work coherent and pragmatic. What I write about has such an intense hold on me, and seems so inappropriate to the world I live in, that it's left me deeply confused and split. My life and my work have been about trying to negotiate between my internal world and my external world. The pull towards horror, for lack of a better term, is very intense for me. It attacks me on so many fronts. It terrifies me, it holds an overwhelming erotic charge, it fascinates me intellectually like a puzzle or problem and it makes me feel insane and deeply emotional. If I have any authority, it derives from my kind of obsessive focus on building a craft that will get me as close as humanly possible to these things that would destroy me if I didn't have language to protect me. It's sort of like each novel is a new attempt to build something that will get me closer to the source, give me more room to move within that area and leave me less protected but safe enough to survive. In *The Tenderness of the Wolves* I found a kind of cold, pragmatic voice that I sensed would be flexible enough to allow me to approach my personal horror. I felt like it could potentially convey deep emotion, logic, the pornographic, the horrific, the analytical, the personal, the impersonal, objectivity, subjectivity, etc., all within the same voice. I wasn't able to do all that much with it at that point, but I sensed that if I experimented with it, I might eventually develop the chops I would need to make a serious effort at writing about the things that preoccupied me so ferociously. For me, the next years were purely about developing my writing. Sometimes an experiment seemed to work, like, say, *My Mark*, which is still one of my favourite things I've written, but I feel like between *The Tenderness of the Wolves* and *Closer* was an awkward phase for me where I was reading, absorbing and trying to incorporate a lot of fiction whose style and structural notions weren't necessarily right for what I wanted to do. I don't know if that answers your question. I just felt like the work I'd done before *ToW* was too personal, too self-indulgent and not critical enough of my relationship to what I was writing about. I think with *ToW* I realized that the best way for me to be the writer I wanted to be was to use myself with all my flaws and strengths as an opportunity to understand my subject matter, rather than use my subject matter as an opportunity to understand me.

RG: I see what you mean: the true feeling, which comes to equal proximity to horror, gets framed by a deadpan along with a lot of other kinds of matter – for example, a mournful isolated lyricism, and a lot of comedy too. In fact, I'd say you were one of the best parodists I can think of, that your aim is dead on. What is the relation between comedy and violence/horror in your writing?

DC: Thanks for that, Bob. Well, I think I learned a lot from the horror movie, which is a form where those things are almost always fused, and of course from Sade, who practically invented that combo. I think of my prose as being made up of a bunch of different systems that are distinct but simultaneous and interdependent. Or I should say that when I'm doing all the laborious rewriting and editing that I need to do to get my work right, I divide the various things going on in the prose into individual systems and attend to each one so that it functions correctly on its own and also services and is serviced by its fellow systems. Comedy is one of the systems, and an important one, because comedy is such a talented tone, yet it has no gravity in and of itself, so it can be used to popularize other systems that are signalling more subjective, meaningful things. It can subvert the visceral effect of represented violence without decentring the actual punch. It can distract readers long enough to ease information into them that would be too confrontational for them to absorb otherwise. It can both deflect the reader's attention away from the emotional meaning of a violent act and indicate that emotion by causing the reader to wonder why that deflection is occurring. It can signal the reader to relax, then betray his or her trust, thereby creating a particular kind of tension that can be really useful. If it's used in a novel or section of a novel where authorial intent is as important as the fiction, comedy can function as superficial entertainment while at the same time indicating a shift or tweak in the fiction's subconscious. Comedy can do a lot, and I try to use it very carefully. That might all sound like gobbledygook, but it's the way I think about comedy. It's interesting that you bring that up, because my first post-cycle novel, *My Loose Thread*, is completely devoid of comedy, and one of the projects I have in mind is a novel that would be nothing but comedy, à la Jacques Tati's great films. I think that would be a really curious challenge.

RG: What conception did you first have for the kind of novel you might want to write?

DC: I was reading a huge number of novels back then, almost all European, the majority of them French. I wanted my fiction to be really direct and complicated at the same time, and I had an idea that I wanted to write a sequence of novels that would combine to form one work, and I had a vague idea at that point that I wanted the structure of that sequence to involve a novel gradually dismembering itself, or being dismembered. So I knew I had to write a first novel that had enough material within it and a strong enough life force to sustain a series of surgeries and attacks, because I wanted to begin by having a pretty strict area to work within. I tried out a lot of different things that didn't quite work. A lot of the pieces collected in *Wrong* were attempts to begin a novel. I didn't figure it out until I moved to Amsterdam, and then *Closer* finally came together because of certain factors in my life combined with the books I read (and music I was listening to) while I was there. I think my experiences and literature and, to a certain extent, music were equally important at that point. On the life front, I'd moved there to be with someone I loved, but our relationship started falling apart almost the day I moved there, and, except for a couple of trips to visit friends in the States, I ended up living alone and basically friendless for over two years. What that did was allow me to live in an experimental and adventurous, sometimes dangerous, way that I would never have done if there'd been people around who cared enough to stop me. I did huge amounts of this strong, very cheap Dutch speed called Pep that induced this kind of psychotic state where the erotic overpowered everything yet I felt extremely objective. That in and of itself hugely influenced my prose, and was a revelation, as well as giving me the need and energy to experience real-life equivalents of my most profound and scariest fantasies first-hand, then to write about them both while I was in that state and when I was sober and myself. It helped me understand the difference between the fantasy of something and its actual nuts and bolts, and having the most extreme experiences available to me helped me understand who I was in relation to them. My experiment escalated over the course of about eight months until I found myself in one situation where things went so out of control that I was forced to make the most important decision of my life, and I made the right one, as well as scaring myself so badly that I stopped the experiment. At the same time that all of that was going on, I'd discovered the *nouveau roman*. There was a used American bookstore in Amsterdam where someone had unloaded about thirty *nouveau roman* novels by Robbe-Grillet, Robert Pinget, Claude Simon, Nathalie Saurraute, Marguerite Duras and Michel Butor, and I bought and read all of them. For some reason, in terms of literary influences, they were the final piece of the puzzle, and *Closer* came together with their help. The books I remember as being particularly helpful were Robbe-Grillet's *For a New Novel, Topography of a Phantom City* and *The Voyeur*; Pinget's *The Inquisitory, Mahu or the Material* and *Fable*; and Simon's *Triptych*. Something about those writers' interest in an objective voice and the way their experiments with narrative were terse and kind of voluptuous at the same time excited me. I should also say that *Closer* was just as heavily influenced by the styles of two rock records: *Psychocandy* by the Jesus and Mary Chain, and Joy Division's *Closer* (hence the title). Also, almost as soon as I stopped doing drugs, I got very ill. I literally couldn't get out of bed for about two months. I was illegally in Holland, and, like I said, had no one around to help me go to a doctor or anything. I thought I was dying, though it turned out that I had a severe case of German measles. That kind of drove me to finish *Closer* too, because I was horrified that I might die without having written what I believed I could.

RG: Can you describe what that most scary experience was? Perhaps it's too much for you to do, but being me, I have to ask.

DC: I can't really isolate that one experience because it was the result of months and months of related, accumulating experiences, and I don't have the space or language to explain what happened. That whole period of experiences was undertaken on behalf of my writing, and my work represents it more accurately than I could do in a situation like this. Basically, I stumbled on the entrance to a kind of secret, utterly amoral little world that existed in the nooks and crannies of Amsterdam where very extreme things went on and were made available to me. I tested myself, and I passed the test. I don't mean to be coy. You have to understand that it's just not possible to talk about those things for many reasons. What's important about that time is that I was able to inhabit a morality and state of mind that were contrary to my own, and this allowed me to write about certain things with a more even-handed understanding and authentic force than I would have had available to me otherwise. It was sort of my own weird living out of Rimbaud's incredibly attractive notion that one could access a kind of transcendent knowledge through a derangement of the senses and all that, only narrowed in this case to knowledge having specifically to do with the erotic. Long story short, what I'd gone through as a kid raised a lot of questions, and what I did in Amsterdam answered a number of them well enough to give me the clarity to write about those questions with a certain confidence.

RG: In our conversation, the way you are framing the violence and horror in your writing, you are describing the working out of inner demons. It is generous of you to do that so candidly. Now I'd like to ask, are those demons individual or global? Do you also believe horror is at the heart of the human condition, as, say, Sade or Baudelaire might have? Is that a naive question? In your books, I sort of climb my way through your voice towards you and your vision – it's a realization that comes to me through my growing friendship with your voice and feeling life as I read a particular book. I wonder if it may be your own version of self-preservation that you locate this matter inside the self – your self – so firmly. Perhaps you sort of soften the blow, or offer us an escape clause, or even try to protect us, by giving us the option of saying, Oh, that's just Dennis and his 'problems,' rather than, Now I see the darkness of my own life.

DC: I think my inclinations, proclivities and experiences provided me with an example that I could use in my work with a certain authority. That's how I think about it anyway.

I think my work is one of a million individualized attempts to understand the human condition. I.e., I'm like any other fiction writer out there. My work becomes very personalized at times, but the only thing remarkable therein is that the ideas and emotions I cop to within that strategy are those that are the most confusing and disturbing to me. I have particular gifts and interests and concerns, and they set my course as a writer, but my pursuit is everyone's pursuit: self-understanding in relationship to global understanding. To break it down, I think the inspiration behind my work is entirely mine. The content of my work is a reconciliation of what's mine to that which is familiar and of essential interest to others. My work's style and form are the result of my attempts to find the perfect balance between the pure product of my mind and a careful if necessarily limited understanding of what it takes to communicate clearly and entertainingly. Honestly, I think my work's inability to communicate with a lot of people has more to do with its politics than with its contents. I don't mean that my work is making a political statement. I just mean that my writing is guided by my world view, which I define as anarchist. When my anarchist principles meet the material I'm interested in exploring, the result is a kind of neutral, pragmatic tone with a lot of internal turmoil. I think that tone is the source a lot of confusion, specifically because it doesn't guard its readers in a traditional way. Anarchism is often confused with amorality, when in fact morality is at the very core of anarchist thought. My work assumes a basic goodness in its readers, and, within that assumption, there's a secondary assumption that this projection will create trust and goodwill. Obviously, this is a flawed strategy on my part, since it seems to lead to a lot of misunderstanding of what I do, but I don't have a choice. I just don't believe in the idea that there is a system already in place that is capable of locating the truth. I think the minute you to start to prioritize one system over another you start deluding yourself. I think if I were able to believe in God or socialism or the narrative or whatever, my work might have a better relationship with the average person who likes to read novels. But if I eliminated the contrariness and confusion in my work, I might write like Clive Barker or Stephen King, and, as much as I enjoy horror as entertainment, I'd rather go for the global the hard, maybe even wrong, way.

Sade's work identifies its enemies and uses the construction of these enemies' principles and rhetoric in the construction of its own narratives and philosophy. My work doesn't see itself as having enemies. I would never ever put myself in a class with Sade as a writer or as a thinker, God knows. But I don't think my work is any less global than his work. I think self-preservation is a motive for me, but I don't think it's the overriding reason why I locate my work inside my own archetypes and tastes and emotional touchstones and so on. I think that decision is more about keeping the work honest, controlled and full of energy.

RG: I find in your work an intense contradiction that is obviously extraordinarily generative. On one hand, isolation, horror, lyrical stasis, an idealism that is almost a gnostic anger at the material world; on the other, a meditation on community and friendship through youth culture (where a young person seeks recognition so urgently) and the tribes of young friends you often depict.

As you say, there's no reason why these two sides – or anything else – should be resolved in fiction when they can't be resolved in the world. That's being honest as a writer, though it may confuse readers who expect to find resolution in a novel. The two sides (and much else!) are not resolved but held together in a kind of performance, where I am watching how far Dennis will go, formally and content-wise. I was wanting to get at how you view the self – your own self – in your work.

I am reminded of a passage by Nabokov, where he says, somewhere in some parenthesis, 'In a first-rate work of fiction the real clash is not between the characters but between the author and the world.'

DC: I'd investigated anarchism a little in my mid-teens, but it hadn't really connected with me. I rediscovered anarchism through my love of punk rock. It was referenced a lot by punk artists and by people writing about punk, so I read a number of books about it. It just made absolute sense to me, especially as articulated by Emma Goldman. The impracticality of revising society into an ideal anarchist state was obvious, so it appealed to me more as a philosophy, although if there's ever a viable revolution I'll definitely join the front lines, and anarchist action groups have my heart. But I do think that all structures created to impose order of any kind are inherently corrupt and that the quest for personal power within the context of America's notion of democracy is at the root of every extant problem here. Obviously, my thinking is a lot more highly detailed than that, but I don't know that it's so useful to this situation to go in to all of that at sufficient length. I think that to live a life informed by anarchist principles in the United States is a reasonably doable if inherently compromised thing that can be boiled way down to a basic rule: as soon as you get power, disperse it. For me, that simple idea reverberates out through instinct into a way of thinking about everything. I think my novels are entirely informed by anarchism on the levels of form, style, approach and philosophy. They enunciate what happens when one anarchist point of view is applied to situations in which the principles behind that form of anarchism are the most severely tested. My characters, however configurative in some cases, act on their own devices, and I think in some way their culture is responsible for the problems that their minds conceive and their actions create. That's why the blame in my work seems so generalized and why its morality seems to lack clear foundations. Anarchy's problem in terms of public perception is that it divests itself of the kinds of signifiers that more politically correct belief systems have no problem utilizing to their advantage. I think my work shares this dilemma. In sort of the same way that an anarchist who acts on his or her principles and attempts to recreate society by the means available to a revolutionary becomes a radical leftist by default, I think the particular nature of my work and the means available to me to make it as public as possible cause it to become an experimental novel by default. That's the huge and insurmountable flaw in the kind of work I've tried to do, and I just try to face the music with an open mind and as much pragmatism as I can muster, I guess.

RG: You put amazing pressure on language and make a distinctive sentence, recognizably yours when it's baroque and when it's truncated and blunt. What is language to you as a medium? How do you think of sentence? How has that thinking changed over the years?

DC: My relationship to the sentence changes all the time, or I feel like it does. Early on, say in *SAFE*, I was interested in overloading my sentences with internal rhymes and rhythms and extensions and shortcuts so that flow of the narrative would feel laboured and unnatural, and the work's artfulness would come off like a meaningful burden. I wanted the work to be about the cruel, self-defeating nature of aestheticism itself, and how art could only short-circuit in relation to experiences that were too deep or frightening or complex to be represented by language. I felt, and still feel, that when language tries to encompass those kinds of experiences, it becomes overly infected with the consciousness of the artist who tries to represent them and, as a result, it flatters the artist and lies to the audience. It's kind of heretical to say, but I think that's a problem in the work of Genet, for instance. In hindsight, I think the approach I took in *SAFE* and other works from that period was kind of at odds with my particular talents. In the cycle of five novels, I pared the prose down while paying the same obsessive attention to the construction of each sentence and the physical relationship between the sentences, and I think I found the right balance. Even so, the cycle ends on a note of surrender – form and style reduced to performing a magic trick that tries and fails to make the content disappear. But at least I think I was able to fully explore and represent the problem in those five novels, and I feel satisfied that I achieved my goals as best I can. Now, post-cycle, I'm interested in making the art in the sentences more invisible, more subterranean, and weighting the work more towards a realistic or documentary-style take on whatever characters and situations I decide to write about. On that level, my new novel *My Loose Thread* is maybe the beginning of the work I want to do. We'll see.

Dislocation

Shiver

Approximate:
Past to Present

Methods

The Sentence

The Novel

Resistance

**The Buzz of
Alternate Meanings**

A Story Is
a Storiage

My Other Self

The Avenue
Laird Hunt

> In my skull is an avenue I stroke
>
> – Clark Coolidge

There is an avenue in my skull too – albeit one that is poorly maintained, cavernously pitted, strewn with rubble, whole segments blasted away; one that is curved, possibly circular, that, like the backgrounds in cartoons, maddeningly repeats itself; one that is ill-marked, with many a false turnoff and many a false vista; one that is skewed of proportion, that is frequently unsafe, almost always unsavoury; one that is troubled by converging lanes, of which there are hundreds, that even resembles a parking lot in places and is probably haunted – *hell of a place*. And yet, *I, narrator*, stroke it, speak through its mess, speak of its mess, multiply it. It's an interesting dilemma – aspects of which are taken up in Adorno's seminal essay on the place of the narrator in the contemporary novel – the narrator, with no story to narrate, *narrates anyway,* a story that has been blown to bits. Of course not everyone sees it that way. We live in *an age of errata, of misinformation, of disinformation, of hoax*; perhaps it is little wonder that there continues to be such a hunger for narratives that, as Adorno describes them, largely by way of nineteenth-century techniques *mimic the real*; that say to us, with disarming earnestness, this, my friends, is *how it was*. In the domain of the fictive narrative, I tend to have little patience for such works. I am much more interested in (and seem capable of constructing only) narratives that are to some degree aware of *the provisional nature of their own authority*, in which *the fictive quality of recollection* is acknowledged, in which *forgetting* is considered the key constituent of memory, and in which, finally, getting it right shares centre stage with getting it wrong.

In my skull is an avenue I stroke
It seems likely I might be alone in seeing in these eight words, words ripped right out of their contexts, a possible model for narrative.

hell of a place
For some years now Brenda Coultas, in her narratives, has been conjuring worlds to which multiple qualities of the preceding

description might apply. Whether in her book *Early Films* or in her recent collection, *A Handmade Museum*, Coultas is engaged in constructing usefully disjunctive, lyric-enhanced investigations into landscapes that have come apart. For me, part of the great thing about Coultas's writing is that she brings an indomitable hunger for beauty to bear on her cracked and spilling subjects.

I, narrator
E.g., Pamela Lu's terrific *Pamela: A Novel*. A *Bildungsroman* of sorts, an intricate chronicle of the coming awake of a highly syntaxed consciousness, in which the greater part of the narrative seems to occur in between commas.

narrates anyway
'The expression that there is nothing to express, nothing with which to express, nothing from which to express, no power to express, no desire to express, together with the obligation to express.' – Samuel Beckett (in a 1949 conversation with Georges Duthuit)[1]

an age of errata, of misinformation, of disinformation, of hoax
The tendered premise in a 1997 episode of *The X-Files*: since World War Two, Americans have had an unquenchable appetite for 'bogus revelation'; having determined this, the United States government has built, presumably as a cover for its more radical weapons-of-mass-destruction programs, an elaborate web of alien abduction and sighting hoaxes. This hoax, we are led to believe, may or may not be one. At the end, intrigued to a ghastly degree, we are left both believing (the elements of documentary inherent in *The X-Files* aiding this process) that there are aliens around and that the government has cooked up (and deployed) weapons even more diabolical than the ones it has copped to. This TV 'fiction' seems to me only slightly less credible than what the evening news, reporting live from the White House! serves up, or than the gamut of what can be found gathered up daily in the *New York Times*. (The day after watching the *X-Files* episode I read allegations by Puerto Rican petitioners at the United Nations that the United States government was testing uranium-capped bullets at its facility on Vieques Island; during the debate an Iraqi delegate stated that similar weapons had been used during the Gulf War.)

mimic the real

Harry Mathews, who, in part of his work, has vertiginously built upon (see *The Conversions* and *Tlooth*, recently reissued by Dalkey Archive) the wonderful, strange narratives of Raymond Roussel, had this to say in a recent interview in *Rain Taxi*: 'The great discovery I made through him [Roussel] was that you didn't have to write about what happened the day you fell in the swimming pool, but that you could invent your own swimming pool that had never existed before, full of quicksilver, lighted by imaginary lamps.'[2] Which, abstracted, might lead to a formula something like: the writer is in the world; the writing is in the writer. Or, looking at it from a reader-oriented perspective, we might arrive at: the writing is in the reader; the reader is in the world. Either way we are dealing with a considerable degree of mediation. One I am interested in.

how it was

'The more strictly the novel adheres to realism in external things, to the gesture that says "this is how it was," the more every word becomes a mere "as if," and the greater becomes the contradiction between this claim and the fact that it was not so.' – Theodor Adorno[3]

the provisional nature of their own authority

Among contemporary works, the narratives of W. G. Sebald are exemplary in this regard, pointing up, as they do, against the backdrop of the bloody twentieth century (and with an aperçu of others), the enormous difficulty of fixing experience, both personal and collective. Keith Waldrop's harrowing memoir *Light While There Is Light* (which calls itself fiction) is another example. As is David Markson's intriguing *Wittgenstein's Mistress*.

the fictive quality of recollection

Ryunosuke Akutagawa brilliantly treats aspects of this in a pair of stories which were later combined and made into the much more famous film *Rashomon* by Akira Kurosawa. Aaron Shurin writes, in passing, in his 1990 essay 'Narrativity,'[4] of the 'irreversible solidity of the past tense.' I've lately begun to marvel, because of this generally ascribed quality, that History continues to be written in it. It was Herodotus, Father of History, who kicked things off – neatly blending directly observed incident/object with reported incident/object with rumoured incident/object with imagined incident/object. At least a good part of what gets built into the past tense, then, hardly irreversible, hardly solid. Pretty slippery, in fact.

forgetting
Walter Benjamin writes beautifully on this in the opening pages of his essay 'The Image of Proust' (*Illuminations*):

> For the important thing for the remembering author is not what he experienced, but the weaving of his memory, the Penelope work of recollection. Or should one call it, rather, a Penelope work of forgetting? Is not the involuntary recollection, Proust's *memoire involuntaire*, much closer to forgetting than what is usually called memory? And is not this work of spontaneous recollection, in which remembering is the woof and forgetting the warf, a counterpart to Penelope's work rather than its likeness? For here the day unravels what the night has woven. When we awake each morning, we hold in our hands, usually weakly and loosely, but a few fringes of the tapestry of lived life, as loomed for us by forgetting. However, with our purposeful activity and, even more, our purposive remembering each day unravels the web and the ornaments of forgetting. This is why Proust finally turned his days into nights, devoting all his hours to undisturbed work in his darkened room with artificial illumination, so that none of those intricate arabesques might escape him.[5]

NOTES

1 Samuel Beckett, 'Three Dialogues with Georges Duthuit,' in *A Samuel Beckett Reader*, ed. John Calder (London: Picador, 1983), 204–5.
2 *Rain Taxi* vol. 3 no. 4 (winter 1998–99).
3 Theodor W. Adorno, 'The Position of the Narrator in the Contemporary Novel,' in *Notes to Literature Vol. 1*, ed. Rolf Tiedermann, trans. Shierry Weber Nicholsen (New York: Columbia University Press, 1991).
4 See <http://www.sfsu.edu/~poetry/narrativity/issue_two/shurin.html>.
5 Walter Benjamin, 'The Image of Proust,' in *Illuminations*, ed. Hannah Arendt, trans. Harry Zohn (New York: Schocken Books, 1969), 202.

Narrative as Determination of the Future Anterior
Michael du Plessis

Narrative, it seems banal to observe, opens a space. This space is not so much a place of play for unlimited possibilities (although in the best of possible worlds it might yet be) as somewhere determined, always, in advance, by the future anterior: what will have happened and how it will already have taken place lure us through stories to their ends, become the end that shines through from the very start. Reading for the ending: in narrative, the end justifies the means; the end is the means.

That is why the distinction so frequently drawn between plot and story, *fabula* and *sjuzhet*, while handy, turns most provocative precisely when it cannot be made, when the temptation is there for us to make it as readers, when the way to do it seems at hand, but we are stopped ultimately from completing it. Too many Cliffs Notes to *The Sound and the Fury* have made modernist plot-story scramblings predictable, easy to read. But still we watch out for when the story turns out to be such that its arrangement prevents us from decrypting, excavating it. The end (the story) stymies the means (the plot) and vice versa.

At the end of 'Leopoldina's Dream' by Silvina Ocampo,[1] we find out that the story has been told, not by a human narrator as we may have assumed in our anthropomorphic self-satisfaction, but by a little dog who, along with his mistress, Leopoldina, has – Virgin Mary-like – been assumed into Heaven. We are left with the puzzle of where this story, this plot, this narrative enunciation, could have come from. Heaven? A dream of Heaven? The end crosses the means; the story undoes the plot. More, since the first part of the story concerns Leopoldina's miraculous ability to bring back objects from her dreams, the tale, narrative itself here, resembles one of these objects, brought back, mysteriously, from some other place, dream world or Heaven. Leopoldina's dream-objects, much to the frustration of the little girls she looks after, are poor things, stones, grass. The narrative, likewise, is a poor object, a mundane miracle, produced by the simple yet frustratingly seductive crossing of narrative options.

Christopher Priest's novel of the everyday miraculous, *The Glamour*,[2] deals with invisibility so as to intertwine plot and story in a way that seems relatively straightforward at the beginning, only to turn into a tangle, a conundrum, at the end, much more so than the flashier (hence, more reassuring) experiments of the *nouveau roman* or overtly experimental fiction. Especially intriguing is that the marvellously banal object in this novel is nothing more than a holiday postcard with the most clichéd of messages, 'Wish you were here,' inscribed on it. At the end of *The Glamour*, we do not know, will never know, who 'you' could be or where even 'here' is. It is a perfect emblem of the entanglements of the future anterior in narrativity, in which every story told seduces us with the ordinary magic, the wish that 'you' (but who?) be 'here' (but where?). Indeed, every narrative, at least for me, seems a charm to produce the effect that you are always, have always been, here in advance. Perhaps that is why narrativity depends on the déjà vu of intertextuality.

In transgender narratives, specifically, the end exculpates the means: this is how I became what I am at the end of the story. What I will have become forms the narrative I am telling. What I will already have been justifies what I will have told. They've 'always already' (surprise) been the sex of their determination, announce the new theory-heads of transgender studies. Much like the coming-out narrative or the *Bildungsroman*, transgender narratives depend on the unification of what is told with the site from which it is told, enounced closed onto enunciation. As such, the distinction that is sometimes drawn between 'traditional' transsexual autobiography (Christine Jorgensen, Mario Martino, Jan Morris) and 'postmodern' transsexual autobiography (Kate Bornstein, Loren Cameron, perhaps Leslie Feinberg) seems untenable. But rock 'n' roll, punk and glam, tore down that distinction, got there first, so the two autobiographies that really matter are Jayne County's *Man Enough to Be a Woman* and Bambi Lake's *The Unsinkable Bambi Lake*. And also Holly Woodlawn's irresistible *A Low Life in High Heels*. The transsexual narrative that seduces, that persuades, is the one that can place transsexuality not as personal anomaly but as socially determined narrative, simultaneously constructed and inevitable. It's a 'conundrum,' to cite the title of Jan Morris's somewhat humdrum transsexual autobiography.

Transsexual subjects, like everyone else, find that our stories are hopelessly entangled with every other story, so there can never be 'a' transsexual narrative, only narratives braided with, placed inside, other narratives. To discover this is to see that transsexuality is never the out-of-place, but there, already, always. By offering narrative implicitly as etiology, autobiography runs the risk of sliding into explanation: 'this is how I became who I am' turns into 'that is why I became who I am.' By accounting for what purportedly causes trans-sexuality, narrative implies that those causes are avoidable, preventa-ble. Etiology and explanation serve then, in the last analysis, to explain transsexuality away, out of existence. Narrative as the neat coordina-tion of plot and story resembles a rabbit-out-of-the-hat trick: here I turn up where I hid myself in the first place. Better than that old trick to make transsexual self-writing a disappearing act. A genuine trick – the lady (or gentleman) vanishes; the magician and his assistant are genuinely puzzled.

'Hormones, Germs, and Cancer (This Is Not an Autobiography)'[3] was written in reaction to the now seemingly inescapable demand for autobiographical narrative ('anecdote' used to be the term) in 'queer theory,' the way that criticism has been overtaken by self-writing of a particularly dull, and un-self-critical sort (the kind of coy self-disclo-sure one finds in the pages of Eve Sedgwick or D. A. Miller). It was also written in response to demands to provide authentication for my own work by accounting for my 'own' gender, my 'self.' After one such request – after I had taught a course on film and transsexuality – a student asked me what my interest in the subject could be. The demand for some narrative production of the self was palpable, if veiled in talk of academic 'interest,' as it often is. I was tempted to reply that I was a college professor by day but a transvestite hooker at night, a tenure-track version of that eighties exploitation film series called *Angel*.[4] Angel, as I recall, was an honour student by day and a new-wave Hollywood streetwalker by night. Angel, I imagined, saved up her money, went to college, then on to graduate school sometime during the heyday of 'theory,' before accepting the inevitable tenure-track position only to find that she still wasn't quite making ends meet. Oh well, Angel soon was back on the streets, forgetting to mention that she was different down there ... If only Angel had realized at the start that college, graduate school and a tenure-track position would bring her back, all these years later, to where she began!

Perhaps one way of making readily packaged and reassuring narra-tives (how I got to be what I already was) a little bit stranger, of giving back to them the everyday oddness they should possess, is to render them not so much as 'I am (will be) where I wished to be (already have been),' but as the more enigmatically familiar 'Wish you were here.' In lieu of a narrative of arrival and appearance (coming out or becoming) what appeals to me is the tale of disappearance: the glamour of invisibility, of rising skywards.

Dream-objects, postcards addressed to no one from nowhere, narrative loops, models of nothing: we search to find what has been written, which may be what we have never read before.

NOTES

1 Silvina Ocampo, 'Leopoldina's Dream,' in *Leopoldina's Dream*, trans. Daniel Balderstam (London: Penguin, 1988), 199–204.

2 Christopher Priest, *The Glamour* (New York: Doubleday, 1985).

3 Michael du Plessis, 'Hormones, Germs, and Cancer (This Is Not an Autobiography),' *Narrativity* 3, <http://www.sfsu.edu/~poetry/narrativity/issuethree_toc.html>.

4 Robert Vincent O'Neil, dir. *Angel*, 1984; Robert Vincent O'Neil, dir. *Avenging Angel*, 1985; Tom De Simone, dir. *Angel 3: The Final Chapter*, 1988.

a narrative of resistance

kari edwards

recently I went to a 'I am a _____(fill in the blank) and I am beautiful and sexy and I am ok with who I am no matter what you say' performance. the fill in the blank in this case could be any word that describes a category or any group of nouns that describe a category that is recognizable within the repeatable patterns of situated narratives. this is not a judgment. the 'I am this _____(fill in the blank)?' is a first step in seeing one's self as other than formlessness situated in social shame. but should this be the stopping point? does it do anything more than reinforce the 'I' as the ultimate achievement, where the endgame is the epiphany of late capitalism – to become a consuming self-controlling anorexic life form on automatic. are we here to be consumers by buying our way into an endless cycle of unexamined representations of the grand tale, a reiteration of the heroic journey, or a story with a moral? I am not interested in morals. morals situate one within the economy of labels and finality. as whatever said in *a day in the life of p.*, writing an article for the *psycalene quarterly*: 'to the funeral ball – to the bat-n-ball, hand shaken going on at the funeral ball.'

I am not interested in situating myself in a state of subjugation, 'or a felonious definition that creates a category.' on the other hand, trying to escape from this multi-labelling assembly line at the commodification factory is like a fish trying to open a franchise of mcdonalds ... it is not a probability, though it might be possible. the possible we live out of has as many options as the impossible ... I want to explore the possibilities hidden away in dark rooms, the unnamed and unseen ... I want to experiment with new ways to articulate which do not situate the inarticulate in 'a larger than persephone cast iron cog with teeth of cement blocks,' and at the same time I want to affirm our humanity while calling attention to flagrant lapses of institutionalized thoughtlessness. whether we were dropped off here by someone's god, or by accident, there is too much suffering and destruction going on for the story to always be about the 'me' theme in personal 'I' narratives.

so then what is a narrative of resistance? what is a narrative that informs and resists at the same time? what is this miracle and how did I get here? is there a stable body? can there be more than twenty pronouns?

words become important in the act of resistance. just for the record, I am a self-proclaimed deviant and all that that can mean. it's just a word, right? *deviant* is like *queer*, but more so; I deviate as much as possible from moral norms ... or social norms, right path or a proper code of conduct, proper spelling, right grammar, right way to be, here to serve someone's god and country. this doesn't mean 'anything goes' – the task remains and is always about reducing suffering.

the implementation of the social contract is not working. there is too much suffering and destruction going on and I/we need to deviate from this path of institutional subjugation. in *a day in the life of p.*, p., the main character, is 'referred to as sometimes, something, whatever – or both.' are we not all a both or whatever sometimes? and a whatever as we glide through our own positional grid, qualitatively changing with each passing event. we can pick and/or choose (as much as one is able) multiple categorie(s) to situate in, if we choose to pick a category at all. there is also the possibility that no matter how (well) positioned we think we are in a category of our choosing, we can experience a sudden shift in position as a result of being subjugated by another's gaze. this dance with a narrative of resistance started for me when I 'discovered I was writing this secret diary, totally unaware of the fact that I was keeping this secret diary ... (but) there was always this feeling I was doing something I didn't know I was doing.' I began reading books that allowed me to say, 'oh, there are others like me, and they all did similar x, y and z things.' finding these connections with others is important, if not critical, to resistance. having a language to speak one's truth is a critical tool for resistance, but if one stays in an identifiable category it does not create an environment of resistance. just the opposite happens. recognizable means something is repeatable enough to be seen as a noun which can be situated in a category. one becomes a target for new markets. or one becomes a member of a group locked into the diagnostic and statistical manual of mental disorders (DSM-IV). so shifting and causing interference, not knowing where the 'I' is going, creates the possible out of the impossible and reinforces resistance with information jolts to the system. you could say practice 'being a campaign of personal espionage,' 'as was done with those who went over niagara falls in a log cabin, or when someone landed in a distant field in the wrong direction.' what becomes important is new systems, 'all split atoms should have their own zip code.' new approaches to open new areas in life which one does not know one does not know, 'write one thing that relates to each of the past 14 million years, in large print.'

we need to explore the hidden possible, 'like truffles on parade,' from out of dark edges or lost words that take place in the path of personal narrative. we need to shift, transform, find multi-connections and use distortion to swerve out of the way of the oncoming train. not the known past which situates into further subjugation. there are new connections. seeking out multiple connections creates new systems that take us into communities where we wouldn't normally go – the more we can get outside ourselves the more we can connect with others. 'truth=maybe.'

all this brings back the question of how, in a language that situates, does one write a narrative of resistance for the inarticulate? lean towards deviation, migration, position shifting, slipping in and out of focus. try to find alliances that go in the same direction by a different track. these corollaries that get lost in their own direction challenge the 'find myself' narrative. this is a tool for disruption, activism, acts of personal and public empowerment. give back to the community, with glorious havoc, and generate new possibilities. as 'p.' stated, 'remember – all prescribed incidents are nothing more than obligatory super rantings ... with a sigh of relief from nowhere.'

NOTES

all quotes are taken from:

kari edwards, *iduna* (Berkeley: OBooks, 2003); *a day in the life of p.* (New York: Subpress, 2002); *diary of lies* (New York: Boog Literature, 2002).

What Story Will Love You Like I Do?

Aja Couchois Duncan

> Come in with your words ... today it is they that are giving
> feast.
>
> – Reb Emat, né Edmond Jabès[1]

More than blood and tendon, fascia and nerve, the body is historic, a
document, a marker of event and time. The body is narrative.

But the body is not solid; it is viscous, almost fluid. You can permeate the
body, but you lose your distinction. The body will swallow you whole.

Writing, like love, is an immersion in the body.

To write is to probe this mucosity, to enter the mess.

Come with me, she says, and I do.

Before we are hungry, after we are consumed. Desire and decay are the
hot breath of language.

*We are but eyes, a nose, the slippery tongue. Such quivering at the briefest
touch.*

Making art is an arrogance of the senses. Writing is an attempt to
resuscitate the pleasures of love.

*'Love, therefore, assumes the status of a cynosure, when in truth it is but an
outward manifestation of the internal discourse of returning.'*[2]

But returning is not closure. And narrative is without end.

*

We know culture the same way we know the body; there are markers,
symbols, rituals, events. And like the body, culture is multitudinous,
discordant, beyond its disparate recordings.

As scribes we document our world. But 'the surfaces are complex, looping.'[3]

Like the continuous and contiguous script, our words are a sketch of ourselves, a map of us looking.

In western cartography, 'the primary document is the physical map ... the conventions of scale, longitude, latitude, direction, and relative location are believed to "scientifically" depict a static landscape.'[4]

'The simple fact of drawing up a map could give an overview and initial mastery of the culture inscribed on the land.' Or so we thought.[5]

The planet shifts and undulates, spits volcanic blood. Particles explode. This movement mirrors a deeper one; our atoms are on fire.

Despite a technology that literally allows us to hover above, seemingly outside, we are not separate from a 'landscape shaped by history, geography, human belief and experience, and an ever-present spiritual world.'[6]

An exploratory narrative resists the fixity of a panoptic view. Not because we are unable to look down, but because we are also always looking up; in neither position are we alone.

'We move in ourselves, as the moon in the gold of its fine skin, as the current in the laugh of the river. Entangled, we are our universe.'[7]

*

I have no idea where the river begins. But to write it births its mouth.

'Tonight, I am the ground, though my hand can hardly endure the next world lying inside of it.'[8]

In the story of myself I am other. In the story of the other, she is I. This is the problem with ethnography.

To describe nature, to define culture, to mark the boundaries of the natural and scientific world, ethnographers document events, make lists, chart births and deaths and name the activities that accompany them. 'Beneath the surface, though, their texts are more unruly, discordant.'[9]

What is ethnography but story? A description of us versus them, through which we are more sharply defined by our onerous absence and they are more actively obscured by their imagined presence. This is the arc of fiction, a story about one figure's journey, one culture's progress through the clearly delineated muck.

In traditional ethnography, the culture is stuck. 'It is easier to register the loss of traditional orders of difference than to perceive the emergence of new ones.'[10] Fiction can be similarly restrictive. The characters form, unravel, reform in known patterns of struggle. The patterns themselves are sentimental gestures.

The author too is looking back. Yet she is invisible, free of subject, distanced from event. Where does she rest? Who is she? What has become of her scent?

*

'One morning ... sitting up in bed, I noticed that I had overnight been sawed apart from top to bottom. Ever since, I have vainly tried to save both halves of myself.'[11]

If the nascent moment of identity occurs before the mirror, then the nascent moment of story occurs with injury, a scab torn free of its wound.

This notion of narrative has emerged as an increasingly influential and, so it is argued, integrating paradigm within psychology. A psychosis is just a different story.

The walls hummed and the bed was a plane of electrical current. This was not surprising. Her greatest fear was a man whose hands conducted electricity.

Delusion, like desire, like loneliness, is not from without, but from within. In the ongoing myth of our madness we speak to god, we witness the mechanizations of a coercive government, we kill because we are told we must. These are the themes of our collective story: religion, society, war. Madness is a seductive author.

Do you feel the ground pulsating, she asks me. Yes, I say, and I do.

*

When we dream, the figures who fill our mindscape are amalgams. Yet we wake knowing the faces were hung incorrectly, the voices dubbed. Our dreams are disorientations, a rupture of our waking narrative structures. But dreams, like madness, create their own order.

She dreams the white-hot current of time. The borders are terrifyingly soothing, a robin's egg blue.

In waking, the borders are walls, the current stagnant air. But between day and night lies possibility, a landscape swelling and sloughing its own geography, so that within dusk and dawn there is no map. It is here we find love, here that language is ravenous and indifferent. A trickster, this story defies your own.

'Give me night itself ... a myriad corner continuing; in your wrist and foot such arrival ... lid and dark lash ... I can hardly say what elbow there is in the course of your river; nor what dark birds fly opposite our sleeping together, what winter oncoming.'[12]

*

If our lives have already been lived, if we are learning and unlearning the same lessons, then we are living a fixed narrative. Such possibility is without colour or sound; it is the absence which I flee.

To write is to leak past the margin of experience into the unknown. Even if we only glimpse this place of saturation, we are drawn to its gaze.

Touch me, she says, and I do.
'The skin contains endlessness.'[13] And our hands hover above this rich

expanse. Though we describe this desire, it is beyond our recounting.

The act of writing is a narrative of suturing, gesture and bounty, damage and mess.

'In fact there is no theory that is not a fragment, carefully prepared, of some autobiography.'[14] And this too is story.

NOTES

1 Edmond Jabès, *The Book of Questions, Volume 1* (Middletown, CT: Wesleyan University Press, 1991).

2 John Keene, *Annotations* (New York: New Directions, 1995).

3 James Clifford, *The Predicament of Culture* (Cambridge, MA: Harvard University Press, 1988).

4 Mark Warhus, *Another America: Native American Maps and the History of Our Land* (New York: St. Martin's Press, 1997).

5 Clifford.

6 Warhus.

7 Jabès.

8 Li-Young Lee, *The Winged Seed* (New York: Simon & Schuster, 1995).

9 Clifford.

10 Ibid.

11 Jabès.

12 Lee.

13 Lyn Hejinian, *The Language of Inquiry* (Berkeley: University of California Press, 2000).

14 Paul Valéry. *Analects* (as quoted in Hejinian).

what is the story here?
Daphne Marlatt

or

Say what?

hearing how language sounds the various aspects of what we live in and how it falls silent against its own structural patterns (limit to what it can articulate). the linearity of the standard english sentence carries the arc of narrative and tends to overwrite what doesn't obviously lead somewhere: the synchronic nature of the perceptual sensorium we inhabit – registered as 'background noise' – the buzz of alternate meanings around the one the sentence keeps building towards.

in this buzz radiates distraction. the dis-parate, the dis-attracted. eddying off the outer edges of a meaning that moves towards some it, some at to which it is fatally attracted.

so, on a larger scale of narrative, the story of 'our' culture – how sound its back-eddies? its gaps? or register who or what gets erased in the momentum of a single-minded narrative impelled to complete itself?

suspicious, then, of narrative and the master-narratives of our time, yet drawn to some form of development (narrative in its un-mastered form – a novel in disparate bits perhaps?), i'm also drawn, if not to poetry, to the intensive use of language that is usual to poetry and the resonating space it occupies. that space on a page that is less silence than sound-box. space that can function as readily between isolated units of prose as between and around the groups of lines we call stanzas.

it seems to me that poetry has ears, not only for sound (music) but also for semantic contiguity, touchings on – even across different keys, various registers of discourse. this reaching to touch another life embodied in speech. brought across in the lightest of connections: semantic branchings, bristly auras of meaning that detour narrative's rush.

so questions keep occurring in the ongoing instant of her/your/my fictive hand as it hovers over the keyboard, about to catch the drift, say, of a particular memory as it crosses the street of public history – is this the beginning of story? and whose? and who else or what else is sounded, standing there in the shadows of the sidetrack?

their relation in a dis(at)tracted narrative

C'est la mer allée[1]

radio, radio *La mer* ...

tuned in, in relation to

upstairs blue birch heaven, birch and apple, houses across the alley obscured by summer's luxuriance, cherry leafage, apple bouyant sea

between each wave the semantic, note(s), a gap –

and she will be late if she keeps playing with water the way her sisters

water 'say what'

you remember – what is it you remember

... *avec le soleil.*

... *at the back of my mind there is always that whisper, that's what makes me so impatient – at cocktail parties, at 'evenings' something cries out 'there isn't time – there isn't time.'*[2]

furor scribendi. rapid gust with frantic signage. twig calligraphy

indie cipherabl

The language is there, one can do what one wants with it. But it is our bodies: right away we are well ordered, already dressed.[3]

where, here

　　　branches

NOTES

1 Arthur Rimbaud, 'L'Eternité,' part iii of 'Fêtes de la patience' (1871), in *Oeuvres*, ed. Henri Matarasso (Paris: Fernand Hazan, 1956), 151.

2 Marian Scott, from her 1937 diary, quoted by Esther Trépannier in *Marian Dale Scott: Pioneer of Modern Art* (Montréal: Musée du Québec, 2000), 93.

3 Hélène Cixous, *Hélène Cixous: Rootprints: Memory and Life Writing*, trans. Eric Prenowitz (London, New York: Routledge, 1997), 61.

Hey, Narrativity
Paul VanDeCarr

I have a tattoo of Bugs Bunny's head on my arm. The original impetus for getting it, well, besides having a tattoo artist friend who offered me some free work, was to have this cross-dressing trickster figure looking up at me as a reminder, or a badge of humour. It did not occur to me then what people have repeatedly told me since, namely that Bugs's pose – with his arms folded behind his head in an expression of relaxed pleasure – gives the distinct impression that he is in the middle of getting a blow job. As I say, I did not think of this when I got the tattoo, but I must admit to liking the added meaning.

Bugs Bunny, like other, more ancient tricksters, is a shape-shifter – switching gender, role, appearance, attitude. I personally associate this kind of protean quality with homosexuality and gender-fucking (an association that is accurate for some trickster figures and their respective folkloric traditions). Add to this the whole blow-job dealie and, for me, what you get is a furry humourist who takes pleasure in changing form. This is all a roundabout way of saying that this is precisely one of my own interests, a kind of literary transvestism, dressing words up in drag so as to change form and person.

In the accompanying pieces, what I mean to do is change form so as to gain access to *Narrativity*. These various submission query letters are, like most any query letter, a way of gaining entry. They vary in their posture to the publication – demanding, dazed, querulous or even blurring the distinction between submitting to the publication in literary and sexual ways. I come knocking on *Narrativity*'s door by turns in the shape of a suitor, a plaintiff, a (hapless) menace. Form interests me partly because of its implied use of expectation on the part of the reader. By dressing up as a query letter (if there can be fairly said to be anything beneath the language, or is it just me?), I mean to shake the reader's proverbial soda can of anticipation about what the query letter intends. (Please pardon the mixed metaphor.)

The sort of shape-shifting or transvestism could be seen as deceptive. But I mean to be no more disingenuous than a sort of bad drag queen. (Believe me, I personally am too gawky to pull off anything but a sort of Halloweenish drag – it's embarrassingly heterosexual-seeming.) Bad drag, or rather, pathetic drag (in that it inspires pathos) is drag as drag. Consider me a Bugs Bunny, all dressed up in fruit as Carmen Miranda, in search of an Oscar.

*

Dear Narrativity:

I came across your 'journal' online, and was intrigued. It is unlike anything I've seen before. The title is out of sight. However, it is suspiciously close to *Native Titty*; do you all sit around jerking off to nudie pictures in *National Geographic*? (LOL!) Or do you just 'deconstruct' it? Or are you *NarrativiTV*, something like a cross-dresser who tells stories. Or is it *NarraTVty*, in which case you like to watch your stories on television? My favourite is *As the World Turns*. (;-)) (A parenthetical smiley-winky face, or maybe a guy with a toupee and a double-chin, like my uncle.) Or better yet, you're like *NarraTVTV*, a cross-dresser on the tube, like Jack on *Will and Grace*!!

Anyway, I would like to write an article for *Narrativity*. Please write and tell me how many words to write and in what format – is e-mail submission okay?

My article or story will be good for *Narrativity* because you'll learn something from it. Perhaps no one has been brave enough to tell you this but your style is kind of weird because (a) you're supposed to be about stories but there are no stories in there at all that I can see, and (b) you're supposed to be a journal but your entries aren't dated and your style is totally unlike a journal – and I should know, because I am the author of this pretty popular weblog which has gotten lots of hits and maybe I could help you publicize your journal because it's pretty hard to find. (LOL!!) So I think you've probably got a lot to learn from whatever article I write for you.

In a lot of my stories on my weblog, I begin at the beginning and middle in the middle and finish at the ending – though I have been known to be 'experimental' at times. Now I have heard some about postmodernism, but some of that ~~shit stuff~~ sh*t is just so boring! Why 'destabilize conventional narrative' as someone once said, when it's much easier to catch bees with honey? I know that what you're trying to do is get people to examine stories – it's like my English teacher Mrs. Weiner says, 'Go back to the text' – but you're going about it all wrong, you're going back to before the text, you have totally overshot your destination!!! Besides, by 'dislocating' people, all you're doing is making them feel lost and angry, and you end up hurting the very same people you say you are trying to help.

Okay, so please tell me how many words you want, and if there are any special formatting requests you have. Thanks and good luck.

Sincerely,
Paul VanDeCarr

P.S. How much do you pay?

*

Dear Editors:

I am writing to submit to your journal. May I suggest? I have some sense of your style – which pocket your hanky is in, so to speak – so let me tell you my intentions.

I am looking for a way into you. You're asking for it, you know, you're bottoms up, but then just when I'm ready you turn. You make me read you, decode you, scale your sheer language – fractured, yes, but sheer.

I am looking for your password, trying all the combinations. I'll quote Althusser, Augustine, Barthes, Benjamin for you, whisper them in your ear. I'll quote Althusser, Augustine, Benjamin, Barthes for you, in the original yet. I'll be Nabokov for you, your pale fire burning slow to dark.

I am trying to cohere, just enough to be something like a story, but loose enough that it all threatens to become unbounded, collage, maybe nonsense. I will scatter, come at you from all sides, invade you maybe infect you. Give you a fever and make you want it.

I am waiting for you now. Follow these words to their beginning, jumping-atop-railroad-cars-up-to-the-locomotive> You'll find me there, wondering if you've been chased. But the scene dissolves, it's all just light anyhow, leaving only a screen of paper-white.

Enough already.

You have exhausted me, exasperated me, outlasted me to the ground where I now lie. Take me, I won't make you pay. Just tell me what you want. Write me, you know how to reach me.

Yours,
Paul VanDeCarr

Narrativity -

I dem and you and every other pu blication on

narrative print m y tract! But I need to know

what form at to pu t it in, so I dem and you

pu t you r su bm ission gu idelines in an u nm

arked white bu siness-size envelope, deposit

them in the pu bli c garbage can at the nor

theast corner of City Hall in San Francisco

this Satu rday at noon. You 'll regret it if

you don't. No police. Don't not do it!

Signed,
Anonym ou s

P.S. Are M LA-style citations okay?!

POLICE ANALYSIS
Memo 164.2478, s f p d Criminal Investigations Unit

• Note irregularities on typewriter – short space after 'u' and 'm' – may suggest overuse, as in 'Marx' or 'Unitarian.' Check for Marxist Unitarians. Also, capital 'N' is below line, capital 'A' is above line – former drug addict?
• Author appears to be alternately clamorous and submissive (e.g., demands, then query in postscript). May indicate unstable personality. Approach with caution.
• Concern over form and style may indicate homosexual inclination.
• Demand links 'northeast' and 'garbage can' – may indicate origin from Northeastern U.S. and troubled relationship with home. New York Jew?
• 'White business-size envelope' may indicate suspect's intention to disguise self as white businessman.
• Check membership lists of Marxist Jewish/Unitarian homophile organizations, other similar underground groups. Do a roundup at Shabbat services at Sha'ar Zahav.

NARRATIVITY!

WE HAVE HoSTAGE ALL THE CITY'S COPies of ALTHUSSER BeCKET LUKACS AND EVEN BALZAC and STEIN For GOOD MeasurE!!! WE deMANd THE RELEASE OF TRADITIONAL NARRATIve! INNOVATION IS alTENATion! STOP Your ASSAULT now! YOUR WEB SITE MUST GO! OR ELSE!!! YOUR PreCIOUS books wILL be buRNED! THE SOciety FoR CUTTing UP NARRativity .com

P S Look OUT We know HTML

POLICE ANALYSIS

Memo 168.3742, SFPD Criminal Investigations Unit

• Note variation in evenness of lines, suggests erratic personality, potentially dangerous. Threat could be real.

• Misspelling of 'Beckett' (Samuel?) as 'Beket' could be a deliberate ruse, or may suggest Slavic or Germanic origin? English usage and orthography is otherwise good.

• Use of lettering from *National Enquirer* (or the *Globe*? – check sources) suggests pop literary/artistic sensibility. Interesting juxtaposition with (apparently) sophisticated literary theory bent. Split personality?

• Note grouping of books being held hostage – first 'Althusser Beket (sic) Lukacs' and second grouping 'Balzac and Stein.' Each grouping in alphabetical order, suggests attempt at egalitarianism, or is the author prioritizing writers? Balzac and Stein in different category ('even Balzac and Stein for good measure') could suggest author holds them in lower esteem, or may just have a markedly more Marxist bent. Check with Literary Crimes Unit.

• Remark that 'Innovation is alienation' seems anti-modernist, or at least reactionary. Not clear if opposition to 'innovation' is on linguistic or historical grounds. Author appears to be relatively untouched by post-structuralism.

• Allusion to SCUM *Manifesto* – check possible connections to radical feminism. (Valerie Solanis still alive? Check with Records department.)

• RECOMMENDATION: Check Slavic/Germanic surnames in MLA and APA membership lists, cross-reference with university police arrest records at Berkeley, Madison, the Ivies, Sisters. Check literary critical dissertation summaries on file, keywords 'The Lie of Overdeterminism,' 'Foucault Eats Turd,' 'Back to Hermeneutics.'

*

Erecting A Solid Foundation
Exclusive Dick Mason Interview

Manstuff recently caught up with porn star Dick Mason. He was on a busy filming schedule, but our very own Ken Wirmy managed to sneak in a quick interview with Mason, who was in between shooting a film and shooting his load. Same difference.

MANSTUFF: Dick, you've been very active recently. Randy House Films has featured you in *Between a Cock and a Hard Place*, *Dick Me Over* and *Dude Ranch* – and that's just in the last two months. How has it been for you, this intense acting schedule?

DICK MASON: It's been a wild ride, I'll tell you that much. I was really looking forward to doing *Dick Me Over*, because I got to act with Mark Samson for the first time. I'd seen some of his work before, and it's good. I mean, you know, he is so fucking hot.

MANSTUFF: Yeah, that scene in the employees' lounge of the steel plant in *Dick Me Over* was one of the hottest in recent memory.

MASON: It's funny you should mention that, because we had to redo parts of that scene so many times. The lighting kept getting screwed up. But for me, I was so hot for Mark Samson that I had no trouble staying hard the whole time. The cum shot in that scene was five star, if you ask me. Not just that it looked good, but it felt great.

MANSTUFF: That's pretty unusual in the business, isn't it, that you're that turned on by another actor?

MASON: It is, yeah. I mean, don't get me wrong, I love my work, and the people I work with are sexy as all get out. It's just that sometimes you have the opportunity to work with a real master of the craft, which Mark Samson definitely is – and to top it off a stud beyond compare. Just look at that guy's cock.

MANSTUFF: I do, as much as possible! [Laughs.] It seems like there are more films lately that use industrial scenes, like the steel plant in *Dick Me Over*, or the factory in *Sex Machine*. Is this a trend?

MASON: Good question. I don't really know. I mean, when I see that kind of shit, I like it. There's the hot sex and the hot metal. Or there's the hard bodies and the hard materials. Or sometimes it's a contrast – flesh against metal. Trend or not, it is most certainly boner-inducing material.

MANSTUFF: That is hot. And then there's the whole worker-manager thing in those two films, and others, too, I guess.

MASON: Yeah, what we meant with that was to break down some boundaries, really push the envelope. Some people say we're just being exploitative. Fuck that, I say. You know, we're just trying to say, maybe if workers and managers screw, then we wouldn't have so many problems. Worker cock in manager's ass. Managers sucking off workers, vice versa. Whatever. The more, the better.

MANSTUFF: So, you're saying that if people of different classes weren't so separated, maybe there wouldn't be so much misunderstanding.

MASON: Something like that. What I'm really saying is that, let's fuck, you know. But if we can break down some of these social categories, that's great. So for me, my work is an attempt to help people cross boundaries sexually, and also transform the categories they put themselves and others in.

MANSTUFF: But it seems to me that can't be done, really. A category is a category, you are who you are.

MASON: It's funny you should put it that way, 'That can't be done.' We might say instead, 'That Kant be done,' because Kant said that we were basically stuck with categories. He didn't envision much flexibility to them. I draw a lot on Kant in my own acting, but I part company with him philosophically when it comes to my work on class and culture.

MANSTUFF: I sort of understand what you mean about these Kantian categories, but I'm not clear on how you reconcile Kantian aesthetic theories – these purist, universalist conceptions – with your own inquiry into class relations.

MASON: Well, you've got to see Kant's aesthetic theories as part of his larger project to analyze universally applicable conditions that enable subjects to have objective knowledge, act morally and make valid aesthetic judgments. As an actor, I'm less interested in Kant's aesthetics than in his epistemological explanation of how objective knowledge is even possible. I believe that acting requires a presumption – a carefully circumscribed presumption, but a presumption nonetheless – of objective knowledge, in order to fully plumb (or should I say, penetrate?) a character. Now, there are problems associated with such notions of universality, to be sure, but Kant's scientific framework – in his *Critique of Pure Reason*, for example – pose some arguments that are essential to any discussion of justice. And even where I disagree with Kant, his arguments are eminently relevant to the vision of class relations that I try to project in films like *Dick Me Over*.

MANSTUFF: That is so hot. One more question. What are you working on next?

MASON: Well, sucking cock and fucking ass. That about sums it up.

MANSTUFF: It's hard work. [Laughs.] But somebody's got to do it. Thanks.

DICK MASON STATS
Birthdate: October 20, 1976
Birthplace: New York City
Hair: Brown
Eyes: Brown
Height: 5′10″
Weight: 160 lbs.

FAVOURITES
Food: Cheeseburgers
Sport: Swimming
Get-away: Miami Beach
Snack: Triscuits
Color: Royal blue
TV show: *Sex and the City*

The Contributors

KATHY ACKER was the author of ten novels, a collection of stories, a screenplay, a play and two books of essays. Her writing and the example of her life continue to influence the sundry communities she belonged to.

D. L. ALVAREZ is an American-born artist and writer who lives and works in Berlin, Germany. His visual work is represented by Derek Eller Gallery in New York and can be found in many prominent collections, including the University Art Museum of Berkeley, the SF MOMA, the Whitney Museum of American Art and the NY MOMA. His writing has been published in various anthologies, and he regularly contributes his interviews with independent filmmakers to *FilmMaker* magazine.

BETSY ANDREWS lives in Brooklyn, NY. She is the author of *She-Devil* (Sardines Press, 2004). Recent publications also include *New Jersey: A Work in Progress* (Furniture Press Pamphlet Series, 2004), poems and essays in *PomPom, X-Connect, Dangerous Families: Queer Writers on Surviving* (Harrington Park Press, 2004) and an upcoming flip book with Bruce Andrews (Boog Press). She writes a review column for *Gay City News* on new queer poetry and creative non-fiction.

Pink Steam, a collection of DODIE BELLAMY's stories, memoirs and memoiresque essays, was published in 2004 by San Francisco's Suspect Thoughts Press. Also in 2004, her infamous epistolary vampire novel, *The Letters of Mina Harker*, was reprinted by the University of Wisconsin Press. Her book *Cunt-Ups* (Tender Buttons) won the 2002 Firecracker Alternative Book Award for poetry. She is currently working on *The Fourth Form*, a multi-dimensional sex novel.

CHRISTIAN BÖK is the author of *Eunoia* (Coach House Books, 2001), a best-selling work of experimental literature which won the 2002 Griffin Prize for Poetic Excellence. *Crystallography* (Coach House Press, 1994), his first book of poetry, earned a nomination for the Gerald Lampert Memorial Award and was reprinted in 2003. Bök has created artificial languages for two television shows: Gene Roddenberry's *Earth: Final Conflict* and Peter Benchley's *Amazon*. Bök has also earned many accolades for his virtuoso performances of sound poetry. His conceptual artworks (which include books built out of

Rubik's Cubes and Lego) have appeared at the Marianne Boesky Gallery in New York City as part of the exhibit Poetry Plastique. He currently teaches English and Creative Writing at the University of Calgary.

BRUCE BOONE currently writes and translates under the name Bruce X. He lives with his queer partner Jamie in San Francisco, and his publications include *My Walk with Bob, Century of Clouds*, many chapbooks and, with Robert Glück, *La Fontaine*. Boone has translated books by Georges Bataille, J-P Lyotard, Pascal Quignard's *Albucius* as well as the same writer's *On Wooden Tablets: Apronenia Avitia*. He's looking for a publisher for his version of Quignard's *Les Ombres errantes*, a book that won Mr. Quignard the Prix Goncourt in 1993.

TAYLOR BRADY is the author of *Microclimates*, a hybrid novel/long poem published by Krupskaya in 2001. A new book, *Occupational Treatment*, is in preparation for Atelos. Other published texts include *Production Notes for Occupation: Location Scouting* (Duration Press e-book, 2002), *33549* (Leroy, 2000) and *Is Placed/Leaves* (Meow, 1996). Recent work has appeared or is forthcoming in journals including *Fourteen Hills, Ambit, Quid*, and in the catalogue accompanying Elliot Anderson's CAMS project. He currently lives in the Bay Area, where he serves on the board of directors of Small Press Traffic.

LAWRENCE YTZHAK BRAITHWAITE is an author and spoken-word performer living in Victoria, British Columbia, Canada. But as Gail Scott wrote in an essay of New Narrative (*Matrix* 62), 'Lawrence Ytzhak Braithwaite's beautiful dangerous novels make him one of the outstanding Canadian prose writers alive, and only the Americans seem to know it.' Braithwaite loves and lives to Dub his prose like Lee 'Scratch' Perry (who he shares physical height with = 5'4) and King Tubby worked with music and voice. His bunker/lab is in New Palestine (AKA the Fernwood district of) Victoria, British Columbia.

Braithwaite is the author of the novels *Wigger* and *Ratz Are Nice* (PSP). He has written many short stories, some appearing in *Fourteen Hills Literary Journal* (San Francisco State University), *Role Call: A Generational Anthology of Social & Political Black Literature and Art, Bluesprints: Anthology of Black British Columbian Literature and Orature* (ed. Wayde Compton), *Redzone: Victoria's Street People Zine*,

Fernwood's Sleeping Dragon, Velvet Mafia, Of the Flesh: Dangerous Fiction, Sleepy Brain web zine (Melbourne, Australia), *nocturnal (re) view* literary journal and appears on the Hurricane Angel's (AKA Jay Cox) full-length CD *luckly, i was half cat.*

A poet, novelist and essayist, NICOLE BROSSARD was born in Montréal in 1943. Since 1965, she has published over thirty books, including *Le centre blanc, La lettre aérienne, Le désert mauve, Hier* and *Cahier de roses et de civilisation.* In recognition of her contributions to the revitalization of francophone poetry in Quebec, Nicole has twice been awarded the Governor General's Award for Poetry, first in 1974, then in 1984. In 1965, she co-founded the literary periodical *La Barre du Jour* and, in 1976, the feminist journal *Les Têtes de Pioche.* That same year, she co-directed the movie *Some American Feminists.* In 1991, Nicole collaborated with Lisette Girouard on an anthology of women's poetry from Quebec entitled *Des origines à nos jours.* She was also awarded the Athanase-David prize, Quebec's highest literary distinction. In 1994, Nicole was made a member of the Académie des Lettres du Québec and, five years later, she accepted, for the second time, the grand prize at the Festival International de la Poésie de Trois-Rivières, this time for her collections *Musée de l'os et de l'eau* and *Au présent des veines.* In 2003, she was awarded the W. O. Mitchell Prize and was given a career bursary from the Conseil des Arts et des Lettres du Québec. Her books have been translated into several languages. Coach House Books will publish the English translation of her novel *Hier* in the spring of 2005. Nicole lives in Montréal.

MARY BURGER is the author of *Nature's Maw Gives and Gives* (Duration Press, 1999), *Bleeding Optimist* (Xurban Press, 1994) and *Thin Straw That I Suck Life Through* (Melodeon, forthcoming). She edits Second Story Books, featuring cross-genre narrative/lyrical works, and co-edited the journal *Proliferation* from 1994 to 1999. Her work can be found online at the St. Mark's Poetry Project Poets and Poems Archives.

DENNIS COOPER is the author of 'The George Miles Cycle,' an interconnected sequence of five novels that includes *Closer* (1989), *Frisk* (1991), *Try* (1994), *Guide* (1997) and *Period* (2000), all published by Grove Press. His most recent novel is *My Loose Thread* (Canongate

Books, 2002). He is editor of Little House on the Bowery, a line of books by adventurous new American fiction writers published under the auspices of Akashic Press. He is a contributing editor of *Artforum* magazine. Cooper's seventh novel, *The Sluts*, and a new collection of poetry, *A Symphony of Confusion About the People I Killed*, are forthcoming in 2005. He is currently collaborating on three multimedia projects with the legendary British band Wire, the French theatre director Giselle Vienne and Detroit-based composer/musician Ian Clarke. He lives in Los Angeles.

LYDIA DAVIS is the author of three collections of short fiction, the latest of which is *Samuel Johnson Is Indignant*, and one novel, *The End of the Story*. Her translation of Proust's *Swann's Way* was published last fall. She is a recipient of the 2003 MacArthur Fellowship.

JEFF DERKSEN is a writer and editor who lives in Vienna and Vancouver: he works at Simon Fraser University. His poetry books include *Transnational Muscle Cars, Dwell* and *Down Time*. His critical writing is found in *Telling It Slant: Avant-Garde Poetry of the Nineties, Assembling Alternatives: Transnational Approaches to Poetry, Stan Douglas: Every Building on the 100 Block of West Hastings* and *Ken Lum Works with Photography*.

AJA COUCHOIS DUNCAN makes a living in the Bay Area as an educator and a troublemaker. Her work has been published in-print in *Clamour, Five Fingers Review, Fourteen Hills, Love Shook Her Heart II* (an anthology published by Alyson Press), *MIRAGE/PERIOD(ICAL)*, *Prosodia, Mungo vs. Ranger, San Jose Manual of Style* and *Tinfish*, and online at *Blithe House Quarterly, How2* and *Narrativity*. New work is forthcoming from the *North American Review*. She holds an MFA in Creative Writing from San Francisco State University.

MICHAEL DU PLESSIS is a Los Angeles-based writer who has taught English and Comparative Literature at the University of Colorado at Boulder, and Comparative Literature and French at the University of Southern California. His writing has appeared in *MFS: Modern Fiction Studies, Discourse*, the *Journal of Literary Studies*, the anthology *RePresenting Bisexualities: Subjects and Cultures of Fluid Desire* and others.

KARI EDWARDS is author of *iduna* (O Books, 2003), *a day in the life of p.* (subpress collective, 2002) and *post/(pink)* (Scarlet Press, 2000). edwards's work can also be found in Scribner's *The Best American Poetry 2004* (fall 2004), *Bisexuality and Transgenderism: InterSEXions of the Others* (Haworth Press, 2004), *Experimental Theology, Public Text 0.2.* (Seattle Research Institute, 2003) and *Blood and Tears: Poems for Matthew Shepard* (Painted Leaf Press, 2000).

COREY FROST lived on Prince Edward Island growing up, and then he lived on the islands of Montréal, Honshu and, most recently, Long (i.e., Brooklyn, NY). A spoken-word performer, he has appeared on hundreds of stages in Canada, the USA and Europe. In 2004 he is touring writers' festivals and events in South Africa, Australia and New Zealand. His first book of short stories, *My Own Devices* (conundrum press, 2002), was shortlisted for both the ReLit awards and the Québec Writers' Federation awards. His second book, *The Worthwhile Flux*, will be released in 2004. He is currently working on a Ph.D. dissertation about text performance.

RENEE GLADMAN is currently publishing Leona, a pamphlet series of experimental prose and poetry, and Leon Works, a perfect-bound series for full-length prose works. From 1999 to 2004, she edited and published Leroy, a chapbook series for emerging or geographically obscured writers. Her own books include *Juice* (Kelsey St. Press, 2000) and *The Activist* (Krupskaya Books, 2003). *Newcomer Can't Swim*, a collective narrative, is forthcoming in 2005. She lives in Brooklyn, New York.

ROBERT GLÜCK is author of nine books of poetry and fiction. His new book, *Denny Smith*, was published by Clear Cut in February 2004. Glück's books include two novels, *Jack the Modernist* and *Margery Kempe*; a book of stories, *Elements of a Coffee Service*; and a book of poems and short prose, *Reader*. He also prefaced *Between Life and Death*, a book of Frank Moore's paintings published by Twin Palms. Glück was an associate editor at Lapis Press, co-director of Small Press Traffic Literary Center and director of the Poetry Center at San Francisco State, where teaches creative writing.

ROB HALPERN is the author of *Rumored Place* (Krupskaya). He lives in San Francisco.

CARLA HARRYMAN is the author of twelve books of experimental prose, poetry, plays and essays. Her published work includes a new volume of prose poetry, *Baby*, forthcoming from Adventures in Poetry; the experimental novels *Gardener of Stars* (2002) and *The Words After Carl Sandburg's Rootabaga Stories and Jean-Paul Sartre* (1999), as well as two volumes of selected writings, *There Never Was a Rose without a Thorn* (1995) and *Animal Instincts: Prose Plays, Essays* (1989). Her most recent plays, *Performing Objects Stationed in the Sub World* (2001–03) and *Mirror Play*, have been variously performed in Oxford, England (2001); Detroit, MI (2002); and San Francisco (2002, 2003, 2004). She has published a number of essays on women's innovative writing: her most recent essay is 'Residues or Revolutions of the Language of Acker and Artaud,' forthcoming from SDSU Press. She is on the faculty of the Department of English at Wayne State University where she teaches Women's Studies, Literature and Creative Writing.

LAIRD HUNT is the author of two novels, *Indiana, Indiana* and *The Impossibly* (both from Coffee House Press). His writings have appeared in *Conjunctions, McSweeney's, Ploughshares, Grand Street, Sulfur* and *Talisman*. He has been a fellow at the MacDowell Colony and the Camargo Foundation and teaches fiction at the University of Denver.

KEVIN KILLIAN, born 1952, is a poet, novelist, critic and playwright. He has written a book of poetry, *Argento Series* (2001); two novels, *Shy* (1989) and *Arctic Summer* (1997); a book of memoirs, *Bedrooms Have Windows* (1989); and a book of stories, *Little Men* (1996), which won the PEN Oakland award for fiction. His new collection, *I Cry Like a Baby*, recently appeared from Painted Leaf Books. For the San Francisco Poets Theater, Killian has written thirty plays, including *Stone Marmalade* (1996, with Leslie Scalapino) and *Often* (2001, with Barbara Guest). His next book will be all about Kylie Minogue.

CHRIS KRAUS'S most recent book is *Video Green: Los Angeles Art and the Triumph of Nothingness*. She is the author of *I Love Dick, Aliens & Anorexia* and the forthcoming novel *Torpor*. She co-edited *Hatred of*

Capitalism: A Semiotexte Reader, with Sylvere Lotringer and co-edits the Semiotexte imprint with Lotringer and Hedi El Kholti. She teaches writing at San Francisco Art Institute and lives in upstate New York and Los Angeles.

PAMELA LU, the author of *Pamela: A Novel*, is currently at work on a collection of stories. She lives at the base of the Santa Cruz mountains, in Neal Cassady's former hometown.

NICOLE MARKOTIC is a poet and fiction writer from Calgary, Alberta. She teaches English Literature and Creative Writing at the University of Calgary, and publishes the chapbook publication Wrinkle Press. Her first book is the prose poetry collection *Connect the Dots* (Wolsak & Wynn), her second book is a fictional biography about Alexander Graham Bell, *Yellow Pages* (RDC Press), and her most recent book is a collection of poetry, *Minotaurs & Other Alphabets* (Wolsak & Wynn). Her chapbook *more excess* won the 1998 bpNichol Poetry Chapbook Award. She is currently completing a novel and a critical book concerning the representations of disability in literature and film.

DAPHNE MARLATT is a West Coast writer. Her most recent title is a chapbook, *Seven Glass Bowls* (Nomados Press, 2003). Her latest collection of poetry, *This Tremor Love Is* (Talonbooks, 2001), was shortlisted for the Dorothy Livesay Poetry Prize, the Pat Lowther Memorial Prize and the Second Annual ReLit Award. She has published two novels, *Taken* and *Ana Historic*; a collection of essays and letters, *Readings from the Labyrinth*; and a number of books of poetry, including *Salvage* (1991), *Ghost Works* (1993), *Touch to My Tongue* (1984) and, in collaboration with Betsy Warland, *Two Women in a Birth*. She has been writer-in-residence at a number of universities across Canada, most recently at the University of Windsor (2001–02), and is currently writing a contemporary version of a Japanese Noh play for a multicultural theatre company in Vancouver.

In addition to two collections of poetry, DOUGLAS A. MARTIN is the author of the novel *Outline of My Lover*, named an International Book of the Year by the *Times Literary Supplement* and adapted in part by the Ballett Frankfurt for their production 'Kammer/Kammer.' He teaches in the continuing education program of the New School for Social Research.

Poet-critic, theorist STEVE MCCAFFERY is the new David Gray Chair of Poetry and Letters at the State University of New York at Buffalo. He is the author of one novel, fifteen volumes of poetry, two dozen chapbooks and four critical works. Most recent to appear are *Bouma Shapes* (Zasterle Press, Gran Canaria, Spain, 2002), *Prior to Meaning: The Protosemantic and Poetics* (Northwestern University Press, 2001) and in two volumes *Seven Pages Missing* (volume 1 *Selected Texts 1969-1999*; volume 2 *Previously Uncollected Texts 1968-2000*), Coach House Books, 2001–02. He was a founding member of the Four Horsemen sound poetry ensemble in 1970, (with bpNichol) of TRG (Toronto Research Group), 1972, and the College of Canadian 'Pataphysics, 1979. Although one of the theoretical founders of Language Poetry, McCaffery's interests have consistently extended into sound, performative and intermedia areas. Before moving to Buffalo, McCaffery taught poetics, philosophy and the paraliterary at York University, and is founding director of NACIP (the North American Centre for Interdisciplinary Poetics). A new volume of poetry, *Slightly Left of Thinking*, is to appear through Chax Press in Tucson.

DEREK MCCORMACK is the author of *The Haunted Hillbilly, Wish Book* and *Dark Rides*. He is the co-author of *Wild Mouse*, a book about the Canadian National Exhibition. He lives in Toronto.

LAURA MORIARTY's newest book is *Self-Destruction* from Post Apollo Press. Recent books are *Nude Memoir* (Krupskaya), *The Case* (O Books), *Like Roads* (Kelsey St. Press), *Cunning* (Spuyten Duyvil), *Spicer's City* (Poetry New York), *L'Archiviste* (Zasterle Press) and *Symmetry* (Avec Books). Her chapbook *Duse* (Coincidence Press, 1987) was reprinted by paradigm press in 2000. Her book *Persia* (Chance Additions) co-won the Poetry Center Book Award in 1983. She received a Wallace Alexander Gerbode Foundation Award in Poetry in 1992, a residency at the Foundation Royaumont in France in 1993 and a New Langton Arts Award in Literature in 1998. From 1986 to 1997 she was archives director at the American Poetry Archives at the Poetry Center at San Francisco State University. She is now acquisition and marketing director at Small Press Distribution.

EILEEN MYLES has written thousands of poems since she gave her first reading at CBGB's in 1974. From 1977 to 1979 she edited a poetry magazine, *dodgems*. From 1984 to 1986 she was artistic director of St. Mark's Poetry Project. She also wrote, acted in and directed plays at St. Mark's and PS 122. In 1992 she conducted an openly female write-in campaign for President of the United States. In 1997 Eileen toured with Sister Spit's Ramblin' Road Show. Her books include *Skies*, (2001), *on my way* (2001), *Cool for You* (a novel, 2000), *School of Fish* (1997), *Maxfield Parrish* (1995), *Not Me*, (1991) and *Chelsea Girls* (stories, 1994). In 1995, with Liz Kotz, she edited *The New Fuck You/ adventures in Lesbian Reading* (Semiotext(e)). She's a frequent contributor to *Book Forum, Art in America, The Village Voice, The Nation, The Stranger, Index* and *Nest*.

DOUG RICE is the author of *Skin Prayer: fragments of abject memory, A Good Cuntboy Is Hard to Find* and *Blood of Mugwump: A Tiresian Tale of Incest*. He is a co-editor of *Federman: A to X-X-X-X* and publishes *Nobodaddies: A Journal of Pirated Desires*. He teaches fiction writing and film at California State University, Sacramento.

LISA ROBERTSON's books of poetry include *XEclogue, Debbie: An Epic* and *The Weather*. Clear Cut Press has recently published the prose work *Occasional Works and Seven Walks from the Office for Soft Architecture* and *Rousseau's Boat* is just out with Nomados. She contributes a regular decorating horoscope to *Nest: A Quarterly of Interiors* under the pen name Swann, and often writes as the Office for Soft Architecture.

CAMILLE ROY is a writer and performer of fiction, poetry and plays. Her most recent book is a work of fiction entitled *SWARM* (Black Star Series). Earlier books include *The Rosy Medallions* (poetry and prose, from Kelsey St.Press, 1995) and *Cold Heaven* (plays, from O Books, 1993). She lives in San Francisco and teaches creative writing privately and at San Francisco State University. Website: www.camilleroy.com.

LESLIE SCALAPINO's works of fiction include *Defoe* (reprinted by Green Integer in 2002), *The Return of Painting, The Pearl, and Orion/A Trilogy* (published by North Point, reprinted by Talisman), *Orchid Jetsam* (Tuumba Press, 2001) and *Dahlia's Iris – Secret Autobiography and Fiction* (FC2 Press, 2003). She has twenty-three books of poetry, fiction, essays and plays.

KATHY LOU SCHULTZ's collections of poetry and experimental fiction include *Some Vague Wife* (Atelos Press, 2002), *Genealogy* (a+bend press, 1999) and *Redress* (San Francisco State University, 1994), winner of the Michael Rubin Award. In addition, her poetry, experimental fiction, critical essays and book reviews have appeared in a variety of journals including the *Electronic Poetry Review, Fence, Fourteen Hills, Hambone, HOW2, Mirage Period(ical), Outlet,* the *Philadelphia Inquirer, Traffic* and *tripwire.* After nearly a decade in the San Francisco Bay Area, Kathy Lou moved to Philadelphia where she is pursuing doctoral studies in literature at the University of Pennsylvania. She is co-editor of *Lipstick Eleven.*

GAIL SCOTT's novel *My Paris,* about a sad diarist in conversation with Gertrude Stein, Walter Benjamin and others, in contemporary Paris, was published at Dalkey Archive Press (Normal, IL: 2003). The Canadian edition of *My Paris* (Toronto: Mercury, 1999) was named one of the Top Ten Canadian novels of 1999 by *Quill and Quire.* Her story collection *Spare Parts Plus Two* (Toronto: Coach House) was reissued in 2002 with new texts. Her other novels are *Main Brides* and *Heroine,* and her essays are collected in *Spaces Like Stairs* and *la théorie, un dimanche* (with Nicole Brossard et al.). Her translation of Michael Delisle's *Le Désarroi du matelot* was shortlisted for the prestigious Governor General's award in translation (2001). She is co-editor of *Narrativity,* and was co-founder of both *Tessera,* a bilingual periodical of new writing by women, and *Spirale,* a French-language critical magazine based in Montréal. Her fiction has been translated into French and German. Scott is working on a new novel, *R., or Exemplary Afternoons.*

X. I. SELENE lives in Montréal, under the sign of the coquillage.

AARON SHURIN's books include the poetry collections *A's Dream, Into Distances, A Door* and *The Paradise of Forms: Selected Poems,* as well as the prose work *Unbound: A Book of AIDS.* He co-directs and teaches in the MFA in Writing Program at the University of San Francisco.

NATHALIE STEPHENS writes in English and French, and is the author of several published works, most recently *L'Injure* (l'Hexagone, 2004), *Paper City* (Coach House, 2003) and *Je Nathanaël* (l'Hexagone, 2003).

Underground (TROIS, 1999) was shortlisted in 2000 for the Grand Prix du Salon du livre de Toronto. Stephens's writing appears in various anthologies, including *Portfolio Milieu* (milieu press, 2004), *A Sentence for Breathing Fire II* (Nightwood, 2004), *The Common Sky: Canadian Writers Against the War* (Three Squares, 2003), *LVNG* (Chicago) and *Tessera* (Montréal). Stephens has performed her work internationally, notably in Barcelona, Chicago, New York and Ljubljana. She is the recipient of a 2002 Chalmers Arts Fellowship and a 2003 British Centre for Literary Translation Residential Bursary. Some of Stephens's work has been translated into Basque, Bulgarian, Portuguese and Slovene. She has translated Catherine Mavrikakis into English and R. M. Vaughan into French. On occasion, she translates herself.

ANNE STONE's first novel, *jacks: a gothic gospel* (Livres DC Books, 1998), is formally and typographically experimental, conveying aspects of the story through the book's design. *Hush* (Insomniac Press, 1999), set in the Eastern Townships of Quebec, explores violence, complicity and sites of resistance. The third one, still in the works, is about Streetsville girls, about sisters, one of whom is gone.

LYNNE TILLMAN's novels are *Haunted Houses, Cast in Doubt, Motion Sickness* and *No Lease on Life* (finalist for the National Book Critics Circle Award, 1998). Her story collections are *The Madame Realism Complex, Absence Makes the Heart* and *This Is Not It*. Her non-fiction books include *The Broad Picture*, an essay collection, and *The Velvet Years: Warhol's Factory 1965–67*, photographs by Stephen Shore. Tillman's writing has been anthologized in, among others, *110 Stories: New York Writes After 9/11, The Norton Anthology of Postmodern Literature, The Time Out Book of New York Short Stories, High Risk* and *The New Gothic*. She is Associate Professor/Writer in Residence at the University at Albany and is currently working on a novel.

ROBIN TREMBLAY-MCGAW's work has appeared in a variety of journals and magazines including *Narrativity, Mirage, Marks, non, How2, Five Fingers Review* and *Poetry Flash*. She has two chapbooks: *after a grand collage* (Dyad Press, 1996) and *making mARKs* (a+bend press, 2000). She is currently a second-year Ph.D. student in Literature at the University of California, Santa Cruz.

PAUL VANDECARR is a writer and filmmaker living in San Francisco. His work has appeared in such publications as the *Advocate*, the *San Francisco Bay Guardian, Storytelling* and on the Pacifica Radio Network, for whose flagship station KPFA he was a news reporter. His short videos have shown nationwide, and he is currently working on a feature-length documentary about Jonestown.

HERIBERTO YÉPEZ was born in Tijuana, Mexico. He is the son of a waitress, and from her he received certain wisdom; keys to understand 'culture.' He has published several books of poetry, essays and fiction in Spanish and won literary prizes for them. He has also translated an anthology of Jerome Rothenberg's poetry into Spanish. His latest book is the experimental novel *El matasellos* (Sudamericana, 2004) and forthcoming *Inventario de mi cuerpo visible*. He teaches philosophy and history of arts classes at the Universidad Autonoma de Baja California, and is currently studying a master's in psychotherapy. He has also participated in art projects and festivals like Insite. Some of his work in English has appeared in *Tripwire, Cross Cultural Poetics, Rattapallax, Chain* and *Shark*. He has two blogs: www.hyepez.blogspot.com (Spanish) and www.mexperimental.blogspot.com (English).

MAGDALENA ZURAWSKI was born in Newark, NJ, in 1972 to Polish immigrants. After graduating from college in 1995, she lived abroad in Berlin, Germany, where she studied as a Fulbright Scholar. Her work has been published in *American Poet: The Journal of the Academy of American Poets, The Poetry Project Newsletter* and *Rattapalax,* among others. In 2000 HopHopHop Press published her chapbook, *Bruised Nickelodeon*. She is currently living in San Francisco and working on her first novel, *The Bruise*. She hopes that publication of *The Bruise* will turn her into a lesbian cult figure and relieve her from many of her present-day woes.